D1453271

Ron Horsley

Jack Ketchum

Tracy Knight

John Maclay

Richard Christian Matheson

Thomas F. Monteleone

Joe Nassise

William F. Nolan

Tom Piccirilli

Mark Powers

Judi Rohrig

Lucy A. Snyder

Thomas Sullivan

Tim Waggoner

MASQUES V

Poppy Z. Brite

MASQUES V

MASQUES V

EDITED BY J.N. WILLIAMSON
AND GARY A. BRAUNBECK

GAUNTLET PUBLICATIONS
■ 2006 ■

Gauntlet Publications
5307 Arroyo Street
Colorado Springs, CO 80922
United States of America
Phone: (719) 591-5566
email: info@gauntletpress.com
Website: www.gauntletpress.com

Table of Contents

In Memory of
J.N. Williamson

1932 — 2005

"What memories have refused to leave your mind and will not rest until you write them down? Will it at last illuminate the world? Will it enlighten us all? Will you write something beautiful? Something beneficial? Will you do that for me, please?"

We have tried to do so in these pages, dear friend. We hope this will make you proud.

Concerns of the Mind and Spirit (Redux): An Introduction

By J.N. Williamson

In 1991, when the last edition of *Masques* was published, the horror genre was all but dead and buried. Most us were just waiting for our invitations to the wake. The 1980s had seen an unprecedented explosion in horror's popularity, and as is wont to happen when a particular genre becomes wildly popular, the wordsmiths in the field could barely turn out enough product to meet the demand; as a result—not surprisingly—much of the work produced in the latter portion of the 80s became progressively weaker in execution and originality. I've no doubt that part of the weakness stemmed from publishers' demand for as much product as possible as soon as possible, thus reducing the time that was left for writers to polish their work before sending it off to market. But if we are to speak honestly about this, then we must also turn the light toward ourselves, the writers. We perhaps became too aware of certain expected formulae in the genre, and so wrote only those types of horror stories that fit within the parameters of those formulae, never daring to journey beyond the accepted borders for fear of losing our place in the publishing schedule.

In short: the glut of horror in the marketplace may have strangled the genre, but we arguably provided the rope.

In the nearly 15 years since the last edition of *Masques*, horror has clawed its way out of the grave once again and reclaimed a goodly amount of its popularity, but there have been changes. While there will always be a place for the vampire, the haunted house, the serial killer, the ghost, were-wolf, demon, and possessed child, the writers at the forefront of horror's newest movement are concerned not so much with shock and gore as they are what it is the *lies behind* those elements.

In *Masques III*, I divided the stories into thematic sections. One of those sections was entitled "Concerns of the Mind and Spirit". With only a few exceptions, all of the stories you're about to encounter could have easily appeared under that title, for in the 15 years since the last edition of *Masques* appeared, the writers in this genre have become more aware of the *internal* horrors of the human condition that far outweigh those external ones listed above. They have returned full force to those concerns of the mind and spirit that make for the richest and most memorable type of horror story.

I needn't list for you all the reminders of how the world we knew back in 1991 has changed; you know them all too well—and if you've by chance forgotten any, you'll find more than a few reminders in these stories.

This is a *Masque* of many firsts and one very important last; it's the first *Masques* in nearly a decade-and-a-half, containing the first professional appearance of several new writers; it's the first *Masques* to contain this many stories; it's the first *Masques* to contain very brief story introductions (because I do not want to keep you from the tales any longer than necessary); and it's the first *Masques* to feature a cover painting done by one of the most popular writers alive, the gracious and marvelous Clive Barker, a true gentleman whose generosity and enthusiasm for this project has touched me beyond articulation, in whose debt I shall always remain.

And the important "last" of which I spoke?

This will be the last *Masques* with myself as the editor, because one other thing has happened in the 15 years since *Masques IV* was published: I became 15 years older, despite my attempts not to, and my body does not hesitate to remind me on a daily basis. In my 70's now, my lifelong problems with diabetes have finally taken their toll on my physical stamina and my eyesight; both are now firing on 4 pistons rather than 8, and a series of minor (knock wood) strokes has further limited my endurance. Plus, I have slapped a mental bumper sticker on the car of my mind: I'D RATHER BE WRITING.

So, dear friends, dear readers, and my dear, dear fellow writers, this will be my final stint as editor of this series. I simply haven't the energy and concentration required for an undertaking of this intensity any longer—and make no mistake, anyone who takes it upon themselves to edit an anthology enters themselves in the literary equivalent of an endurance test worthy of reality television contests. I have decided to do the wise thing, and vote myself off of the island.

If and when *Masques VI* appears, it will be billed as *J.N. Williamson's Masques*, Edited by (insert name here). Such good friends as Mort Castle, John Maclay, and Tracy Knight have already agreed to serve as future editors of this series, and I could not hope to leave it in better or more caring hands. (In fact, when this 5th edition sees print, if I have my way, you will see Gary A. Braunbeck listed as my co-editor, despite his loud protestations to the contrary; it is because of Gary's dedication and determination—as well as that of publisher Barry Hoffman, a true bulldog when he sets his will to something—that this anthology has made it past the finish line. So there you go, Gary—you're my first *Masques* co-editor, whether you want the credit or not. We'll duke it out later.)

It has been my very great honor to serve as editor of this series, to have introduced you to several writers who are now household names, and to have had the privilege of reading so many stories to choose from. Of all the *Masques* volumes, I think I am the proudest of this one; not only because of the Herculean effort it took to finally make this anthology a reality, but because it has proven to me that horror—like rock and roll—will always be, it will never die; and regardless of what the future holds for the genre (and for humankind)—be it days of bright promise or nights of bleakest despair—we will always, *always* be able to find our storytellers, those men and women whose imaginations will never stop exciting, entertaining, and enrapturing our own, articulating those concerns of the mind and spirit that we must never ignore or forget.

And so, for one last time, permit me the honor of acting as ringmaster to this particular circus of the imagination; allow me to sidestep from the spotlight, remove my top hat, and with a sweeping flourish of my arm, proclaim that it is once again time:

Let the masque begin!

J.N. Williamson
October 3, 2005
Noblesville, IN

Poppy Z. Brite

*Any traditional Masque celebration always starts with an incantation to the spirits, and I can think of no better way to begin this fifth installment of the **Masques** series than with this evocative and subtly unsettling tone-poem from a writer who has more than proven her mettle with the unsettling.*

*Though still primarily known as a horror writer, Poppy Brite has in the past few years shifted her focus to a series of intoxicatingly atmospheric mysteries set in the world of New Orleans restaurateurs Rickey and G-man. **Liquor** and **Prime** are the first novels in this marvelous series, and I look forward to many more.*

—JNW

Wandering the Borderlands

✠ BY POPPY Z. BRITE ✠

I have worked with dead bodies for most of my life. I've been a morgue assistant, a medical student, and for one terrible summer, a member of a cleanup service that cleaned not household grime but the results of murders and suicides. Presently I am the coroner of Orleans Parish. I handle bodies and things that no longer even look like bodies; I sit alone with them late at night; I look into their faces and try to see what, if anything, they knew at the end. I do not fear them.

And yet not long ago I had a dream. In this dream, I knew somehow that my neighbor was in trouble, and I climbed her porch steps to see if I could help. As I stood at her door, I knew with the unquestionable logic of dreams that she was in there, violated and dead. When I touched the door, it swung open, and I could see that the furniture inside was tumbled and smashed.

"I can't go in," I said (to whom?), "the burglar might still be in there. I'll go back home and call the police." And that was sound reasoning. But truly, I could not enter the house because I feared seeing the body.

It's not that I am close to this neighbor; with the modern passion for privacy, we've spoken no more than twenty words in the years we've lived beside each other. It was not *her* specific body I feared in the dream. I can explain it no more clearly than this: *I feared seeing what her body had become.*

When I woke up, I couldn't understand exactly what I had been afraid of. But I know that if the dream ever returns, I will be just as coldly terrified, and just as helpless.

I saw a man die at my gym recently. I have a bad back from lifting so much inert human weight, and I keep it at bay by exercising on Nautilus machines. On my way to the locker room one hot afternoon, I became aware of a commotion in the swimming pool area. A man had just been found on the bottom of the pool. It seemed likely that he had gone into cardiac arrest, and no one knew how long he had been underwater. Two people—another doctor I know and a personal trainer—were giving him CPR as various gym staffers and members swarmed around. There was nothing I could do. I knew the man was probably dying, and I realized that while I had seen thousands of dead people, I had never actually seen anyone die. I didn't want to see it now, but I couldn't make myself turn away. He was barely visible through the crowd of people trying to help him: a pale pot belly; a pair of white legs jerking with the motion of artificial respiration but otherwise dreadfully still; the wrinkled soles of his feet; his swim trunks still wet. Somehow the wet swim trunks were the worst. *Of course they're still wet*, I thought; *he was just pulled out of the pool.* But they brought home to me the fact that he was never going to go back to the locker room and pull off the trunks, glad to be rid of their clinging clamminess. They could cling to him throughout eternity and he wouldn't care.

Eventually the paramedics showed up and shocked him with their defibrillator, put a breathing tube down his throat, gave him a shot of adrenaline. None of it worked. I'm not sure if the man was dead or alive when they finally took him out to the ambulance. The saddest thing was that nobody seemed to know his name. Apparently he'd just joined the gym, another fat New Orleanian determined to finally get in shape, but unable to pace himself. I saw them on my table all the time. People kept asking each other who he was, but no one knew. I hated the idea that he might have died in a place where not only did no one love him, but no one even knew him.

From the moment I realized I couldn't help him to the moment they strapped him to the stretcher and carried him out, I felt that I shouldn't be watching. It felt wrong somehow to be looking at him, even though I was holding my St. Joseph medal and praying for him. When I performed autopsies, I didn't feel this way at all. I knew those people were dead and didn't give a damn who looked at them, and in many cases I was performing one of the last kind (if brutal) acts anyone was ever going to do for them. But this man was not alive, not dead, not yet ready for my table, no longer a part of the laughing, eating, living world. He was in the borderlands, and it seemed a very personal moment that all of us strangers shouldn't be looking at...but we all did, as if he might give us the answer to the question we'd been yearning for ever since we were old enough to conceive of our own deaths.

There is no profession, no occupation, no state of jadedness that confers immunity from fear of death. The taboo is too strong; we can lessen it through exposure but never eliminate it entirely. The horror movies are riveting, but, I think, wrong: we do not believe the dead will come back to life and hurt us. Rather, we fear them because they will *never* come back to life, and because we can never know where they have gone. In that way, we are the ones wandering the borderlands. We are lost and they are found. They know a terrible secret, and they will never share it with us.

⁂

Richard Matheson

Occasionally—albeit unconsciously—I'll find that writers submitting stories to **Masques** *will repeat certain motifs. You'll find a trio of ghost stories this time around, as well as 2 stories from legends in the field that are set in a barbershop. Here is the first, and a wickedly funny, chilling visit it is, courtesy of one of the greatest writers ever to grace this field, Richard Matheson, author of* **The Shrinking Man***,* **"Duel"***,* **I Am Legend***, and—oh, come on! Do I* **really** *need to introduce this towering figure of imaginative fiction?*

Didn't think so…

—JNW

Haircut

✠ By Richard Matheson ✠

Angelo was down the block having lunch at Temple's Cafeteria and Joe was alone, sitting in one of the barber chairs reading the morning paper.

It was hot in the shop. The air seemed heavy with the smell of lotions and tonics and shaving soap. There were dark swirls of hair lying on the tiles. In the stillness, a big fly buzzed around in lazy circles. **HEAT WAVE CONTINUES**—Joe read.

He was rubbing at his neck with a handkerchief when the screen door creaked open and shut with a thud. Joe looked across the shop at the man who was moving toward him.

"Yes, sir," Joe said automatically, folding the newspaper and sliding off the black leather of the chair.

As he put the newspaper on one of the wireback chairs along the wall, the man shuffled over to the chair and sat down on it, his hands in the coat pockets of his wrinkled brown gabardine suit. He slumped down in the chair, waiting, as Joe turned around.

"Yes, sir," Joe said again, looking at the man's sallow, dry-skinned face. He took a towel from the glass-floored cabinet. "Like to take your coat off, sir?" he asked. "Pretty hot today."

The man said nothing. Joe's smile faltered for a moment, then returned.

"Yes, sir," he said, tucking the towel under the collar of the man's faded shirt, feeling how dry and cool the man's skin was. He put the striped cloth over the man's coat and pinned it in place.

"Looks like we're havin' another scorcher," he said.

The man was silent. Joe cleared his throat.

"Shave?" he asked.

The man shook his head once.

"Haircut," Joe said and the man nodded slowly.

Joe picked up the electric shaver and flicked it on. The high-pitched buzzing filled the air.

"Uh...could you sit up a little, sir?" Joe asked.

Without a sound or change of expression, the man pressed his elbows down on the arms of the chair and raised himself a little.

Joe ran the shaver up the man's neck, noticing now white the skin was where the hair had been. The man hadn't been to a barber in a long time; for a haircut anyway.

"Well, it sure looks like the heat ain't plannin' to leave," Joe said.

"Keeps growing," the man said.

"You said it," Joe answered. "Gets hotter and hotter. Like I told the missus the other night..."

As he talked, he kept shaving off the hair on the back of the man's neck. The lank hair fluttered darkly down onto the man's shoulders.

Joe put a different head on the electric shaver and started cutting again.

"You want it short?" he asked.

The man nodded slowly and Joe had to draw away the shaver to keep from cutting him.

"It keeps growin'," the man said.

Joe chuckled self-consciously. "Ain't it the way?" he said. Then his face grew studious. "Course hair always grows a lot faster in the summertime. It's the heat. Makes the glands work faster or somethin'. Cut it short, I always say."

"Yes," the man said, "short." His voice was flat and without tone.

Joe put down the shaver and pulled the creased handkerchief from his back trouser pocket. He mopped at his brow.

"*Hot,*" he said and blew out a heavy breath.

The man said nothing and Joe put away his handkerchief. He picked up the scissors and comb and turned back to the chair. He clicked the scissor blades a few times and started trimming. He grimaced a little as he smelled the man's breath. Bad teeth, he thought.

"And my nails," the man said.

"Beg pardon?" Joe asked.

"They keep growing," the man said.

Joe hesitated a moment, glancing up at the mirror on the opposite wall. The man was staring into his lap.

Joe swallowed and started cutting again. He ran the thin comb through the man's hair and snipped off bunches of it. The dark, dry hair fell down on the striped cloth. Some of it fluttered down to the floor.

"Cut?" the man said.

"What's that?" Joe asked.

"My nails," the man answered.

"Oh. No. We ain't got no manicurist," Joe said. He laughed apologetically. "We ain't that high-class."

The man's face didn't change at all and Joe's smile faded.

"You want a manicure, though," he said, "there's a big

barber shop up on Atlantic Avenue in the bank. They got a manicurist there."

"They keep growing," the man said.

"Yeah," Joe said distractedly. "Uh...you want any off the top?"

"I can't stop it," the man said.

"Huh?" Joe looked across the way again at the reflection of the man's unchanging face. He saw how still the man's eyes were, how sunken.

He went back to his cutting and decided not to talk anymore.

As he cut, the smell kept getting worse. It wasn't the man's breath, Joe decided, it was his body. The man probably hadn't taken a bath in weeks. Joe breathed through gritted teeth. If there's anything I can't stand, he thought.

In a little while, he finished cutting with the scissors and comb. Laying them down on the counter, be took off the striped cloth and shook the dark hair onto the floor.

He rearranged the towel and pinned the striped cloth on again. Then he flicked on the black dispenser and let about an inch and a half of white lather push out onto the palm of his left hand.

He rubbed it into the men's temples and around the ears, his fingers twitching at the cool dryness of the man's flesh. He's *sick*, he thought worriedly, hope to hell it isn't contagious. Some people just ain't got no consideration at all.

Joe stropped the straight razor, humming nervously to himself while the man sat motionless in the chair.

"Hurry," the man said.

"Yes, sir," Joe said, "right away." He stropped the razor blade once more, then let go of the black strap. It swung down and bumped once against the back of the chair.

Joe drew the skin taut and shaved around the man's right ear.

"I should have stayed," the man said.

28

"Sir?"

The man said nothing. Joe swallowed uneasily and went on shaving, breathing through his mouth in order to avoid the smell which kept getting worse.

"Hurry," the man said.

"Goin' as fast as I can," Joe said, a little irritably.

"I should have stayed."

Joe shivered for some reason. "Be finished in a second," he said. The man kept staring at his lap, his body motionless on the chair, his hands still in his coat pockets.

"Why?" the man said.

"What?" Joe asked.

"Does it keep growing?"

Joe looked blank. He glanced at the man's reflection again, feeling something tighten in his stomach. He tried to grin.

"That's life," he said, weakly, and finished up with the shaving as quickly as he could. He wiped off the lather with a clean towel, noticing how starkly white the man's skin was where the hair had been shaved away.

He started automatically for the water bottle to clean off the man's neck and around the ears. Then he stopped himself and turned back. He sprinkled powder on the brush and spread it around the man's neck. The sweetish smell of the clouding powder mixed with the other heavier smell.

"Comb it wet or dry?" Joe asked.

The man didn't answer. Nervously, trying not to breathe anymore than necessary, Joe ran the comb through the man's hair without touching it with his fingers. He parted it on the left side and combed and brushed it back.

Now, for the first time, the man's lifeless eyes raised and he looked into the mirror at himself.

"Yes," he said slowly. "That's better."

With a lethargic movement, he stood up and Joe had to move around the chair to get the towel and the striped cloth off.

"Yes, sir," he said, automatically.

The man started shuffling for the door, his hands still in the side pockets of his coat.

"Hey, wait a minute," Joe said, a surprised look on his face.

The man turned slowly and Joe swallowed as the dark-circled eyes looked at him.

"That's a buck-fifty," he said, nervously.

The man stared at him with glazed, unblinking eyes.

"What?" he said.

"A buck-fifty," Joe said again. "For the cut."

A moment more, the man looked at Joe. Then, slowly, as if he weren't sure he was looking in the right place, the man looked down at his coat pockets.

Slowly, jerkingly, he drew out his hands.

Joe felt himself go rigid. He caught his breath and moved back a step, eyes staring at the man's white hands, at the nails which grew almost an inch past the finger tips.

"But I have no money," the man said as he slowly opened his hands.

Joe didn't even hear the gasp that filled this throat.

He stood there, staring open-mouthed at the black dirt sifting through the man's white fingers.

He stood there, paralyzed, until the man had turned and, with a heavy shuffle, walked to the screen door and left the shop.

Then, he walked numbly to the doorway and out onto the sun-drenched sidewalk.

He stood there for a long time, blank-faced, watching the man hobble slowly across the street and walk up toward Atlantic Avenue and the bank.

Ray Garton

*Ray Garton is the author of numerous novels, among them the modern-day classic **Live Girls** and its sequel, **Night Life**, as well as **Crucifax Autumn**, **Trade Secrets**, **Lot Lizards**, and the Grand Guignol comedy/horror masterpiece **Scissors**. Usually known for his more extreme horror, Garton has recently begun shifting his focus into dark humor—as this marvelous **Twilight Zone**-esque story illustrates.*

—JNW

Recall

✠ BY RAY GARTON ✠

Monday was Dan Griffin's favorite day of the week, always had been. This particular Monday also happened to be his fortieth birthday. As he showered and dressed for work, Dan had ambivalent feelings about the Big Four-Oh, but he was not going to let them get him down. The fact that his fortieth had fallen on a Monday was, he thought, a good omen, since it was, after all, his favorite day of the week.

As a boy, Monday had meant he could go back to school after two deadly-dull days with his parents. His mother had always been on him to practice playing the piano, and his dad pestered him about practicing the clarinet. When they weren't pushing him to practice, they were discussing his college years and where he might spend them—they'd even spoken a few times of getting Dan into Juilliard. They were always arranging performances for church—he would perform a solo on his clarinet, or accompany himself on the piano as he sang. When he turned thirteen, they let Dan decide whether or not he wanted to continue going to church—they did not believe in forcing religion on him. He'd never gone to church again. It had felt good to quit, to know he'd never have to perform for anyone again. But his parents continued to urge him to practice his piano and clarinet, and to keep his voice in shape with exercises. They also encouraged him to draw and paint, something for which he'd shown a talent since he was quite young. He wanted no part of any of it, though.

His parents had told him again and again that his talents were gifts, but Dan had never seen them that way. They made him different, extraordinary, they set him apart from others—Dan had never wanted any of those things. He'd wanted only to be normal and to lead a normal life.

Dad had been a salesman for American Ranch Security Insurance all his life, and he wanted something better for Dan. He'd wanted Dan to nurture his talents and pursue them professionally. He and Mom had expected Dan to become a great musician and singer. During his freshman year at Lincoln High School, Dan had auditioned for the Lincolnaires, the school's choir, only to satisfy his parents, to get them off his back. He'd made no effort to sing well for the audition—and yet Mr. Sherman, the choir's director, had told Dan he had the best voice he'd heard in twenty years. He urged Dan to join the Lincolnaires. "You have the kind of voice that goes places," Mr. Sherman had said. After getting a good look at the music geeks he saw in the halls of the music building, Dan refused and tried out instead for football. With his height, broad shoulders, and deep chest, he made the team easily, and when Mom found out, she'd cried. Dad had been furious. But Dan was determined to play football and date cheerleaders, like a normal teenager. He'd decided then that *he* had to live his life, not his parents, and he did not want to live it as a music geek, as some kind of freak.

He was good at football, and he loved the game. He made some friends on the team, the sons of wealthy and important people in town, and by the time he was a senior, he moved in those social circles. He hoped to use those connections later. One of his friends was the son of Dad's boss at ARS Insurance. Dan had continued playing football in college, but was serious about his study of business at Berkeley. He knew a career as a professional football player was not in the cards for him—he was good, but not *that* good—and he'd decided to follow in Dad's footsteps and go into the insurance business after college. But because of the connection he'd made playing football, it wasn't his dad who'd helped him get a job selling insurance, it was his dad's boss who'd given him an office job in the San Francisco branch. Now Dan was a junior executive there, midway up the corporate ladder, in a corner office with a nice view of the city.

Dan had an English muffin with his coffee. He missed his ex-wife's breakfasts, the muffins she'd made, the perfect pancakes. But Pamela had left him three years ago, and she'd taken their son and daughter with her. He was scheduled to see fifteen-year-old Royce and thirteen-year-old Lauren every two weeks, but he didn't always make it, and he knew they didn't care. They were indifferent to him, and they never complained when he didn't show up.

He drove to work in his Porsche. Everyone at work was driving BMWs these days, but Dan did his own thinking, and happily parked his Porsche among the Beemers every day. His personalized license plate didn't read RISK-TKR for nothing.

He drove the car down into the building's subterranean garage and parked in his reserved slot, which was near an elevator. He carried his briefcase from the car to the elevator, punched the button with his thumb. The door slid open, he stepped inside, punched a button, and the door closed. ARS insurance occupied floors eighteen through twenty in the forty-story building, and Dan's office was on nineteen.

His work was sometimes monotonous, but it was much easier to do in a corner office with a view.

He punched the 19 button and the elevator went up. Dan waited, briefcase in hand.

It bumped to a stop. He frowned because it felt too soon for the elevator to stop. He looked up at the row of floor numbers above the door, expecting 19 to be lit. But all the numbers were dark.

The door slid open.

Still frowning, Dan stared open-mouthed out of the elevator. It opened on a small, narrow office with a desk, a chair behind it, another in front facing the desk. There was a blotter on the desktop, a shiny black pen in a holder, a telephone with a console of buttons, a gooseneck lamp, and an address caddy. At the front of the desk was a brass frame holding a rectangular placque that read IDA CRENSHAW. On a credenza behind the desk stood a pitcher of icewater and two glasses on a round tray. There was no window, nothing on the beige walls, no bookshelves or filing cabinets, no computer. The office was lit by a single overhead light. There was a closed unmarked door to the right of the desk.

He stepped out of the elevator and looked to his right, then his left. There was no corridor extending to either side, only beige walls. The lobby and reception desk from the nineteenth floor were nowhere in sight—there was only the small, stark office. The elevator door closed behind him.

The door to the right of the desk opened and a tall woman in her sixties with short silver hair walked in. She wore a pantsuit of lime green and pale yellow and held a thick manila folder in her right hand. Her resemblance to actress Bea Arthur was so striking that, for a moment, Dan thought it was she.

The woman flashed a quick smile and said, "Hello, Mr. Griffin. I'm Ida Crenshaw." She had a husky whisky-voice. She sat down at the desk and opened the folder before her.

"How do you know my name?" he asked.

"Sit down and I'll explain."

"How can this be?" he said as he looked around again. "This is some kind of mistake. I was going to my office and—"

"You won't be going to your office anymore, Mr. Griffin. Now please, sit down so we can get started."

Dan turned around where he stood and exclaimed with a single expelled breath. Behind him, there was only a bare beige wall. The elevator door was gone.

"You have nowhere else to go, Mr. Griffin," she said, "so you might as well just sit down and roll with this. Would you like some water?"

Dan nodded as he turned around again to face the desk.

Ida Crenshaw stood and went to the credenza, brought the tray over and set it at the front of her desk. Ice jingled as she poured water into a glass, then held it out to him. Dan took it, sipped the water.

"Now, please, sit down," she said.

Mouth open again, Dan lowered himself into the chair facing the desk and set his briefcase down on the floor beside it.

"Now, about your soul," Ida Crenshaw said.

Dan took another sip of water, then put the glass back on the tray. He said, "Look, Miss, uh, Crenshaw, there's obviously been some sort of mist—I beg your pardon? My...*soul*, did you say?"

"Yes, it's being recalled. There's been no mistake. Well, actually, there has been a mistake, but not today. The mistake seems to have been in giving you this particular soul in the first place. It's been the source of some controversy, I'm afraid. I'm your caseworker."

"My...caseworker."

"That's right."

Dan looked at his watch. It was eight fifty-three. He

stroked his jaw—the skin was smooth, so he had shaved. He was awake, he'd established that much.

"I realize this is a little startling," Ida Crenshaw said. "And please, call me Ida. This is hardly formal. Now, tell me, Dan—you don't mind if I call you Dan, I hope—tell me, what seems to be your problem with the soul?"

"Problem? With…my soul? I…I'm afraid I don't have the faintest idea what the hell you're talking about."

"Well, you hardly use it, you're seldom in touch with it, but most troubling of all is the fact that—" Her eyebrows bunched together as her eyes scanned page after page in the folder. Then she closed the folder and slid it aside, put her elbows on the desktop, and rested her chin on the interlaced fingers of both hands. She smiled and said, "Why don't you sing, Dan?"

"Sing? Why don't I—did you just ask me why don't I sing?"

"Yes."

Dan's eyes darted all over the office. "Is there a—am I being videotaped? Is this some kind of hidden camera thing?"

Ida rolled her eyes. "No, this is not a hidden camera thing. This is real. Well, sort of. It's as real as it needs to be. Could I get you to concentrate on our little talk here, Dan? Please?"

"On our talk?"

"That's right. Just think about my questions and answer them, okay?"

Dan was quite sure things were *not* okay. He took another swallow of icewater, wished it was vodka, then put the glass back. He nodded. "Yes. All right."

"Now, tell me. Why don't you sing?"

"You mean…right now?"

"No, I mean in your life."

"I sing in the shower," he said.

"Not if you think someone's listening."

"Well, yeah, I've always been kind of…shy about it."

"Why? You know you have a good voice. What was it the man said? The director of the Lincolnaires?"

Half of Dan's mouth turned up in a partial smile. "That I had the best voice he'd heard in twenty years."

"And when did he say that to you?" Ida asked.

"When I auditioned to be in the Lincolnaires."

"So, you auditioned, and you were accepted. But you never sang with the Lincolnaires."

"I didn't want to. I just auditioned to satisfy my parents."

"Surely that was a case of youthful rebellion—you didn't want to do it because your parents *wanted* you to do it."

"No, I really didn't want to sing."

Ida tilted her head slightly to one side and frowned. She opened the folder again. "What about your piano lessons?" She flipped through the pages, found the one she wanted, and quickly read it. "Can you still play?"

He shrugged. "Maybe. A song or two. I haven't been anywhere near a piano in years."

"Why not?"

"Why not? What kind of question is that? I'm an insurance executive, for God's sake, not a musician."

"Why not?"

"Why am I not a musician? Because I live in the *real* world, where you have to pay bills and plan for the future."

Ida flipped through the pages again and read another, then folded her hands on the open folder. She turned her head slowly from side to side as she said, "You had music in you, Dan, you know that. Music and art. What about your drawing and painting? You didn't keep up with that, either, did you?"

Dan shook his head in a silent no.

Ida said, "Why? Because you can't make deals while you're painting the way you can on the golf course?"

"I wasn't *that* good," he said.

"You weren't that good at golf, either, but you spent plenty of time on the course. You had a talent for drawing and painting, don't say you didn't." She took in a deep breath as she sat back in her chair, let it out slowly. "You're a very unusual case, Daniel Griffin."

"Me? Why am I so unusual?"

She thought a moment, as if choosing her words carefully. "Because you were given the soul of an artist, Dan — and you're an insurance executive. You had a soul filled with music and art and poetry, but you had a brain filled with statistics and actuarial tables and dollar signs. That's not the way it works. Normally, when we give a body the soul of an artist, that body goes on to be an artist of some kind. Without fail. You're here because we want to know what went wrong in your case."

"Nothing went wrong," Dan said with tension in his voice. He suddenly felt scrutinized and it made him nervous and defensive. He fidgeted in the chair and cracked his knuckles without realizing he was doing it. "I did other things with my life, that's all."

"As simple as that?"

"As simple as that."

"You don't seem to understand, Dan." Ida leaned forward over her arms, which were folded on the desktop. "The soul of an artist — it demands release. It is a force that cannot simply be ignored or suppressed, it *must* have release. Those who try to suppress it become ill with despair, alcoholism, drug addiction, even insanity. And yet, without any resistance at all — in fact, in the face of your enormously proud and supportive parents who were devastated by your choices — you somehow managed to ignore it. You buried it deep, or you turned it off, or *some*thing. That's a first for us, Dan. How did you do it?"

Dan spoke softly: "I didn't ignore it entirely. I sang sometimes. Alone in my car, I've always got a CD playing, and I always sing along. I sing in the shower. I used to sing to my children when they were little."

"But aside from singing for your children, you never really sang *for* anyone, did you? You never shared that ability with anyone. You never sang because you *had* to, just for the joy of it."

"Singers sing," he said. "I wasn't a singer. I've never been a singer. Or a painter."

"And that's what we find so mysterious—that you could have a soul so filled with music and art and poetry, but feel no great urge to release any of it." She flipped back a few pages and made a note. "I suppose it's possible there might be something faulty about the soul itself, but that's *highly* unlikely. Didn't you ever feel a pressing need to express yourself artistically?"

"The only pressing need I felt," he said, "was my desire to be normal. If anything, I wanted to *hide* my talents."

The creases in Ida's forehead were deep. "So you could be *normal*? Dan, anyone can be normal. Not many can sing a song so beautifully that it brings tears to someone's eyes." She tapped the folder with a fingernail. "You had that in you. But you wanted to be *normal*." There was quiet astonishment in her voice.

"You say that as if it's a crime, or something," he said. "What's wrong with wanting to be normal."

"But you had the soul of an artist, Dan."

"But I didn't want the *life* of an artist, Ida."

"But when you have the soul of an artist, you have no *choice*, Dan, that's what I'm trying to make clear to you. So what happened with *you*?"

"I don't know, how am *I* supposed to know?" He fidgeted in the chair again. "I released plenty of creativity before I turned thirteen, believe me. My parents had me playing the piano, the clarinet, singing."

"They recognized your talents," Ida said. "They recognized their importance and wanted you to nurture them."

"Yeah. And they nearly drove me nuts. They finally let me stop going to church, so I didn't have to do anymore performing for the brethren and sistern, or whatever they call them. You have no idea how happy that made me."

41

"You were happy that you wouldn't be performing anymore?"

"That's right. I did everything I could after that to be *normal*, not one of those malfunctioning music geeks. All I wanted to do was get good grades, go to college, meet a beautiful woman, and start some kind of career that would make money. With emphasis on the money, frankly."

"So you buried those talents, and any urges you had to express them."

"I didn't *have* any urges to express them. I didn't *want* them."

"And yet you seem to be reasonably stable."

"I'm not an alcoholic or drug addict, if that's what you mean," he said. "I experienced some depression in high school and college. I've never told anyone about it. It was pretty bad for awhile. I actually thought about killing myself. But it passed. Maybe that was a side effect of not releasing all that art and music and poetry."

Ida nodded. "That's possible. Depression, of course, is a part of the artist's soul because it's a soul that feels everything in such extremes, good and bad. Perhaps that depression is the only part of this soul you experienced." She scribbled a note in the folder. "I suppose there's the possiblity that the soul malfunctioned, somehow, although it still seems doubtful. It's never happened before. It will have to be carefully examined, of course. But we were hoping we'd get more information than this from the consciousness."

"The...consciousness?"

"Yes. You. You know, we were sup*posed* to recall this soul twelve years ago, but we got backed up, then the recall date was moved a couple times. It's a little embarassing that we haven't gotten to you until your fortieth birthday." Ida read something in the folder. It seemed to interest her and she kept reading for several seconds, eyes moving quickly over the pages. She nodded once and said, "I see. I understand now. It makes perfect sense."

"Wait a second," Dan said. He looked at his watch

again—it was gone. He looked across the desk at Ida. "Where did my watch go?"

She smiled. "It's on your wrist, sweetheart."

He looked again, and there it was. It was twelve minutes after nine. "You know, I really have to get to work," he said.

"I told you, Dan, you won't be going to work anymore."

A heavy feeling of dread suddenly fell over him. "What...what are you talking about?"

"I told you. Your soul has been recalled. And I think I've solved the mystery of Daniel Griffin."

Dan frowned as something occurred to him, something that made goosebumps break out on his shoulders. "You've been speaking in the past tense," he said.

"You are the consciousness of Dan Griffin," Ida said. "We brought you here like this to see what you could tell us about your soul. Obviously, you don't know as much as we'd hoped. But I think I have the answer."

"Does...does that have something to do with the fact that you look almost exactly like Bea Arthur?"

She smiled. "We wanted to make you comfortable. *Maude* made you laugh when you were a boy, and you associate good feelings with that television series. So I look the way I look. But it's not really me." She gestured around the office with a liver-spotted hand. "This room, this desk, your body—none of this is real."

"But...where am I? I mean, where am I *really*?"

"Your body is lying in the elevator, either dead or dying. You—meaning the consciousness of Dan Griffin— will be recycled, while the soul will be examined for malfunctions and defects."

Dan suddenly felt a bit short of breath and heard his heart beat in his ears, felt it throb in his fingertips—all illusions, it seemed, if it was true that he was nothing more than *consciousness*. He said, "What is it?"

"What is what?"

"You said you'd solved the mystery of...well, of me. What did you mean?"

Ida said, "We're so understaffed around here, I don't have time to read every word of the file of each and every case. I just happened to read something here in your file, and after a couple pages, I realized the price you've paid for denying your soul release."

Dan realized his hands were trembling. "What? What is it?"

"You were a very bitter person, Dan. You've always been bitter. And no one liked you because of that. I'm not sure how Pamela put up with you as long as she did. You had no real friends. You devastated your loving, supportive parents, who died heartbroken. People just didn't like you, and you didn't give them any reason to."

Dan's eyes were open wide beneath a frowning brow. "But...at work..."

"People at work *especially* didn't like you." She closed the folder. "But I shouldn't be telling you any of this. It's very irregular, you know. You were a very special case, which is why we had this meeting, otherwise you would've gone directly to Recycling. Which is where you'll be going now."

Dan shot to his feet and said breathlessly, "Wait, you can't do this, you can't, it's a mistake."

"Calm down, Dan," Ida said.

"I will *not* calm down. You have to give me a second chance. Look, I've read Dickens, I know Scrooge got a second chance, so you have to give *me* a second chance. I'm only forty, I've got another good thirty or forty years in me, I'm healthy. I can *do* all those things! I can!"

"This is precisely why we never meet before recycling. Dan, it's been decided, and now it's—"

"It can be *re*decided. I'll sing. I'll sing anywhere people will listen. I'll paint. I'll get a piano and take more lessons. I'll paint the piano and sing *a capella*. I'll do whatever it—"

"You've already decided the course of your life, Dan," she said. "Even your wife couldn't get you to pay attention to her, or to your children, or your *life*, for that matter."

As she spoke, Dan's hands closed into fists at his side. Tears burned his eyes.

"Your work was your life," she said. "Your statistics, your charts and graphs. Your life had the order of one who works with numbers, but it was just as cold as those numbers because you allowed it to become that way, because you *made* it that way. You had no passion, because your true passion was music and art, but you somehow suppressed those feelings, buried them so deep you couldn't feel them anymore. Instead, you felt only bitterness—and you didn't even know why. Some suffer from alcoholism, drug addiction, insanity—you were crippled emotionally. And your vanity license plate—*risk taker*—really, that's pretty funny. Buying that Porsche, which you really couldn't afford, instead of the more popular BMW was probably the riskiest thing you've *ever* done, Dan, and surely you realize how...how pathetic that is. You didn't take risks any more than you made commitments. The only thing you were ever committed to was your work, and how committed were you to *that*, really? How long have you been a junior executive in that corner office? How many others your age have ambitiously passed you by on the corporate ladder? You're whole life has been the result of your decision to ignore your own soul, it all comes from—"

"All right, all *right*. I made mistakes. I...I ignored...my soul. I admit it. I'm not arguing with you. And that bitterness—I know where it comes from. It comes from a lot of what-ifs lived over and over in my head. I never told anyone about them, not even Pamela. I barely acknowledged them myself. Like I said, I'm not arguing with you."

"And now it's time for you to go to Recycling."

Dan put both palms flat on the desktop and leaned on his arms with elbows locked. "That's where you lose me. You can't do this, you can't *tell* me all this and then not give me a chance to change things. Who *are* you, anyway?"

"I'm Ida Cren—"

"No, I mean...*what* are you?"

"Something you couldn't possibly begin to understand, and I'm only a very small piece of a much larger picture, which would probably make your head explode. If you really had one. Let's stay on topic here, all right? I'm not up for discussion."

"Has it occurred to you that there might not be anything wrong with the soul?" Dan said. "Maybe *I'm* the problem, did you think about that?"

"Yes, of *course* we thought about that," Ida said. "And we were right, as I just pointed out."

Dan said, "Then you'd be pulling a perfectly good soul out of circulation, right? So why not give me a chance, now that I know what a mess I've made of my life—well, look, it's not that I didn't *know* my life was a mess, I just didn't...I guess I just didn't think about it much. You know? But now you've got to give me a chance to fix things, to use that soul and get in touch with it."

Ida said, "The soul will not be, uh, 'taken out of circulation,' as you put it. It will still be examined just in case, but my report will read that the soul functioned perfectly. We *had* discussed the possibility of giving you a second chance, but frankly, we didn't expect you to react like this, and I—"

"Well, I *am* reacting like this. How the hell did you *expect* me to react? I'll do *all* those things, and I'll *keep* doing them. I'm not talking about some quick fix-it, here, I'm talking about long-term, permanent change, a change to which I will firmly and fully commit myself. You've got to give me that chance, now that you've told me all this, now that you've let me know, you've *got* to."

Ida drummed her fingers on the blotter a few times, studied him with intense eyes. She took a deep breath, and as she let it out, she picked up the telephone receiver, punched a button on the console, and put the receiver to her ear.

"What do you think?" she said. "Is it possible? Or is it too late?" After a moment, she nodded. "Yes, I agree. What do the others say?" Her fingers drummed again. "But what are the chances he'll—yes, I know, but—" More drumming. "All right then." She replaced the receiver and smiled briefly at Dan. "Well, Mr. Scrooge, you're getting your second chance. But we can't guarantee your health."

Everything slowly blurred together until the office became a dull beige smear.

"What do you mean?" Dan said, and his voice broke up like a fading radio signal.

Ida's voice was far off now, faint with distance. He barely heard her last words: "You've suffered a stroke, Dan."

Darkness. Silence.

When Dan opened his eyes again, it was on another blurry colorless smear of images. They slowly coalesced, formed figures, sharpened in clarity.

He lay on his back in what appeared to be a hospital room. Tubes that seemed to come from everywhere at once were attached to various parts of his body. His ex-wife Pamela stood beside his bed on the left. She was talking to a man at the foot of the bed, a doctor in a white coat with a stethoscope around his neck and a clipboard in his hand. As the doctor's lips moved, Dan made an effort to isolate his voice amid the roar of what sounded like a jet engine inside his head.

"...stroke that will...complete paralysis on the right side...brain damage, but to what extent we don't know yet."

Dan attempted to move, to sit up, and the world tilted and spun around him. It frightened and nauseated him, and he stopped trying to move.

"...possible partial rehabilitation...but we don't know what limitations the brain damage will bring."

Dan tried to talk, but his tongue would not work properly and his lips were numb. He made a gurgling sound, like a cooing infant.

He closed his eyes and thought vaguely, *Take me back,*

Ida, please, take me back! But after awhile, he wondered who Ida was, and then he forgot all about her. His mind seemed to slowly collapse on itself. The doctor was still talking, but Dan could no longer understand what he was saying.

Only seconds later, Dan forgot his own name as he lay there with his mouth open, tongue lolling in one corner.

He gurgled.

⋆⋆⋆

Christopher Conlon

*I said earlier that there will always be a place in **Masques** for the well-told ghost story; here's another, and quite a poetic one it is, which is no surprise, seeing as how Christopher Conlon is an accomplished poet (**Gilbert and Garbo in Love**, **The Weeping Season**) as well as short story writer (track down a copy of his brilliant collection **Saying Secrets: American Stories** and you'll be treated to some of the most exquisite prose being written today). As an editor, Christopher has given us **The Twilight Zone Scripts of Jerry Sohl** and **Poe's Lighthouse**, two invaluable volumes for **Twilight Zone** aficionados. For more about Christopher's work, visit his website, www.christopherconlon.com. I know you'll be going there after you read this wonderful tale.*

—JNW

Ghost in Autumn

✠ BY CHRISTOPHER CONLON ✠

I had been out rowing that afternoon, just light paddling around the cove, and was nearly to shore when I noticed the figure standing there waiting for me in the twilight. It was a woman, and she stood very still. It took me only an instant to realize that it was my mother. She had been dead for twenty years.

I rowed close enough that I could step from the boat and begin to haul it up onto the sand. The light was rose and violet behind the trees and long grasses that held this spot of the Patuxent River in such pleasant isolation; a late formation of Canada geese honked by overhead and as I pulled the boat up I could feel the wet sand between my toes.

"Mom," I said, pausing to look at her. She hadn't changed.

"Hello, Jon," she smiled tentatively. We stared at each other for a moment.

"Let me just finish with this," I said finally, and hauled the boat from the river. Sand stuck to my wet feet and I kicked them lightly in the water again.

"It still looks good," she said, studying the wooden boat closely. My father had built it, years before. It was varnished a deep rich red which I periodically touched up in the garage. Other than that, I'd never had to provide much upkeep to it.

"Dad knew how to build things," I said, sitting at the shoreline with my feet in the water.

"He did." She came over and sat beside me in the sand. "You don't look so good, Jonny."

"I'm forty years old."

"I know. I didn't mean that."

I looked at her. She was wearing a suede jacket I remembered, fringed all around the bottom in a style common twenty years ago. She had on blue jeans rolled up at the cuffs and high-top leather boots. Her yellow-tinted aviator glasses were in place, and her blonde hair, long and straight and parted down the middle, was as I recalled it. She was thin, not as thin as she'd once been, but thinner than she would be later when the drinking got out of control and she ran to fat. She was about my age, I supposed. Quite pretty.

"I'm all right," I said at last. "Lost my hair, that's all." We watched the sky darken. It was early October, beginning to turn cool, and I knew I would not be able to spend many more afternoons rowing, at least not comfortably. I would miss it. I missed it every year.

I listened as frogs and crickets started their nightly chirruping somewhere behind us. "Did you want something to eat?" I asked finally.

"That would be nice," she said, nodding appreciatively.

We walked up the beach to the house. She carefully wiped her boots on the mat before stepping over the threshold even though, after all, it was her house. She had bought it with my father as a summer residence a quarter of a century ago; it was my idea, much later, after they were both dead, to move in permanently. I ran a towel over myself quickly and moved barefoot into the kitchen, ran water into the teapot and set it to boil.

She was standing uncertainly in the living room, glancing around in the semidarkness. My living room has a stark look: an old throw rug on the wood floor, hard wicker chairs for furniture, some books haphazardly in the homemade cases. No TV. No pictures on the walls.

"You've changed it so much," she said.

"It's been twenty years. Ten, since Dad died."

"Yes." She looked out the window at the road which follows the shoreline to a few more homes, a little bar and restaurant a mile or so up. "There's more houses now," she said.

"Yeah. We try to keep them out. Sometimes we succeed."

"Good. Keep at it." She looked at me.

"Sit down." I gestured toward one of the chairs. She moved to it gingerly, sat on its edge, as if at any moment she might have to leap up and run.

I sat on the chair facing hers. "What are you doing here, Mom?"

"I wanted to see you."

"Is it that simple?"

"It depends."

"Where have you been, anyway? Where...?"

She shook her head lightly in a gesture I remembered, smiled a little and put her finger over her mouth: Don't ask.

"Do you see Dad?"

"No."

There was silence again. A car passed on the road outside.

In a few minutes the tea kettle began to whistle. "Let me help," she said, starting to rise. But I was up ahead of her, saying, "No, I've got it," and instinctively touching her shoulder. It was no different from touching anyone's shoulder.

I made tea from bags, cut what late-season fruit I still had—cantaloupe, honeydew melon, a last peach—together into bowls, and sliced bread.

"Maybe we should eat in the kitchen," I suggested. "It's more comfortable, and at least there's a table."

"Oh, yes. All right."

We sat together. I watched her eat but was unsure whether she did it the same way or not. I didn't recall ever noticing how my mother ate. She was polite about it, anyway, well-mannered; almost dainty. She took a lot of milk in her tea.

"Do you think you'll stay here a while?" I asked when we finished.

"A little while," she said. "But only if it's all right."

"Of course it's all right. Do you want your old room back? I sleep in it now, you know."

"No, your room is fine for me."

"There's a futon in it. Maybe a little hard for you."

"No, sweetheart, really, I'll be all right."

The light over the kitchen table enveloped us and seemed to keep out the creeping darkness that filled the rest of the house, the night, the world.

The next day we went out in the boat together. She had on a bright yellow bikini, very much in the style of the nineteen seventies, as was everything she wore. She sat at the bow, leaning on her elbows, looking at the sky and at me. She'd left her glasses behind; I wasn't sure how clearly she could see me, or anything, but she was happy. Her eyes were a sparkling blue. She smiled and stretched luxuriously, like a cat in the sun.

"I'd forgotten this," she said. "Doing this. Being out in the water, in the sun."

"Not many days left," I said. "You've come late in the season."

"I know." She draped the ends of her hair down into the water. I watched it floating there as I rowed, lazily. It was like some kind of sea grass and seemed perfectly natural here. I was aware of her body, of how young and supple it still was, and this was another thing I'd never noticed when I was young, never *seen*. It did not surprise me when she reached around behind her and removed her bikini top; she was always very open about her body. There was nothing incestuous in it. My mother and I were not like other people. But somehow, here, she was real in a way she'd never been before. I knew I was with someone, a person, and this person was my mother, and here she was still young, young even though she was my age and I was old.

"So what do you know?" I asked, watching as she took handfuls of glistening sun-warmed water and dribbled them over herself.

"About what?" she said.

"Anything. The past, the present. The fate of the world."

"*Nada.*" She grinned. "Sorry, Jonny. I'm not privy to that kind of information."

"You must know some things."

"Some, yes, some."

"Do you know when I'll die?"

"No." She said this very firmly and finally.

"Did you know it when Dad died?"

She seemed to ponder it, her eyes bright and thoughtful. "It's hard to say, Jonny. I know that sounds like a cop-out, but it's really hard to say."

I stopped rowing and got my water bottle, squirted some into my mouth.

"A plastic bottle?" she said, reaching for it. I handed it to her. "Just for water?"

I smiled. "They're all the rage now."

"I mean, it's just water?"

55

"Just water. Purified, supposedly."

"And people pay for it?"

"People pay for it."

She shook her head, smiling, and tilted the bottle back. She squeezed too hard and it shot her in the face. We both laughed. Finally she got the hang of it.

"Just tastes like water to me," she smiled, handing it back. "But it's good."

"You've missed a lot in the past twenty years," I said. "You don't notice it so much in my house. I still write on a manual typewriter, something absolutely nobody in the world does anymore."

"All electrics now?"

"All computers now."

She grinned. "That sounds like those sci-fi stories you used to read."

"A lot of the world is sci-fi now," I said. "Maybe that's why I live here at the shore, to hide out from it. My neighbors have computers. We should go over and look at one. Ha! Wait 'til you see the Internet."

She didn't pursue it. "What else? I like listening to you talk about your world."

"Well, I pretty much rejected my world. I just stay here and write. When I need money I take on a couple of courses at one of the community colleges around here for a semester."

"So you finished college."

"Yes. But come on, you must have known that. You must know *something*."

"Okay, I knew it." She grinned again. "But I still like to hear you say it."

"And you know about my divorce. You know that my daughter died."

She looked down. "I know."

I looked out at the rippling water. It was bright, very bright, hundreds of silver coins flashing across the sea. I did not want to admit to her that my daughter had committed suicide, but I knew she knew that.

"It's all right, Jon," she said.

"It's not."

"You were a good father."

"The evidence," I said dryly, "suggests otherwise."

"Come on," she said, tugging my knee, "this is our time. Let's be together now."

I tried to smile. "Okay. Sorry."

She sat back again, crunching into an apple she'd found in the bag I packed. "You'll find someone else," she said. "Another woman, a wife."

"Is that encouragement, or a prediction based on inside information?"

"I choose not to reveal my sources," she said, grinning, her mouth full. Bits of white apple were on her teeth.

"There's a lot you don't reveal," I said with a smile.

"Jonny, it's just that I don't know. I know that's hard to believe, but it's the truth."

"Okay."

"I wish I did. I wish I could sit here in this boat on this lovely day and tell you that you're going to be rich and famous and have a beautiful wife and seventeen children. But I don't know. I could lie."

"I don't want you to lie."

"Well, then." She finished with the apple and sat up in the boat, threw the core with all her strength as far as it would go: I watched her arm muscles ripple as she did it. She looked at me. "Do you mind if I smoke? You do mind, I know."

"I do, but it's all right."

"Thanks." She brought a package of cigarettes out of our bag. I hadn't put them there. I was fairly sure the brand had gone out of business years ago.

"Mom," I said finally, watching her smoke, "why are you here? Really."

She smiled at me and shook her head. "I don't know. I'm just here."

"For a while."

"For a while."

"And you know some things but not most."

"Something like that."

"Tell me something else you know."

"You're so insistent!" She looked at me with a mischievous gleam in her eye. "All right. I know that you do it in the shower. How's that? With your left hand."

I laughed. It felt good in the cooling afternoon. "You and Dad tried to turn me into a rightie," I said. "I remember you moving forks and pencils into my right hand all the time." I shook my head. "Didn't work."

"Obviously not!"

The boat drifted through the afternoon light, the water cradling us gently, happily toward no destination I knew.

She started drinking again a few weeks later. We had had good times; we'd gone for long walks along the shore and talked about things from times past. We cooked meals together. I drove her up to the little grocery store a couple of miles away and watched her marvel at things and laugh at them: the convenience foods especially, pre-packaged salads and pre-grated cheese, big plastic two-liter bottles of soda, and of course the cash register, which, after we'd returned to the car, she remarked on by saying, "I thought that thing was going to fly off into outer space!" She was fascinated with my compact discs and the little portable player; she even asked me to find CDs of old Willie Nelson and Tanya Tucker albums for her, her favorite singers, which I did, and it was quite a sight, my mother, forty years old, charming and beautiful and from another age, dancing around my house with an anachronistic disc player in her hands and little earphones on her head.

But soon she began to seem bored, and started going for walks by herself. I immediately suspected where she was walking to: there was a rustic little bar and restaurant just up the road, a dark place with wood floors and a fire-place. All very civilized and pleasant, and though I do not drink I sometimes went there for a meal. It was the only place you could buy alcohol for several miles, and it was the kind of place my mother would like. I wondered what kind of conversations she had with people, this woman who looked to have stepped directly out of the early nineteen seventies and whose memories stopped cold in nineteen seventy-nine. Maybe she didn't talk at all, I thought; maybe she just sat and drank, as she did in her later years. I did not know, did not want to know. I was disturbed by the whiskey odor on her breath, a smell I was all too familiar with and which brought back memories I didn't want, but the days were still good, at least for a while.

It's true that she began to age before my eyes. I would be shocked, by November, at how much older she'd become: her blonde hair was streaked with white now, and her skin seemed to be growing harder and more deeply lined. Her eyes lost their extraordinary luster. At night I would hear her muttering in her sleep in the next room, turning again and again, tossing the bed sheets away. Finally, one night, I heard her crying.

"Mom?" I whispered, coming into the room. "What is it?"

"It's all right, Jonny," she said, her voice fractured with weeping. "Go back to bed. I'm sorry I woke you, honey."

"Mom, tell me what it is." I knelt by her bedside, touched her cheek softly.

"I don't know what it is." Her face was contorted, anguished.

"Are you sick? What can I do?"

"I'm not sick. Not that way. But I'm sick, that's it. I'm sick."

"Mom…"

"I'm sick and I can't stop being sick."

I looked at her, her body grown heavy. Her face was

rounder now and had an unhealthy pallor. Her arms were thicker, her fingers puffy. I took hold of her hand in a way I never had the first time, when I first knew her. But I was older now.

"Mom, you'll be all right," I said. "It doesn't have to be like this. I can take you to a hospital."

"No. It's not that kind of sickness."

"It is."

"I'm all right. Go to sleep now."

I stood, looked down at her, a desolate wind flying through my heart. *I'm all right. Go to sleep now.* Exactly what my daughter would say. And of course my mother knew that.

By Thanksgiving I would find my mother wandering along the road in the middle of the night, looking for the house in the darkness. My headlights would shine straight through her as they touched her body. And yet her body was solid: thick, ill, yellow with jaundice.

She would rally. One day she would tell me, "Son, I'm stopping, I'm absolutely stopping, I'm not going to drink anymore." And for show she would pour the whiskey bottle she'd brought into the house down the drain, every last drop. "Done. Done for good!" But by nightfall she would be at the bar again.

It all happened insanely fast, as if her life were a speeded-up film. The gray in her hair. The heaviness. The permanently slurred speech. Sometimes I wished my dad were there, but he had not been there for the worst of it anyway: they'd long left each other by then. It had been the two of us in the house, alone together, night after night, just as it was now. And I was as helpless now as I'd been then.

"Why are you here?" I finally asked her one night when she wasn't too drunk to respond. "Why are you here, Mom? To torture me? *Why*?"

She looked up at me from the wicker chair, arms wrapped around the bottle like a baby, eyes black with tears and sickness and despair.

"Don't hate me, Jonny," she pleaded quietly. "Please don't hate me."

"You're going to die. You know that."

She shook her head.

"You will. You did once."

"Not really. And maybe that's why...why I won't die now."

"You'll go on like this? For how long?"

She looked up at me again, eyes huge. "I don't know. *I don't know*."

Winter.

Rain pounded down onto the roof in mad sheets, the wind whipping the trees outside and whistling through the cracks in the windows. My mother spent most of her time in bed or else in the wicker chair in the main room, curled up fetally with a bottle in her hand. She did not cause me any trouble. There were no scenes. I went about my business. But always, she was there, hovering in my consciousness like some dark wraith. I wanted her to leave, but I could not imagine where she might go. How could she live? How could she get money? She did not belong here but was trapped. Somehow I'd begun to understand that she was trapped, that her coming here had had little to do with her and was not something she understood.

"I think..." she said once, in the darkness.

"What, Mom?"

"I think maybe...maybe it's you who keeps me here."

"Me?"

She looked at me. "Maybe."

"How can it be me?"

"I don't know. Maybe it is."

"No," I said. "If I controlled things like that, you'd be gone."

"I didn't say you did it consciously."

"So, unconsciously. Why you? Why not Dad?" I felt a flash of anger. "Why not my daughter?"

She sat unmoving for a long time. I heard her sigh, a strange, distant sound that reminded me of a faraway train.

"I was your first," she said.

I stopped writing. I spent a great deal of time walking or driving, as often as not finding her staggering along the road in the middle of the night, walking home in the wrong direction. The rain stopped, but the skies remained black-clouded and dim. I chopped wood, did little things outside the house, anything to keep myself busy.

Finally I put on a heavy coat and dragged the boat out into the winter water. My feet got wet through my boots but I didn't care. I jumped in, paddled hard. The water was rough and gray, splattering in my face again and again. I just rowed, as hard as I could, feeling my upper body muscles groan with the effort. I had no destination, no goal, just a sudden need to escape, to be elsewhere, anywhere.

I rowed for a long time, directionless, in circles. The sky grew dark as evening came on and a light rain, hardly more than a mist, began to drizzle down. I hugged myself closely, breathing through gritted teeth, and let night fall around me.

At last I heard voices and looked up. I'd drifted to the bar and my mother was saying goodbye to someone there, walking—stumbling—from the building. I watched her as she made her way slowly, fumblingly, through the dark. A cigarette glowed in one hand. A bottle was in the other.

Occasionally she stopped and drank from it, then kept moving. I paddled quietly, keeping up with her from a distance, maybe fifty yards from her. She passed through a grove of trees, keeping to the path better than she usually did. It took her perhaps twenty minutes to get to the house, which had just the kitchen light on, shining weakly out onto the little strip of grass that passes for my lawn.

She dropped down onto the grass, this fat, faintly pathetic-looking woman, and sat there looking out at the water. Her hair drooped limply in front of her face but she did not move to touch it. I did not know if she saw me. If she did, she made no sign. She sat motionless and looked tired, exhausted, a weariness that seemed to come from another dimension, another world, like none that could exist on this planet. It did not seem that she would ever move again. Her entire body seemed about to collapse, to molder into the earth.

I stared at her, feeling the empty wind in my heart. This would have no simple ending, I knew now. No. She would be here for a long time, possibly forever, and there was nothing either of us could do about it. The other ghosts of my life were just that, ghosts, but my mother was more. She had pride of place. I knew it should have been someone else there, a young girl who told me it was all right, go to sleep now, and I did, and her absence from the shore before me left me desolate and in physical pain, a pain that began in my stomach and emanated through every inch of me, bathing me in bitter anguish so deep I could not cry or scream. The darkness around me bloomed but it seemed not to come from the sky, rather from myself, a giant darkness overflowing my mind and body and filling the night and the world with my weakness, my agony, a darkness that was my own and which I could not escape and which had, so far as I could see from my place in the still waters, no end.

Ray Russell

*My late friend Ray Russell (1924—1999) was one of the finest writers and human beings it has ever been my privilege to know. The author of such exquisite and terrifying novels as **The Case Against Satan, The Colony,** and **The Bishop's Daughter,** Ray was also an accomplished screenwriter and short story author. While many of his stories have been gathered into such collections as **Sardonicus and Other Stories, Unholy Trinity,** and **The Book of Hell,** there are still many of his wonderful tales that have never appeared in book form. I'm honored to be able to correct that with at least one of them here, a talke in the Gothic tradition that showcases Ray's writing at its most lean and powerful.*

—JNW

The Black Wench

✠ By Ray Russell ✠

"Mainwaring'" said Bud Kallen from the back seat of the humming car. "So that's the way you spell it over here." He folded up the deed he'd been studying.

"Yes," replied Nigel Sloane, a slim, silver-haired man as smooth as the Bentley he was driving. "But not *pronounced* 'Maine Wearing,' as you did. We pronounce it 'Mannering'…" He turned to the young woman in the passenger seat to his left. "…Which, I take it, is the way your late mother *spelled* her maiden name, Mrs. Kallen?"

"That's right," Elena Kallen answered. "Americans said it wrong so often that my great-grandfather Humphrey changed the spelling when he settled in the States right after the First World War."

"Sensible of him."

"Settling in the States?" asked Bud Kallen.

"Simplifying the name," said Nigel Sloane.

He had disliked Kallen the instant he'd met him, and had tried in vain to suppress the emotion. He told himself that he resented the man's youth, and the fact that he was an American; but that didn't wash, because Mrs. Kallen was young and American, too, and Sloane didn't dislike her. Was that only because she was a woman? he asked himself; a beautiful woman with large brown eyes and sable hair? He hoped he was not so biased. The Warwickshire countryside, green as broccoli in the midday sun, rolled majestically past his window as he guided the car around a subtle bend in the road.

Elena was saying, "The name died out when my mother married. She didn't have any brothers. And her unmarried sister died a long time ago. That must have mad it hard for you to find me."

"A bit," Sloane admitted. "But we are a diligent firm, Mrs. Kallen. We kept on the scent until we discovered that Helen Mannering, the grand-daughter of Humphrey, had married a gentleman attached to one of the Central American consulates in your country, a Mr. Enrique Castillo, and that their union had produced two offspring: Henry and Elena. If your brother Henry had not been killed in Vietnam, he, being the elder, would have been my passenger today. As fate decreed, however, you are the closest surviving blood relation of Sir Giles Mainwaring."

The firm's enquiry agents had found the former Elena Castillo living in a small apartment with her husband in Los Angeles, where Kallen ran a not very successful public relations company called Images Unlimited.

"I still can hardly believe it," said Elena, shaking her head. "It seems incredible that there isn't anybody closer to Sir Giles here in England."

"I can assure you that we searched for them," said Sloane. "As his solicitors, we were duty bound to leave no stone unturned. But Sir Giles was a widower whose only child died without issue a few years ago, and his only branches of the family tree still here—cousins *many* times removed, and whatnot—but you have the most direct lineal connection to him, genealogically speaking. Therefore, according to the terms of his will, you are the legatee of his entire estate, including Mainwaring Hall."

Bud said, "I guess it'll be Kallen Hall from now on, right, honey?"

Before Elena could respond to her husband's impudent assumption, Nigel Sloane said frostily over his shoulder, "It has been called Mainwaring Hall since Jacobean times, Mr. Kallen. Sir Giles was descended in a direct line from one of the first baronets in the kingdom, Sir Edred Mainwaring, who received his baronetcy from King James the First."

"Of the King James Bible?" asked Elena.

"The same. It was a new rank in those days, you see, created by the king to provide a new dignity higher than knight but lower than baron."

"Why?" Bud asked.

"To raise money for the treasury."

Bud laughed. "You mean the king *sold* this new 'dignity' to old Edred? For filthy lucre?"

"In a manner of speaking."

Bud laughed again and slapped his knee. "I love it!" he said. "*Love* it!"

Doing his best to ignore Bud, Nigel Sloane addressed Elena: "Speaking of filthy lucre, Mrs. Kallen, there will of course be a heavy toll in death duties—what I believe you call inheritance taxes—but even after the Inland Revenue has taken its ton of flesh there will be a substantial cash settlement. One might call it, without fear of hyperbole, a small fortune."

"Not a large fortune?" asked Bud.

Nigel Sloane shrugged. "These things are relative. And then we must not forget Mainwaring Hall itself, which we could arrange to sell for you, should you decide not to live there."

"Why would we decide that?" asked Elena.

"Well, for one thing, it's so very large for two people; and for another...but there, see for yourself." The car slowed down and came to a stop. To their left in the middle distance, looming in the center of spacious grounds, stood an enormous old house.

It seemed to grow out of the earth from roots almost four centuries old, as if it had been not so much built as planted. It sucked its strength from the soil and the air, squatted on the landscape like an exotic bloated organism, surveying its dominion with the unblinking eyes of its many windows. If the Kallens had known anything about Jacobean architectural style, they would have recognized instantly that Mainwaring Hall was a typical example of it. The uneasy mixture of late Perpendicular Gothic motives and crudely misused classic details boldly announced its period as surely as a fanfare of trumpets. The Flemish influence, characteristically, was strong, and the Tudor pointed arch was much in evidence. Nearer them, glinting in the weeds at the roadside, an empty Coca-Cola can, flung there by some irreverent motorist, provided an ironic contrast that spanned the centuries at a glance.

Noting this anomaly, Elena said, "It's like time doesn't exist."

"Perhaps it doesn't," said Sloane. "Perhaps it's an illusion. When Pythagoras was asked to define time, he said it was the soul of this world. I've never quite understood what he meant by that, but I've always liked the sound of it."

"The old place must be expensive to keep up," said Bud.

"Precisely," said Sloane, agreeing with Kallen for the first time all day.

"But we have money now," Elena reminded her husband. "A small fortune. You heard Mr. Sloane."

Bud spoke to the solicitor: "You said the house is awfully big for just the two of us, and you were going to say something else..."

"Was I? I don't remember. I suppose I was about to say

that Jacobean isn't to everyone's fancy. Some people even consider it to be in rather bad taste."

"*I* don't," said Elena stoutly. "I think it's beautiful."

Sloane was too much of a gentleman to voice his opinion of her opinion. He purred diplomatically, "Ah, there speaks the family pride of a true Mainwaring. Shall we drive in?"

He started the Bentley again and drove it slowly through the open gates, up a curving path past trees and hedges, formal gardens, and weathered stone statuary of indeterminate age. "Warwickshire is Shakespeare country, you know," Sloane said as he drove. "Stratford, if you care for that sort of thing, is a pleasant motoring journey from here." At length, the car drew up to the main entrance of the massive house.

"It's in pretty good shape for its age," Bud commented.

"Restoration and renovation through the years," Sloane explained, "not to mention added wings and what-not. Very few of the mod cons, though, I fear."

"Beg pardon?" said Elena.

"Modern conveniences. No central heating, air conditioning, television antennae..."

"No phone?"

"Oh, yes. Mainwaring Hall is on the telephone. And electricity has been laid on. It also has one other contemporary feature that should interest a Californian couple like you: a swimming pool."

"Really?"

Sloane nodded. "Sir Giles had it installed some twenty years ago, when the doctors prescribed swimming as healthful exercise for his heart. He tried it once, said he loathed the chlorinated water, and never got into it again. Lived to the age of eighty-six and died of emphysema, not a heart attack."

"Well, I'll give the pool plenty of use," said Elena. "I love to swim."

"Yeah," said Bud, "I'm more of a scuba diving nut

myself, but show her a pool and she's happy as a pig in slop."

"What a colorful expression," said Sloane. "Not much opportunity for scuba diving around here, however. Shall we look at the interior?" They climbed out of the car and walked up to the formidable oaken portal. As he lifted the heavy brass knocker and struck sharply several times against the thick door, the solicitor said, "There's been only a skeleton staff here since Sir Giles died."

"And here's one of the skeletons now," murmured Bud as the door was opened by a cadaverous and very old butler.

"Ah, there you are, Coles," said Sloane, as the aged manservant blinked first at the solicitor, then at his clients, and, with a long, lung-emptying sigh, toppled forward as if bludgeoned, into the arms of a startled Nigel Sloane.

"Help me get him inside," Sloane said to Bud, and the two men clumsily carried the inert butler into the house to the first available chair, an ornate relic of wood at the foot of the no less ornate staircase. Into this chair they deposited their load as gently as possible, while Elena hovered behind them, uttering helpless moans of sympathy.

"Oh, the poor old man," she said. "What's wrong with him?"

"He's an extremely antiquated chap," said Sloane, "and the death of Sir Giles has put a great strain on him."

"He's not *dead*, is he?" she asked.

"No," said Bud, "he's coming around."

The butler's eyelids fluttered several times. He lifted his head from his chest.

"Now then, Coles," said the solicitor, "do you know me?"

"Mr...Sloane..."

"Well done. These two young people are your new master and mistress..."

He seemed reluctant to meet his new employers, so Elena said, "I think introductions can wait. He should go and lie down until he's feeling better."

Sloane endorsed that idea, and in moments the housekeeper, Mrs. Thayer, who was temporarily doubling as cook, was summoned to convoy the butler to his quarters. While she was thus occupied, Sloane conducted the Kallens on a quick, informal tour of the first floor.

Every room was done in either true Jacobean or later pseudo-Jacobean style: main hall, galleries, staircases, dining room, library, drawing room, billiard room. Richly carved walnut paneling covered every inch of every wall: representations of spaniels, squirrels, woodcocks, partridges, pheasants all stood out in vivid relief. The library was spacious enough to accommodate, in addition to endless shelves of books, no less than six commodious sofas for browsing and lounging. Sloane, as he led them through the rooms, kept up a running commentary: "As you see, the doorways, fireplaces, and the like are all frames with classic forms, and both inside *and* outside there is a wide use of gains, pilasters, and S scrolls...The paintings in *this* gallery have very little intrinsic value, for the most part, but serve as a family album. Most of the Mainwarings are here except for a few black sheep like Sir Percival, who wrote bad checks and died of venereal disease. The last Lady Mainwaring kept his picture in her sitting room, as a joke. Here is that lady, and her husband, Sir Giles, both painted some forty years ago. The gentleman at the far end is the first baronet of the line, Sir Edred, painted, the family claim, by Daniel Mytens, who also painted James the First, but some experts dispute that claim. Wart and all, eh?" Sir Edred indeed had a large hairy mole to the left of his prominent nose, Elena saw as she drew closer to the painting. He also had a gray beard and moustaches, and glaring pale eyes. A close-fitting cloth headpiece or hood covered his possibly bald head, even his ears. A large ring of fur encollared his throat. "The *north* gallery," Sloane continued, "has some Constables and Gainsboroughs, even a Holbein, all of great artistic and financial interest..."

The billiard room was pronounced by Bud to be his favorite. He immediately took down a cue from the wall rack and broke the balls with a resounding clatter.

"Can we see the pool?" Elena asked.

"To be sure. And then we can stroll out to the stables."

"There are horses here?" she marveled.

"Not for some time," Sloane said. "Just motor cars. A Mercedes, a Jaguar, a bright red Ferrari that will probably suit *you*, Mr. Kallen, and a very, *very* old Rolls-Royce."

"Who drove the Ferrari?" Elena asked.

"Why, Sir Giles. He was quite the dashing old gentleman."

He led them out a back entrance of the house to the pool—which was empty and dry, its floor carpeted with dead leaves. Elena groaned with disappointment, but Sloane said, "Not to worry. I'll arrange to have it cleaned and filled for you. Leave everything to me."

"It's so nice and private out here," she said, "I have a feeling I could sunbathe in my birthday suit..."

"Birthday suit?" the bewildered solicitor inquired.

Bud sniggered. "With nobody but the hired help cheering you on from the servants' quarters!"

"Actually," said Sloane, "the servants' quarters do not overlook the pool; they are in a remote section of the house—but our English sun is no match for the sun of Southern California or the French Riviera, I'm afraid. One doesn't tan under its rays, one pinks. We're a bit too north, you see. Shall we have a look at your stable of thoroughbred motor cars?..."

Mrs. Thayer appeared from the house at that moment. She was a stout woman of forty-odd years, with an air of imperturbable dignity. "Excuse me, sir," she said to the solicitor, "but Mr. Coles would like to speak to you. Can you come upstairs?"

"Now?"

"Please."

"Oh, very well." He told the Kallens how to find their way to the stables, and followed Mrs. Thayer into the house.

The stables were larger than they had expected, and their walls were covered by the biggest magnolias Elena had ever seen. All the cars were there, conforming to Nigel Sloane's spoken catalogue, and in gleaming condition. Sure enough, Bud was drawn to the red Ferrari as if to a smiling girl, and he looked at it with undisguised lust. As they were leaving the stables, Elena said, "Hey, look at this."

She pointed to a group of four words cut into the wood of a dark and cobwebbed corner of the stables. The letters were crude, but worn smooth at the edges, their depths engrained with dirt, bespeaking the passage of unnumbered years since they had been carved there. The words were:

Beware the Blacke-wench

"Probably a horse," said Bud. "An ornery black mare that threw her riders."

In the house again, Nigel Sloane told them that the ancient butler, Coles, had announced his intention to retire from service and spend his declining years with a niece near Ipswich.

"Kind of sudden, isn't it?" said Bud.

"Perhaps," Sloane conceded, "but it's difficult for the old boy to adjust to new young masters. He served Sir Giles for almost fifty years! And, to speak frankly, I think you will be better off with a younger man in the post. Poor old Coles is past his prime. I'll put you in touch with one or two good employment agencies. You'll be wanting a cook, as well, and gardeners, of course...other servants, too...leave all that to me and to Mrs. Thayer. We'll arrange the interviews for you."

A taxicab from the nearby village called for Coles that very afternoon. The old man climbed in with his cases and boxes, and was off to the railroad station without another word. "He sure was in a big hurry," said Bud.

Mrs. Thayer subsequently showed the Kallens the rest of the house—the upstairs bedrooms, sitting rooms, nurseries, and servants' quarters; belowstairs, the kitchen, pantry, and wine cellar—while Sloane telephoned employment agencies, arranged for the reactivating of the pool, and generally made himself indispensable.

After a simple tea prepared an served by Mrs. Thayer, Sloane said, "I should be getting back now. If you have any questions, if there is anything I can do, anything at all, please have no hesitation in telephoning. You have my number." He addressed these remarks to Elena. "And if you should reconsider, and wish to dispose of this valuable property at an attractive price..."

"I wouldn't dream of it," she declared. "I love the place, I belong here, I'm a Mainwaring. Why should I get rid of it? Is it haunted or something?"

Bud said, "Sure it is. All these old English houses have ghosts, don't they?"

Nigel Sloane chuckled. "Your husband is right. All old English houses are reputed to harbor ghosts, and Mainwaring Hall is no exception."

"Really?" squeaked Elena. "Ghosts?"

"Just one. So the old wives' tales would have it, at any rate. It's the reason Mainwaring Hall has always had difficulty keeping servants, and why most of them left after Sir Giles died. Country folk are terribly superstitious. But I've never seen the ghost, and I don't believe that Sir Giles ever saw it. That's the one common denominator about ghosts: nobody ever actually sees them; but everybody has a friend of a friend who knows somebody whose great-aunt says that her mother had a servant who saw one. Humans are very gullible animals."

"But what's it supposed to be like?"

"The ghost of Mainwaring Hall?"

"Yes! Tell us! I'm dying to know!"

The solicitor sighed. "Oh, dear. Well, then. It's purported to take the form of a naked woman, a black woman, which is why it's known as The Black Wench..." Elena and Bud exchanged quick glances. "Some versions say that its presence is felt, rather than seen, felt as a cold wet hand or an expanse of clammy bare flesh...but I'm upsetting you, Mrs. Kallen."

"No, no! Please go on."

"The Mainwarings of old, some say, were heavily invested in the African slave traffic as early as 1620 and made the bulk of their wealth by financing the capture, transport, and sale of the poor wretches to the American colonies. This conveniently accounts for the apparition's color, you see...a female slave who died in some cruel manner, perhaps, flogged or what-you-will, and who blamed the Mainwarings for her harsh fate."

"How long has she been haunting Mainwaring Hall?" Elena asked.

"The first recorded sighting was by Sir Edred Mainwaring. He wrote that he saw her in the room that is now the library, but which in his time was much smaller and served as his study, what he called his 'closet.' She allegedly came to him there late one night in 1624 while he was reading his Bible, this naked black woman, glistening as if covered with perspiration from head to foot, and, in Sir Edred's words, 'reeking with the stench of Hell.' He was a religious man, and he believed that she was 'asweat from the fires of Perdition,' whither she'd been sent as a demon or succubus to tempt him to damnation with her naked body."

"Wow," said Bud, "if a guy has got to see a ghost, that's the kind of ghost to see, huh?"

Sloane said, "I take your meaning. Sir Giles, after Lady Mainwaring had passed away, once told me that he wouldn't have minded an occasional visit from a naked wench. But I don't think he was ever favored by the black lady's attentions. As far as Sir Edred is concerned, a modern psychiatrist would no doubt say that he was having a sexual fantasy about a voluptuous African woman, but that his religious convictions wouldn't allow him to enjoy the fantasy without those pious distortions. I do hope I haven't offended you, Mrs. Kallen, or frightened you."

"No, of course not. Goodness, I don't believe in ghosts."

"Very sensible," said the solicitor as he rose to leave. "Do you?"

Nivel Sloane smiled. "I've always admired what Sir Osbert Sitwell said when he was asked that same question," he told her. "'Only at night.'"

That evening after dinner, Bud killed some time at the billiard table, but soon grew bored without an opponent. He roamed restlessly through the library and several other rooms, finally joining Elena in the drawing room, where she was writing postcards to friends in the States.

"It isn't exactly L.A., is it?" he said. "Or London. I *liked* London, what we saw of it on the way in. Theatres, movies, restaurants, gambling casinos. It's alive. Not so dead quiet, like this place. We'll have to get a TV."

"If you want to."

He rested on the arm of her chair and, with an excruciating attempt at an English accent, whispered in her ear, "I say, my deah, what about initiating the mahster bedroom?"

She giggled. "It's early."

"Almost ten. And this country air"—he yawned theatrically—"makes me sleepy."

"We have had a busy day." She, too, was overcome by a yawn. "Give me ten minutes to get ready, then come up."

He bowed deeply from the waist. "As you wish, milady." She left the room.

The master bedroom boasted two adjoining sitting rooms where husband and wife might dress and undress in privacy, visible to no eyes other than their own and those of their valet and maid. To the sitting room with the more feminine décor, where her bags had been taken and unpacked by Mrs. Thayer, Elena now retreated and took off her clothes. When she was without a stitch, she admired herself in a tall old looking glass, smiling with total absence of false modesty. Her body was sumptuous and full-bosomed, satin to the touch, with the olive skin of her father, and a curly nest at center like a swatch of soft fur. Her brushes had been set out on the dressing tables. She selected one, but instead of sitting down to brush her dark hair, she did it standing up, nude, in front of the full-length mirror, watching her breasts bob and quiver as she brushed the gleaming thick mass in long strokes. Once, she winked at herself.

The gaze of a cold, unmoving eye made her drop the brush and catch her breath in sudden fright when she glimpsed it in the glass.

Turning quickly, her hands covering breasts and thatch in a reflexive movement, she saw that the eye belonged to a personage at the opposite side of the room: insolent, dissolute, clad in the tight breeches, cutaway coat, and tall silk hat of a Regency rake, he might have been taken for Beau Brummel had not a small brass plate on the picture's frame identified him as Sir Percival Mainwaring (1785-1826). He appraised her nudity coolly through a lorgnette. She stuck her tongue out at him.

Downstairs, Bud impatiently waited only six minutes, not ten, before climbing the staircase to the master bedroom. Even so, she was already in bed when he walked into the room: the lights were turned off, but he had no difficulty discerning the familiar curves of her shape under the coverlet, thrown into relief by a cool wash of moonlight from the windows.

"My little eager beaver," he muttered playfully, as he began to undress there in the bedroom. No sitting room for him: he was in no mood to stand on ceremony, and he let the clothes fall to the floor. Nude in the moonlight, he was a well-proportioned, muscular young man, and, at the moment, spectacularly virile. "Here I come, ready or not," he crooned, and climbed under the coverlet.

She was lying on one side, her naked back to him. He pressed the whole length of his body to hers, then immediately recoiled.

"*Damn*, you're cold!" he complained. "And you're all wet...soaking...what did you do, take a cold shower and come to bed without toweling off?"

"What did you say, dear?" Elena asked as she walked through the door from her sitting room, clad in a filmy nightgown.

"*Christ*!"

Bud sprang from the bed as if kissed by a scorpion.

"What's the matter?"

He crouched naked in the dark, on the carpet next to the bed, gasping. "Who..." he said in choked fragments, "who's that...in the bed?"

"Nobody!"

He stretched out a trembling arm and pointed his finger to the bed. "I felt her...she's *there*..."

Elena snapped a switch, flooding the room with light. "Where?" The bed was empty.

"She *was* there!"

"Who?"

"How the hell should I know? I thought it was you. And then...you walked through the door." His face was chalky.

She handed him his robe. "Come on, dear, get up off the floor. Put this on. You had a dream, that's all."

He got to his feet and wrapped himself in the robe. "A dream...no...couldn't be..."

"Sure, don't you see? You got into bed to wait for me, and you dozed off just for a few seconds and dreamt I was already in bed beside you."

"Cold," he said. "She was cold. Naked and wet." He yanked the coverlet all the way off the bed. "If it was a dream," he said, "how do you explain *that*?"

On one side, the sheet was wrinkled from top to bottom by the long, sodden stain of a drenched and recent occupant.

Bud Kallen refused ever to sleep in that bed. He claimed it was "clammy," even after the sheets had been changed, even after the mattress had been replaced. The young couple slept in one of the other bedrooms, he clinging to his wife all night, every night, like a child clinging to its mother.

It was not a conjugal embrace. The spearhead of his virility had been shattered that night, and did not regain its former edge. Elena began to feel it was her fault.

"No, honey, it's not you," he insisted one morning at breakfast. "It's this damn house. Why don't we sell it? Sloane said he could get us a good price for it."

"Sell the house?" she wailed. "Just when we've got the pool ready again, and a TV, and a new butler and a cook, and—"

"What's that got to do with it? The pool and the TV antenna are good selling points."

"I don't *want* to sell it. Don't you understand?"

"But why not? The cars alone are worth a mint, even if we keep one or two of them. That classic Rolls? It's a collector's item. And those priceless paintings! Gainsboroughs and Constables and…"

"You're not a Mainwaring, that's why you don't understand. But I am."

He laughed metallically. "You're a *Kallen*, that's what you are. And before that, you were a Castillo—a spic, for Christ's sake! Don't pull that lady of the manor stuff with me."

Her dark eyes had brimmed with hurt and fury. Now she tore away from the table, knocking over her coffee cup, and ran weeping from the room.

He found her huddled on a stone bench in the garden, her tear-streaked face held in her hands. He talked to her gently and contritely, apologizing, asking to be forgiven. He could be persuasively charming when it suited him. By the time they had returned to the house, she had agreed to invite Nigel Sloane to dinner at Mainwaring Hall some time that week.

Two evenings later, the solicitor was enjoying an excellent meal prepared by their new cook: turtle soup, halibut mousse, beef Wellington, fresh asparagus vinaigrette, with appropriate wines from the well-stocked cellar of the late Sir Giles. Offered his choice of either sherry trifle or Stilton cheese and biscuits "for afters," he chose both, causing Elena to ask him how he kept his trim figure. She and Bud, true to American custom, were on perpetual diets. "Do you exercise?"

"Never," he proudly replied, and asked if Elena were enjoying her swimming pool.

"I swim every day," she told him, "and sometimes at night."

"Sir Giles would have been happy about that."

Coffee and cognac followed in the drawing room, and as Sloane touched a flame to a Havana cigar, he said, "Am I to understand that you have had second thoughts about selling?"

Bud thought it polite to let Elena speak. She said, "That's the word, Mr. Sloane. Thoughts. Just thoughts, for now. Could we talk about it?"

"Of course. Any particular reason?"

She shrugged. "No."

Bud rubbed his arms and said, "Chilly in here. We ought to have a fire. I'll ring for the butler."

"Dear, you'll broil us alive. I feel fine." Her smooth arms and back were bare in her dinner gown. "The cognac will warm you up."

Sloane returned to the subject of selling. "Yes, we can certainly investigate one or two avenues of possibility." He smiled. "But you two seemed to have been settling in so nicely. Haven't seen The Black Wench, by any chance?"

"No," Bud said, too quickly.

Elena asked, "Have you ever known anyone who *has* seen her?"

"Ah," replied Sloane, "one can never say that one has known somebody who's seen a ghost. The most one can say is that one knows somebody who *says* he's seen a ghost."

"And did you ever know anybody who said he saw the Black Wench?"

"In point of fact, yes."

"Who?" asked Bud.

"Coles."

"What? That old guy who quit the day we got here?"

Sloane nodded. "A few years ago, Sir Giles told me — laughing as he did so — 'I believe old Coles has gone dotty. Claims to have seen the Wench. In the billiard room, of all places. Called him by name, he says. Gave him quite a turn. I told him to stop knocking back the cooking sherry or I'd sack him.'"

Elena asked, "Did Coles ever see her again?"

"He said he did — the very day the two of you arrived. He told me that was why he wanted to leave. All for the best, to my way of thinking. High time he'd been put out to pasture. And I did smell drink on his breath that day."

Bud leaned forward. "How did Coles describe her? Was she naked? And black?"

"I don't know. I didn't cross-examine him." His cigar had gone out. As he rekindled it, he said, "I wouldn't place too much importance on that word 'black,' you know." A long plume of smoke unfurled from his mouth. "Or 'naked,' for the matter of that."

"What do you mean?" asked Elena.

"Well 'black' hasn't always meant the same thing, when applied to the color of people. Samuel Pepys, in his diary, refers to the wife of a Mr. Hater as a 'very pretty, modest, black woman,' but she was certainly no Negress, simply a woman of dark complexion. Shakespeare, in *Love's Labour's Lost* and *The Two Gentlemen of Verona*, for example, calls 'black' characters who are obviously what we would call white. And in four or five sonnets about his beloved Dark Lady, he calls *her* 'black,' although it's now believed that she was of Italian descent. The same is true of the word 'naked,' which in older parlance sometimes meant clad only in underclothing. So," he concluded with a twinkle, "Sir Edred's 'naked black woman' may have been no more than a late-night lady-love of his steward's, a scullery maid, more than like, thoroughly English if a touch swarthy, and caught in her skivvies on the way back to her own bed. Wandered into the master's closet by mistake, no doubt."

Elena smiled. "More cognac, Mr. Sloane?"

"Just a drop, perhaps. Thank you. Now then: a sale of this property could begin with an auction of the paintings, motor cars, and other valuables; or, on the other hand—"

"I've changed my mind," she said. "Talking to you has helped me think more clearly. I don't want to sell, after all."

When Nigel Sloane had left, Bud held his temper until he was certain all the servants had gone to bed. Then he exploded: "*What the hell's the matter with you?*"

"He was so sensible," said Elena. "So level-headed. He let me see that so-called ghost for what it really is: nothing at all. A servant girl in her underwear. A senile butler who'd been hitting the bottle. I'm not going to give up all this for some fairy tale."

"'*All this*'? This white elephant? This drafty old museum?"

"I have a right to change my mind."

"*What* mind? You dumb spic!"

"That's the second time in less than a week you've used that word. I know you're sexually frustrated, and I'm sorry for you, but—"

"Just *shut up* about that! Getting out of this damn house is all the cure I need!"

She turned and walked away.

"*Where are you going?*" he shouted.

"For a swim," she said, and ran swiftly upstairs, where she stripped and squeezed into a brief bikini she would have hesitated to wear on a public beach, and tripped quickly downstairs again on bare toes, out to the moonlit pool. The night-silence was cloven by a splash when, sleek as a dolphin, she dove cleanly into the water.

She swam the length of the pool, her arms slicing the water in strong, graceful strokes; then she reversed, swimming back towards the other end again. The exercise and the bracing effect of the chill water calmed her, draining the anger and tension from her body and mind. Having touched pool's end, she decided to swim just one more length—no sense overdoing it—so she turned around and started once again for the deep end.

But now her heart was jolted by something she saw in the moonlight, moving toward the pool. It was luminous in the lunar glow, with the opalescence of bare flesh, vaguely human in outline, and yet not human.

Not human because—although it had two arms that hung at its sides, two legs that were bringing it nearer and nearer the pool—it had no face.

She tried to scream but could only whimper.

Where a face should have been, there was an oval void, eyeless, soulless...

It drew even closer.

Suddenly she laughed with relief and recognition. It was her husband, in his swim trunks and scuba mask. The oxygen tank was strapped to his back.

"Bud, you idiot!" she said affectionately. "Scuba diving in a swimming pool?"

Without a word, he dove under the surface of the water. She giggled at his eccentric foolery, grateful that he was no longer angry and had chosen this bit of clowning as a way of making up.

She felt her ankles seized by his powerful hands. She laughed again. They had often played like this back home, when they were young surfers on the beach at Santa Monica. She kicked coquettishly, not really wanting to free her legs from his grasp.

She was pulled down, under the surface.

He continued to hold onto her ankles with hands that gripped like steel clamps. She kicked frantically now, coquetry forgotten, roiling the water, struggling to escape. Fear rushed into her very bone marrow as water filled her nostrils, her mouth. She beat upon him with her fists, but he eluded her. She tried to rip off his oxygen tank, his breathing tube, but he was too quick and too strong for her.

Freezing thoughts stabbed her. Why was he doing it? Because she wouldn't sell? Even if she had sold, would he have done it later anyway, to get all the money for himself? If only the servants hadn't gone to bed. If only their quarters overlooked the pool. But there was no one, no help...

The awful pressure of water was in her lungs, and it hurt. It *hurt* to drown, she realized through her panic, there was *pain*; hideous nauseating fear and *pain*. But soon the pain ebbed, and a numbness set in, and a softness, and a darkness...

When she emerged from the pool, she staggered away aimlessly, unsure of her own intentions. She felt giddy, she couldn't see very well, everything looked distorted, she didn't walk normally, she felt as if she were floating. Well, that wasn't surprising, she told herself, after what she'd just been through. She was lucky to be alive.

Had she lost consciousness at some point? She couldn't be sure. How long had she been held underwater? It had seemed like hours, but time, as Mr. Sloane had said, was only an illusion.

She found herself nearing the stables, and the horses whinnied and reared as she passed.

Horses? She peered at the animals. Yes, there were horses in the stables, all right. No cars. Although that puzzled her, she knew there had to be a logical explanation, and she made her way toward the house.

She still couldn't see clearly. The house looked different, somehow. It wavered before her eyes, throbbing and pulsating. She wandered without purpose into the strangely mist-softened billiard room, startling old Coles, the butler...

"Coles?" she said aloud. But *he* shouldn't have been there. He'd left Mainwaring Hall the day they'd arrived. In that moment, Elena knew she was dreaming. And that explained the horses in the stable. She hoped it explained Bud's attempt to kill her, too. Please God, let *that* be part of the nightmare.

The house twirled and gyrated—or was it the world, the universe?—and a wave of dizziness swept over her, a vast roaring filled her ears, she felt as if she were in the center of a tornado's raging dark funnel. The feeling passed.

She entered the library, as it rippled and miraculously shrank to a small den of a chamber. A man sat at a desk, reading an immense book by the light of a guttering candle. He was gray-bearded, with a large nose and a mole, and he wore a cloth hood over his head. He looked up at her. His eyes bulged. His mouth fell open.

"Who art thou?" he croaked. "Dost seek to tempt me? Avaunt, thou black devil! In the Name of Jesu, I charge thee, take thy nakedness hence!" He fell back into his chair, trembling.

Elena backed out of the shrunken library, shattered by the vivid reality of this dream, and moved toward the undulating staircase. She felt she was not climbing it so much as riding it, as she might ride a smooth, silent escalator. Her bare feet could not even feel the stairs; but that was the way of dreams.

When she entered her husband's sitting room, she saw his wet swim trunks and scuba gear in a heap on the floor.

(And lightning flashes of knowledge seared her.)

His back turned to her, Bud was now dressed in crisp pajamas and robe, fluffing his hair with her blow dryer.

(She came to know that time is not a river flowing in one direction, but a whirlpool spinning round and round; that a spirit released from the prison of flesh can spiral unfettered into Past, recent Past, distant Past, years, centuries before its own death, its own birth.)

After stuffing the damp scuba gear into a duffel bag and throwing the bag into a cupboard, Bud picked up the phone and dialed. "Is this the police?..."

(She knew why Coles had fainted at the door upon seeing her the day they arrived: he had recognized her from the earlier sighting in the billiard room some years before.)

"This is Mr. Kallen at Maine Wearing Hall. Something terrible has happened out here..."

(She knew how naked her bikini-clad body must have looked to Sir Edred in his seventeenth-century study; how black her olive skin and dark hair were by his standards.)

"An accident in the swimming pool...my wife...I'm afraid she's..."

(And finally she knew that none of this was a dream; that she had been murdered; that the legendary ghost of Mainwaring Hall was no scullery maid or African slave girl; that she herself, Elena Kallen, was, always had been, forever would be, the Black Wench.)

A split second before he felt her, Bud smelled the pungent chlorine of the pool—Sir Edred's "stench of Hell"—and then she reached out and laid a hand of ice upon his shoulder.

With a cry, he spun around and saw his wife, in her bikini, glistening with the water that had killed her. Water trickled from her ears, her nostrils, her gaping mouth, ran in a rivulet between her breasts, formed a glittering gem in her navel, snaked down her tapered legs into a puddle at her feet. Howling, Bud Kallen leaped backward, pressed his spine to the wall, and slid slowly down the flocked wallpaper as if he were a lump of custard flung there by a spoiled child, until he was huddled on the floor, eyes distended, moaning, vomiting, fouling his clothes, a mass of quivering, whining terror.

When the police arrived and woke the sleeping servants, they found two bodies: those of Elena Kallen, drowned in the pool, and her husband, on the floor of his sitting room, dead from a massive coronary. The telephone was still in his hand.

Mort Castle

Mort Castle, author of **Cursed Be The Child**, **The Strangers**, and **Moon on the Water** (one of the finest and most eclectic short story collections you'll ever encounter) is a poet, musician, teacher, and all-around Renaissance Man (in the dictionary sense of the word). He is also the only writer to have stories appear in all five of the **Masques** volumes. The following tale—undoubtedly one of Mort's most frightening—serves as a lesson to up-and-coming writers that one doesn't need to resort to vulgarity or graphic descriptions of brutality in order to terrify one's readers or oneself.

—JNW

FYI

✠ By Mort Castle ✠

This is not a confession. Confession might be good for the soul, but I do not believe in a soul. Confession with proper demonstration of remorse might save your life in a court of law, but I am not concerned with such matters.

Remorse? I do have regrets—heartfelt—and I anticipate more, but my stating that is strictly FYI, strictly for your information and not my benefit.

FYI. That is what this is all about.

This is what you need to know. This is what I mean you to know and it is being told to you in the way I mean you to know it.

So, then. So.

FYI. Yesterday, I killed my children.

I loved my children and I love them still in the profound and weighted echoes of their absence.

MASQUES V

I loved them.
And I killed them.

Who were my children?
FYI. Bob. Adam. Tammy Lee.
Ages: Bob, eight, Adam, ten, and Tammy Lee, 12.
Sometimes Tammy Lee used to ask, used to demand, "I am your favorite, right, Daddy?"
She was. Sometimes. Sometimes Adam was and sometimes Bob was and sometimes I could honestly answer, satisfying none of them, "You are all my favorite."
That's how it is with your children, isn't it?
So, then. So.
I loved them and I killed them.
I killed them and I will never see them again and knowing that is an intense and angled emptiness within me. That is the pain. That's what this pain feels like for me.
They say nobody can truly know another's pain.
Perhaps not.
But you can get an inkling of it, can't you?
FYI.

FYI. This is how I killed my children.
They are at the beach. It is perfect beach day. The water is shifting greens and blues and the sun becomes scooped out broken angles on the always moving water.
It is only the three of them at the beach. I am not yet with them, not yet.
They wait, patient, on an old, green, pill-nappy blanket. They smell of sun block and popsicles.
Beautiful, they were beautiful, my three children, Bob and Adam and Tammy Lee. They are waiting.

They know I am coming.

They are waiting for Daddy.

This time they have no idea what I mean to do.

So, then. So. Then I am there. Inside me is a great sorrow and a great resolve.

It makes my movements solemn and slow.

Then I tell them what I will do. I do not attempt an explanation. This is nothing that can be explained. Not to them, the innocent.

They submit, one by one, each in turn, Bob and Adam and Tammy Lee, fearing eyes, sick yellow paleness, give themselves to me without struggle, surrender to me and to death, as I will myself to be so strong, and then, one by one, each in turn, Bob and Adam and Tammy Lee.

I break their necks and marvel each time at the cracking sharpness of that breaking, at each body's frantic, senseless thrashing at disruption of signals from the brain, the furious seizures of disconnection and shutting down and dying.

They are dead. Beautiful children. I lay them side by side by side on the blanket. They look wrong, the heads are tipped wrong. I cannot set them right. Adam's eyes will not close. I shut the right one with a gentle thumb, then the left, but then the right pops open and then the left opens.

There is no accusation in Adam's eyes.

There is only death.

I recognize what I see and I weep.

FYI. This is how I killed my children.

This time, it is only my three children and I in the house, of course.

I fill the bathtub. I make sure the water is pleasantly warm. Not too hot. Not cold. There will be enough shock without that of the wrong water temperature.

Then I call Bob.

He doesn't know. There's no need for him to know, not really, and I don't need him to know, because I must do this in the way I must do this, building up from worse to worst to beyond that.

I tell Bob to take off his clothes.

Bob doesn't like to take a bath. He is eight years old. Eight year old boys do not like baths.

You know, I am sure. Little boys have no natural affinity for the tub. It is different with girls.

Bob argues.

I joke. I tell him terrible toe jams will come curling around his ankles, climbing up his shins, tell him kids will call him old Nasty Butt Bob, tell him the silly old stuff about potatoes sprouting behind his ears and mushrooms springing from his disgusting scalp.

He strips. I pop him in the tub, and slide skinny legs forward, scoot him along on his bottom, and then I tip him back and push him below the water and hold his shoulders, and he twists, head breaks the surface of the water, so the heel of my hand is on his forehead and my elbow is locked and then for a second's foolish comfort perhaps he thinks it's a game it's all a game it's a game.

But it is a game he does not like and he is such a skinny little boy, so bony, and he tries to wriggle free, to lift his head, to breathe, and he is making foolish and crazy sounds and bubbles and I hold him down in the water and hold him down and his eyes grow huge and there's a writhing snake of a blue vein in his forehead I've never before noticed and somehow a thin hand claws at my face, claws into my face, and I feel skin tear under nails, and I hold him and I watch him drown and I watch him drown and I watch him die and I kill him and I murder my Bob.

So, then. So.

Then I murder Adam.

FYI. I want it to be harder this time, harder for Adam

and harder for me. We go to the backyard. The fence is high and there are no neighbors, inquisitive or otherwise. This is the place I have made for us, this place where we live, my children, my three children Bob and Adam and Tammy Lee. We have only one another here. That is the way it has always been.

Adam wants to know about the baseball bat. I don't like baseball, don't like sports and especially team sports, and my son, my Adam, of course does not like baseball and so we don't play baseball.

But now I have a baseball bat.

Because, I tell Adam, I am going to hit him with the baseball bat and hit him and I have set my mind to just keep on hitting him until he is dead. I am kidding. I have to be kidding, is what Adam says.

I told him because he had to know, because that was part of it, too.

Then I swing the baseball bat, swing it hard, a low and whooshing arc and I catch him at an angle across the shins. The shock comes all the way through the shaft of the baseball bat and my wrists thrum painfully and Adam screams loud so loud but of course there is nobody to hear screams. Adam falls. Adam cannot run. His face is teary and he's gulping and there's a milky looking wad of snot at his nostril as he rolls and tries to crawl, a crawl that's mostly with his arms.

So I bring the bat down. I have the incongruous thought that I probably look like a cartoon character chopping wood or something like that.

And I set to chop-chop-chopping and there are streamers of blood in the air and Adam looks dented and I think he's yelling don't don't don't and I find a rhythm synched to that yelling and then a wet and muddy noise and no more yelling.

He is not moving.

Not now.

But he is not dead.

Not yet.

I want to stop right there, I want to undo it all, to save alive my Adam and my Bob and my Tammy Lee, but I cannot no I cannot.

So I use all my force and smash in his head and there's not all that much to it, just a rotten busting thump like a cantaloupe dropped to the floor in the produce department.

It is finished with Adam for now.

It is time to kill Tammy Lee.

We are in the kitchen. I tell her what I have done to Bob and Adam, tell her what I mean to do to her. I state it simply and directly, neither understatement nor hyperbole, just what has to be. I show her the serrated bread knife.

Tammy Lee's tears ball up and ooze out like clear oil. No, don't kill her, please don't kill her, please...I have tried to avoid melodrama, to present only the reality of these situations, but we know children are theatrical by nature, and so Tammy Lee begs and she does so on her knees, hands clasped together like a prayerful angel cliche.

No, don't kill her, just slap her, beat her with your fists or with your belt, don't kill her don't kill her don't kill, oh, she doesn't know exactly what it is bad men sometimes do to little girls, but she knows it is very bad, but whatever it is, it is not death it is not dying so do that do that to her instead please oh please.

That is how she begs.

FYI. It makes me almost angry, I think I am angry, and I don't want to hear that anymore and maybe that's all it takes sometimes, do you think, the simple need not to hear anymore.

I yank her up by her hair. I bend her back onto the table.

I slash her throat, and I keep doing it as she stops making anything like intelligible sounds. I concentrate on the subtle flesh and steel interplay between the serrations on the blade and the coils of her windpipe.

When I stop cutting, Tammy Lee's head is held to her body by only a somehow unyielding strap of neck skin.

Then I rest.

I need to rest.

So, then. So.

I rest and as I often do, I think about Mr. G. Gordon Liddy. In the quiet house of my dead children, I think about Mr. G. Gordon Liddy.

FYI. I'm not political, not at all. I think you need to be informed to vote and I don't seek to be informed and I don't vote nor do I imagine my vote might matter in the least should I cast it. I therefore do not concern myself with Mr. G. Gordon Liddy's politics or those actions judged illegal by the courts for which he was sent to prison.

In a book he wrote, a true book, Mr. G. Gordon Liddy tells how he held his hand over the flame of a candle until the flesh bubbled and blackened. He burned his hand and accepted the pain and he did not flinch.

Here is how I think he did it. I think he first saw himself doing it, saw it in a wonderful vivid place in his mind, and he held onto that scene seeing himself doing it seeing the flame tickle the palm of his hand and seeing the steadiness of his arm and seeing his own face as expressionless as a countertop. Then he made himself see that scene again and again and again, holding onto it, making it more real than ever dream could be and more real than most of the mundane and pointless moments of daily life.

And when there was no question, only an affirmation, when he did not doubt, doubting neither the reality of the pain nor his ability to inflict it on himself and to bear it, then he did in fact and deed hold his hand over the candle and I think, perhaps at least the first time, I think he might have had just a hint of a smile on his lips.

FYI. The title of Mr. G. Gordon Liddy's book is *Will*.

I'm sure you want to know who I am. Now you want to know that.

There's irony there. You never wanted to know me until I started telling you all this, FYI.

You know I am someone who has read a book.

I read a poem, too. I might have read more than just one, actually, but there is only the one I recall. It was years ago and the writer was named Emily Dickinson, a woman poet.

"I'm nobody, who are you?" That was, I think, the first line of the poem, or maybe the first two lines.

I remember that because I am nobody. I'm the one who washes your windshield and through suds and squeegee blurs you take little notice of the name in the oval above the pocket of my blue shirt and do not see my face, not really. So, then. So. I'm the bagger the supermarket checker signals to provide a "carry-out" but you don't want help, don't want my help, as you roll the cart past me into the parking lot. FYI. I'm the one you do not apologize to when your elbow strikes me as you board the 5:38 commuter train. I'm the telephone solicitor who doesn't even get the courtesy of a rude "Go to hell," just a quiet hang up, as you reach for the remote to watch a rerun of *NYPD Blue*.

I'm the one who never had a hand in the air in grade school or junior high or high school and the teacher never noticed and never asked and the other students never said anything about it, not even anything derogatory. I'm the guy across the way who lives in a neighborhood and has no neighbors, who gets pink slipped with no mid-level manager picking up on the empty cubicle for at least a month, the one at the deli who holds Number 57 and listens to the call of "55...56...58...59."

FYI. I am nobody.

That is who I am.

I think without even saying it, I am answering, too, the question implicit in Ms. Dickinson's poem, "Who are you?"

FYI.

So, then. So.

Yesterday, I killed my children.

After I killed them at the beach, after I snapped the necks, drowned, beat to death, cut the throat of my children, after I killed them by these means, I killed them again and again and again, killed them with rope and shotgun and rat poison, smothered them with pillows, shocked them with electricity, locked them away and set them aflame, I killed them and killed them and stopped killing only when I no longer had imagination or innovation to conjure up a method.

I killed my Bob and Adam and Tammy Lee and it hurt.

And as I am sure you've realized, realized because you are so perceptive, so smart, wise even, the sort of person who is the pillar of society, a community leader, a true heart of the nation, a leader and a follower both as you choose, an upstanding, righteous citizen, you comprehend that my children were imaginary.

In a wonderful vivid place in my mind, I had three beautiful children.

So, then. So.

This is what you need to know. This is what I mean you to know and it is being told to you in the way I mean you to know it. FYI—strictly for your information and not my benefit.

I told you that at the beginning, didn't I?

With your discerning mind, with your keen intuition and highly developed interpersonal skills, you surely cannot believe this is merely a nasty shaggy dog story contrived as an ugly joke by a nobody.

FYI. No, not so.

Believe me, killing my children, my Bob and Adam and Tammy Lee, that hurt me. The hurt is not imaginary. It is agony and the promise of anguish without end; that is what it is to lose your children. You have to know that.

Maybe there is something else you understand by now, but if not, I will state it for you. FYI.

I hate you. I hate you not for hating me but for not even acknowledging my presence on this Earth.

So, then. So.

FYI.

Yesterday, I killed my children.

FYI.

Tomorrow, I will kill yours.

Thomas Sullivan

*Thomas Sullivan has been a professional gambler, a Rube Goldberg-style innovator, a coach, a teacher, and a born-again athlete. His short stories have been published in a wide range of magazines from **Omni to Espionage**. His novel **The Martyring** was nominated for the World Fantasy Award, and another novel, **The Phases of Harry Moon**, was nominated for the Pulitzer Prize. Sullivan brings a wealth of skill and experience to all his work, as well as a lean literary sensibility that is rare in any genre. I couldn't be more proud to include this marvelous story here in **Masques V**.*

—JNW

Phantom of the Rainbow

✠ BY THOMAS SULLIVAN ✠

The drive-in theater is crumbling now, a single massive sarsen rearing out of the weeds with the name Bel-Air ghosting away with the paint. Ruddy bushes choke the lanes and a weathered board fence complies with the state of decay. The speaker poles are still there, empty wire baskets clutching at nothing, a few crowned with electrical cables like the hemorrhaged veins of some traumatic decapitation. The refreshment stand remains, a tight, low structure hunkered down for eternity. Nothing moves, nothing speaks, except the faintly murmuring dust devils which prowl incessantly in search of parking spots.

There are always vacant spots. All but one, in fact, are vacant—and that one is taken only on Friday nights. Because Friday night is when Debbie comes...

"I could kill her! She's done it again, and I could just kill her!"

Abby at forty-two, six years younger than her sister Debbie, and clawing for social respect in lieu of the life she has lost. She blames Debbie because they are both unmarried pariahs in the self-contained town where they have spent their lives.

"Your sister has been getting dressed up and parking in an abandoned drive-in every Friday night for thirty years," Ruth, their mother, replies in the timeworn tone of a mantra. Whatever she says comes out in this monotone of calm. "What's the harm now? Why do you let it bother you all of a sudden?"

"It's always bothered me. The reason it bothers me more now is because she's been seen. Everyone knows. They even drive by to look!"

"Then it's their problem, and they can go to hell."

She says hell calmly, and she wears the faint smile of one who has long since discovered that life is a bitter joke.

"Here we go again," Abby says evenly, trying to match her mother's composure. But her haggard face bloats with blood as if she were strangling on a gallows. "The gawkers can go to hell. The gossips can go to hell. You and I can go to hell. *Or we can lock Debbie up somewhere and get on with our lives!*"

"She's not hurting anyone."

"She's hurting us! Me!"

"You."

It is where they are at. Where they have been more or less for three decades. But Ruth is nearly seventy, and the boil between her daughters will soon overflow the kettle she has watched all these years.

Debbie knows this, too.

She is fat and oily and her skin has lost its tension, like unpicked fruit that has begun to atrophy. But she is not stupid. What she does, she does for love lost. She is not unlike her sister in this. The difference is that no one has ever loved Abby, whereas Debbie...ah, well, that is why she goes to the drive-in every Friday night.

She drives herself in an old Fairlane 500 now, but once she went in gleaming T-Birds, Capris and Impalas. The drivers were the virile young men of her generation who wore pink shirts, sported DA's and smoked cigarettes as sensuously as James Dean. Sometimes they watched the movies through their sunglasses.

"Hey, Deb, whatya say we make some steam at the Bel-Air Friday night?"

"You mean in case your jalopy makes it that far, the radiator will boil over?"

"Nix and negatorio, doll. I got my old man's Fleetwood with the radio."

The radio. Who could resist the songs? They turned your blood vessels into lit fuses. They exploded with passion or ached with despair. Rock 'n' roll breathed out of a hundred radios, and the kids danced 'n' on car tops at the Bel-Air before the movie started. The world danced. And she—Debbie Miller—whirled the fastest, exuding heat and perfume and the vitality of never-ending youth in a season of desire.

Every Friday night.

That's what Abby missed and Debbie longs for. That's what she goes back to.

Tonight it is Eddie who will take her. The car is a Mercury Monterey V-8. The movies are a couple of Elvis throbs.

At 6:35 she decides he has arrived, and she rushes past her mother and her sister, pretending she hears him honking in the driveway, pretending she does not see Abby's face ugly and gray with what Debbie believes is jealousy.

She enters her old rusted Fairlane from the passenger side and slides into the driver's seat.

"Hi, Eddie."

"Yeah."

Eddie is cool.

She starts the engine and the radio, already tuned to an "oldies" station, bursts into "Burn that Candle"—Bill Haley and the Comets. That at least is real. The rest is memory and association. She rolls the window down and feels the warm vitality of youth flooding in as it did then, caressing her earlobes, her lips, her eyes. The twilight is organic with earthy fragrance and neon blushes. Young lions prowl the dragways, and every stoplight is a rite of passage. She remembers to ask Eddie questions that will allow him to brag about the Monterey.

They take the old roads, Saginaw to Apple Lane to North Haven. And there it is, the bright white slab of concrete rising up on the horizon, slightly curved, defining and sheltering the private perfection of Friday nights. They circle the fence, passing the marquee. The real Debbie, aging and alone at the wheel, ignores the movie listed there in broken letters: _HE ____TOM O_ _HE _P_RA. That was the last film before the theater closed. The last date. She doesn't want to think about the last date.

Eddie pays for the tickets and they gun through, turning too fast perhaps, heading for the back row. All her dates park in the back row. For just a second or two she thinks she glimpses Tommy Chandler behind the concession counter as they coast past. She even thinks he sees her. Somehow. His huge, dark eyes and homely face lifting suddenly through the glass doors, sharply pained and intense. If she goes for popcorn, she'll see him for sure. But she won't speak. Because she hadn't really known him then. This night thirty years ago. That didn't happen until the last date either.

"Let's get comfortable," Eddie says.

"I'm comfortable."

"Be a shame to waste all the space in a Fleetwood."

"I'll stretch every five minutes."

"We could stretch out better in the back seat."

Eddie is like the rest of them. No romance, just sex. That's okay, though. A smart girl can put any boy through the motions. You have to have your fantasies, and you have to stretch them out as long as you can. Debbie was always good at fantasies. Thirty years good. She makes Eddie watch all of *Jailhouse Rock* and half of *Loving You* before she lets him play around. And when the front seat of the Monterey gets too hot, she sends him for popcorn.

Tommy Chandler is in charge of the popcorn. He does silly things whenever she sends one of her dates, like adding extra butter or slipping a Hershey chocolate kiss in the bottom of the box. She didn't know it then. That it was for her. That he was spying on her all the time. But she knows it now, and it has become the essential link between fantasy and reality.

"Is that all you want, Eddie? To get your hand under my skirt?"

"What's wrong with that?"

"You're not even subtle. You don't care a thing about me. Me, Eddie."

But Tommy does. And he is watching her now. And that's why he has taken his place among the legends of love on the screen who romance her every Friday night. In the exhaust of a car passing in front of the projection booth, or even in the steamy exhalations of a cool night, you can see them come off the screen sometimes, cast onto the haze by the projector. They flicker and dance and reach out so seductively that she imagines they are three-dimensional in the air. Once freed, they are in her drive-in forever. She has only to remember them and they will reaggregate whenever she wishes. Lovers, heroes, villains.

And monsters.

❖ ❖ ❖

"What's wrong with you, Debbie?"

"Nothing is wrong with me."

"Then why do you keep going back there? Why do you have to humiliate mother and me every Friday night? Thirty years is long enough to get over the shock."

"No one is humiliating you, Abby."

"You've been humiliating me since I was twelve. My sister the whore, my sister the man-killer, my sister the fruitcake—"

"I didn't kill anyone."

"No. You were just so fast and loose that it had to happen."

"I didn't kill anyone!" she exclaims, and you can hear the pain bouncing off some inner fortification perhaps three decades thick.

"How we've suffered for you," Abby continues the attack, low urgency in her voice. It goes beyond the tone of their mother's mantra, because it is a single phrase: *Mother and me...* "Mother and me have been humiliated all our lives because of you. People shun *us*.That's how crazy you are, people shun us. Mother and me. We're not crazy, you are. But they shun us because we keep you here."

"I'm more normal than you are. At least I had something once."

Abby's small eyes go round and her mouth yawns, exposing her front teeth like a rodent's. "The whole town knows you should be put away," she quavers.

"Mother won't let them touch me."

"Mother is getting old. What will you do when she dies, Debbie? Run away from home? Do you think anyone will challenge who is in charge of the family then? I'm warning you, don't go to the drive-in anymore."

"I'll do whatever I please, little sister."

They are at the childish end of a childish argument,

and all that is left is a childish response. Abby snags her sister's hair. "Don't tell me what you're going to do! Not when it humiliates mother and me!"

Debbie submits because Abby is stronger, but the victory is hers. "You...can't...stop...me," she whispers in pain-shortened gasps.

"I can. I will. If you go again, I'll come and get you. It's not right. It's not fair."

Fair?

Jealousy.

It was, is and forever shall be jealousy between them. Not scandal. Abby was jealous of the reality then and she is jealous of the memory now. But how can Debbie stop being eighteen? For six and a half days a week she waits for the Technicolor features to return in her *film noir* life, for roses to be red and re-acquire fragrance, for the magic of "Honky Tonk" and "Blueberry Hill" to come pulsing out of the past with the promise of youth everlasting.

Her sister cannot have these things. No one ever took Abby to the drive-in Friday night.

Abby lives in the cruel continuum of real time. And if there is a chance, a way, she will block the road back for Debbie. She is younger, physically stronger. And it has come down to that. Friday nights are endangered.

That is why Debbie must do the thing she has not done for thirty years. She has saved this one all that time. Saved it because it is the best and the worst. Saved it because she couldn't face it. But now she must or lose it forever.

The last date.

Rain clears the afternoon air, and her anticipation of twilight tastes like water with a cut of lemon in it. Her date is Bo Cummings, the car is a Nash Rambler custom convertible. She wears a pink shell, a black poodle skirt, bobbysox and saddle shoes. Bo has on a long-sleeve lavender shirt and baggy black trousers. The song on the radio when he picks her up is "Sea Cruise," and the movie...yes, yes, the movie is the one that still clings with its last remaining letters to the marquee, only now it is complete: THE PHANTOM OF THE OPERA.

She tries to slip out of the house at dusk without being seen, but the single anachronism in the whole sequence is Abby's face, dark and scowling, in an upstairs window as she drives away. Debbie fears then that her sister will come, just as she said she would. Perhaps when their mother goes to bed, Abby will slip out and come roaring down on her in the big Buick Electra, spoiling Friday night, spoiling everything.

The great stone slab of the Bel-Air rises as before. *Tabula rasa.* Write upon me. Write romance and unspent youth. And there is the fence, quite black against the embered horizon, and the marquee. The other movie is *Dracula*—part of a monster film review—but she will only have time to watch the one she saw thirty years ago, the one that arrested her life and still imprisons it.

It is the 1943 version, starring Nelson Eddy, Claude Rains and Susanna Foster. A bore, they say, but not to her. And not to Tommy Chandler who sells popcorn. She gets her usual glimpse of him as they speed past the concession, and then she is in the back row where the heavy make-outs park. Bo is all over her before the cartoons are even finished.

"If you don't want to watch the movie, I do," she scolds.

"We can watch and feel at the same time," he says.

"I can't see with the windshield steaming up."

For a while he keeps his hands to himself, but then he starts the engine, turns on the defroster and strokes her knee.

"Stop it, Bo."

"Rambler defroster works great. What's the problem?"

"I mean it, Bo, if you don't stop, I'm going to watch from the concession stand."

She really does want to watch the movie now. Three men are vying for the girl, and all of them are romantic. But the most romantic is Claude Rains, the old violinist who is fired from the orchestra, who has been secretly paying for the girl's voice lessons, who is disfigured when he tries to sell his concerto to keep paying for them. Beauty and the beast. Love from afar. How different from the pawing in the back row of the drive-in. Is it this that draws her to the concession stand where she knows Tommy Chandler is, homely Tommy Chandler who watches her from afar?

She arrives at the stand flushed and disheveled. There is a speaker inside and a single large window adjacent to the projection booth, through which she can watch the movie. Bo is right behind her.

"Hey! What's wrong with you?" he demands.

"Don't make a scene, Bo," she says.

She smells buttered popcorn and out of the corner of her eye she sees Tommy Chandler's stark stare swallowing them. Behind him, through the window, Susanna Foster is in her dressing room and the disembodied voice of Claude Rains, now the phantom of the opera, is telling her that he'll help her.

"Come on back to the car," Bo says.

"No."

"Come on. I'm not gonna do nothin'."

"If you weren't, you wouldn't want me to go back."

He laughs and tries to pull her arm. Her eyes flash to Tommy Chandler's for no particular reason, and he looks away.

"I ought to stay right here...where it's *safe*," she says with a glance at Tommy.

"Come on, you can't watch a movie on your feet."

Thirty years ago she went on arguing. Bo had to half drag her, and Tommy Chandler was visibly agitated. But now there isn't time. (*Because Abby is coming.*)

"Okay," she says, "but I'd like a box of popcorn."

"Hey! Popcorn for the lady," Bo orders up, fumbling through his wallet.

Tommy Chandler ladles on the butter and hands her the box with a look more penetrating than anything her Friday night dates have ever done to her, and she and Bo return to the car.

The phantom has just poisoned someone who is in Susanna Foster's way. Debbie lets Bo eat the rest of the popcorn. It keeps his hands busy. But as soon as he finishes, he starts to maul her again.

She can't stop thinking of the look Tommy Chandler gave her. "Bo, honey," she says.

"What?"

"They were giving away phantom masks at the concession. I think I'd like one as a souvenir."

"I'll get you one when the movie ends."

"They were almost all gone. Besides, there'll be a crowd then. Go get one now or there won't be any left." He makes no move, and she says, "I'll get one myself."

"Okay, okay," he grumbles. And he opens the door and disappears into the darkness.

This is the last time she will see him alive. There will be a glimpse of him later when the men bring him out of the restroom, his head crimson and cleaved by a pipe that was used to brace the window open, but the casket will be closed at the funeral. She thinks very hard about Tommy Chandler now. She hadn't thought about him at all then, but that was before he did what he did. In retrospect, she has put together the timing. It is just about here in the movie—the phantom has strangled two more victims—and Tommy is watching, seething, inflamed by the parallel between himself and the ugly phantom who cannot hope to declare his love. The movie is a mockery of his circumstances, a fun house mirror belittling his passion. He is a seller of popcorn in a drive-in, while the phantom is a tragic artist, ennobled by evening dress and the architectural grandeur of the Paris Opera House. The parallel extends only to the agony of his helplessness. And that is when Bo shows up—the night's villain—asking for a mask.

Meanwhile, too much time is passing as she waits in the car. She knows something is wrong, but she isn't really alarmed until the lights come on and the police cruiser begins searching. It doesn't even dawn on her who the youth is who is approaching the car now. He has one of the phantom masks on, and he is going to tell her what's wrong or maybe what happened to Bo. But he opens the door on the driver's side and slides in with quiet trepidation. He is breathing rapidly and silently, and he stares at her through that great, mute mask.

"Yes?" she asks, starting to get alarmed.

"You know I won't hurt you," he says, trembling. "I ...took care of him...that's all."

"What?" she asks incredulously.

And that is when the fear and hate merge. He tries to explain, but all she understands is that he has done something to Bo, and that the crowd gathering at the concession stand is looking at something bad, and that people who know Bo's car are pointing toward them. She doesn't scream, though a scream climbs in her throat, and she tears off Tommy's mask and stares at him as if he really is a monster. And it is the look that he gives her in return—a look of perfect pain and betrayal—that she will come most to regret. Through the months of hate for Tommy Chandler it is this look that will make her reflect, review and ultimately redeem him.

At least in memory.

How much he must have loved her! Enough to kill for her, die for her. It was all wrong that night, but not in

Tommy Chandler's mind. Not on the screen for those few fateful moments when he seized an opportunity that must have seemed presented to him like destiny. If only she had realized, understood...perhaps she would not have to see those great stark eyes welling up with fear again this night, his face collapsing into something as vapid as a death mask. "Tommy! Come back!" she cries, but he is thirty years away, fleeing along the fence to the front of the drive-in. Above him on film, the phantom is fleeing to the lake and the subterranean labyrinth of the Paris Opera House. The movie, pale and disembodied in the tower lights, makes a scale-model mockery of Tommy Chandler's intense passion. His lake and labyrinth are a playground and a pond in front of the screen.

A score of pursuers almost catch him there, but he manages to cut back into the parking lot and commandeer an empty car. Tires fluming dust, he spins in the wrong direction and tears out of the lot, taking the speaker phone with him. Having the speaker is one of the ironies, Debbie has come to realize, because it is just then that the phantom plays his concerto for Susanna. And Tommy's speaker is dead.

In another twenty seconds Tommy will be dead.

Two turns against the right-of-way, up the entrance lane, and then onto North Haven where the crash drowns out the collapse of a subterranean wall in the Paris Opera House. After thirty years, Debbie's footnote is another regret: that Tommy Chandler never got to hear Susanna Foster sing for the phantom of the opera.

That was how it was...

And now Debbie sits weeping in the front seat of a rusting hulk in the ruins of a past she must leave. She cannot redeem it after all, and her hateful sister is on her way. Civilization has had its outrage and its revenge on her phantom. She has called upon her masked lover, and he cannot answer. How could she expect him to sustain himself thirty years on her cold look of loathing and disgust? She has kept the others alive because they wanted her, more or less, and she wanted them. But Tommy Chandler is dead. The only one that mattered, and she let him die. The last credits are scrolling up the screen of her imagination. There are Eddies and Bos, but there is no Tommy Chandler, and the tears that roll lugubriously down her fat cheeks onto her pink shell are because she never sang his concerto for him.

It is the sound of a heavy car in the night that brings her out of it. The Buick Electra roaring along North Haven, around the great fence. Abby has waited for their mother to fall asleep and is bearing down on Debbie like the coach of death come to carry her off to the hell of reality.

No matter. There is nothing more to see.

No more boys.

No more movies.

No more Friday nights.

The brakes, when they are hit, bite hard, and Debbie's reaction is so instantaneous that it seems to last forever. Her pulse leaps and a gap in her expectations soars open. But at last it comes, and her heart sings with it. Tommy's concerto: the scream of rubber, the rending of metal, the shower of glass. Only it is Abby, of course. Abby out on North Haven crashing into...what? The police will say it was the pole that killed her. But the amount of damage will suggest otherwise. It is over in three seconds, a wonderfully self-contained score that yields to the night. In a little while the sirens come and the ambulance — slowly, no rush — and then all is peaceful again.

It is harmless, of course.

Every Friday night, aging Debbie Miller parks her Fairlane 500 in the back row of a crumbling, weed-choked drive-in. Rock 'n' roll breathes out of a hundred radios, and the screen in her imagination lights up. THE PHANTOM OF THE OPERA is the movie, and it is always 1958.

It is harmless. Fantasy. Imagination. Memory.

The town may gossip about it, if they wish. Be shocked, or filled with pity.

But who is bringing her popcorn from the concession stand?

Sharon Cullars

*Sharon Cullars is another writer who makes their debut story appearance here, and we couldn't be happier. The host of the Short Story section at **Bella Online** (www.bellaonline.com), a web site for women, Sharon recently signed a 2-book deal with Brava/Kensington Publishing and—as you're about to discover—she has a unique and poignant take on the supernatural. Not too much, but...*

—JNW

JUST A LITTLE, JUST ENOUGH

✠ BY SHARON CULLARS ✠

A memory flowed through her. Intoxicating. She loved it. Some sort of meat…roast beef maybe. No, more like sirloin. Yes, that was it. Steak with sauce. And twice-baked potato. She tasted the cream of the melted butter on her tongue, the tang of cheese. Cheddar. The sensation lasted several glorious minutes, then was gone. She peeked at the woman sitting in the seat next to her, took in the abundant hips and waist. Obviously the rich meal was one of many the woman had eaten. Overindulgence had turned the skin sallow, saggy, adipose. Her chin wobbled with the motion of the bus. Lena shuddered in disgust, no longer savoring the pleasure. She hated when the pleasure left. She craved for more.

A couple of stops later, the woman rang the bell and Lena moved to let her out of the seat.

MASQUES V

Mabel sat down at the dinner table later that night. Earl looked at his plate, then looked up at her as though he wasn't sure where her head was at.

"What?" she asked.

"Steak again? And twice-baked potatoes. We had that last night."

"What're you talking about? We haven't had this in weeks."

"We had this last night, woman!"

"Earl, you're losing it! Don't you think I know what I cooked last night...?

"Oh yeah? Then tell me what we had." His lip was curled in a self-righteous snarl. A regular mask for him.

She started to speak, then stumbled as she tried to retrieve the memory. "Why I...I..." For the life of her she couldn't remember last night's meal.

"That's funny, I don't seem to be able to..."

"You going through the change or somethin'?" She hated that sarcastic tone. Twenty-eight years hadn't mellowed his meanness, had only made it worse.

She didn't answer, resisting the question and the thought that she was losing her mind.

Sensations. She craved them. She and her kind. Taking the treasure into their bodies—feeling, tasting, touching lives that weren't their own. That was how they lived. The alternative was life without sensations, without feelings—a living death. To live, they took.

Their hunger moved them. Their desire for humanity chose the lives they would feed from. They who called themselves "The Ones". The divergence in their desires framed their "personalities"; sometimes they absorbed the needs of their prey, and it only compounded their nascent desires. A taste might grow into a need, sometimes even an obsession.

She studied the ones she would take. Studied them on the streets. Pondered their images in magazines, on television. Wondered about them. Longed for their lives, longed to have feelings and sensations that were her own. To know that she would live long enough to savor life. Not to steal it. She could sit down and mimic their motions, put a spoon to her mouth, ingest the food. Could let a man touch her in places that would bring an orgasm to a human. And feel nothing.

The irony was that they felt the absence. Knew the void that dwelt inside. And tried desperately to fill it in the short time (sometimes only months, rarely years) that they had.

The brevity of their time impelled them to live as humanly as possible, to adapt themselves to the world. Some took jobs (she worked as a sales rep in the Perfumery at Macy's), rented apartments, and found ways to fit in. To feel "normal." In the seven months she had been alive, she had learned so much. And knew that there was so much more she would never know.

For her, a little was enough. Just one memory, one exquisite memory, was enough to sustain her. She never knew if the memory was missed. Still, she tried not to take too much. Only once had she done so, over a period of time.

The victim had been a woman in her apartment building, a few doors down from her. Her memories were so alluring. Traveller, lover, friend...sensations and memories that were banked up like a well-guarded treasure. And each day, in the elevator, just a brush and she would retrieve parts and segments of the woman's life.

Then one day, an ambulance stopped in front of the building, and paramedics wheeled the woman out of her apartment. Lena had opened her door and looked at the vacant eyes as her neighbor lay on the gurney. The super told her later that they had taken the woman to a mental hospital. Lena did not experience guilt unless she haphazardly picked it up from a stray touch. Still, she could not forget the woman and what she had done to her. And she had promised herself never again.

Right now, a mother bent down to adjust the rubber band on her daughter's hair. Lena only now realized that she had been tracking them. Maybe a touch had clued her. The loving way the mother caressed her child. The adoring way she looked at the girl.

Expressions drew Lena, seduced her.

She followed them for several blocks.

The next time they paused, she would draw close, feign a brush, take a memory, savor the feelings of a mother's love. Something she could not experience on her own. She had no children, had not known a mother.

The opportunity came and she started for the woman who had stopped in front of a window display of dolls. Both mother and daughter stood mesmerized by the glory of plastic, synthetic, lace, and velvet. She eased up on the mother, just a touch away from them both. She was hungry for them. She had touched both mothers and children before, remembered how a mother's love smelled of perfume and baked bread, how little girls sometimes tasted of bubble gum and smelled of shampoo, but she only craved the good ones, the ones whose thoughts and hearts weren't shelters for unspeakable pain.

"Excuse me," Lena said as she brushed against the mother. She meant to take just a little, just enough. But from nowhere a passerby bumped into her, pressing Lena into the woman, almost knocking both of them over. A flood of memories came gushing in, breaking through the seams, tearing at the foundation of her mind. Smells, sounds, touches...a baby's whimper; talcum powder masking the pungency of soiled diapers nearby; a little girl's breath against her ear as she laughed at some inanity; Winnie the Pooh being read in soft, bedroom tones; trusting eyes looking up; a ribbon coaxed around unruly curls…other memories, not so pleasant. A man who hurt them both. Who loved them both. Who didn't know where love and pain left off. So much sensation. Too much. She shuddered with the onslaught.

The woman recovered from her stumble, looked at Lena blankly, then turned confused eyes on her daughter, who looked up at the woman calling "Mama?" The woman didn't respond, looked like she didn't know she was supposed to.

Lena escaped into the cluster of passersby, feeling a guilt that must have come from the woman. Guilt for what, Lena couldn't discern. It was uncomfortable, a contradiction, a need to protect, a resentment that she couldn't do so. A desire to escape the pain and never look back.

She could barely stand it. She walked faster, trying to escape it, this terrible accident. And she knew that she would feel this feeling for some time. And would probably seek it out again.

Mabel stared at the local anchor of the 11:00 news. Earl was asleep in his Lazyboy, his mouth agape, snoring.

"And in local news, a woman has been charged with abandoning her eight-year old daughter downtown…"

Mabel shook her head, wondering at the state of the world, at the same time trying to retrieve something she was sure she had lost, but didn't know what.

Jack Ketchum &
P.D. Cacek

Were I to try and list the credits and awards amassed by either Jack Ketchum or P.D. Cacek separately, they'd take up most of this page; to try and list them together is a Herculean task that daunts even me. Suffice to say that, between the two of them, they have either won or been nominated for every major award the horror/dark fantasy field has to offer, and justifiably so. These two powerful writers have combined forces here to offer us a contemporary cautionary tale of which, were she still among us, the late Shirley Jackson would undoubtedly approve.

—JNW

THE NET

✠ BY JACK KETCHUM & P.D. CACEK ✠

5/6/2003 11:22 PM
Andrew—
I can't BELIEVE you picked me over all the other women in that chatroom!

5/6/2003 11:31 PM
Cassandra—
Are you kidding? I liked a lot of the others well enough— Mugu, Wicked. But some of them...jeez...when the hell is Maya gonna get off her high horse? Or Babycrazed for that matter. And tell me, please, when is Flit gonna develop a brain?

But I'd think my reasons for wanting to write just to you ought to be pretty obvious. You're smart, youíre funny, and from the way you wrote about little kids the other day I know you're caring too. Do you have kids, by the way? Odd thing about chat rooms. You can be on for weeks and never really get to know the people you're talking to. Anyhow, glad you accepted my invitation. Look forward to hearing from you.

Best,
Andrew

5/7/2003 10:01 PM
Andrew—
No, I don't have any kids of my own...but I'd love to. One day. Right now I have to be satisfied with spoiling my niece and nephew. They're just babies, only two and four, but I figure if their only aunt can't spoil them, who can?

And you're right...sometimes you can chat to someone for months and never really get a clear idea of who—or what they are. It's funny, though, because I feel I know more about you than I do some of the people I've known for years. For instance—that time you and Tigerman got "into it" about experimenting on animals and how mad he got because you said animals have just as much right to live without fear and pain as people do...and he told you to go "F" yourself. You could have said that, too, but you didn't. You stayed a gentleman to the end and that's what I suspect you are, Andrew...a gentle man. Hope to hear from you soon. Bye—

Cassandra

P.S.: Call me Cassie...all my real friends do. :-)

P.P.S: What kind of music do you like? I just love the stuff from 80's! 'Bye again

5/7/2003 11:00 PM
Cassie—
Tigerman's a jerk. I didn't want to say that with everybody else listening in but since it's just you and me now I feel freer. I never liked the guy much, tell the truth. He always seemed…I dunno…either to be hiding something or hiding behind something. Getting "into it" with me was about as open as he got. So maybe I accomplished something :-) Who knows?

Are you planning on going back there again? To Singlechat I mean. Don't really think I want to. I guess I'd just like to stay with talking to you for a while if you don't mind.

Music? All kinds. No headbanger or rap though. 50's stuff, Beatles-era, country—I even listen to opera and show tunes now and then. THERE, I'VE SAID IT! SHOW TUNES! Hope it doesn't cost me our relationship:-) But my favorite's definitely the blues. I can listen to the blues all night long. It's good no matter how you're feeling—happy, sad, whatever. It seems to touch something in me. Always has.

Gotta go. Need to go change the litterbox. My desk and computer are in a little alcove right off the bathroom. It's a kind of dressing-room I adaped into a study. But when Cujo's just used the litter it can get pretty stinky. One of the problems living in New York is that you can't let 'em go outside. They'd be meat in minutes. Don't suppose you're a cat-lover, are you?

Stay in touch, okay?
Andrew

P.S.: Thanks for calling me a gentleman. And a gentle man. I try to be.

Best,
Andrew

5/7/2003 11:20 PM
Andrew—
I know what you mean about Tigerman. It did seem like he was hiding something—the way he got so angry when anybody challenged him. He really was beginning to creep me out. I felt the same way when Maya started talking about...you know...about how she thought it was okay to have as many boyfriends as she wanted just so long as they didn't know each other. I don't think it's okay and I wanted to tell her so—but I didn't feel I could. Like you said, not with everybody listening. Guess I'm just old fashioned in some ways...which is why I don't think I'll ever go back to Singlechat. Besides, I don't have to now. I'd much rather "chat" with you :-)

I LOVE show tunes, too, so our relationship's fine. <blush> And I really like the Blues—especially on rainy nights. I like to turn the music way down, so the rain against the window sounds like it's part of the song and just lay in bed and listen. Sometimes I even fall asleep listening, it's so beautiful.

OHMYGOD...I LOVE cats and Cujo's a great name! (Please tell me Cujo's not as big as that dog in Stephen King's book! If he/she is you'd better go change that litter box QUICK! Eek!) I've had cats all my life...but not right now. I lost my cat, Sgt. Stripes, last Halloween. He was fifteen when he died and I'd had him since he was seven weeks old. It was hard...still is hard to think about him without wanting to cry. He was a BIG guy—twenty-eight pounds before he got sick—an orange tabby with gold eyes. I think he thought he was a dog because he used to follow me around the house and "wag" his tail...and sleep with me at night. It was nice, you know, feeling him next to me. That's the hardest part...being alone at night. I miss him so much.

Wow—got a little blue there. Sorry.

You live in New York City. That is so cool! We're practically neighbors! I live in Pennsylvania, a little town called Warminster—which I think is Lenni Lenape (Native American) for "Wide Spot in Road. Don't Blink."

Gotta go, too. Have a ton of paperwork to do. Give Cujo a hug for me.

—Cassie

5/8/2003 9:22 PM
Cassie—
Fact is, Cujo was the runt of her litter. She's about half the size of most cats. And guess what? She's an orange tabby just like Sgt. Stripes—though her eyes are green. How about that? Something else we have in common!

It's okay to get blue sometimes. I sure do.

It's okay to be old-fashioned too, especially when it comes to relationships. Last relationship I had lasted a year, the one before that two years, and the one before that three years. Oooops—I guess they're getting shorter and shorter! But I've always been a one-woman guy. Even here in New York, where I guess there are plenty of opportunities, I've never dated more than one woman at a time. Don't believe in it.

Warminster, Pennsylvania. I looked it up on the map. Damn! That really isn't very far. What is it, about two-and-a-half, three hours from NY? Funny. On the Net you never know where people are writing from unless for some reason they tell you. You could have lived in L.A. or Michigan or Alaska for godsakes! Neighbors! Cool!

If this is too forward, let me know. No problem. But I'm

wondering what you look like. I'd tell you what I look like but you called me a gentleman, right? And a gentleman always figures, ladies first.

All best,
Andrew

5/8/2003 11:32 PM
Dear Andrew, (hope you don't mind the "dear"…but that's part of being "old fashioned" too…)

And I'm glad you're old-fashioned. I sort of knew you would be. I'm sorry your last relationship ended so soon after it started but that just means it wasn't the right one. I know about that too. My last "serious" one lasted almost two years and…well, let's just say it didn't end on a very happy note. He wanted something I wasn't prepared to give…

I don't date a lot. Never really saw much use in just "going out" with someone. Maybe that's because I hadn't found a gentleman yet. Til now, that is…

Ooops. That was a little forward, wasn't it? <BLUSH!>

Okay, you asked me what I looked like…well, first clue — Cujo and I have something in common. No, I don't have orange stripes! My eyes are green…but that's all I'm going to say for now… :-)

I don't know what it's like where you are but Spring doesn't seem to know what it wants this year. 70s one day and 50s the next and RAIN, humidity. Humidity makes my hair go all curly. Ooops! Now you know I have hair! Okay, it's dark brown hair in fact with red highlighs. It used to be very long, down to my waist when I was little, but that would take FOREVER to dry. Hope you're not disappointed but my hair's short now, curly in summer and kind of "shaggy" the rest of the time.

Okay, I'm sort of tall…all legs, was what my father used to say. Still does when he wants to get me to blush. Which isn't hard to do. <blush>

Can I tell you something? I've always thought a man is as handsome as he acts, what he does and how he behaves. Looks aren't as important to me as what's inside. But…it's YOUR turn now. Tell me what Andrew looks like. If you want, that is. Gotta go now…more later…promise.

OO (hugs)
Cassie
P.S.: New York's only an hour and forty-five minutes away. I checked Map-Quest. :-)

5/9/2003 1:03 AM
Dear Cassie,

I used to have long hair too—way back in the hippie days —and cut it for the same reason. Pain in the butt to dry...I'm 5'10", about 140 pounds, dark hair, in pretty good shape for a guy my age. My eyes change slightly depending on what I'm wearing. My driver's licenses says "blue" but they range from blue to gray to amber.

You're only an hour and forty-five minutes away? Guess I didn't read that map too well.

Tell me more. Are your mom and dad alive? Mine are both gone, my mother for many years now, my father for seven. I think I mentioned back in Singlechat that I'm an only child. You said you have a sister. Any other siblings? Just curious. Family seems to get more important to me as I grow older—or in my case, the lack of one. Don't mean to sound sorry for myself—it's just a fact I deal with. I've got some aunts and uncles and cousins but I'm not really close to them. Probably that's why I like cats so much—surrogate family. :-)

Write soon, okay?
XOXOXOX
Andrew

5/9/2003 6:34 PM
Dear Andrew,

Your eyes sound remarkable—magical in fact. Makes me wish my eyes were something other than plain old green. I'd say jade green, but I wouldn't want to lie to you. :-)

There is one thing…I hate talking about myself, as I'm sure you noticed in Singlechat, I'm basically shy and pretty uninteresting when you come right down to it…but…okay—my friends say I look "hot" in a bathing suit. <BLUSH!!!!!!!!!>

Anyhow, you wanted to know about my parents (still blushing, by the way.) They're both alive and quite active. My Mother was a "Stay-at-Home-Mom" when my sister and I were little, but has recently gone back to school! She wants to get her Teaching Credential and my dad and I think it's great. My Dad, by the way, ownes his own Travel Agency—we've had a LOT of great vacations! In fact, my Mom and Dad will be going on a "Second Honeymoon" in a few days—to Hawaii for a week. Don't know what I'll do with myself while they're gone—since I live with them (saves on rent)—but I'm sure I'll think of something.

I understand about feeling distant from family. My sister

and I are a bit distant. I'd never tell her this but I think she tends to put her career (Real Estate) before her children, while I think being a mom is the best "job" a woman can have. On the other hand, her being so into work lets me spend a lot more time with Mandy and Jamie (my niece and nephew) so I guess there's an upside to everything. Like tonight…which is why this e-mail's so short—my sister's asked me to baby-sit and I plan to spoil those kids ROT-TEN! I've rented MONSTERS, INC., SHREK and MY favorites, ARISTOCATS and GAY PURR-EE!

Probably sounds like a really boring night…right? So what are YOUR favorite movies? Color? Books? Inquiring minds want to know. Hugs to your kitty…and you.
x
Cassie

5/9/2003 7:10 PM
Dear Cassie,

Your movie-night doesn't sound boring at all. I think it's great you're into kids. Favorite movies, books? That's hard. Color is easy. Black. But the reason the other two are hard is that although what I do for a living is write freelance ad copy, my goal's to become a real writer. Fiction. Been trying for about five years now, ever since I quit my nine-to-five at the agency. So far, lots of rejection letters but not much else, though some of them have been very encouraging. Point is, because of that I read constantly, and I see movies all the time. Need to see what's out there. So to pick favorites is almost impossible. The book I'm reading right now is great—Dennis Lehane's SHUTTER ISLAND, about two detectives investigating an escape from a mental institution. I rented REMAINS OF THE DAY again the night before last. Love that movie. So lonely, so sad. But the list would have to go on and on…

You live with your parents, huh? God! you must have a hell of a good relationship! I remember I couldn't WAIT to get out of there, on my own, as soon as possible. I know that rents being what they are these days a lot of younger folks are doing that but there's no way I could have. How old are you, anyway? If you don't mind my asking. I'm going to risk something now and tell you that I'll be forty-six in November—I suspect that's more than a few years older than you. And I hope it doesn't change things between us. Say it ain't so! :-)

And as long as I'm in a risky mood tonight I'll admit to one other thing. We're completely on the same page, you and I, about what the important things are between people. But long legs, green eyes, brown-red hair and "hot in a bathing suit..." I'm getting a mental picture of you. And I gotta admit that I like what I see. :-)

XOXOXOXOX
Andrew

5/10/2003 1:05 AM
Dear Andrew...

Sorry it took me so long to get back to you but the evening was a DISASTER! My loving sister didn't tell me that Jamie was sick—let's just say "leaking" at both ends, poor baby. I had to make sure Mandy didn't get too close and that was hard because she loves her big brother SO much. So she started crying and Jamie started crying and...needless to say they weren't very interested in watching movies. :-(
I'm exhausted, but couldn't collapse until I answered you. See how important you are? <g>

Black's another thing we have in common! I love it and always try to wear something black every day (sometimes you can't see it, but it's there.) And OMYGOD! you're a writer! I've never known a real writer. That is so…awesome (as the kids say.) I hope this isn't pushy or anything but could you send me a story? I'd love to read one. Honest. I really do need something to read anyway. Just finished a book you'd probably love—A DANCE FOR EMILIA by Peter S. Beagle. It's about a man who comes back from the dead in his cat. It's beautiful and made me cry at the end. What can I say, I'm a big softie. I love stories that have a bittersweet ending. I did see REMAINS OF THE DAY. And cried.

Then I saw Anthony Hopkins in SILENCE OF THE LAMBS. EEEEEEEEK!

But, Sir (spoken with a heavy Southern Belle accent beneath a fluttering fan,) y'all should know better'n to ask a lady her age. (Flutter, flutter.) Let's just say ah'm old enough.

Can you really SEE me? It's funny but I think you can. You can see the REAL me and that makes me feel very…special. See me right now as I write this, in bed, on my laptop…in my very short, very RED nightgown.

Can you see that?

Goodnight and XOXOXOXOXOX back.
Luv,
Cassie

5/10/2003 1:25 AM
Dear Cassie,

"Very short, very red nightgown…?" Phew! And you expect me to SLEEP now? <g>

139

I'll get a copy of the Beagle book. Sounds good. And I'll be glad to send you a story, too. I know just the one. It's called RETURNS, and it's also about a cat...and believe it or not, a ghost! The coincidences just keep piling up here. It really is wonderful. Thank god we got out of that damn chat room and into this.

Sometimes late-night e-mails seem almost like distress calls to me, you know? Like some sad lonely S.O.S. tapped out into cyberspace. But yours aren't like that at all. They make my day, Cassie. They really do.

Luv back atcha, and
XOXOXOXOXOXOXOXOXOXOXOXOXOXOXOXOX
Andrew

p.s.: Whoops, forgot. I don't know your address. I guess I got a little bit carried away back there...
Andrew

5/10/2003 8:15 AM
:-) I don't think you got carried away at all. I think you're pretty wonderful. I know we haven't known each other for very long—on or off the chat-room—but I already feel a connection with you that I've never really had with anyone else. Does that sound really weird to you? Hope not, because I wanted to be honest with you about this.

My address. 119 North Street Road, Warminster, Pa. 18974. But you could send the story as an attachment...so I could read it sooner. Hint, hint, HINT. Now I HAVE to get going or I'll be LATE!

XoXoXoXoXoXo
Cassie

5/10/2003 2:01 PM
Dear Cassie,

Okay...gulp...the story's attached. I can only hope you're kinder to it than some editors have been.

Early riser, huh? Me, I'm a night person. Don't even want to TALK to anybody before ten in the morning...

It occurs to me now that it's awfully good of you to trust me with your street address after only knowing me from Singlechat and these e-mails. A lot of women wouldn't. I guess I must be doing something right :-) And you...well, you tell me I'm wonderful and I'm kinda floored by that, it's been a long time since anybody's called me that, and I just want to say...hell, I dunno what I want to say...only that (and don't get scared now, okay?) I may be falling for you just a little. Just a little. Is it okay to say that? Jeez—I better sign off now before I put my entire LEG into my mouth, not just my foot.

Love,
Andrew

5/10/2003 4:00 PM
Dearest Andrew,

Haven't even opened your story but I had to send this first—it's more than OKAY because I think I'm...falling for you too. And I do trust you. More than I've trusted anyone for a very long time.

Okay. Just HAD to say that. Now...on to your story. I"ll write as soon as I read it. Promise, promise, promise.

<kiss>
Cassie

MASQUES V

5/10/2003 5:15 PM
Dearest Andrew —

Oh. My. God.

Your story is...beyond beautiful. Those editors must be crazy. I started crying after I read it the first time and I'm still crying. But don't get me wrong...I'm crying because it's so BEAUTIFUL. You're brilliant! At first I thought the man came back as a ghost for his girlfriend, and then, when I realized it was for his cat...Andrew, that was so touching. And then when the girlfriend has the guy from the pound come over to have the cat destroyed...

Wait a minute. I'm crying again. Gotta get more Kleenex.

Okay, I'm back.

But that part...I wanted the ghost to hit her, beat her up, do SOMETHING to stop her. Then I realized it was okay, that he was there to see his cat through. Andrew, you touched my heart and let me finally get all the grief for Stripes out in a good way. Thank you so very much. I loved the story, Andrew. Really. And I love you for sharing it with me.

What else is there to say?

XOXOXOXOXOX
Cassie

5/10/2003 7:33 PM
My god, Cassie...

You can't begin to know how much this means to me. You really can't. I was cooking dinner, something reheatable that would last me for a few days. Just something simple, y'know? Chicken tarragon in a garlic/wine sauce. Anyhow I was letting it simmer a while before I started on the rice and asparagus and I thought, check your e-mail, maybe she's read the attachment by now. And I'm amazed by your response. Not so much to the writing, though nobody's ever exactly called me brilliant before, but your response to the heart of the story, that I touched you so deeply, that you felt the story had even helped you heal a bit. That's so fulfilling, so important and beautiful to hear.

And Cassie? You know what? You just said you loved me...

I know you mean you loved me because of the story. I understand that. But do you think it's possible for two people to fall in love—REALLY in love—just by writing back and forth like this? Never having met? Never having touched or kissed? Never having even used the phone for godsakes? It feels so strange to me but know what? it feels good. Better than I've felt in years.

Uh-oh. Cujo's throwing up again. Only thing wrong with cats are furballs. Though she's been doing it a lot lately, dammit. I better go attend to it. But furball or no furball, I'm smiling now. Can you see it? Big wide grin.

Love you, Cassie,
Andrew

5/10/2003 9:58 PM
Dearest Andrew,

It wasn't just the story. And I do believe that people can fall in love without ever having touched or seen each other. I think we're proof. I love you, Andrew. Not your words. Not your talent. Not your brilliance. You. The real you. Your heart.

Plus hey, you can cook! My mother says I'd better find a man who can cook because I can barely boil water. One thing we DON'T have in common is garlic, though. I'm allergic. Does that make you think less of me? :-)

Poor Cujo. Hope her tummy feels better soon. Send her my love...as I send it to you.

All my love,
Cassie

5/12/2003 3:34 AM
Oh Cassie, I wish I could tell you how much I care, how much your last e-mail makes me feel. But right now I think something awful's happened—or something awful's about to happen. I don't want to go into it right away and alarm you because maybe that would turn out to be unnecessary and everything will be fine. But I gotta sign off right now. I'll write when I can.

I love you too, Cassie! I love you too!
A

5/12/2003 8:05 AM
Dear Andrew,

What's wrong? Tell me. Please. I love you, and that's all that matters.

Love,
Cassie

5/12/2003 11:25 PM
Andrew? What's going on? Please write. PLEASE...

Love, Cassie

5/13/2003 8:10 AM
Andrew—what's happened? Can't you tell me? Is it something I said? Please let me know. Whatever it is, we can work it out. I know we can.

I REALLY love you—Cassie

5/15/2003 12:45 AM
Andrew? What did I DO?

5/15/2003 9:55 PM
Oh jesus, Cassie, honey, I'm so sorry to have put you through this. I can't believe I was so thoughtless. I haven't even looked at the computer. Couldn't bring myself to. I should have written so much sooner. I'd better explain.

Friday afternoon I was working on some ad copy and I heard Cujo coughing in the kitchen. She didn't sound like she does when she's throwing a fur ball. It was this hacking cough. I went in and there she was on the floor, this cough hacking away at her from deep within. I almost thought she was choking. I got her some olive oil, which she'll take when it IS a fur ball but she wouldn't have anything to do with it.

Finally it subsided and she retreated to the hall closet—there's a box of books there where she likes to sleep sometimes. I went back to work, worried but thinking maybe it was just some passing cat-thing. Then at dinnertime she wouldn't eat. I figured it was probably a bug or something but I kept an eye on her anyway. She seemed peaceful enough. Purred when I petted her. She wouldn't come out of the closet though. And then that night, about two in the morning, she woke me up coughing again, worse this time, hunched on her box and her eyes were tearing and it was like she couldn't get her breath, you know? So I wet a dish towel under warm water and wiped her eyes and mouth and nose and saw she was frothing at the mouth. And that scared the hell out of me. So I got her in her cat box and got a cab to the vet's. They have an emergency service all night long.

The vet was somebody I'd never seen before and she was awfully young but she was very kind. She could see I was a mess. She diagnosed acute respiratory distress and gave her a shot of cortizone to ease her breathing and it did help, I could see pretty much right away. I waited while they took her upstairs for an x-ray and a while later Dr. Morris—that was her name—came down and showed it to me on the light-board. Her lungs were completely flecked with what looked like motes of dust, but were really droplets of moisture. They looked like photos you see of the milky way there were so many. They were THAT DENSE, Cassie. And now I was really afraid for her.

Dr. Morris said she wanted to drain the lungs immediately and start her on a heavy dose of antibiotics, that they wanted to keep her overnight for observation. If worse came to worse, they could knock her out and intubate her until hopefully the antibiotics took hold. I said whatever it takes. She said it was going to be expensive and I said I don't care about the money, never mind the money, whatever it takes. By then I was practically crying. She told me to go home and get some sleep, that they'd call me if there was any change. I went home and wrote to you. That last e-mail. I drank a glass full of straight scotch and it did was it was supposed to do, knocked me out, and I went to sleep.

They called at quarter to five in the morning. Almost dawn. Said Cujo was failing fast and what did I want to do? I said just hold her for me if you can, I'll be right there. I got there just in time to feel her breathing stop, her heart stop, her eyes wide open looking straight into mine as though she could see me. I buried my face in her neck and cried and cried.

I'm crying now.

You see why I couldn't write, Cassie? I wish I could call you. Can I call you? I need to talk to somebody now or I'll go crazy and the only creature on earth other than you I could talk to is gone now.

Love,
Andrew

5/15/2003 9:25 PM
Oh God, Andrew...just got your message. I'm crying too. Can't talk right now. Can't write anymore. Give me a minute—I'll write back. I promise. I promi

5/15/2003 11:20 PM
My love.

I said I'd write back in a moment—and here it is, almost two hours later. I'm so sorry for not being able to get back to you sooner but...your loss, your horrible loss brought all the memories of Stripes back and I lost it, too. God that sounds so selfish...I hate myself for that, for failing you like that. But please, don't hate me—I couldn't stand it. I'm back and I'm here for you now. If you still want me to be...

Andrew, my darling Andrew I'm so sorry about Cujo. All I can say is how sorry I am and that I wish I could hold you and comfort you right now...I want to hold you, Andrew, so you'll feel safe to cry out all the sadness you feel. No one held me when Stripes died. I hid in my room...like now...and cried silently...like now.

But I AM holding you, Andrew—can you feel my arms around you? I hope you can, I really do. Because I love you and want to help you through. And I wish I could call…but my stupid father is still on the phone…making stupid last-minute "vacation arrangements" that HAVE to be done RIGHT THIS MINUTE! God! I wish I had my own place because if I did I'd be on the phone, talking to you…and telling you to come here, to come to me, to be with me so I can share what you feel.

And maybe you can. My parents leave tomorrow, Andrew…and maybe by morning you'll feel a little better—not a lot, I know, but a little maybe. If you do, why don't you think about coming down? You said you needed me. But I need you, too, Andrew. I need to help you through this because I LOVE YOU. I love you, Andrew. And I wish I could hold you right now.

What else can I do?

Love always,
Cassie
P.S.: You called me honey.

5/15/2003 11:25 PM
Cassie—

When do they leave? I'm THERE. God, yes!

XOXOXOXOXOX
A.

5/15/2003 11:28 PM
My love,

They leave tomorrow afternoon. I'll be here, alone. Whole house to myself. Please come…please.

XOXOXOXOXOXOXOXOXOXOXOXOXOXOXOXOX-
OXOXOXOXOXOXOXOXOXOXO
All my love,
Cassie

FROM THE JOURNAL OF ANDREW SKY:

I wish she'd sent me her phone number. Wonder why she didn't? It could be she's afraid of just this—that I might be tempted to chicken out at the last minute. Which I am. Maybe she anticipated that.

There's a real temptation not to show.

If I want to be there by nightfall I've got to leave in about an hour. No later. I've been procrastinating on leaving all day, ever since this morning staring into the mirror doing what I do every morning, shaving, brushing my teeth, looking at the same face I see every day. For the first time it struck me as a hard face, too few smile-lines and too many traces of frowns.

What can she possibly see in me?

I woke up all excited and an hour later I was depressed and worried and I've stayed that way all afternoon. I went out shopping at the Food Emporium. I corrected the Iona College ad copy that's due in the mail on Tuesday. I answered some e-mail—hoping, I think, that there'd be one from Chrissie saying please don't come, this is a mistake, I'm not ready. There wasn't any.

It's me who's not ready.

I haven't even met her yet and I feel like I've lost her already.

What a fucking mess I am, huh?

I think of Laura and all I'd hoped for with her and I still get a knot in my gut, I still want to smash something. Hell, back then I did smash a few things—half the dishes in the sink, the lamp beside the bed—and all it got me were credit card bills for replacing them. What I needed to replace was Laura. But there was no replacing Laura. No way.

I couldn't replace the feeling of her beside me asleep in my bed or how cool I felt walking down the street with my arm around her waist, my woman, this woman more beautiful and successful than I'd ever thought could possibly be attracted to a guy like me but who said who said that she was mine and I was hers now, made me promise to always be hers no matter what. I remember laughing and saying who else's could I be?

And it was true. Who else's?

Nobody's. Before or since.

Not a single human being even touched me after Laura.

Not until Cassie.

I don't even know for sure why I surfed my way into that dumb chatroom.

I think I was looking for a porn chat, really. Or maybe I was warming up to that. I looked at a lot of porn for a while. Another dumb escape. So it could very well be that I was building up the courage for a little porno-chat that day. Something at least remotely exciting. Maybe I'll flip back through these pages at some point and see if I entered it here.

Not that it matters.

But for a over year I'd felt as hard as my goddamn wall. Harder. It was a way to get by I guess. Tough it out. What few friends I had left that goddamn Laura didn't take along with her I put off and continue to put off and make excuses for not seeing because I know damn well I've become a bore on the subject as on most subjects like the goddamn copy I write for a living and the goddamn city I live in that won't even let you smoke in a bar anymore. And I will not be a bore. I have some pride.

I talked to my cat instead. You couldn't bore Cujo.

But if this building weren't pretty well soundproofed

the neighbors might have had me locked up. I ranted and raved. I cried. I was howling at the moon here.

Cujo didn't mind.

Cujo was unshakable.

She could cure any hurt with that purr of hers. At least for a little while, until the hurt came back again.

But without her now this being alone just kills me. I'm in a city of how many million people? And I've never felt so completely cut off and alone. I might as well be some loony old hermit off in the Maine woods somewhere.

And whose fault is that? Mine of course.

Laura didn't leave for no reason. She left me for the same reason I'm pretty much unemployable—except as what I am, a free-lancer.

I never had a boss in my entire life who I didn't go off on at one time or another. I've lost more jobs than my TV has cable stations. I have this problem with authority figures I guess, with anybody who has power over me. Back when I could afford a shrink instead of just this journal Marty and I talked about it a lot. Goes all the way back to my parents we decided. A hell of lot of good that did me.

But Laura had power over me. The kind of power only a woman you love can have. More than I should have let her have. I realize that now. And I had this temper. We fought like cats and dogs half the time.

But then that's all here in this journal.

I know I expected too much of her. I expected her to realize that despite the damn rejection letters I was a writer, a serious writer, that I had a writer's sensitivity and a writer's soul. I expected supportive. I expected quiet and gentle. From a New York City bitch born and bred, working her way up the ladder on Mad Ave and whose parents had left her oh, only about a million and a half.

I must have been out of my fucking mind.

I've got to remember not to expect too much from Cassie. Not right off the bat anyway. She could be ugly as a post for one thing. Despite the long legs, green eyes, "hot in a bathing suit" stuff. Green eyes do not a face make, right? But somehow I think her looks aren't going to matter to me all that much. She's the first one who's touched me in so long, who's really cared about me. And somehow I think she's what I guess you'd call a "real woman." With a real woman's wisdom. Not like Laura, who turned out in the end to be a spoiled little girl when you get right down to it. Who couldn't put up with the real Andrew Sky, occasional temper-tantrum and all.

But I've got to admit, I'm a little scared.

I've got a lot riding on this.

It may be that Cassie's my last hope for any real happiness on this earth. It's possible.

I'm not getting any younger after all. I smoke too much and probably I drink too much. I've only got twenty-five grand or so in the bank. I'm not bad looking but I'm no fucking Tom Cruise either.

She cares for me, though. I know that through her e-mails. So I've got reason to hope that my looks and all the rest of it won't mean any more to her than hers will to me. She seems to see right down into my soul sometimes. And that's an amazing thing, an amazing feeling. I might be driving off in a little while to meet my entire future. I'm scared, but shit, I'm excited too now. Writing this helped...and damn! It's filled the whole hour!

Jesus! I'd better get going. Better hit the road.

FROM THE DIARY OF CASSIE HOGAN

He's coming! Andrew's really coming to see me! ME!! I'm so excited. I can't sleep...I just had to get out of bed and write this down or I'll burst!!!

Mom's been a bitch all night. First she yelled at me about doing my homework...like I'll need to know Geometry...then she told me she made "arrangements" for me to stay with Aunt Kay while they're in Hawaii! No way. What does she think I am? A baby?

I hate her! She'll be sorry when they get back and find out I left to be with Andrew. I'm not even going to leave them a note. Let them worry about what happened to me.

No. I can't do that to Daddy. I'll leave them a note and tell them the truth. That I love Andrew and we're going to get married and live happily ever after so they don't have to worry about me anymore. I'm a big girl (Note: cross "big girl" out) No...I'm a WOMAN.

I'm Andrew's woman. And he's my man. My love. My lover.

I wonder if he'll want to "do it" when he gets here? If he does that's okay...because I found some of those things in Daddy's end-table and took one. A rubber. And my mother thinks I'm too young to stay by myself! Well, I'm old enough to know about rubbers, aren't I?

I wonder if one will be enough?

Heather is going to be SO jealous!!! She thinks she's so hot because she's dating that dork from the junior college...but HE'S only nineteen and Andrew's in his forties. He's a REAL man! And he's mine. He loves me...he said so. And I love him!

And he's really, really coming!

God, I'm so excited. I just wish I looked better!!! I tried to get mom to drive me to the mall so I could get a haircut—I HATE my hair—but she wouldn't. Said she had too much to do and that my hair is fine the way it is. The BITCH! I wanted my hair to be perfect for Andrew but now it's just—UGH!

But I know my face will be okay. I took some of The Bitch's facial mask and scrub and used it on those stupid pimples on my chin. They're all red now but I think they'll be okay by morning. If they aren't I'll die! I'll kill myself if they aren't! Because Andrew deserves the best...and I want to be the best for him. I love him! And he loves me! But I'll still die if those pimples aren't better!!!

But really, I know he won't care about my hair or my skin. He loves me. The real me inside. Just like I love the real him inside.

I'm going to SURPRISE him! I'm going to wear my red nightgown when I open the door! That will REALLY make him happy!

I'll do anything to make him happy because I love him and his cat died.

Maybe we can go to the pet store after we do it and buy a kitten! I would just LOVE that!

God, I'm so nervous. I know I won't be able to sleep, but I have to. I HAVE to so I'll look good for Andrew. G'night, Dear Diary. I'll tell you all about it tomorrow…when Andrew comes for me!

TRANSCRIPT OF AN INTERVIEW GIVEN BY ANDREW J. SKY, OF 233 WEST 73RD STREET, N.Y., N.Y., WITNESSED BY LT. DONALD SEBALD, WARMINSTER P.D., 5/16/03

SKY: So I'm late because of this goddamn tire blowing out on me so a trip that should have taken me what, an hour and a half? Took me about two and a half so I'm nervous, right? Nervous about meeting her and nervous about being late and I'm also filthy from changing the tire, anyhow I finally find the place in the dark and I ring the bell and she comes to the door wearing that little…

SEBALD: The red nightgown.

SKY: Yeah, and well, you know, she's not leaving a whole lot to the imagination and she's really pretty as hell but I can tell right away she's not happy to see me. I mean, there's no hugs or kisses or anything like in the e-mails and she's kind of frowning but damned if I know why. I'm not that ugly and I'm not that dirty and I'm dressed okay. Anyhow, she invites me in and asks if I want something to drink and I tell her I could sure use a beer and I tell her about the flat and ask could I wash up somewhere so she points me to the bathroom and I do. When I come out she's lightened up a bit and there's a beer open for me and a pepsi for her and we're both on the couch in the living room only she's way over to one side while I'm over on the other and I'm wondering, why the frost? and it's making me even more nervous so I figure, you better just go ahead and ask her so that's what I do.

SEBALD: You ask her what, exactly?

SKY: I ask her what's wrong. She says she's been waiting for me all day. Like we'd set some specific time.

SEBALD: And you hadn't?

SKY: No, never. I don't know what she expected, that I was going to be there first thing in the morning or something so I tell her that. That I'm really sorry but that it was just a misunderstanding because we really hadn't set a particular time but I'm really, really sorry and that's when she tells me she didn't even go to school today, she stayed home waiting for me and that's when I start looking at her. I mean really looking at her. Up close, y'know? I guess I'd been afraid to do that before. I guess I was too fucking nervous at first and then there was all that frost. That plus the nightgown. But anyway, I look at her and realize that there's hardly a line on her face. Hardly a single line. I mean, I knew she was young, that was obvious right away. But still I figure, got to be college she's talking about. She skipped classes today waiting for me and I feel real bad about that so I tell her but jesus! then all of a sudden she's about to cry! I can't believe it! And I feel like, I don't know, I feel like I've probably fucked up again. Just by being late. Even though I'm not late. Not really. But then she stands up and says, come on, I want to show you something so I do, I follow her, and she walks me into her bedroom.

SEBALD: She leads you in? Of her own volition? That's what you're saying?

SKY: That's right. Of course of her own volition. And the first thing I notice, the first thing that anybody would notice is that this is a bedroom, right? And now I'm confused. I mean, she's just met me for the first time and she's damn near crying and she's led me right into her fucking bedroom! There's the bed, and there are all these posters on the wall, rock stars and movie stars and whatever, and there's her desk with the computer. And I'm looking at all this. Taking it in. But she's not interested in what I'm doing. She's pointing down beside the bed and she's got two suitcases there, sitting on the floor and she says look at that. So I ask her, suitcases? And she says I was going to run away with you tonight, you know that? Something like that, anyway, I don't remember exactly because by now I'm barely listening to her. It's like this whole thing is washing over me finally. I'm finally beginning to get it.

SEBALD: Get what?

SKY: The posters, the goddamn pennants on the walls. The teddybears on the shelves over her desk. The photos on the mirror. She's a kid! She's a goddamn fucking kid! So I ask her. I get myself under control and I say, Cassie, exactly how old are you? And she says something like old enough and now she's crying for real but I don't give a damn, I'm having all I can do to stay calm enough to ask her one more time but I do, I ask her how fucking old, Cassie? And she says fifteen. Just like that. Fifteen! Defiant, like. Can you believe it? She's jailbait! All this time she's been conning me! Leading me on! I can show you the goddamn e-mails for chrissake! And now she wants to run away with me? Is she out of her fucking mind? Shit! Fuck!

SEBALD: Take it easy, Mr. Sky. Unless you want those cuffs again. Just go on telling us what happened.

SKY: Sorry. I'm sorry. It's just that...never mind. I just...jesus, I guess I just lost it at that point, you know? Went ballistic I guess. I grabbed her and slapped her and told her what I thought of her, called her a stupid little bitch, and she's crying, really going at it, and I remember grabbing her by the arm and throwing her across the bed so hard she fell all the way over to the floor on the other side. Then I trashed the room.

SEBALD: Trashed the room. Be explicit, please, for the record.

SKY: Tore down the posters, the pennants, broke the mirror with my fist, which is where these cuts come from, kicked in the full-length mirror on the door, knocked all the cosmetics and whatever shit she had there off her dresser and the dolls and bears off the shelf, tore up books, papers, whatever. (Pause.)

SEBALD: Go on, Mr. Sky. And where was she all this time?

SKY: She'd gotten up. She was standing on the far side of the bed and she was screaming for me to stop, she had a little cut on her forehead and I remember her face was all streaked and red from the crying. But she stayed right there yelling at me. Right up until I went for the computer. It was the computer, I guess, that did it for both of us. It was our link, you know? For me it meant one thing. For her I guess it meant another. But it was our link. Like a totem. She came at me as soon as I tore the wire off the mouse.

SEBALD: You're saying she came at you?

SKY: I guess she was trying to protect the computer. She kept calling me a bastard. I'm not a bastard. I was in love with her. Anyhow, before she made it around the bed I'd kicked in the side of the printer and by the time she actually reached me I'd torn the keyboard loose and I hit her with that, swung it at the side of her head.

SEBALD: Left side or right side?

SKY: What? Oh, left side, over the ear. And she went right down. Hit the floor at the foot of the bed, you know? Kneeling there, her arms on the bed, bleeding a little onto the bed, her legs curled under her on the floor.

SEBALD: She was alive then?

SKY: Oh yeah, she was alive. But she wasn't cursing at me anymore. She just sat there staring at me like I was dogshit, like I was the lowest thing she'd ever seen. And like she was afraid of me too, you know? Both things together. And I'd only seen that one other time on one other face, that combination I guess you'd say. On my ex. My girlfriend Laura. That she was scared of me and disgusted with me at the same time. So that was when I tore loose the monitor and used it on her. (Pause.)

SEBALD: Mr. Sky?

SKY: She loved that computer. So believe me, it wasn't easy.

Barry Hoffman

*Barry Hoffman is the author of the acclaimed novel **Born Bad**, as well as the **Eyes** series of horror/suspense novels (including **Hungry Eyes**, **Judas Eyes**, **Eyes of Prey**). Longtime editor and publisher of **Gauntlet**, a magazine that explores and challenges the limits of free expression, Hoffman is also an accomplished (if far too infrequent for my tastes) short story writer. As the following tale shows, Hoffman's writing is hard, lean, fast…and merciless.*

—JNW

DISAPPEARING ACT

✠ BY BARRY HOFFMAN ✠

She didn't know when the thought of retirement had grabbed hold of her. Fifty-eight years old, a teacher for thirty-four years, and for some ungodly reason she was sitting with her best friend at a meeting where retirement options were being outlined.

Her discontent, in hindsight, had been creeping up on her for some time, she knew. Sitting there, trying to focus on the words of the retirement representative, she recalled a time when retirement wasn't a part of her vocabulary. She'd loved her job. She'd loved the kids. She'd craved the daily challenge. She'd enthusiastically put in hour after hour at home coming up with innovative lesson plans. She had come to school early to tutor children or just let them bend her ear. She had taken ten-year olds on trips weekends, allowing some to venture out of the inner-city for the first time.

When had it all gone wrong? she wondered.

As they'd entered the spacious auditorium she and Jodi had joked about the others in attendance. At fifty-eight both she and Jodi were clearly the youngest. The others seemed like walking cadavers; lifeless, morose, battered and beaten. Not only had they been sapped of their passion, but their souls seemed stolen. Retirement for them would be a death sentence within a year or two. They'd given *too much*, could take no more of the bureaucratic nonsense that plagued them daily, yet, she sensed, they were being pushed reluctantly out the door. Had they been accorded the respect they deserved, respect they'd spent a lifetime earning, they would have stayed to the bitter end with a smile on their face. Now they reeked of resentment, bitterness and defeat.

Was she any different? She, too, felt like a punching bag. The media, without mercy, attacked teachers; parents were either belligerent or apathetic; and she and her co-workers were convenient scapegoats for politicians looking for press. And her principal, don't get her talking. He was a weasel of a man whose goal in life was to remain the faithful house nigger. He was a yes-man, a team player, who without question did as he was told, solely to retain his job. When the shit hit the fan, as it inevitably did countless times during the course of the year, he immediately cast his glance for a convenient scapegoat. Anyone could be sacrificed, as long as he remained unscathed. How many times had he betrayed she and her colleagues, broken promises and stabbed them in the back? Too many times to count.

The man up front was talking about a host of options. There was one option if you were single, another if you had only a spouse to support, still third if you still had children living at home, and countless variations within each that had her mind spinning. She was divorced, her children were grown, the house paid, so she just wanted to take her money and run. She thought there would be countless questions, as the various options were more than a little confusing, but those in the auditorium merely sat, eyes glazed, totally unresponsive.

A white-haired light-skinned black woman, a few seats over, seemed to be dozing. Every few moments she'd jerk her head up, confusion etched in her features, as if some seemingly essential piece of information had passed her by. She looked sixty-five if she were a day, heavyset with her white hair askew. A lifer, Mya thought, who for some reason had finally had enough. Mya, also a light-skinned black, wondered if she'd look as beaten in a few years time. *Maybe you do already*, a voice in her head chided her. She hushed the voice before it made her consider whether it had a ring of truth to it.

Mya blinked her eyes. Could she have nodded off? she wondered, as the woman began to fade right in front of her eyes. Trying to concentrate on what was being said, Mya would steal a glance at the woman every few seconds. She was there, but Mya swore she could see through her to several other women to her left. Then the woman was gone. She hadn't up and left, Mya knew. Mya had been watching her. No, she'd simply disappeared. She had nothing to retire to, Mya guessed, yet there was no way she could take the daily grind any longer. With no alternative, she'd opted out—*literally*.

Mya wondered what she'd do if she actually retired. Her life had been teaching. She had no hobbies nor outside interests. Sure, she could travel, but the idea had little appeal. Sightseeing was not her thing. She had no desire to go on a cruise, explore Europe, visit the Holy Land...*go anywhere*. There had been a time, when she was young and svelte, when the Bahamas or French Riviera would have beckoned, but she was old—hell, *ancient*—and those curves that had once drawn stares were mere memories.

Focus, she told herself. She didn't want to come to another of these meetings. It was depressing as hell.

She blinked again, wondering if she'd dozed off,

knowing she hadn't. But where were the two men who'd been sitting just a few seats in front of her? Though sitting next to each other, the two hadn't spoken to one another once the meeting had begun. She had wondered if they were asleep, as they hardly moved. They took no notes, asked no questions. And finally, the two had faded before her eyes, like the light-skinned black woman, and were now gone.

She recalled Jodi's words, as they were waiting for the meeting to begin. Jodi was bitching of the inequities of life. As a youth and adolescent Jodi insisted you were too inexperienced and self-absorbed to grab life by the throat and enjoy it to its fullest. Then you slaved for thirty or more years, and when you *could* retire you were too old and infirm to make your dreams reality.

Mya had argued that she'd exaggerated, but realized Jodi hadn't been far off base. There were times, when Mya was thirty, even forty, when she was full of desires and ambitions. Times when she would have loved to take a few years to go off with some handsome stranger where no commitment was necessary. Or maybe start her own business. But divorced, with three kids to raise, she couldn't. There were bills to pay, and that weekly paycheck, small as it was for a professional like her, was sorely needed. And, summers were given to spending quality time with her children. During the school year their schedules and hers allowed for too little time together. Too often they were ships passing in the night. No, Mya was intent to provide a moral and emotional foundation for her own children, so their needs dominated her summers.

And, yes, now that she *could* enjoy herself—her children having fled the nest, scattered around the country—this was *her* time. But, though she refused to admit it to Jodi, her friend had been right. She likened herself to the Titanic after it had struck the infamous iceberg. She was overweight and out of shape. Her blood pressure was a bit too high as was her cholesterol. A chronic backache made both sitting *and* standing for long periods a trial. Her knees ached after climbing stairs. And creeping arthritis meant she could no longer play the piano, which had been her one passion. She was too aged and decrepit to enjoy these golden years she'd be allowed, without any need to worry about stretching her paycheck week to week.

Glancing to her left and right, Mya saw that more than half of the two dozen people who'd been in the auditorium when she and Jodi had arrived were now gone. Not one had risen and left. With no hope they'd simply disappeared. Yet, the man at the front continued, talking now about health plan options.

Mya turned to Jodi to share her thoughts, but her friend was just a mere shadow of herself. Mya whispered something to Jodi, but she didn't respond. Jodi had almost a serene look on her face, and then she, too, was gone.

Mya looked around and now she was the only one remaining.

The man up front went on for a few minutes more, then asked if there were any questions. Mya raised her hand, not certain what she'd ask, but desperate for recognition. He looked at her. No, she corrected herself, *looked through her*, then put his papers in his satchel, and walked past her as if she weren't there.

❧❧❧

Kealan Patrick Burke

*Say what you will about horror always reverting to the old tropes, but for my money and reading time there will **always** be a place in **Masques** for the well-told ghost story—and this one is simply exquisite.*

*Kealan Burke has already made a name for himself as both a writer (**The Turtle Boy**) and an editor (**Quietly Now**, **Taverns of the Dead**). His work is marked by a unique worldview and a distinctive narrative voice. Coming from Ireland, it's no surprise that there is such melancholy musicality to his prose.*

—JNW

STIRRINGS

✠ BY KEALAN PATRICK BURKE ✠

The mulberry trees stand like March's dark soldiers at the bottom of the garden, soaked in shadow as they contemplate the birth of dawn, their ragged silhouettes conspiring to send extensions of themselves sprawling without grace across the freshly tended yard. Dew glistens and the insects begin the first tentative strains of their morning overture. Night creatures shrug off the responsibility of dawn and seek out the dark until the curtain deigns to drop on the world once more.

A beautiful morning.

In the large white tract house where his wife lies shrouded in the security of dreams, Cole stands by the window, arms folded, reveling in the feel of the terry cloth beneath his fingers. His reflection is a tortured ghost peering back at him without the faint smile he knows has creased his lips. A stranger watches in the glass, hollow-eyed with disapproval.

A cardinal, a flying splash of newly shed blood, alights on the twisted limb of a withering tree bent low to the ground. Though the bark on the striated bole is crumbling, the oak wears this armor of decades with sagging pride.

From the bedroom, Marion moans, teased by wakefulness. Cole listens as she glides on the waves of an ethereal ocean wave back into the soporific dark of oblivion. He closes his eyes—shutters against a world of hurt—and imagines her there in that peaceful world, devoid of sharp edges and the madness that runs rampant round the waking world like a rabid black dog. She will be safe there.

Untouchable.

Unhaunted.

He huffs breath against the windowpane; it fills the yard with morning mist. The sight of it gives him an almost perverse delight, but not nearly as much as the raising of his finger, the writing of three simple words; so common, so devoid of meaning until now. With child-like care, he draws his finger down through the condensation and leaves his mark.

Stirrings. The bedroom. Not long now. He hears his name whispered and this time even the man in the glass, watching him from a face almost but not quite obliterated by his own breath, smiles with him. She is dreaming. Dreaming of him, and he hopes, happier times.

Or perhaps not. Perhaps she is snared in a ruthless dream, much like the one that trapped him for months until he awoke weeping and clawing for the air that had been denied his daughter. Perhaps she is at the pond with Samantha.

The thought makes a monster of his reflection, a seething thing with cold, lifeless eyes burning with self-hatred and accusation. Something akin to heartbreak ripples through his being, but of course it is just a memory. Old broken hearts seldom break again, or so often.

"*Cole.*" Her sigh floats through the crack in the oaken door that seals the lavender bedroom. The lace curtains on either side of him shift slightly, whisper against his finger and once again he closes his eyes, immersing himself in the smells, the sensations, the sounds of the old house, sounds he might have hated before, sounds he might have thought of as nothing more than the creak and groan of old bones settling around his cage of despair. Now he yearns to bear audience to its unique and aged symphony, for it is no longer commonplace.

"Cole?" He is jolted from his appreciation by a sudden and terrifying spike of horror driven deep into his skin. He is frozen, rooted to the spot before the mist-clouded window, an alien trembling holding him in place. The reflection is gone, unwilling to be privy to this blatant shattering of rules, rules so carefully dictated by the circumstances that have made his presence here possible. The cardinal takes flight, abandoning his post as sentry atop the wizened oak. The sun peeks a sleep-blurred golden eye above the blanket of the horizon. The shadows in the yard creep slowly closer; drawn to the occurrence of something ever so curious in the sunroom of the house.

"Cole?" *Not a whisper*. Not this time. *She's here. She's awake.* Stirrings, as of fabric whipping against the legs of the walker. Marion's pallid face floats specter-like over his shoulder in the glass. Eyes even darker than his own, hair tousled in paralyzed waves of gray. He does not turn around. Cannot turn around for surely this is some cosmic trick, some divine sleight of hand, a momentary lapse in the concentration of the puppeteer. Because she cannot be awake. It is not possible. And yet…he prays it is.

"You're awake," he dares to whisper, his voice a chill breeze over an October lake. As soon as he has spoken he waits for one of them to wink out of existence now that the unthinkable has happened. Her hand touches his shoulder, recoils at the coldness it finds there. Then it returns, albeit restrained by the weight of uncertainty. Barely there. The shake of Cole's head is slight. "You *can't* be."

"I thought you were gone," she tells him, her beautiful voice marred by grief and sleep he knows she is afraid to completely abandon in a reality she has grown to distrust. "I thought you left me."

Cole is caught in his own cocoon of bewilderment even as her breath tickles the hair on the nape of his neck. *Why am I still here?*

"I thought you were gone from me," she says again, but this time the words are spoken through the fingers of a hand anguish has summoned to her lips.

We're a stage play, Cole thinks then, his innards tugged by hope and pain and dread. *A silent movie with the quiet as the soundtrack to our stalemate.* They remain still and quiet, afraid to move, lest all of this suddenly reveal itself to be nothing but a joke, a fleeting tantalizing glimpse of hope never to be caught again. On the window the ghost of Cole's breath begins to vanish; the words he wrote there fading. *They will come again*, he knows. *They will come with the rain when I am gone.*

"We better not wake Samantha," Marion whispers and it is such an unexpected thing to say, such a peculiar statement that Cole finally turns around to face her, dragged by uncertainty to look full upon her. Her eyes are at half-mast and with a heart split between relief and mourning, he realizes they have been all along.

"Samantha is sleeping," she says softly, weaving slightly where she stands atop slumbering feet. Her sleep-tangled hair frames a face aged by loss, carved with the rough hand of grief at watching her husband and daughter die before her very eyes. Cole sighs and the morning light warms them as he lays a trembling hand on his wife's elbow and carefully guides her back to her room, to what was once *their* room, where they laughed and cried and made love. Where nothing could get them until the pond took their child and anguish made Cole follow her into the dark.

Sad times which even death does not allow escape

from. Sad times which have left Cole—once a loving father, once a loving husband—a haunter of morning, a husk of trapped and awful emotions, condemned to live on in the twilight of his wife's dreaming, a shadow wandering the borderland between sleep and waking. Where she can never see him.

Gently, so gently, he lays her down among the frozen white waves of the sheets. She frowns at the abrupt end to a hopeful dream as her eyes drift closed and she turns away from him. The motion is symbolic. So many nights, so many times they needed each other did they turn their backs and suffer alone. As they suffer now.

Cole, gripped by sadness, steps back and gazes down at her, the memory of weeping shifting inside him. A fleeting ghost. Gold light burns beneath the door as the day catches fire. His shadow rises on the wall next to the bed. There is a small crack in the plaster. There is a small crack in everything and both of them have just shared one. Marion stirs, moans. For a moment he wishes her awake.

Her breathing grows shallow. Cole brushes his lips against her forehead, watches an aborted smile slip from her lips and leaves the room. The sunlight has filled the window, lacing the words with an amber glow; the signature, the childish but so very significant mark he has left on the glass:

I WAS HERE

He feels another tugging inside, this one more painful than the last and altogether different. The sun fills his eyes with liquid sadness. He looks back over his shoulder, through the crack in the bedroom door at the sleeping woman, at his wife, and chokes the yearning to run to her, to cast off the concerns of what might happen should he rush to her, grab her tight and never let her go. Would she come with him? Dust feigns emotion and surges up his throat. It is too late for such frenetic desires. It is time. He waits a heartbeat, watches the sheets. The rise and fall of her breathing.

She moans.

"Marion," he says, softly.

Now.

She sits bolt upright, her face a mask of grief-stricken horror, her skin pulled tight at the behest of a mouth open in silent screaming. Black sleep flees her eyes and she looks at Cole through the narrow space between door and jamb. A whine. Cole feels the tugging try to shear him in half. Marion shrieks, a deafening, horrifying sound of utter loss, of unending pain and suffering. Of pleading.

The sunlight is cold.

Finally, she yells his name.

And he is gone.

For Charles L. Grant, to avoiding that coin at all cost...

Lucy A. Snyder

Lucy A. Snyder is a writer, editor, and web designer who holds degrees in biology and journalism. She formerly published the long-running webzine **Dark Planet** *and was a poetry editor for the prozines* **Strange Horizons** *and* **HMS Beagle**. *Her work has appeared in publications such as* **Lady Churchill's Rosebud Wristlet**, **Chiaroscuro**, *and in the anthologies* **Villains Victorious**, **Guardian Angels**, **Bedtime Stories to Darken Your Dreams**, *and* **Civil War Fantastic**.

I've rarely accepted a story for this series without asking for at least minor revisions, but when I pulled this manuscript from its envelope and gave it a read, I realized that I had in my hands what is arguably a perfect **Masques** *tale. I think you'll agree—when a storyteller gets it right, they get it right.*

—JNW

THE SHEETS WERE CLEAN AND DRY

✠ BY LUCY A. SNYDER ✠

B reathless, Kathy slipped into the fabric shop. Xander would be furious if he discovered she'd left the house. Her blouse was sticking to the welts on her back she'd received as punishment for disappointing him. The night before, she'd mistakenly cracked open the '82 Chateau Margaux instead of the '80 as he'd ordered. An expensive mistake, and she'd paid for it in skin and blood.

Once he'd tired of exercising his belt, he curtly demanded she make a new suit for him by the next Tuesday. She hadn't any good suit fabric left in the house. But she'd known better than to tell him that. He'd beat her for not being prepared.

Kathy stared around the shop. The cabbie didn't understand English very well, and instead of taking her downtown, he'd deposited her in Chinatown. She decided to see if a nearby store—Chen's Fabric Shoppe—had something useful.

"Can I help you?" asked the stooped old woman behind the counter. Her thick white hair was pulled up in a bun secured by two lacquered chopsticks.

"Do you have any wool? Something in a gray, good for a man's suit?"

"Mmm-hm." The old woman limped through the shop to some bolts of slate-gray cloth with a fine herringbone twill. "Tibetan wool. Feel very nice on your man."

Kathy touched the fabric. It *was* quite nice, soft but substantial and had an excellent drape.

"I think he'll like it," Kathy said.

At least I hope he'll like it, she thought, biting her lip. It was becoming impossible to please Xander. He'd been so sweet and attentive at first, but now he found fault with everything she did. She'd make the wine mistake because she'd been working 36 hours straight. She'd spent the night baking bread to replace the loaves he'd thrown out because he claimed the wheat was bitter. And then she'd spent the entire day cleaning the fifteen-room house. She'd been so tired when she'd gone down to the wine cellar, she'd barely been able to keep her eyes open.

At least he'd let her sleep after he'd whipped her.

Kathy realized she was clenching her fists, and made herself relax. She had no right to be angry with Xander. He let her live in a mansion and had taken her on trips around the world. Without him, she'd probably still be stuck in their cramped tract house in Atlanta, picking up after her little brothers and listening to her parents scream at each other when she wasn't working nine-hour shifts at the dry cleaner's. Without him, she wouldn't even know what Chateau Margaux *was*.

She'd met him when he brought one of his suits in to be dry cleaned while he was on an extended business trip. The cleaners' was right by the airport. Lots of businessmen came through the place, but the moment Xander stepped inside, Kathy knew he was different. It was in his walk, the way he held himself, the way he looked at her. Power and confidence were his pheromone, and the sound of his voice made her instantly weak in the knees. They chatted a bit as she took his suit and wrote down his information, and that might have been the last she'd seen of him if she had not slipped a note into his suit pocket.

He called her that night, and took her to Phillipe's Resturant where they dined in candlelight and split a bottle of Dom Perignon. The fanciest date she'd had before then was when one of her high school boyfriends took her to the Outback Steakhouse before the prom.

Their courtship lasted eight months. He treated her like a princess, and Kathy was entranced by how absolutely *cool* Xander was. He gave her the kind of lifestyle she'd only read about in her mother's romance novels. Only after she became his wife did she finally discover that the perfect sangfroid he displayed to the world required volcanic ventings in private.

Her mother had always said a woman should count her blessings. So what if Xander forbade her to leave the house without him? So what if she couldn't go to college, or have her own friends, or visit her family? He was an important man, and had worked hard for his money and position. As he always said, he *deserved* a good woman to make sure everything in his household suited him. He *needed* her. He only hit her because he loved her, and wanted her to be a better person.

Kathy realized she was digging her nails into her palms. She took a deep breath and smiled at the old woman.

"I'll take ten yards of this, thanks."

"Anything for you? You make man happy, you make something make you happy."

"Oh, no, I—"

The old woman produced a bolt of the black satin, so lustrous it seemed almost to glow. Kathy stroked it with her index finger; it was the smoothest, softest cloth she'd ever touched. Slightly warm, even.

"Silk?" Kathy asked.

179

The old woman nodded. "From spiders in the Mekong Valley. Fabric made for bedsheets. 800 thread count. Woven tight to trap dreams."

Kathy stroked the material again. Slowly. To lie naked on sheets of that satin would be absolute heaven.

She immediately tried to tamp down her desire. She couldn't think of herself; she had to consider what Xander would want.

"No, I really shouldn't," she stammered, pulling away.

The old woman's gaze now rested on some old, yellow bruises on Kathy's wrist; they were surely from Xander grabbing her too roughly, but she couldn't remember when he'd marked her. Kathy tried to pull her sleeve down to cover them, but it was too short.

"You make something make *you* happy," the old woman insisted. "Nothing make man unhappier than unhappy woman. It take a lot of strength to take care of house; you need sleep. Silk bedsheets just the thing to keep you strong."

"Well…" Xander seldom slept in her bed, but she could always use the satin for his jacket lining. Yes, he'd like that very much, she decided.

Kathy worked long and hard on the suit and when she finished, it was a wonder to behold. The luster of the satin lining seemed to spread to the twill, and when Xander put it on he glowed with power and confidence.

He posed frowning in front of his mirror, turning this way and that, searching for some small flaw. His frown deepened when he could find nothing to criticize. Finally, his face relaxed into a neutral smile.

"Fine job," he said, then gave her a quick kiss on the forehead as he headed toward the door. "I'll be back in two nights."

When he was gone, Kathy went back to her sewing room. She pulled out the rest of the satin and set to making her sheets. The fabric came together easily, almost seemed eager to join under the needle. She re-made her bed with its new clothes, pulled the goosedown comforter up to her chin, and fell asleep.

She woke with a cry on her lips and an orgasm in her loins. She'd dreamed that Xander whipped her with a great cat o' nine tails. Each lash brought as much pleasure as a kiss to her vulva. He beat her harder and harder 'til the walls were covered in bits of her flesh.

She rolled over and tried to go back to sleep. Her naked body was drenched in sweat, but the sheets were dry.

The next night, she dreamed it was Xander on the rack, and she with the whip.

Silk bedsheets just the thing to keep you strong.

She beat him, again and again, flaying the flesh from his body until he came and died in the same great groan. Then she fell on his body, tearing out handfuls of his sweet-salty flesh that she devoured him in greedy slurps. She ripped loose a bloody rib, and pleasured herself with it, driving it into her own flesh until at last she came.

Kathy awoke with a horrified start and stumbled into the bathroom, her belly aching. She'd started her period in the night, a whole week early, and was bleeding profusely. She swore softly; surely she'd ruined the sheets. After she put in a tampon and went back to bed, she discovered that the sheets were clean and dry.

Xander stumbled in early the next evening, rumpled and red-eyed from his flight, still wearing the suit she'd made him. His eyes burned with the dark glow of his jacket's satin lining.

"I dreamed of you," he accused hoarsely. "On the plane, at the meeting, I could think of nothing but you. Go upstairs."

She stepped back, shaking her head, even though her parts were swollen with sudden desire. "I'm bleeding a little—"

"Then I'll make you bleed a lot!"

She ran, and he chased her through the kitchen and up the stairs. He caught her outside her bedroom; she wasn't sure if she'd truly been trying to escape him. It wasn't right to have sex in her condition, but oh God, she wanted it so bad.

He dragged her to the bed, tore off her clothes, and they had savage, frenzied, bestial sex. They sweated and bled and came until they were practically empty, and throughout it all the sheets stayed perfectly dry. Xander was in a frenzy that neither orgasms nor ordinary pain seemed to satisfy.

"I want to fuck your heart," he said, reaching over the edge of the bed to pull something shiny out of his jacket pocket. A slim double-bladed dagger. "I want to feel your heart pulse around my cock."

Death was more than she could submit to. She grabbed Xander's wrist and they wrestled for the dagger on the slippery bed.

Kathy fought and kicked, trying to pry the blade from his hand. Xander hit her across the face with his free hand—

—and she remembered her first kiss from redheaded Sean who sat beside her in her middle school English class.

He hit her again—

—and she remembered the sweet pain of losing her virginity to Mike Wilson; she could no longer remember his face clearly, but she'd never forget the smell of his aftershave.

A third blow fell on her shoulder, and she felt her muscles start to tremble and weaken—

—then she remembered her childhood dreams. The dreams she had as young girl before the gauntlet of adolescence and the dulling grind of school and work made her lose herself: she had not dreamed of being Rapunzel waiting for her Prince, she had dreamed of donning armor and slaying dragons; she had not dreamed of being Lois Lane fainting for her Superman, she had dreamed of being Catwoman on the prowl—and she certainly had not dreamed of slaving as a rich man's bitch; she had dreamed of battling pirates for their gold.

Silk bedsheets just the thing to keep you strong.

With a scream, she heaved Xander over onto his own blade. He gasped as it plunged deep into his chest. Dark blood flowed over the bedclothes.

The sheets writhed and shimmered and drank down the blood.

Kathy watched, mesmerized, as the moisture was sucked from Xander's body until he was a husk, then ashes, then dust, then nothing.

Five minutes after he was dead, nothing remained on the sheets but the dagger and a few gold fillings from his teeth.

The sheets rustled, the serpentine hiss of the satin whispering to her softly:

I will keep you strong if you bring me what I need...

❖ ❖ ❖

The next evening, she put on her best cocktail dress and headed out to the downtown bars to look for a luscious young Lothario.

Maybe he'd buy her dinner first; that would be nice. She was hungry.

But more importantly, so were the sheets.

Joe Nassise

*Joe Nassise is the former president of the Horror Writers'
Association and the author of the acclaimed novel
Riverwatch and the powerful novella **More Than Life
Itself**. His latest novel, **Heretic: Book One of the Templar
Chronicles**, hails the arrival of an important new series in
the field of horror/dark fantasy. Joe's writing is deceptively
uncomplicated on the surface, in much the way a prism
seems uncomplicated until one holds it up to the light.*

—JNW

SAINTKILLER

✠ BY JOE NASSISE ✠

The first time it happened, Memphis Stone was standing over the rapidly cooling body of a young girl.

It was just after 9:00 pm, mid-summer, the streets of
Boston still reflecting the heat they had soaked up during
the day under the combination of the 90 degree temperature
and the even higher percentage humidity. It had been a long,
grueling month with heat-frayed tempers and the corre-
sponding hike in violent crime that always accompanied
such a stretch.

Stone had been fostering a mild headache for most of
the afternoon. The pain made him tense, irritable, and the
fact that he was still standing there two hours after he was
supposed to have gone off shift did nothing to assuage that.
Just the opposite, in fact, as it sent his headache rocketing
up several levels higher on the pain scale.

He stared down at the body, wondering. *Who was she? Why did she have to come along right when she did? Couldn't she have taken a different way home?*

She was the fourth victim this month. All of them young, all of them seemingly innocent, at least to this world-weary detective. Apparently he wasn't the only one who thought so, for the press had taken to calling it the work of the Saintkiller.

He rubbed at his forehead, his hand over his eyes as he tried to ease the rapidly tightening band of tension churning there. When he took his hand away, the scene before him wavered and then changed...

The alley was all but empty. The detectives, the crime scene technicians, the mob of curious onlookers that had gathered like leeches just beyond the tape-line, were all gone.

Memphis could see that the girl remained, still looking as lost and forlorn as she had when he'd first arrived on the scene.

The girl remained, though now her body was still warm to the touch as the last remnants of her life fled her young frame.

The girl remained, but she was no longer alone.

It stood about five feet tall and was wrapped in a long cowled robe that was several sizes too big, a robe which hung in dirty folds about its frame as it stood hunched over the girl. Its hood hid its face from his view.

Memphis was suddenly struck with the bizarre notion that if he had been able to see it he would have see only a flat, barren surface devoid of feature or function, a face that wasn't really a face at all.

Kneeling down beside the body, the thing reached out and grasped the girl's leg. Its hand had only four fingers, overly long appendages with thick misshapen knuckles and nails several inches in length that rasped together as they closed around the girl's calf. It leaned forward and out of the depths of its hood came a long, molted tongue of sickly hue. It quivered in the air, inches from an exposed section of the girl's tender flesh, as if anticipating the taste to come.

Suddenly it stopped. Its head came up slightly and Memphis could hear it sniffing, like a dog searching for a scent. Once, twice, and then it stiffened. Its head swiveled in Stone's direction. Two points of greenish flame flared within the darkness inside that hood where the creature's eyes should have been.

Memphis gasped...

...and with a start came back to himself. His partner, Jefferson Brooks, was holding his arm tightly, an odd look, part concern, part horror, on his face as he pulled him away from the crime scene.

"I said, get a hold of yourself, Stone."

Memphis shook the man's arm away. "I'm fine. What are you doing?"

Nash snorted. "Fine my ass. You were down on your hands and knees sniffing the body, for heaven's sake. Get a grip, man."

Memphis stared at him in disbelief. Sniffing the body? Then the memory of what he had seen in his vision came rushing back and he almost fell over in his haste to get away from the corpse before him.

Sudden pain flared in the detective's hands, enough to tear his gaze away from the tableau before him. Looking down, he found blood pouring out of a hole the size of a quarter in the center of each palm, wide enough that he could see the street beneath through the ragged opening in his flesh. The dark arterial blood seemed to spurt free in time with each beat of his heart.

It happened again three days later.

Memphis was up most of the night trying to piece

together the few leads he had into something he hoped might actually move the investigation forward a step or two, but to no avail. The lingering unease he felt from the odd event in the alley was not helping. Frustrated and angry, he returned to his apartment only to spend several hours in a fit of uneasy sleep, chased by dreams full of dark and terrifying creatures that stalked him through lonely streets and empty buildings. He gave up trying to rest around six, went out for his morning jog, showered, shaved, and then gulped down a sparse breakfast.

Now he stood by the counter pouring himself another cup of coffee. In the adjoining room the television was tuned to a local newscast. He was reaching for the sugar when he heard the anchorman break in with a Special Report.

As he turned to listen, blood splashed across the countertop.

Memphis lost his grip on the newly-filled cup, the ceramic shattering as it smashed on the floor tiles, but he barely noticed as he stared in amazement at the holes that had suddenly erupted in the center of each palm again.

Blood flowed like a fountain from the wounds, scarlet against the white of the kitchen counters.

The room around him wavered and then changed...

...A warehouse.

The smell of machine oil, sweat, and pain. Darkness pooling in the corners and overhead. The steady rhythmic sound of a pump working in the background.

A scream erupted from somewhere off to his right; harsh, discordant, full of anguish and fear.

He moved in that direction, his footsteps sounding hollow and unwelcome in the silence that immediately followed that cry, past shroud-covered hulks of machinery, down a short corridor, and into another opened room.

Memphis stood in the doorway, staring in dazed bewilderment.

The room was enormous. Far bigger than should have been possible. All but the closest wall was lost somewhere in the distance. The room itself was filled with row upon row of mobile autopsy tables, like those used in morgues, each one holding the naked form of an unconscious teenager strapped to its surface with thick leather belts. A maze of tubes and wires ran from a monitoring device beside each table to the body atop it, though their individual purposes were not easily discernible. A sense of despair and decay filled the room with a thick and cloying presence, accentuated with the occasional scream from one of the patients/prisoners as they encountered some idle terror in their dreams.

Between the tables, tending their occupants, were dozens of creatures like the one he had encountered in the alley.

As one, they turned to look at him.

Terrified, Memphis took a step backward, away from those burning green eyes, and...

...returned to his kitchen, where his blood continued to paint the floor tiles crimson.

He stared at his hands, astonished and more than a little afraid now. Behind him, in the other room, the announcer's voice suddenly seemed overly loud.

"Tonight, the Saintkiller has claimed another victim..."

"I am not going crazy. I'm not."

But it certainly felt like he was. The visions, dreams, whatever the hell they were, had intensified over the last week, becoming more frequent and more vivid until he could no longer tell reality from imagination.

He tried working himself to exhaustion, but the dreams still came. He tried drinking himself into unconsciousness, hoping that the sweet oblivion of alcohol could hold the visions at bay, but the dreams still came. He even gulped down a handful of tranquilizers the night before last, but even that had failed.

He didn't go into work for over a week. No doubt the investigation had stalled, but he couldn't care less. At first the office tried to track him down, calling at all hours, leaving messages, demanding his presence. When he grew tired of listening, he ripped the phone out of the wall and threw it out the window into the backyard. He even stopped answering his door, afraid of whom or what he might find waiting outside each time the buzzer rang.

Memphis was not a religious individual. Truth be told, he hadn't set foot inside a church in years and so the whole stigmata thing was confusing the hell out of him. He sat there with his hands wrapped in cotton gauze, having discovered that it proved rather effective in soaking up the blood when the stigmata appeared for the third time late last night. He didn't have a clue what was causing it all. *Well, that's not quite true*, he admitted to himself. He hadn't needed the morning paper to know that the Saintkiller had claimed another victim. Somehow he and the murderer were connected and that knowledge was both simultaneously fascinating and revolting.

What if this guy doesn't stop? he thought. *What then? Will I have to live with this the rest of my life?* He snorted derisively at the idea. *What life? I can't even make it a week. No way could I make it a month, never mind longer. I'd be better off putting a bullet in my head now and saving myself a lot of trouble.*

Not that he hadn't considered it. That's how bad it was getting.

He sat at the kitchen table playing idly with the blood-caked bandage on his left hand, considering some of the things he'd seen over the last few days. Deep caverns where phantoms lie resting quietly...dark rites performed in shadowy tenements over the bodies of sacrificial lambs, both human and otherwise…unearthly battlefields where bodies lay piled in the sun, their pale-feathered wings ruffling in the breeze.

And blood.

Seemingly endless streams of blood.

Memphis cringed at the memories.

His fear made him uncomfortable. He got up from the table and moved into the living room, where he noticed that the day had fled and darkness now covered the land. *Where had the day gone?* Leaving the lights off, he took a seat near the window and stared out into the darkness, wondering where the killer was at that moment, wondering if his own hands would soon be signaling the death of another victim.

As he looked out the window, his view was abruptly cut-off by the sudden flaring of a brilliant light reflecting in the glass from the corner behind him.

Turning to look, he discovered that he was no longer alone.

"Do not be afraid," his visitor said. "I am Ashariel and I have come bearing a message."

The stranger's voice was strong, commanding, even a little overwhelming. It seemed to have hidden depths, echoes upon echoes, and Memphis found himself trying to catch each separate layer, as if there was another message beneath the obvious one that he desperately needed to understand.

Memphis might have spent the last week or two hounded by visions and half-convinced he was going out of his mind, but that didn't make him any less a cop. He had his service revolver out and pointed at the other before his visitor had even finished speaking.

It was only then that he noticed the other man's wings.

"What the hell…?"

The newcomer chuckled. "Not quite," he said, "but close."

"Who? What…?" The gun was forgotten in his overwhelming amazement. He might not be religious, but he could certainly recognize an angel—particularly when it was standing in his living room.

"You are not going crazy, Memphis Stone. I have a message for you, one of great importance, and the visions were necessary to prepare your mortal mind so that you might receive it properly. You have been chosen and there is much you will need to do."

"Chosen? For what? And why me? I'm not even a believer."

"There is no need for you to believe, Memphis. Others believe in you."

And with that the angel reached out a hand. The room around Memphis tipped, swayed, and then spun downward out of control. The last thing Memphis saw before the darkness closed in was the solid black of his visitor's eyes.

The warehouse was just where the vision had shown it would be, nestled in an all-but-forgotten lot just south of Jessup on Decatur. Memphis stood across the street, lost in the concealing shadows of a neighboring doorway, and watched the place closely for over an hour.

The usual street traffic was out in abundance, from hookers to gangbangers and derelicts. The building was not only ignored, but universally shunned. The detective had seen it before—the street folk knew trouble when they saw it and avoided it instinctively.

He waited a several moments longer, until the few stragglers were no longer in sight, then crossed the street and slipped through a hole in the chain-link fence surrounding the property. He crossed the ground quickly, not wanting to be caught in the open. When he reached the building itself he headed around to the back where his vision had shown he would find a broken window. He used that to gain entrance.

Memphis then made his way quietly through the interior of the warehouse, moving from room to room, following the course the archangel had laid out in the vision he experienced back in his living room.

Then, with an eerie sense of déjà vu he found himself standing just outside the entrance of the room he sought.

He knew now that the creatures he had seen in the alley and in his vision were real. Ashariel had explained their true nature to him, had imparted their need to harness the life force of the innocent to maintain their infernal forms, their complete hatred for the joy that freedom can bring and their innate desire to force humans into a life of servitude. He didn't recall having made the decision to go along with Ashariel's plan, yet he found himself standing in the darkened hallway just beyond the entrance, a semi-automatic pistol held firmly in a shooter's grip.

He took several deep breaths, preparing himself for what he knew he was about to see and then stepped into view in the doorway of the room, the pistol raised and ready.

There were six of them scattered throughout the room, tending to their charges. As one they looked up at Memphis' appearance.

Without hesitation, the detective-turned-avenger opened fire.

The gunfire echoed in the enclosed space, Memphis' first three shots were perfectly on target, striking the nearest creature in the chest and face. He shifted his aim as it went down, only to find the other five were already rushing across the room toward him, their arms raised high, their claw-like fingernails ready to be used as weapons.

Lord they're fast! he thought, as he put three more bullets into the next closest one.

Still the others came on. By now they had crossed half the distance toward him.

Two down, four to go. This was going to be close. His gun barked again and again, his aim near perfect.

Four left, the closest twenty feet away.

Three left, fifteen feet.

Two left, less than ten.

The final creature made it within striking distance. Memphis was forced to duck as the thing swung those vicious claws in his direction. This close, he could smell the fetid stink of the creature and could see the ragged, raw flesh that served as its face.

He came back up shooting, putting two bullets dead center into the thing's hood.

It was tossed over backward with the force of the shots to lie unmoving on the floor in front of the doorway in which Memphis still stood.

The detective bent down, placed the muzzle of his weapon against the back of the thing's head and used his final bullet, just for good measure.

With that, the battle was over.

Memphis stepped over the corpse and approached the nearest table.

Once beautiful, the girl before him was now frightfully thin. Her skin, thin and yellowed like old parchment, was stretched tightly across bones that jutted forth far more than they should. She was all harsh angles and shadowed hollows. Strange tubes of some kind of flexible crystal-like substance pierced her body in a vertical line running down the center of her form, the first attached to the center of her forehead, the last just above her groin, seven in all. Other smaller tubes were twined about her limbs and attached at the elbows, knees, and wrists. Blood and other unidentifiable fluids were being pumped in and out of her form through these connections.

As the detective leaned closer to get a better look, the girl's eyes snapped open.

Memphis recoiled in horror.

She turned her head to follow him, a desperate, pleading look in her eyes. Her lips parted and she appeared to say something, but Memphis was unable to understand what she said over the thump and hiss of the machinery around her.

Overcoming his revulsion, he returned to her side. He bent down, placing his ear near to her lips.

"Please…" she said.

Memphis understood. He'd known it would come to this; he'd seen it in the vision the angel had put before him. He'd just hadn't realized that the girl, and all of her companions, might actually be conscious and aware.

Gritting his teeth, he reached for the tube that went into her throat.

It moved beneath his touch as it if were itself aware, squirming away from his grasp in an attempt to prevent him from carrying out his designs. Using both hands, he grasped it firmly, preventing it from getting away.

The girl watched him with eyes opened wide.

When he was ready, his hand gripping the tube tightly, he met her gaze.

She smiled.

He did the same.

Then he pulled.

The tube came out of her throat with a small sucking sound and without another sound the girl was dead.

Blood gushed from Memphis' hands and splashed across the girl's corpse beneath him, the stigmata appearing again at the sudden death of another innocent, this time at his own hands.

Tears in his eyes, the detective turned to the next table and the form strapped helplessly to it.

It took him three hours.

By the time he was finished, he was sick at heart and weak from loss of blood.

But the children had been set free.

He carefully made his way back across the room, his eyes on the ground, avoiding the stares of those he had sent on to a better life. After what seemed like forever, he left the

self-created graveyard behind and traversed the maze of
corridors that had led him there, until he could once more
see the moonlight coming in through the window he had
used to gain entrance.

He stumbled once, as he prepared to leave the building, and barely caught himself with a quick grab for the
nearest wall. Once the wave of dizziness had passed, he
slipped back out through the opening and disappeared into
the night.

"They were awake. Aware. They knew what I was
there for."

Ashariel nodded, but did not comment further.

"They're free now. That's good, isn't it?"

"Of course. You did well. The Lord is pleased."

Memphis stared down at the slowly closing wounds in
his hands. "But if I was doing the Lord's work, why did His
wounds appear?" That part of it just wasn't making any
sense to him. The stigmata appeared when the Saintkiller
murdered an innocent victim. Why then did it appear when
he released the prisoners from their pain?

Ashariel's answer proved to be no help at all.

"We all have our crosses to bear."

When Memphis turned to respond, he found his visitor
had vanished as abruptly as he had appeared on that first
night.

Across town, in an abandoned warehouse located
south of Jessup on Decatur, a set of tracks were visible on
the floor of an empty, oversized room. The tracks moved in
a haphazard pattern through years of accumulated dust,
from a broken window in the rear corner, around the center
of the room, and back to the window again.

Aside from the tracks, the only evidence that anyone had been in the room in years was a handprint on the wall near the window.

A handprint made in blood, with a curious hole in the middle of the palm.

Gary A. Braunbeck

*When I discovered that Gary A. Braunbeck's highly-acclaimed novel **In Silent Graves** began life as a short story (never published in its original version), I absolutely insisted on seeing it and, upon finishing it, knew that it had to be included in this fifth **Masques** volume. I once described him as being a writer "...who can break your heart even while he's showing you shocking horror in places you've never before noticed it." That has not changed, as you are about to discover.*

—JNW

IN A HAND OR FACE

❖ By Gary A. Braunbeck ❖

A weary remnant of the young woman she once was, Fran McLachlan stood in the center of the midway holding her five-year-old son's hand and trying not to think about the way her life had gone wrong.

"Mommy," Eric said, "what's wrong?"

Fran was glad that the massive bruises on his cheek and jaw looked far less discolored and painful today. If only she could say the same for her own abrasions—but, after all, wasn't that why God created makeup and Tylenol?

"*Mommy?*"

"Wha—? Oh, I'm sorry, hon. What did you say?"

"Did that lady say something bad to you?"

"No, hon, she didn't."

"Then how come you look so sad?" He clutched his balloon-doll as if his very life depended on it.

Oh, Christ! How could she answer that question honestly now, after what Madame Ariadne had shown her? How could she tell her son—the only good thing she had—that she was thinking about abandoning him on a fairgrounds nearly a hundred miles from home because of a palm-reading?

You didn't give her a definite answer, she thought. *The group's not going to head back to the shelter for another hour—you can at least make this time count. You can make sure he has so much fun that nothing will ever taint the memory for him, ever.*

God, Eric, do you know how much I love you?

"Hey, you," she said, tugging on his hand and smiling.

"Hey, *you!*" he replied, grinning.

"We'll have to…to be leaving soon, so what say until then we do whatever you want?"

"*Really?*"

"Uh-huh. You pick."

"Then I wanna go on the merry-go-round."

This surprised her. "Why? We've been on it three times today."

" 'Cause you laughed when the tiger started bouncing and it wasn't a pretend-laugh like all the other ladies. I liked it."

Oh for the love of God, kiddo—why'd you have to go and say something like that?

Fran kissed her son's cheek and told herself she. Would. Not. Start. Crying.

"Okay," she whispered. "The merry-go-round and then…then m-maybe we'll meet your new friend and get some hot dogs."

"*Hot dogs!*" shouted Eric, dragging her down the midway, his balloon-doll thrust in front of him as if it were flying.

For a moment there, Fran could've sworn that her son's face actually shone with happiness.

And not pretend-happiness, either.

It began three hours before. Fran and Eric were having lunch at a long picnic table with several other women from the Cedar Hill Women's Shelter and their children, the kids occupying themselves by pointing out all the sights to one another while the mothers took the time to regroup and count the money they had (or, in most cases, *didn't* have) left.

"You look a lot better today, Fran," said one of the women. "So does Eric."

"Yeah," Fran said. "We're both feeling better."

"Have you thought about, well...about Ted?"

Fran shook her head. "No—I mean, yes, I have, but Eric hasn't mentioned him and I'd appreciate it if none of you would bring up his father today, okay? I don't want anything to spoil the day for him."

Eric and most of the other children wandered over to watch a group of balloon-toting clowns breeze by. One of the clowns stopped to make balloon-dolls for several of the children. Fran saw this and smiled. "Just...*look* at them will you? Everything's still *new* to them. Even with what's happened to them, they still laugh and giggle and...I don't know...*hope*, I guess. Remember when you were that young? How nothing bad ever followed you to the next morning? Moment to moment, with a new excitement each time; that's what I think 'childhood innocence' is. Maybe something bad happened *this morning*, but *now*...now's fun, you've got a ball to bounce or a model plane to fly or a doll to pretend with, and the day's full of mystery and wonder and things to look forward to and...and—"

You're babbling. Shut up.

They scattered shortly thereafter, instructed to meet back at the south entrance at six p.m.

Fran and Eric rode the merry-go-round for the third time that day, but from the way Eric acted you'd have sworn this was the first time he'd ever been on it. Fran envied him his joy, but was at the same time aware of how precious it was, and knew by the wide smile on his face and the gleeful shimmer of his eyes that she'd made the right decision to leave Ted and take Eric to the shelter where he wouldn't have to worry about Daddy coming at him with the belt or his fists, or be forced to cower upstairs in his room while Daddy thrashed Mommy into a whimpering, broken, swollen zombie who shuffled around, whispering, never looking up, afraid of the violence the next five minutes might or might not bring.

Since they'd moved to the shelter two weeks ago, Eric—who before had been a good fifteen pounds underweight, nearly skeletal—had begun eating again and laughing again and was able to sleep soundly for the first time in his short life. God, how she cursed herself for having waited so long, for having kept Eric in such a brutal, hateful, terrifying environment!

At first it was just a couple of slaps every now and then, and Ted was always sorry afterward, so Fran allowed herself to believe that he really was going to get better about things, that he was going to get some counseling, but then he went on graveyard shift at the plant, sleeping during the day, refusing to see a counselor on the weekends, and as Eric grew older Ted's violent outbursts grew not only in number but in brutality—a couple of slaps turned into a bunch of slaps, a bunch of slaps turned into fists to the chest, stomach, and face, which evolved into slamming her against walls and choking her, sometimes knocking her down to the floor where, until the night she'd sneaked out of the house with Eric, he'd begun to give her a couple of kicks to the side—

—she was, for a moment, so numb with the weight of her thoughts that she didn't even realize the merry-go-round had stopped, then she noticed that Eric was standing outside the circular gate of the ride talking to a little girl who looked to be around seven or eight.

"Eric!" she called to him. "You stay right there."

Better watch it, you, she thought. *That's how kids wind up with their pictures on the sides of milk cartons. "I only turned away for a minute," says the mother/father.*

She quickly exited through the gate, sprinting to where Eric and the little girl—who looked vaguely familiar to Fran—were still standing.

"Hey, you," she said, taking Eric's hand in hers.

"Hey, *you!*" he replied, giggling.

The little girl seemed to hear someone calling her, said a quick good-bye to Eric, then turned and ran—but not before shoving a piece of paper into Eric's hand.

"Who's your friend?"

"I dunno," said Eric. "She was telling me 'bout her hand." He offered the piece of paper to Fran.

It was some kind of special fair pass. On the front were the words: **Good For Two Free Readings**! The back read:

> *Each line, be it in a hand or face, masks another; lines hidden within lines, a secret Hand beneath the surface of the one with which you touch the world and those you love. It is only in the secret lines on the hidden hand that your true destiny can be mapped, and only one who possesses Certain Sight can make an accurate reading. If you're content with mere showmen, then please take your business to any of the fortune-teller tents—but if you want the truth, see Madame Ariadne.*

"So, kiddo—wanna get your palm read?"

"Wha's that?"

Fran turned over Eric's hand, sticking the tip of her finger into the middle of his palm. "A lady looks at your hand and tells you what's gonna happen to you."

"*Aw*," he said, grinning. "I saw that on a TV show. It was *neat*."

"Does that mean 'yes'?" She couldn't resist tickling his palm.

"*Stop!*"

She did. "Wanna go?"

"Sure. It'll be like on TV."

The interior of Madame Ariadne's tent was not what Fran expected—no crystal ball or beaded curtains, no candles or spicy incense or stuffed ram's head or shelves overflowing with philtres and potions; if anything, the interior more resembled the white sterilized rooms where a veterinarian might examine a family pet: white rolled-tile floor, white partition walls, chairs, and a table upon which sat—most surprising of all—a computer. Next to the computer was something Fran assumed was a flatbed scanner.

"This is Weird City, kiddo."

"Like on *X-Files*!"

"That doesn't make me feel any better."

Eric laughed, then a door opened in one of the back partitions and Madame Ariadne entered. If things didn't feel off-kilter enough, Madame Ariadne—instead of being a weathered, sinister Maria Ouspenskaya clone—looked to be no older than thirty-three, her cheeks flushed as if she'd just finished a good aerobic workout; judging from the light grey cotton warmup suit she wore, that was probably the case.

"Well, *hi*," she said, brushing a thick strand of strawberry-blonde hair from her eyes and kneeling down to face Eric. "My name's Ariadne. What's yours?"

"Eric."

"Ah, that's a good name."

"Uh-huh."

She offered her hand. "Well, it's a pleasure to meet you, Eric."

Eric looked at Fran, who gestured *Go on.*

He shook it. "Hi."

It happened so quickly that Fran almost missed it; as soon as Eric's hand was enfolded in her grip, Madame Ariadne visibly flinched—not in such a way as to cause Eric any alarm, but to the eyes of an adult it was clear that she'd felt something that startled—maybe even frightened—her.

Fran cautioned herself to be careful, that this could be part of an act—scare the parent with some crap about "bad vibrations," then con them into a more complicated and expensive reading.

"We have a pass for two *free* readings," said Fran.

"I know," said Ariadne, smiling at Eric and releasing his hand. "This isn't a scam operation, Fran. The pass says free and free it shall be."

"How did you know—?"

"So, Eric," said the fortune-teller, "how would you like to go first?"

"'Kay."

She led him over to the table, then took her place behind the computer and typed in a few commands, activating the scanner. "Eric, I want you to take your—are you left-handed?"

"Uh-huh."

"I thought so. Take your left hand and press it down on the glass right there."

"On the box?"

"Mmm-hmm. Don't worry, it won't hurt. It's just going to take a picture of your hand."

"Promise?"

Ariadne's smile was spring itself. "Promise."

Eric pressed his palm onto the scanner. Ariadne took a plastic cover device and placed it on top of Eric's hand, which now was completely hidden from sight.

"Arm's in a box," he said to Fran, grinning.

"Oh, boy."

"Hey, Eric," said Ariadne cheerfully, "did you know that each part of your hand was given to you by an angel?"

"*Nuh-uh!*"

"Uh-huh. As a reward for their love and friendship, God allowed each angel to add one small part to the hand of every human being; thumbs, lines, bumps, every part of your hand's a gift from an angel." She winked at him. "I read that in a book when I was a little girl. I don't know if it's true, but I think it's kinda neat, don't you?"

"Uh-huh."

There was a slight hum, a slow roll of blue light from under the cover, and it was over.

By now Fran was standing behind Ariadne, staring at the computer screen as a holographic copy of Eric's hand—composed mostly of grid lines—appeared on the monitor.

Ariadne playfully poked Eric with her elbow. "Now watch this—it's so *cool!*" She hit a key and a dark blue line rolled down from the top of the screen, passing over the grid-hand and changing it to a three-dimensional, flesh-colored hand that looked so real Fran almost expected it to reach out and tweak her nose (a favorite past-time of Eric's).

Eric squealed with delight. "Izzat mine? *Izzat my hand?*"

"It sure is," said Ariadne. "And it's a good, strong hand, with strong lines. See that line right there? That means you're a good boy, and this line means you've got lots of imagination—I'll bet you like to make things, don't you? Like models, and draw, and build things with clay."

"Oh, yeah!"

"I knew it! The lines never lie. This line right here—

ah, this one's very special, because it means that you're going to grow up"—she gave Fran a quick, secretive look—"to be someone really special—even more special than you are right now. Oh, you've got a good life ahead of you, Eric. You should be so happy!"

"Oh, boy!"

This went on for a few more moments, until the little girl from the merry-go-round came out of the same door from which Ariadne had entered and said to Eric, "You want to come and watch a video with me? I got *The Great Mouse Detective.*"

"*Mouse Detective!*" shouted Eric. He turned to Fran. "Can I, Mommy? Can I go watch *Mouse Detective?*"

Fran was once again struck by the notion that she knew this little girl from somewhere. "I don't...I don't know, hon—"

"That's one of my daughters, Sarah," said Ariadne. "I've got a little play room set up for her right back there. Toys, books, a TV/VCR unit, and—God!—*tons* of Disney videos—I swear she'll bankrupt me with those things. I'll have them leave the door open so you can keep an eye on them.

"He'll not be out of your sight for one second, Fran. I swear it."

Fran looked down at Eric. "You really want to watch the movie?"

"Yeah!"

"Okay, then. But be polite."

The only things faster than light is the speed at which some children rush to watch a Disney video—a principle that Eric and Sarah proved a second later: *Whoosh-Bang!*—Disney rules.

Fran stood in silence for a moment, watching the two children through the door as they took their seats in front of the television.

"That's quite a collection of bruises on his face, Fran,"

said the fortune-teller. "Ted must've really clobbered him."

A breath in, a breath out; one, two, three; then Fran whirled toward Ariadne and said: "How the hell did you know my name?"

"The same way I know that you've been at the Cedar Hill Women's Shelter for the last fifteen days. The same way I know that both you and Eric were in Licking Memorial's ER *sixteen* days ago because the two of you 'fell while taking in the groceries.'

"The same way I know that Ted spotted you at the free clinic five days ago and followed you back to the shelter."

"He *what?*"

"You heard me. He—don't get panicky, he didn't follow the group here today. He's on swing until the first of next week, but you have to believe me when I tell you that he *is* going to be waiting for you outside the shelter sometime in the next eight days, resplendent in his remorse."

"You can't possibly know that."

"Do you think I'm trying to scare you? You're damned right I am."

"How did you—?"

Ariadne hit a key, and Eric's hand disappeared, replaced by scrolling records: Fran's birth certificate; the date of her high school graduation; a copy of her marriage license; Eric's birth certificate (complete with foot- and hand-prints made at the hospital); her student loan application for college tuition (check returned, full amount, student withdrew from school before deadline, no monies owed); copies of police reports (three domestic calls, no charges filed); and several hospital records detailing treatments given to one Francine Alicia McLachlan and Eric Carl McLachlan, some together, most separate—including at least two doctors' handwritten notations, nearly indecipherable except for "abuse?" and "possible mistreatment."

"So?" snapped Fran, trying to keep the anxiety from her voice. "You or someone who works with you is a hacker, so what? Anyone with a computer could get this information these days."

"True enough," said Ariadne. "But would they also know that you once came very close to killing Ted while he was asleep?"

Fran blanched, shocked into silence.

"December 22, two years ago," said Ariadne. "He'd lost his temper and started pounding on you and Eric came running downstairs and put himself between you and Ted—something he does quite a bit, doesn't he?—and Ted pushed him down. Eric fell against a coffee table and the corner missed his left eye by less than half-an-inch. Five stitches in the ER took care of the gash, and in the cab on the way home Eric said he wanted to go away because Daddy scared him. Ted was already asleep when you got home, so you put Eric to bed, waited until he was asleep, then you went to the downstairs hall closet and took out Ted's .357 Magnum, put in one bullet, then wrapped the muzzle in an old towel to muffle the sound of the shot—"

"Stop it!"

"You never told anyone about that, did you, Fran?"

"...no...I mean, I don't *think* I..."

"So I couldn't have hacked that information from any computer, could I?"

"...no..."

Ariadne placed a warm, tender hand against Fran's cheek. "Listen to me very carefully. I don't want to frighten you, but I have to. Eric's in danger."

Fran's legs suddenly felt like rubber, and she just barely made it into the chair facing the computer. "...someone..." she whispered. "I...I must have told someone about...about wanting to kill Ted, and you...you..."

Ariadne placed a finger against Fran's lips, silencing her, and in a soft voice, the whisper of leaves caught in the wind brushing across an autumn sidewalk, spoke of other things that only Fran knew, intimate details of solitary experiences, hopes, desires, petty jealousies and silly girl-hood fantasies extending back through nearly three decades, and when she'd finished (by describing in detail Fran's first childhood memory of getting her arm caught in the toilet when she was ten months old because she wanted to see where the water went after you flushed), Fran—confused, frightened, and feeling so godawful helpless—was certain of one thing:

Madame Ariadne had...*powers* of some kind, incomprehensible, unknowable, incredible.

"What...what *are* you?"

Ariadne leaned over Fran's shoulder and typed a command. "First you need to see something."

The screen blinked, display Eric's hand once again.

"Both you and Eric have Conic hands. See the shape of his fingers? Just like yours—they're very smooth and taper from the base, gradually lessening toward the rounded tip. The Conic Hand is the Hand of Imagination. Just from the shape of Eric's hand any fortune-teller would know that he's very sensitive, often highly emotional—but not emotionally unstable. He's like you in that way, isn't he?"

Fran nodded. "He's pretty anxious a lot of the time but he tries to hide it because he doesn't want to upset me."

"Not surprising." The image of Eric's hand turned slightly to the left, displaying the height of the mounts on the surface of the palm. "See this rise here at the base of the middle finger? This is called the 'Mount of Saturn'—also known as 'The Mount Which Brings Sadness.' If you've got a Conic hand with a pronounced Mount of Saturn, you constantly worry about the safety of the ones you love, even above your own well-being—which would explain why Eric always tries to get between you and Ted when—"

"—he wants to protect me," whispered Fran.

"Of course he does; he loves you very, very much."

"I know."

"Good."

Eric's hand turned toward them, palm facing outward. "Why do you use a computer and scanner?" asked Fran. "I mean, most fortune-tellers—"

"—would whip out the candles and crystal balls and hold your hand in theirs as they made the reading, yeah, yeah, yeah—believe me, I know this is a bit weird. I use this because...because the naked eye—even mine—cannot clearly see the lines within the lines, the—"

"—hidden hand within the hand?"

"Yes. This equipment was designed specifically to reveal those hidden lines, the secret hand."

Fran looked at the image on the screen. "Okay...?"

"Can you recognize any of the lines?"

Fran leaned in, squinting. "I can see that his life line is really long." Her mood brightened. "He'll have a long life."

Ariadne shook her head. "A long life line doesn't nec- essarily mean a person will live to be very old. I mean, sure, in places where it weakens or breaks you can expect some health problems, but a lot of people have life lines that are incredibly short—some fade entirely—and they still live to piss on their enemies' graves. No, we're interested in one of the Fate Lines, Saturn—right here, staring at the base of the wrist and going straight up to intersect with its sister mount." She altered the image so that it now displayed only a flat red outline of Eric's hand, with the Fate Line of Saturn enhanced in bright blue, the Mount of Saturn in bright green—

—and at the point where the two intersected, a cluster of small markings in jaundiced yellow.

"What are those?" asked Fran.

Ariadne magnified the cluster.

Fran puzzled at the sight. "They look...almost like stars."

"They are. On the Mount of Jupiter or Apollo, they mean great success and wealth. On Mercury they mean a glorious, happy marriage...."

Fran faced Ariadne. "What aren't you telling me?"

The fortune-teller looked back at the children happily watching their video and singing along with the voice of Vincent Price, then pulled in a deep breath and released it in a series of staggered bursts.

"Jesus," said Fran. "If you want my attention, you got it."

"Have you talked to your husband since moving to the shelter?"

"What's that got to do with—?"

"Have you?"

"Once—okay, twice. The psychologist says it's good for us to call our husbands or boyfriends, let them know we're all right—if they care—and to get things off our chests. The shelter gets part of its funding from Catholic Services, so they're kind of big on aiming for reconciliation if it's possible."

"Do you think there's any chance you and Ted will get back together?"

Fran shrugged. "I don't know. Maybe. If he gets his ass into counseling and does something about his temper, if he admits that there're emotional problems he's been carrying around and stops treating me like—okay, okay, please don't look at me like that.

"Maybe. *Maybe* we'll get back together."

Ariadne took Fran's hand in hers, examining it. "You still love him?"

"...yeah..."

"Sounds like you wish you didn't."

"Sometimes I do wish that, but—" She pulled her hand away. "Why do you need to know?"

Ariadne pointed at the screen. "When a Conic hand has a direct intersecting of the Line and Mount of Saturn, and when that intersection is marked by stars, it has only one meaning, and it's never, *never* wrong: death by violence."

Deep within Fran McLachlan's core, at the center of

216

her interior world where all hopes, regrets, dreams, emotions, experiences, and sensations coalesced into something beyond articulation, a crack spread across the base, threatening to bring it all crashing down.

Very quietly, words carefully measured, heart triphammering against her chest, she managed to get it out: "Say it."

"Ted's going to kill Eric. I knew it the moment I held his hand."

"...no...no...he w-w-wouldn't do something like...like that..."

"On purpose, no, probably not. But you know what happens when he loses his temper—"

"—he doesn't...he doesn't *think*, he just—"

"—lashes out at what- or whomever happens to be in his path, which is you and Eric—"

"—don't know how many times I've told him that he should just stay in his room when Daddy gets that way, but he won't, he doesn't like it when Ted hits me—"

Ariadne cupped Fran's face in her hands. "Fran? Look at me. Look at—there you go. Take a deep breath, hold it, hold it, now let it out. Good. Do you trust me?"

"I...I d-don't know—"

"Yes, you do."

Fran looked into the face of the woman before her, and saw there nothing but concern, kindness, and deep, abiding compassion. "Yeah, I guess I do."

"Then you believe what I'm telling you?"

"Oh, God, I...I don't know...."

The fortune-teller looked over her shoulder and called, "Sarah? Honey, would you come here for a minute?"

"Aw, they're just getting to the part with the clock!"

"You've seen it before. Just come here for a second, okay?"

"'Kay."

She appeared a few seconds later.

"Sarah, I'd like you to meet Eric's mother."

The little girl held out her hand. "Pleased to meet you, ma'am."

Fran saw the little girl's hand, saw the scar that ran from between her index and middle finger all the way down to her wrist (from when her father had gone at her with a pair of scissors), then looked up into her eyes and thought, *Please, don't let them be two different colors*, but they were—the left gray, the right soft blue—and she tried to get her mouth to form words but everything was clogged in the bottom of her throat.

"You okay, ma'am?" asked Sarah.

"I'm...I'm fine," Fran managed to say, shaking her hand. "Do you like Bobby Sherman records, Sarah?"

The little girl's face brightened. "Oh, yes! My favorite song is—"

"'Julie, Julie,'" said Fran.

"How'd you know?"

"Lucky guess."

Ariadne touched her daughter's face. "Sorry that I interrupted your movie. Just for that, I'm buying pizza tonight."

"*Pizza! Oh, boy!*" And Sarah surpassed the speed of light once again to bring the news to Eric.

"Don't bother trying to tell yourself that you didn't see her," said Ariadne. "In her way, she's as real as you or I."

Fran was shaking. "That w-was *Connie* Jacks! She w-was my best friend when I was a little girl. Her father used t-to hit her all the time, knock her around, but she never told anyone but me. She died when I was seven. Everyone thought that she'd fallen down the stairs and hit her head on the r-r-radiator, but I always thought that—"

"—he did," said Ariadne. "He beat her to death. If it's any consolation, he blew his brains out about ten years ago. Guilt usually catches up with you, eventually."

Fran looked at Ariadne—having now decided that the woman couldn't be human—and said: "*What are you?*"

"I am a Hallower: a half-human descendant of the *Grigori*, who were among the Fallen Angels. In retaliation for God's not having shared all Knowledge with them, the Fallen Angels stole the Book of Forbidden Wisdom and came down to Earth and gave countless Secrets to Man. Most of the *Grigori* coupled with human women during their time on Earth, and my race was the issue of that coupling. I am a direct descendant of the Fallen Angel Kokabel. He gave mankind the Forbidden Knowledge of Time and Science and assisted the *Grigori* Penemue in giving children the Knowledge of the lonely, bitter, and painful." She lifted her left hand, palm facing outward. "He also tainted the Mark of the Archangel Iofiel, who holds dominion over the planet Saturn." She placed the tip of her right index finger at the base of her left middle finger. "It's because of Kokabel that the Mount of Saturn brings such deep sadness with it.

"That's why I've chosen to do what I do. In a hand or face, Fran, the mark of my ancestor's sin can be found; I am the only being who can read the signs, and I will spend eternity trying to ease what sadness and pain I can.

"Maybe you won't ever reconcile with Ted, I can't say—but what I *do* know is that there are six stars on Eric's hand—one for each year that he will live, and the stars are in the Patriarchal Configuration—meaning the danger will come from Eric's father. Maybe he'll do it after you guys get back together, maybe he'll do it after your divorce when it's his turn to have Eric for the weekend—hell, who knows? He might come by Eric's school and take him, he might snatch him from your backyard when you get your own place—it's secondary to the fact that somehow *he will kill Eric* and you can't prevent it. But I can.

"Which is why you have to leave him with me. Take Eric with you, and he won't live to see his seventh birthday."

Fran laughed; she couldn't help it; it's how she fought back panic. Rising from the chair, she felt light-headed.

"You know, you really...really don't give a person a chance to cath her breath."

"There's not much time. What can I do to convince you?—and don't ask me to sprout wings or perform some tacky parlor trick, though I can do either as a last resort."

Fran glared at her. "Tell me how Connie Jacks can still be alive, how she can still be a little girl after all this time."

Ariadne rubbed her eyes. "I suppose the simplest explanation is to say that she's a ghost who doesn't *know* she's a ghost."

"Buy you said she was as real as—"

"—and she is. She can bruise, throw a temper tantrum, break a bone, muddy her good shoes, get a stomach-ache...sometime in the next eight months she's going to need to have her appendix removed and in a year or so she's going to have to get braces on her front teeth and she's *not* going to be happy about it.

"When a child—*any* child—perishes at someone else's hand, their body dies, yes, but their *promise* lives on. What they *should have* grow up to be doesn't cease to exist because the child is dead, it simply wanders alone on a different, more abstract plane that ours. Because I am what I am, I have the ability to...*guide* that potential into a new corporeality. Do you understand?"

"You can...you can bring them back to life?"

"Not in the way you're thinking, no hocus-pocus or *Frankenstein* stuff. I give their displaced potential a new home—flesh—so that it can take up at the point where everything was snuffed. That girl in there, Sarah, is the girl Connie Jacks *should have* lived to become. The only thing different is her name and her memories, because as far as she knows *I'm* her mother. She has no memory of being beaten to death, of whimpering in lonely agony for someone to come help her because it never happened to her. To Sarah, the world is a new and wondrous place, filled with fairs and pizzas and mouse detectives, and she'll never have to be afraid."

Fran tried to catch her breath. "I still don't understand how—"

Ariadne put a finger to her lips. "Shhh, not so loud—I don't want them to hear you.

"There are two kinds of time, Fran: *chronos* and *kairos*. Kairos is not measurable. In kairos, you simply *are*, from the moment of your birth on. You *are*, wholly and positively. Kairos is especially strong in children, because they haven't learned to understand, let alone accept, concepts such as time and age and death. In children, kairos can break through chronos: when they're playing safely, drawing a picture for Mommy or Daddy, taking the first taste of the first ice-cream cone of summer, when they sing along to songs in a Disney cartoon, there is only kairos. As long as a child thinks it's immortal, it is.

"Think of every living child as being the burning bush that Moses saw; surrounded by the flames of chronos, but untouched by the fire. In chronos you're nothing more than a set of records, fingerprints, your social-security number, you're always watching the clock, aware of time passing— but in kairos, you are *Francine*.

"Children don't know about chronos, and in my care, that's how it remains.

"Sarah's not my only child, Fran. I've got hundreds more just like her, too many of whom died at the hands of a parent who was supposed to love them, care for them, protect them from harm. Some died at the hands of family friends, or suffered unspeakable deaths inflicted on them by people who stole them away for their twisted pleasures. I have *babies*, some who lived less than a month because they were starved or beaten or dumped in trash cans or left out in the cold to freeze to death or locked in cars on summer days to slowly suffocate—but that can't touch them now because in my care they live only in kairos. Chronos isn't part of them any longer.

"I will save as many living children as I can from having to die at abusive, neglectful, violent hands." She entered a series of commands, and the flesh-colored, holographic copy of Eric's hand was restored to the screen. The image magnified to focus on the stars, then focused deeper, to a series of markings beneath the stars.

"Look closely, Fran. Do you see them?"

"They look like...like squares."

"Those are the mark of kairos. They're called the 'Walls of Redress.' They're very faint on Eric's hand, but you can see that there are six of them, one for each of the stars, and that if they were more solid, each would hold a star inside of it. The Walls of Redress are the promise of protection. No matter what danger is marked on the hand, if there is a square near or around it, the person can escape the danger if the signs are read in time."

"Why are they so faint?"

"Because the part of the world in which they might or might not exist in still in flux; they can fully form in kairos or they can fade away in chronos. It depends on the decision you make."

Fran's eyes began to tear. "...*ohgod*..."

Ariadne grabbed Fran's shoulders. "It's all been arranged. When you leave here, take him around the fair once more, do whatever you want, but make certain that the last thing you do is ride the merry-go-round, and that you get off the ride before he does—who'll notice? A tired mother walking a few steps ahead of her kid when the ride's done?"

"Who will—?"

"Sarah will be there with some of her brothers or sisters and they'll bring him back to me."

"But...*Christ!*...h-h-how can I...wh-what would I s-say to—?"

"There are over six thousand people here today. Countless children disappear each year on fairgrounds, at carnivals or amusement parks. He won't be living among only children like Sarah, there are hundreds of other children just like Eric in my care, children I got to *before* violence claimed them."

Fran gulped in air, trying to staunch her sobs. "I…I'll…can I…come with you?"

Slowly, sadly, Ariadne shook her head.

Something inside Fran crumpled. *"Why?"*

"Because the place we're going is only for Hallowers and the children in their care." A small, melancholy grin. "Think of it as the ultimate kids' clubhouse: No Grownups Allowed."

"Will I ever…ever see him again? I don't know if…if I could live without—"

"Yes. It won't be soon, but you'll see him again. He'll—and I know this isn't much comfort—but he'll write to you. A letter a week, a videotaped message four times a year; that's my rule. Don't worry if you move because his letters will arrive wherever you are every Friday, even if it's a national holiday." A short, wind-chime laugh. "We sort of have our own private delivery service."

She touched Fran's cheek, lovingly. "I promise you, Fran, I *swear* he won't forget about you, he won't feel angry for your leaving him with me. He'll miss you, because he loves you so much, but it will get easier as time goes on. He'll never lose his love for you, and he'll grow up to be everything you hoped and more. You will have your son back, one day, and there will be no love lost.

"Don't say anything right now. You've got a little while, so go on, take your son to the fair and make him laugh, make him smile, and be certain that you miss nothing—not a word, not a look, a touch, a whisper, nose-tweak, or kiss. The next few hours will have to last you for a good while. Waste no moment.

"Go on. I'll know your decision soon enough."

Fran called for Eric, then wiped her eyes and stared at Ariadne. "I don't really believe in God, you know?"

Ariadne shrugged. "Not a prerequisite for the service. The belief you're talking about only has to work one way, anyhow."

"Good-bye, Ariadne."

"So long, Fran. Catch you on the flip side."

As they were leaving the tent, Eric turned back to Madame Ariadne and flashed his palm. "I got a angel hand."

The fortune-teller smiled. "You are a strange and goofy kid, Eric McLachlan."

"Yes, I am!"

They stopped to play a few games (Eric won a small toy fire truck at the ring-toss booth), watched some clowns parade around, shared a soft pretzel, and then, suddenly, feeling as if she were a weary remnant of the young woman she once was, Fran McLachlan stood in the center of the midway holding her five-year-old son's hand and trying not to think about the way her life had gone wrong.

"Mommy," said Eric, "what's wrong? Did that lady say something bad to you?"

She told him no, and asked him what he wanted to do, and he chose the merry-go-round.

This time both of them rode on the tiger, and Eric's laughter, in his mother's ears, during those final moments of the ride, was the voice of forgiveness itself.

"Can I go again?" he asked as Fran climbed down.

"Sure, honey. Of course you can." The attendant was walking by at that moment, so Fran gave him the last ticket.

"You have fun," she said to Eric.

A happy bounce. "'Kay. You...you stand out there and watch me, okay?"

"...okay..."

Steady.

"I'll wave at you when I go by."

Hang on.

"Have you had a...a good time today, honey?"

"*Yeah!* This was the best fun ever!"

Oh shit, don't let him see it.

"I'm g-glad." She leaned in and kissed his cheek. "I love you, Eric."

"Love you, too—better get off now, Mommy, so they can start the ride."

Not daring to look at her son's face, Fran McLachlan turned around and left, catching a peripheral glimpse of Sarah getting onto the ride with a two younger children whose hands she was holding: the protective big sister.

Fran looked down at her hand and wondered what secrets were hidden there in the lines within the lines, the hand beneath the hand.

Walking away from the merry-go-round, she was startled when a sudden, strong breeze whipped past, pulling the balloon-doll from her grip and sending it upward, soaring, free, rising on the wind toward a place where chronos had no place, where the children were safe and never wept or knew fear.

Good-bye, she thought. *Be happy.*

And was surprised to feel a smile on her face.

Tracy Knight

Tracy Knight is a clinical psychologist and writer who lives in western Illinois. His short fiction has been published in a variety of anthologies in the science fiction, horror, mystery and western genres. He is the author of two novels: **The Astonished Eye** *and* **Beneath a Whiskey Sky,** *and is currently on the psychology faculty at Western Illinois University. Tracy's gift for focusing on the telling detail of a scene to offer a startling parallax effect is on full throttle in this haunting offering.*

—JNW

MOTHS IN DAMP GRASS

✠ BY TRACY KNIGHT ✠

Nine-year-old Timmy Rees had never before seen anything quite like the young man sitting coiled in the wheelchair, his entire body folded into itself, limbs wrenched this way and that as if they had a thousand ideas what to do and couldn't settle on any one. The man held his right hand horizontally, palm down, directly in front of his eyes; his fingers were rigid, bowed, and he gracefully waggled the hand back and forth, left and right, all the time smiling as he minded its every motion. Occasionally he scrubbed his other hand through his mussy shock of black hair, which was crookedly cut, likely because he couldn't hold his head still for the barber.

His wasn't an obvious smile, an innate expression of savored pleasure. Rather, it was as though a smile had been vaguely described to him and he was simply trying to follow directions. His bared upper teeth were splayed like reaching fingers, his lips wrested and trembling.

When Mother saw the doctor approaching, she tugged Timmy toward a chair in the corner of the psychiatric unit's Day Room. The boy sat politely and, although he kept tabs on Mother, he also continued to intently examine the gnarled, happy man.

"Dr. Clark?" Mother winked when she caught the young psychiatrist's eye, and smiled her winsome smile, her shiny lipstick the color of an old, deep bruise.

"Valerie, how's my favorite psychiatric nurse?" Dr. Clark was six feet tall with piercing green eyes and dark hair with splashes of gray at the temples. His white coat hung nobly from his body. "We've missed you here the past few days. The unit's been hopping. We're almost to over-flow."

"I'm concerned," Mother said in her special tone full of both concern and commitment. She patted the platinum blonde hairdo she'd just had done yesterday. "So concerned I had to take a few days off. I hope you understand."

"Timmy?"

She nodded. "I checked his stool this morning. There was blood in it again. And what appeared to be glass. I've seen him eating mud, pebbles, aluminum foil, chips of paint. He had a fever of 102 earlier this week, Lord knows from what."

"Thank God you're his mom," said Dr. Clark. "Most mothers these days—especially single mothers as busy as you—wouldn't even have noticed. Look, let's raise the dosage on the Seroquel for a few days, see if it helps." He scribbled a note to himself.

"Thanks," Mother said, wiping away an invisible tear carefully so she wouldn't smear her bold mascara. "But what am I going to do? I'm not sure how much longer I can deal with this."

Dr. Clark squeezed her shoulder. "I understand. It is

frustrating. To be honest, I've never seen a case of diagnosable *pica* suddenly appearing in a nine-year-old; eating bizarre, non-nutritional things is typically seen in much younger kids. And his loss of speech is equally puzzling. Normally I'd say we should admit him—"

Mother raised her hand to her mouth and crinkled her perfectly shaped eyebrows. "Oh, but I don't want that. I've always taken such good care of Timmy."

"I know, Valerie, I know. You've got good reason to be proud of yourself. Most parents aren't mental health professionals, aren't capable keeping such a close eye on things. You are. So I'm comfortable not admitting him today. But really, Val: If this continues for another week, or if he eats something more dangerous, we'll need to keep him here, take a closer look. In the meantime, let's move his outpatient appointment up to Monday."

"That would be wonderful, Matt..." Mother blushed. "I mean, Dr. Clark."

"Matt's fine," the doctor said, grasping her forearm, then rubbing up and down it. "See you in two days then?"

She fluttered her eyelashes as if he'd proposed. "We'll be there. I wish I knew how to thank you."

Although Timmy heard every word of his mother's predictable conversation with the doctor, he still couldn't take his eyes off the tangled, smiling man for more than a few seconds. The man continued to wag his hand rhythmically in front of his eyes, now and again cooing pleasantly, like a mourning dove.

Timmy pulled his chair closer and whispered so Mother wouldn't hear him. "You're smiling," he said to the man. "Does that mean you're happy?"

No response. The man didn't even seem to notice Timmy was there.

"I wonder what it's like inside," Timmy continued, "where you're at."

The man tipped his head to one side and his eyes

twitched toward Timmy several times, although they always returned to the moving hand.

Timmy thought harder. He was desperate to know. "Please," he whispered, almost too loudly. "Are you happy? What's it like?"

The strangely melodious voice was like a breeze breathing through Timmy's mind.

Moths in damp grass, it said. *Soft and calm and warm and safe.*

Timmy returned the tangled-up man's unfailing smile.

Driving toward home, Mother's expression filled with such joyful satisfaction that Timmy half-expected her to say she'd been kidding this past year, or that she had just gone temporarily mad when she began forcing him to eat glass shards and metal shavings and injecting him with dirt to give him a fever. But she didn't. Instead she spoke about how interested Dr. Clark was in her—not only as the dedicated mother of an emotionally disturbed child, but as a woman.

"Would you like to have a new, good Daddy?" she asked, checking her lipstick in the rearview mirror. "Not like your old Daddy, someone who would leave us, but a kind, smart Daddy."

Timmy turned toward her but knew better than to respond. He understood the rules, such as they were. Mother had told him never to say anything when she fed him the things he didn't want to eat, and renewed her demand every time she injected him with dirt. Within two weeks of the first time she'd forced thumbtacks down his throat, Timmy had decided he didn't know anymore what he could say and what he couldn't, so he determined the best resolution possible. He quit speaking.

She reached over and tousled his hair. "Ah, sweetie.

Someday you'll talk again. I can't wait to hear that beautiful voice. Dr. Clark said if we continue to see him and you take your medicine like a good boy, you'll speak again. You'll be perfect in every way."

She turned toward Timmy, so he nodded his agreement.

"I'll make you supper as soon as we get home," Mother said.

Timmy stared straight ahead. He didn't want to think about it.

"After you eat, it'll be time to take a bath and go to bed," Mother said as she drizzled melted butter over the pile of tiny nuts and bolts lying in the center of the paper plate. Timmy wanted to say it was only six o'clock, much too early for bedtime, but of course he didn't.

Mother carefully scooped up a spoonful of the nuts and bolts and opened her mouth as if she were going to be the one eating them, but it was to show him what she expected. "Come on now, honey," she said, "open wide."

He clenched his eyelids, just to see if the world would go away.

Mother's voice lowered and he heard the first traces of the rage he wanted, above all else, to avoid. "Now, it's easy, Timmy. Just open your throat and let them slide. You can wash them down with your iced tea."

Hot tears escaped his closed eyes, but he did as she said.

The nuts and bolts landed on his tongue. The mingling of warm butter and oily metal grime made him want to gag, but instead he did as he had so many times before. He relaxed his throat until it was wide open, tipped back his head and let the tiny nuts and bolts scuttle down his throat and into his waiting stomach.

"What a good boy you are," said Mother, cupping her palm against his cheek. "Now get your PJs on. Time for bed."

Timmy lay in his curtained bedroom, which was illuminated only by a sickly green night light, and felt his stomach clenching and churning and fussing about what horrible new stuff had been thrust into it.

He breathed deeply and tried to relax, mindful that if he vomited up what Mother had fed him, he simply would have to eat it all again. Perhaps if he calmed himself it wouldn't be long until his stomach, convinced there was nothing useful to be gained from the nuts and bolts, would surrender them, pass them down to its organ neighbors and, finally, completely out of him.

That thought alone was so soothing that Timmy began drifting away from the bed, the room, the roiling pain. The outer world became fuzzy and far away.

"Wheeeeeeeeeeeeee!"

The high-pitched cry snapped Timmy back to consciousness, and he had to squint to see what it was that was suspended five feet above his bed, whirling like a pinwheel.

"Wheeeeeeeeeeeeee!"

The spinning slowed.

Timmy gripped his sheets and pulled them over his nose, but kept his eyes free. He had to see.

What floated above his bed wasn't familiar at first, not until the figure came to a complete stop.

It was the young man from the hospital, the twisted-up man, floating face down, lit only by the green night light.

The man's body was at rest in the air, arms and legs outstretched. But he was different than before. He seemed in absolute control of his body and his eyes were locked directly on Timmy's.

What Timmy noticed, most of all, was that despite the fact that there was a man hovering above his bed, he didn't feel the least bit scared. Perhaps living an uncertain, painful life had its blessings.

The man laughed gently. "Pleasant here, this place where you live," he said. "Nice in this room with you."

Timmy didn't know what to say and sure didn't want his mother to hear either the floating man or him talking. No telling what she'd do to him then.

"Please," the man said. "Talk to me. I spun out of me, to this place. You did this for me. A gift."

Finally, Timmy couldn't resist but kept his voice as hushed as he could. Meeting the man's gaze, he said, "I didn't do anything. How did you get here? How are you floating up there?"

The man shrugged and, as he did, his body swayed delicately. "Unsure. You noticed me, talked to me, made it inside me. Different than everyone else. Listened. Magic. Connected."

"You're...okay now?" The man seemed happy, happier even than he'd seemed back in the hospital. "How did you get all twisted up like you were before?"

The man narrowed his eyes and smiled. "Don't remember. Always been that way, or almost always. When I was little, there was a fever, hot. The world became loud, so loud. Roars of color and smell and sound and sensation. Thought I'd explode. So I folded up. Found a way to bring order. The best I could do."

With each fractured sentence the floating man uttered, Timmy became more curious. "You wave your hand in front of your eyes. What's that?"

"When I folded, pulled inside," the man said, nodding, his body bobbing like a cork on a pond, "found ways to bring sequence, cadence, predictability to my world. I stay inside. Focus on my hand. Sometimes rock back and forth, back and forth. Then there's rhythm in life, form to guide me, life that won't drown me or sweep me away. Like a moth in damp grass."

"What? A moth?"

"Still see them sometimes, the moths, when they let me sit outside. They drowse in the grass, tiny moths—white and tan—comfortable, warm, quiet. They wake if someone comes to them. They fly away. Before then, their world is peace and they're invisible."

"You found a secret. Your life's been good. When I asked if you were happy, I bet you would have said yes if you could."

"Mostly, but miss a lot. Miss feeling my parents. When they hug and talk, can't feel it or hear it very well."

That stopped Timmy for a moment, after which he said, "I miss those things, too."

"How? Why? Out here the world hasn't gone loud, bright, confused."

"Yes, it has." Timmy pushed the covers down to his waist. His stomach wailed more loudly now so he rubbed his tummy with his hands.

"You hurt," the floating man said, concern softening his handsome face. "No reason you should. It's a good world out there where you live."

"I thought so, too," Timmy said, voice strained. "I used to, at least. But my Dad left us. My Mother...well, she makes me sick on purpose so she can take me to the hospital. Tonight she fed me—" the memory clamped his throat. "—nuts and bolts. She gets all sorts of attention that way. People tell her how good of a mother she is, how she saves my life. I think she wants the doctor to fall in love with her. I wish...I wish I could be away from her. I wish I could find the things *I* miss, just like you do. I'm sick all the time. Lonely. I don't even go to school anymore."

The floating man brought his index finger to his chin and scratched it. "Hmm. Never imagined such things out there."

"I never imagined such a thing as you either."

The man allowed his body to spin for a few moments, his belt buckle reflecting the green light. Then he stopped again. "How do you live, then, without everything being too loud?"

Timmy shrugged. "I guess I learned to ignore things. Lots of things. My brain does it for me. It isn't hard. It just takes practice."

Glancing left to right, a smile of satisfaction spread across the man's face. "Yes. Yes. I guess I hadn't developed that ability—*omitting*—when the roaring began. But...now it's different. Now I think I can. Thanks to you. You came to me, the moth in damp grass. I awoke. I flew. No longer invisible."

"I'm happy," Timmy said, letting his warm hand rest on his rumbling stomach. "I'm happy you're happy."

"Wonder if I can find my way back," the man said. Then his body rotated, slowly at first, increasing in speed until he was a circular, fizzing blur throwing off a warm, aromatic breeze that buffeted Timmy's hair.

A sharp *pop*. He was gone.

Timmy lay there for hours, his bedroom silent save for his stomach's grumblings, and marveled over the visit from the tangled-up man. When he finally slept, he dreamed of tiny moths, with feathery white wings, slumbering in damp grass.

Dr. Clark's eyes were wide open, showing too much white, and he nervously wiped his hands, one over the other, as he spoke to the parents.

"Mr. and Mrs. Banner," he said almost breathlessly, "please have a seat. This is something I've never seen before. I don't know—"

Charlie Banner, a small and weary man of forty,

grabbed Dr. Clark's arm as though he wanted to slap him into sobriety. "Just tell us, Doctor. Ever since you called, Rita's been beside herself. Tell us!"

"Wait here," said Dr. Clark, who then bolted down the hall, returning moments later pushing the wheelchair holding Mark, the Banner's twenty-three year old son.

"What...?" Rita Banner said. Her body began to give way until her husband steadied her.

"Stand tall, Rita," Charlie said, voice tremoring. "It's our boy."

"Mom? Dad?" Mark said. These were the first words he'd uttered in over twenty years. He smiled and it was a real smile. His body was entirely unknotted and relaxed.

"Mark?" Charlie Banner said, tears rolling down his cheeks as he enfolded his son in his arms and began sobbing.

Rita laid her head against her husband's back and embraced them both.

"I've never seen either cerebral palsy or an autistic disorder act like this," Dr. Clark said. "These conditions just don't go into spontaneous remission. I'll be reviewing his chart today. Perhaps it was a combination of his medications, or...hell, I don't know. It's impossible."

"Oh God, my boy's back with us," Rita said. "We love you so much, Mark."

"I love you, too, Mom." He turned to Dr. Clark and winked.

Dr. Clark, although visibly gratified, seemed unsure what to do next. Finally he said, "I'll just let you folks visit a while. I'll be in my office if you need me."

"I want him home," Rita said.

Nodding, Dr. Clark said, "I understand. But we need to keep him a couple of days, check him over completely, call in a few consultants. I'll discharge him by the weekend if he stays stable. I promise."

"Thank you, Doctor," Charlie said, reaching up to shake the doctor's hand.

"They say everyone gets one miracle a year," Dr. Clark said, clasping Charlie's hand. "There's no doubt this is mine. And yours. I'll leave you folks alone now."

Dr. Clark started down the hallway, but his body's little twitches said he wanted to hop up and down, maybe even sing.

"Are you okay, son?" Rita asked. "How do you feel?"

"I'm weak, but I feel good. Real good." Then Mark turned and called, "Doctor?"

Dr. Clark spun around. "Yes, Mark?"

"There was a boy in here yesterday, a boy who was brought by his mother. He eats things he's not supposed to."

Recognition, then confusion, fanned out over Dr. Clark's face. "Yes?"

Mark pressed his chin against his fist. "I'm not sure—it seems like another world now—but I think that's one of the reasons I came back from wherever I was…so I could tell you that he's not eating them…by choice. His mother's feeding him that stuff, forcing it down him. She's wanting attention, wanting you to admire her. She's killing her son because she thinks you'll love her."

Dr. Clark cleared his throat. "I can't say anything about my patients. Confidentiality." The chalky cast to his complexion told Mark he needn't say more.

Scratching his scalp, Dr. Clark walked out of sight.

"Let's see about taking you outside," Charlie said, "let you get some fresh air. How about it, son?"

Mark smiled. "Thanks, Dad. I'd like that. I'd like that a lot."

Mother hustled him from the parking lot and, when Timmy didn't move quickly enough to suit her, she dramatically swept him up in her arms. Because he was taller than he was a year ago, she ran clumsily and he worried she'd drop him.

"We'll be in the Emergency Room in a minute, honey," she said.

Timmy had awakened this morning in excruciating pain, but also in a state of mind he couldn't remember ever before having. He felt resolute, confident. He felt safe.

"Mother?" he said.

She stopped in her tracks and set him down on his feet.

"Timmy. My Timmy! You're talking!"

"Can I ride in a wheelchair, instead of you carrying me? Please?"

"Of course, dear, of course." She grabbed his hand and pulled him into the ER entrance, then barked at the nearest nurse to get them a wheelchair and call Dr. Clark.

The wheelchair was dutifully delivered. Timmy sat down in it and his mother pushed him toward the elevator.

Once the elevator doors slid closed and they were alone, Mother said, "Timmy, I'm happy you're talking, but remember: You're to say nothing about...our secret. Understand? Never."

Timmy nodded. "I won't say a word, Mother."

"I just want you to be safe and loved," Mother said. "I want you to be well."

"Me, too," said Timmy.

Then he closed his eyes and concentrated harder than he'd ever concentrated before, until desire and possibility — angled rays of glorious light — converged. Seconds later, Timmy heard and felt his hip crack and dislocate as his right leg spun inward, inward, until the toe of his shoe pointed nearly backward. His left leg tensed, strained upward, twisting from its socket. His arms went rigid then snapped together in a flash, the backs of his hands slapping against one another as his fingers splayed, extended, reached. When he lost control of his neck, his head reeled sideways. His cheeks swelled and strained into a jungle of muscles. His upper lip curled and rose until he felt his breath sliding in and out between his teeth.

There was a little pain, not much, and what pain existed quickly faded.

He shouted with joy but it sounded like a roar.

"Somebody help me!" Valerie screamed as soon as the elevator doors opened. She propelled her son's wheelchair with such force that she lost her traction and slipped, falling face-first to the carpeted floor.

Timmy's wheelchair rolled out of control until Dr. Clark stepped in front of it, reached down and grabbed the armrests. Timmy's writhing body nearly tumbled out.

Rising to her feet, Mother yelled, "Something's happened to Timmy! Look! Something awful!"

Dr. Clark knelt and tried to make eye contact with the boy, but it was impossible. Timmy's eyes sailed back and forth, back and forth, as he traced the trembling movements of the hand he held before his face.

"Timmy?" Dr. Clark said, shaking the boy by the shoulders. "Timmy!"

Timmy smiled and felt a thread of drool escaping the corner of his mouth. The doctor's voice sounded far away, as if it were in a thick forest beyond a lofty, sloping hill. He glanced briefly at the doctor's terrified expression, but quickly returned his gaze to the palm-down hand he waved in front of him. Such a gorgeous, peaceful rhythm.

Dr. Clark stood up and faced Mother, who by now was pressing her hands against her temples, eyes wild.

"It doesn't make any sense, Valerie," Dr. Clark said. "What in the hell did you do to this boy?"

"Nothing," she whimpered, eyes never leaving Timmy.

"We'll need to admit him, get a scan. This condition

doesn't make sense, coming out of nowhere like this. There's something going on in his brain. And while we're at it, we'll get some X-rays. I think we'll find a lot in this boy's stomach, a lot of shit that *you've* been forcing down him."

She glanced up. "What?"

Dr. Clark looked past her and nodded. Two uniformed officers appeared to each side of Valerie and grabbed her biceps.

"We've got a witness," Dr. Clark said. "Someone Timmy talked to yesterday. We know what you've been doing to your boy. You're going to jail."

"But...but what about my Timmy? My son."

Dr. Clark, face crimson, said, "He's here for now and, the way it looks, maybe for a long time. If we need to, we'll go to court and get guardianship."

An officer tugged at Valerie's arm. She nodded dumbly and was led away.

Dr. Clark fell to his knees again, then placed his hand on Timmy's quaking leg. "I'm sorry I didn't figure this out, Timmy. I should have. But don't you worry. We're going to take good care of you. I promise."

Timmy arched his back, almost falling from the wheelchair. He craned his neck and bellowed boundless sounds that Dr. Clark couldn't understand.

Dr. Clark led the new nurses' aide to the boy sitting in the wheelchair near the window. He faced the rising sun, his features glowing gold.

"Jenny, I want you to give special attention to Timmy here," Dr. Clark said, pulling out his handkerchief and wiping spittle from the boy's chin. "He's been through a lot and we still don't know what he's going to need to get better. Give him all the love and care you can...and then some."

Jenny leaned down and grasped Timmy's waving, flapping hand. He relaxed and even cooed.

"Hi, Timmy," she said in a sweet, soft voice that—even at this infinite distance—Timmy knew he'd love to hear every day.

She turned to Dr. Clark. "He's smiling," she said. "Does that mean he's happy?"

Dr. Clark shook his head. "I don't know. I hope so."

And though Timmy had happily surrendered his speech and rendered himself as invisible as his small body would allow, at that instant he wanted so much to return if for only a moment, and to tell them of the rapture to be found resting silently in a shrouded place surrounded by velvet life. About drowsing far from the pain and the noise and the confusion. About being forever safe, consoled, warm, away. About moths in damp grass.

Judi Rohrig

*Judi Rohrig's fiction has appeared in **Cemetery Dance Magazine**, **Extremes 5**, **Dreaming of Angels**, and online at **HorrorFind**. Editor and publisher of HELLNOTES, a weekly newsletter that serves the horror community, Rohrig has also worked as a newspaper columnist, marketing director, teacher, and school administrator. She is currently working on two book-length works. She may be visited online: http://www.judirohrig.com. Judi makes her first **Masques** appearance with this disquieting cautionary tale about those whose obsession with capturing the perfect image can lead to the imprisonment of more than one's sanity. After all, every picture is worth...*

—JNW

A THOUSAND WORDS

❖ BY JUDI ROHRIG ❖

Sun-Herald Reporter: *Photographers shoot lots and lots of bad pictures to get that perfect one. How many 'bad ones' would you estimate you shot to wind up with the awesome fifty you have here in the gallery?*

Mikaela James: I don't know that there really are any 'bad' pictures. Sure there are a lot of pictures that can't be used, but it's the 'bad ones' that can sometimes make you recognize something you hadn't seen in a way that will make you recognize it when you see it again. Only when you see it again—whatever "it" is—you can zoom in and capture its soul.

"These suck."

"You're being too hard on yourself again, Miki."

"No, I'm not. These truly suck."

"Come to bed, hon."

I studied the images on the contact sheet again, unsure how I had done such a disastrous job. It was a pud assignment, for crissakes.

"Miki...be-e-ed. With me-e-e-e!"

A no-brainer.

"C'mon, sweetheart. Look! I'm that Casanova snake charmer. Do-do-do-o-o-do-o-do. Do-do-do-dododo-do..."

The lighting had been perfect inside the sideshow tent: murky shadows loitering in the folds of the crinkled canvas; dangerous reds from the midway pulsating through the flap, stabbing bloody wounds in the snake charmer's eyes. I remember what I'd seen through the lens. It was more than what the editor had asked for. It was a cover on Smithsonian magazine, another gallery showing, and most of all, an ecstatic note from Wesley proclaiming me a gifted bitch. One worthy enough—

"Look, hon, it's rising...rising..."

I glanced toward the futon in the corner. Alex was stretched diagonally across the striped sheets, his legs apart, his hands wagging *Mr. Dixie* at me.

"Woo hoo!"

"You're not funny, Alex."

"Funny? I'm wounded. Mr. Dixie's wounded, too."

"I have a deadline on this. You know that."

I left him there. Outside. Shut myself in my tiny darkroom just as I had dozens of times before. When I finally had all the rolls developed—black film twisting from their clips—the prints I'd settled on drying from the makeshift clothesline—and all my chemicals tucked away for the night, I emerged to find the bedroom lights still burning, and dear, sweet Alex buzzing peacefully in all his nakedness. Mr. Dixie had obliged Taps, too, and lay quite uncharming.

That's when it hit me.

Thirty-five minutes later I was tooling into the area where the multi-colored lights had mesmerized throngs of excited carnival goers only hours before. It didn't matter that the place lay shrouded in slumber. I had to be there, had to follow my gut.

The metal caravan lay well behind the main drag of the midway, trailers and trucks angled among sweet gums and tall paper birches. A few of the larger campers bore yellow night lights near their doors, but most were blanketed by the night. For the week, this would be home to the strange people whose images I'd sucked into my Minolta, and frankly, the place looked comfortably settled. Normal.

The little road that circled the park must have been recently topped with a fresh load of cinders and rock because the tires of my Cherokee sounded as though they were crunching glass as I pulled in next to the snake charmer's trailer.

He'd been the last of the "ten-in-one" freaks I'd snapped. His name was Jesse Lee Davies, but he called himself "Benhudi the Snake Charmer." He wasn't East Indian, and for the shows he'd obviously stained his skin a deep, rich tan and talked as though he'd just arrived from Bombay. His thin, wiry body reminded me of Ghandi. Alex insisted he favored Nehru more.

What had impressed me was how affable he and all the other "freaks" had been. I figured they would all cringe and run at the sight of all my photographic equipment. Instead, I'd been surrounded and curiously ogled by the very oddities I'd come to capture.

From their grinning huddle, the most emaciated woman I'd ever seen ran to me on her stick-like legs. Her face beamed with an inviting smile. "Will you take my picture? Oh, please! Please!" She jumped up and down the same way Alex's six-year-old daughter Annie usually did when she was excited. I was afraid the woman's fragile bones would break in two if I didn't oblige.

She'd insisted on posing in front of the banner that bore a painted rendering of her that made her look rail thin, yet surprisingly heavier than she was in person. Billed as "Willow Reed, the World's Thinnest Woman," she whispered later that her real name was Frances Miller. "But I truly like 'Willow' better, so please just use that in anything you write."

"I don't write," I told her. "I just take pictures."

"A picture's worth a thousand words, don't they say?" she shot back.

I was about to explain, but she'd already extended her arms like a runway model and poked another huge grin at me.

It was the same with the others. They all bounced and giggled like children, posing almost vaingloriously in front of their gigantic painted images. The whole experience had been so like a silly party that I'd expected the Mad Hatter to push back the flap of their performance tent and invite me in for a cup of tea.

"I thought these shows weren't PC, anymore," Alex had warned on the way over that afternoon. "I thought gawkers were just insensitive assholes."

Willow laughed when I broached that very subject with her. "As compared to the sniveling, laughing-behind-my-back assholes I used to work with at the bank, you mean?" Her smile faded. "Look, honey, we're different, and some of us not by our own choice. Dave the Human Rubberband has this skin condition. *Cutis hyperelastica* or something like that. I just think of 'cute elastic.' Makes him sound like a super hero, doesn't it?" She'd pressed her skeletal fingers to her toothy mouth and guffawed more than giggled. "Then there's Lori the gorilla woman. She just got tired of having to work two thankless jobs to buy more razors than food. We're 'freaks,' plain and simple. You take your best holt, honey."

I know my confusion showed.

Willow laughed. "You do anything to get the money."

Harold Goss, the Human Pumpkin, a squat man whose skin held an orangish tinge, rattled off a series of chuckles before he spoke: "People stare at us anyway. This way at least they have to pay to do it."

The "Talker" avoided me. Willow, who'd proven to be a helpful guide, said there had been too many reporters who'd called him a "Barker," and that wasn't what he was at all. "He's not a dog! He 'lectures.' You remember that when you write it down, honey."

"I don't write, I—"

"He's a very smart man, and *rrrr* would I love to share his bunk some night."

Of course, Willow also made that very same comment and growling noise about Scott the Penguin Boy, Kris/Chris the Girl/Boy, and two muscled young men named Lance and Gene who did the grunt work. She didn't make any comment in a lustful tone about Jesse Lee though.

"There really aren't many shows like ours anymore," Jesse Lee added after most of the others had been satisfied that they'd exhausted any possible pose I could shoot. "Some *well-intentioned* person killed them. Now carnivals are mostly about rides thrilling enough to make the boys puke up their corndogs and the girls scared enough to not notice getting felt up. Oh, and the food: greasy corndogs, sticky cotton candy, and 'the largest tenderloin outside of Texas.'" His smile seemed less measured somehow than the others.

He'd posed for only a few shots, claiming the colorful snakes he allowed to twine and twist around his body needed their rest before the evening performance. "Catch me later," he said.

As I sat in the Cherokee, watching the broad summer leaves dance shadows on the snake charmers' trailer, I doubted he meant this much later. I had questions though, and a gnawing sensation in my gut that he could answer them better than anybody else with the show.

My soft rap on the metal door of his trailer caused a light to go on inside almost instantly. When he pushed out the door, his eyes seemed even deeper than I remembered. He didn't look as though I'd awakened him.

"I know it's late." I offered him what Alex called my "please, indulge me" smile. "You said to catch you later."

"It's okay," he said quietly, extending his arm, inviting me inside.

The interior wasn't what I'd expected to find at all. Glassed cages had been built into the sides of the trailer in the space where most anyone else allowed a couch—one that might fold down into a small bed—or a chair or two.

"My fellow performers," Jesse Lee said, bowing slightly. He wore a long, beige tunic over matching loose pants. Pajamas, I surmised. It was night. Still, considering the weather had been warm, the outfit seemed a little odd. He was sans his East Indian coloring.

"I never thought..." I stammered as I eyed the enclosures.

"I suppose people would assume those of us with animals would have some special trailer for them. I certainly don't. But then again, I'm really the only 'wonder worker' with this show. The rest are *freaks*."

His stress on the last word struck me as amazingly odd. My face must have betrayed the thought.

"Shocked I would call the others 'freaks'? That's what they are. Abnormalities of nature or by their own hand."

Inside the cage nearest me something shoved the thick wood shavings against the glass, but there was no noise at all.

"I can make us some tea, if you'd like."

I nodded, offering what I hoped was a polite smile, but as I followed Jesse Lee into the kitchette area, I glanced back at the other cages, seeing more disturbances. Slitherings.

I'd never thought much about snakes actually. I'd

grown up living near enough to several streams and ponds to have happened on one or two, but I don't remember ever being afraid of them. They just *were*. I kept my distance; they kept theirs.

"What's a 'wonder worker'?" I asked when he finally sat down with our mugs of hot tea.

His eyes reached across the table, burrowing into me in a way I don't think I'd ever experienced before. "Let *me* ask one question before I answer yours."

"Okay."

"Why do want to take pictures of us?"

My nervous laugh spilled out before I realized it. "It's what I do."

"Capture people's souls?"

I thought he was joking, so I laughed again.

"You think you don't capture a soul in your camera?" He was stone cold serious.

"There are some cultures that believe that, I suppose."

"You took their pictures anyway?"

"No."

"Amish? You've taken pictures of them?"

Slam dunk. Two points. My best gallery exhibit ever had been of an Amish community in Indiana. They hadn't objected to my picture-taking, had been more than generous with their time and most hospitable in every other way, too, in fact. Though to honor their ways I had shot carefully, avoiding capturing any full faces. The critics had been effusive in their praise on that showing. I had the "eye," they'd said. Wesley Muench, my mentor, the one photographer I had adored since I was a teen, had stroked my back, smiled, and told me I was earning my way toward becoming a "talented bitch."

The attention had earned me a couple of plum assignments including this one.

"You saw my Amish exhibit?"

He took a long minute to answer, stirring the liquid

with little clatter, blowing the steam away from his over-sized tea cup before sipping. When he looked at me, his eyes stabbed again darkly. "No. I've never seen any of your work."

For the first time, I noticed his hands, his fingers. They were smooth and long, oddly effeminate for a man. Alex's fingers were rough, course almost, especially the calluses on the tips caused by his guitar-playing. The only other hands I'd ever really studied had been Wesley's. His fingers were large and broad, discolored at places and scarred. When I'd studied photography under him, I'd often wondered what it would be like to be touched—

"He would have hurt you. He's very into pain."

"What?"

"The man you were thinking of. You wouldn't have enjoyed his touch. He's cruel to his women."

The steam curled upward from Jesse Lee's cup, looking every bit as charmed as one of the snakes in his acts. I leaned back hard against the booth's cushion unsure what to say.

Then his head dropped a bit, his brow hooding his deep, piercing eyes. " 'A wonder worker' isn't a freak. We work very hard at what we do. I studied snake charmers in India. You know they've fallen on hard times there, too. Everyone wants to protect the animals but shit on the people. It's very sad. I didn't start out as a snake charmer, you know. The first job I had was as a—"

"Wait," I said. "Go back to what you said about Wesley."

"Wesley? Wesley who?"

"Wesley Muench. You said he was into pain. How do you know that?"

His eyes changed. Suddenly, he was offering me an innocent, puzzled look. "I thought you woke me so I could help you understand the freaks you've come to capture."

"You weren't asleep."

"How do you know?"

"Jesus, you were waiting for me to come back!"

"And if I was..."

I considered what to say next.

"What are you looking for Ms. James? What do you see when you look through your lens? What did you see when you took my picture?"

I didn't know how to answer because I knew what I'd seen in the tent. Yet I'd been totally stumped by the *nothing* images I'd developed and printed. What I had captured was a man with a large snake wrapped around his body. Nothing more, and there had been more. But what? And what had happened to it?

Jesse Lee leaned back in his chair, the edge of his lip lifting into a half sneer/half smile. "Okay, then what did you write about me?"

"Dammit! I don't use words. I keep telling everybody that. I just see!"

"See what?"

I couldn't explain it.

"Did you see my death?"

"What?"

"The end of me?"

"No, why would I?"

"You took part of my soul, Ms. James. When you developed your pictures, when all those chemicals washed over your paper and my image appeared, what did you see then? What did my soul look like?"

I said nothing. My mind was riffling through the several dozen prints I had made of this man. He'd been the one I'd felt I'd failed the most.

"How did you fail me, Ms. James?"

The hair stood up on the back of my neck, and I clutched the warm tea cup more firmly. "Is this something else you've studied?" I asked, trying to be cool, trying not to let him hear my thudding heart, trying not to think any thoughts for him to read.

He laughed. "You think I'm a mentalist, is that it? That I can read your mind?" He leaned toward me over the table, the lamp above illumining his menacing glower. "I thought *you* could read mine!" He let go a laugh that chilled me. "But you don't use words, do you?"

I slid out from behind the table. I'd expected him to try and stop me, only he hadn't.

My arms and body had gone all gooseflesh as I stumbled past the glass enclosures, and from each one, sharp eyes, eyes just like Jesse Lee's, looked out from wood-shredded shadows.

I hadn't remembered the three metal steps, hadn't remembered it was a trailer. I'd nearly fallen out the door when I shoved it open with my shoulder.

Outside, morning had somehow arrived. Birds chattered excitedly from the sweet gums as I jumped in the Cherokee and bolted from Beecher Park. I'd driven all the way back to the apartment shaking. Then I sat outside in the parking lot trying to figure myself out.

This was all incredibly stupid. He'd been playing mind games with me. He was scaring me off with what were probably educated guesses. Sure, he was used to reading people. That's what they did. "You do anything to get the money," Willow had said.

Only I couldn't figure out why he was picking on me. I didn't have any money. I'd only wanted a few pictures for an anthology that would contain some dumb stories about freaks. Some editor had been taken with the play of natural light I'd used in the Amish exhibit. I'd been careful not to use any artificial lights or flashes.

"I want you to capture that feel with freaks," she'd said. "Real freaks. They're out there. Maybe harder to find because Barnum's dead and too many people think the old carnival freak shows were inhumane. It's that 'inhumanity' I want to see. I want to see the brutal truth reflected in their eyes."

She'd pointed out that I had somehow found the niche in the Amish community, discovered and honored their ways and captured that.

"Captured." There was that word again.

I spent the better part of the day looking at what I had "captured." Not some horrible glint or mournful glower that the editor was seeking; not parts of the soul Jesse Lee admonished me for stealing. I saw smiles and laughter. Glee.

It felt wrong. Very, very wrong.

Reporter: Then what makes you choose exactly which picture is right? What elements does it have to have? A certain balance, color, what?

James: I don't choose. The print chooses me.

Sitting behind the wheel of the Cherokee just at the edge of the main drag of the midway, I let the throbbing hues of lights explode and burst. It wasn't cajoling as it had been the first day. I felt no draw, no excitement.

Before me a grand display, a mini Mardi Gras paraded: men in jeans, shorts, or slacks with T-shirts, tanks, or polos walked arm-in-arm or several feet behind or in front of women in jeans, shorts, or fluttering dresses with plunging necklines—nipples poking through the flimsy fabrics. Some wrangled children dressed in all manner of clothing paying homage to their favorite cartoon, movie, or toy. Attired in everything from snapped bottomed pants to school colors, they ambled, scooted, or raced past, making their way boiterously from the long line of whirling rides, grease-laden concessions, and rowdy games-of-chance over to the long canvas tent where the Talker's voice blared in muffled tones as he offered a genuine *Ballyhoo*. The "sacrificial" freak that people could view freely changed from hour to hour, but each one helped the Talker spin his spiel in his bid to hustle the baited crowds into coughing up their money and ushering their curious selves beyond the flap of the tent into the show.

I watched. I waited.

Finally the number of people dwindled to a few scantily clad, heavily made up young women who had dreams of adventures with the slick, sinewy grunts who ran the rides. That's when I snapped up my sturdy companion, the Minolta Wesley had chosen for me to buy, and made my way around to the back of the performance tent.

Showtime had ended. Nobody had to pretend anymore. Not for the "holt" or the gawkers or the camera lens.

Or so they thought.

From the back flap, the freaks stumbled out just like the last mainstays at Clifford's Tavern in town after "last call." And there was as much commotion. At first.

Lori the gorilla woman laughed raucously at something Kris/Chris had whispered from the corner of his boyside mouth while his girlside hand fought to turn his head away.

I snapped.

Then a thin whisp emerged, weaving through the night air like gentle smoke as it glided past me. Willow's winsome smile had been furrowed back into the soil of her face, making her a walking stick of twisted vanilla licorice.

Snap. Snap.

Harold Goss's orangish tinge glowed an odd green under the sulphur safety lights. His body sloshed as he moved while his mouth twitched nervously. I noted he carved a wide swath of avoidance around the others.

Snap. Snap.

One after the other they came. The "cute elastic" man smoothing down the Atlanta Braves T-shirt he'd donned to cover his naked torso, his face drawn into a pinched frown, his gait not the bouncing one I seen him display earlier.

Snap.

Scott the Penguin Boy waddled hurriedly across the gravel road to catch up with Flip the Human Seal whose vestigial hands punctuated whatever he was saying to Gene the grunt who cradled him in his strong arms.

Snap. Snap. Snap.

I'd watched them all from behind the dim shelter of a perched stack of crates. Again and again, I pressed the shutter button, zooming in and out with no real thought or plan. Sorting would come later.

Finally, only Jesse Lee remained inside.

I waited for a long time, but he must have exited some other way. Before I called it a night, I crept past his trailer. Inside the lights shown brightly from the kitchette area. I toyed with knocking at his door, but instead decided to go home, and like a child at Halloween, to empty my bag and see what goodies I'd managed to collect.

A lot of the images were difficult to look at too long especially when I juxtaposed them with the before/posed shots. Cloying smiles hung next to runnels of painfilled frowns. Disparity leaped from the photo papers where I'd tacked them on the wall of my small apartment.

The disingenuous smiles before had been wrong because they had revealed half-truths rather than bold-faced lies. But was this then the raw truth the editor was looking for?

Reporter: How long did it take you to do this shoot?

James: The carnival was in town for the week, and I used every minute I could. I shot day and night, letting my darkroom tell me where I was in this project.

Large knuckled and hairy, stained yellow with nicotine from the chain of Camels he insisted were his only vice, scarred where he'd barked them on countless equipment setups, discolored from all the chemicals he handled, and broad when he splayed them on the table as he viewed student contact sheets, Wesley's hands became a fascination for me when I was his apprentice. I so ached to have those rough fingers peel off my clothes slowly, methodically, and then explore my very being. I wanted to be his only vice.

Maybe that's why I wasn't really concerned when the first rough patches and bumps appeared on my own hands. Who knew what plants I could have shoved through as I sought to capture the freaks without their knowing it?

Or maybe I was overusing the chemicals. This was really the first time I had worked for so many days in a row without a break. Dektol, the developing chemical I used, was known to cause allergic reactions in some people. I couldn't bother myself with worrying about it though. I needed to make the puzzle work, needed to complete it so my living room wall could just be a wall again and not some permanent concoction of mine much like Jesse Lee's animal home.

Some nights my head would spin as I shifted my tired eyes from the contact sheets to the blow-ups I'd made.

Side by side the photos allowed the people to come alive through their physical burdens. On Wednesday, I had switched to black and white film. The absence of the distracting color became like the breath of God. I wasn't a talented bitch anymore. I *was* God, creating my own world.

"You'll write something good about me now, won't you, honey," Willow told me when I showed her a couple pictures I'd taken. The freaks were all curious, but it was Willow who'd asked so many questions, made so many comments. "I don't want people to think I don't like what I do, you know."

I'd given up explaining how I only took pictures.

Jesse Lee didn't make any inquiries about the project. He'd offer me a smug smile or two and disappear. I avoided taking his picture when he was around, rationalizing that I didn't want to rob him of any more of his soul. Really, I was afraid of what might stare back at me from the developing tray.

I slept little. Mostly, I became a fixture. Me and my other eye. I was at the carnival so much the freaks had taken to ignoring me or overlooking me. Occasionally one would offer up a toothy grin—Willow had flipped up her dress, mooning me once—but pretty much the façade they'd forced on Monday was gone. They performed for the crowds.

Willow warned me on Thursday that this was there last gig this season. Although she and a few others were planning on heading south to form a new show, most would be scattering. If I didn't get what I needed by Saturday night, all the work I had done up to that time would be lost.

On Friday morning, I found a note from Alex:

Miki,
When you come up for air from this project, give me a
call. I'm back at my place in case you didn't notice.
Love you,
Alex

I didn't know when exactly he'd left it, couldn't remember even when I'd seen him last. The bed. I'd left him naked and sleeping. That was Monday.

Jesus.

"Alex can't come to the phone right now, but if you'll leave a message, he'll get right back to you, I swear!" The machine may have been Alex's; the voice was mine. I'd even bought him the machine in the first place so he could maintain the guise that he was still living in his apartment.

We didn't want his daughter Annie to know her father was shacking up with that nutty photographer.

The hands were mine, too. I'd noticed them as I placed the phone back in the cradle. Though I hardly recognized them.

When I was in college I had a ganglion on my left hand. The family doctor had offered surgery but only as a last resort. "You know what I'd do," Doctor Phil had said, "I hit that with a big book or something. That'll break it up. There's just some stuff in there like applesauce really."

I searched my brain to remember when it had disappeared because as I looked at my hands, I found large patches of scaling. I know I'd suffered with "Lizard skin" during some winter months when the heated air inside was dry, but my hands had never been this awful.

On Friday night, or was it really Saturday morning, I collapsed in a beaten heap on the futon. I was lost. Whatever magic I had tapped into for the Amish exhibit was gone. I tasted defeat in my mouth and felt it as my withering, marred hands wiped away the tears that rolled into my hair and onto my unused bed.

"Alex can't come to the phone right now, but if you'll leave a message, he'll get right back to you, I swear!" I didn't have the energy to cuss much less slam down the phone. Frustration? I was too tired for that, too.

I didn't have to knock. Jesse Lee threw open his trailer door before I was even near it. His eyes flashed red as though the bulbs from the Tilt-A-Whirl were flickering instead of being silent and asleep like everything else in the late summer's ground fog.

"Did you find my death?"

"I found I wasn't God."

"I thought you were merely aiming to be a 'talented bitch.'"

I stared at him, wondering what I had come for, knowing *he* knew. He'd known all along. "'Would you tell me please which way I ought to go from here?'" I remembered the line from my childhood. It seemed so fitting since I had become as lost as Alice in this strange wonderland.

He smiled. Smiled like the Cheshire cat. Then he held out his hand, invitingly. "'That depends on where you want to get to.'"

"'I don't want to go among mad people,'" I said, touching his smooth fingers as they drew me in.

"'Oh, you can't help that, we're all mad here. I'm mad. You're mad.'"

Until dawn we worked inside his trailer, but his snakes never left the harbor of their cages. Jesse Lee disrobed and stretched himself out on the Persian rug he'd unrolled. I let my Minolta touch him, stroke him, discover him. Capture a bit of his soul.

Back in my darkroom, I held the photo paper in my hands just before I slid it into the Dektol. And before any image could appear, I sank both my ravaged hands into the solution.

The hissing came first, softly like the first steam from a tea kettle, and I felt the tiny snakes slithering over my hands, between my fingers, up my arms and into my ears. After they crawled inside my head, they fed me their words, the words of raw truth.

I spent the rest of the last day snapping Willow and Scott, Lori and Harold, Kris/Chris, Dave, Flip and the others. All of them. And then when their images began forming on the paper, I plunged my hands into the developing solution, letting the pustules break open and the words slink knowingly onto the paper.

"I am a person!" The dark words tattooed themselves on Willow's naked torso, her skin opaque over fragile bones.

"No one hears me scream!" Flip's wrinkled forehead blared. Another line slanted downward entwining itself around his seal-like feet: "I am like you. I am a real man!"

The editor of the anthology called the pictures too brutal for what she needed. Wesley called me a mad bitch, and I suppose I had gone that way, but...

Alex helped me mat my work and frame them and carry each one into the small gallery. We waited for the gawkers. And hoped they could see the truth.

Reporter: I have to ask about the last picture in the show. It's the only color photo, a severed, bloody finger. There are no words tattooed on this one alone. Why is that?

James: Remember I said sometimes the bad pictures make you recognize something you hadn't seen in a way that will make you recognize it when you see it again? That's when you can zoom in and capture its soul... or let it capture yours.

I held up my left hand: one thumb; three fingers.

There are more carnivals. I have more film.

Tom Piccirilli

Tom Piccirilli is the author of 14 novels including **November Mourns**, **A Choir of Ill Children**, **Headstone City**, and **The Night Class**. He's a hardcore fan of noir fiction and film, Asian cinema, and grade z-horror flicks. He has won multiple Bram Stoker Awards as both a fiction writer and a poet, and his work—as you're about to experience for yourself—is hallucinatory, challenging, and genuinely disturbing. You can learn more about Tom and his work at his official website: www.tompiccirilli.com.

—JNW

MAKING FACES

✠ BY TOM PICCIRILLI ✠

Usually Lash wakes up thinking, This is it, you're finally dead. It lets him start the day off with an overwhelming sense of relief.

The dog is chewing into his chest, about to crack through the breastbone and get to the thick meat of his heart inside. Lash took the little bastard in because it was shivering under an abandoned Chevy with six saturate tickets beneath the busted wiper, rain sluicing off the hood and running high in the gutter. Three distended bodies stacked face-down in the backseat. The dog there with its tiny front paw held up–offering it out to Lash like, oh please take me home, look how cute I am, my name is Iwuvyou. Lash has tried this with girls in bars and they just scowl at him, move a few stools down.

Talk about loyalty. Now Iwuvyou's snout-deep in your torso, tail wagging like crazy, wippity-wappity.

267

But no, Lash realizes, You're still kicking, and the dog is only licking your chest hair, catching it in his teeth. Because Lash has been sweating in the night and it's pooled there and dried in a salty line down to his belly button.

There's something that needs to be said this morning, that's clear, but he hasn't managed to grasp the essence of it yet. He reaches up and puts his hand to his mouth, trying to see if there are any words there. He tugs his lips apart, pinches his tongue. He tastes charcoal on his fingertips.

What needed to be said has been drawn on the wall.

Today You Must Make a Change.

"Dammit," Lash says. He already understands it's true, but he really hates to see it smeared all over the place like that.

The canvas stretched on the easel looks like a first-grader's been going at it with finger paints. Once, he had promise. His professors knew it, and so did his parents. They encouraged, advised, and applauded until Lash couldn't take the ridiculous hope in their eyes anymore. Mom looking at him so lovingly, with such misplaced pride, that he wanted to rip his own teeth out. Jesus, you talk about pressure, the way they stared at you waiting for the genius to bleed out. The disappointment always close behind. Come on, come on, we're waiting.

Since then he keeps up the pretense because life, somehow, means even less without it. He calls himself an artist. He used to say he was a painter but everybody kept wanting him to do their houses, their apartment ceilings. Now he asks the chicks in the bar to sit for him, he'd love to do their portraits, and would they mind posing nude? They gag on their Banana daiquiris and move their seats.

What he is, is unemployed, paying his rent with some of the insurance money his mother left him. He lives meager, which is a personality trait rather than a well-thought out plan. Every few days he throws some color at the easel and swirls the brush around, yearning for his subconscious to take over and carry the ball. If he's feeling particularly passionate, he uses the charcoal. That hasn't happened for a while.

There's a storm outside.

Wind drives the thrashing rain down upon the city and the madmen and murdered float and roll in the alleys. Families crawl onto half-submerged buses as great surges and swells of water funnel over the dispossessed pedestrians. Lash's mother would have called this the end of the world, and she would have said it happily. He knows it's only another bad day.

The church directly across from his window is full of black motion, music, and activity. In this part of the city, the buildings have gargoyles doing what they were made to do: their mouths are spigots designed to ease rain overflow.

Lash knows that the word gargoyle is actually a bastardization of "gurgling." The stone beasts are named for the sounds they make. He's full of useless information like that. It's just more shit that doesn't make him money.

A child stands framed by stained glass and stares at Lash, with a strange intent, perhaps a great and worthwhile purpose.

Okay, so Lash tries not to let his urban paranoia carry him away, but you really gotta see this kid. Tow-headed, huge brown eyes, acutely pale skin, and dressed well in black slacks and a white formal shirt buttoned all the way to the collar. In the movies, creepy ten-year-olds are always ghosts come back to fuck up your week.

The kid sticks his tongue out.

You know what you have to do. Lash remains an adult for about three seconds, and then the undying adolescent takes over, makes him growl at the boy. They watch each other through throbbing sheets of water bursting and boiling on the windows. The kid sticks his thumbs in his ears, wriggles his fingers, miming laughter. Lash sticks his pinkies in his nostrils, yanks his nose wide, cocks his head.

These are all faces he's painted many times before, back when he tried to hone his small amount of talent. Sketching passers by while seated in front of the museums and ritzy tourist traps. Children used to get pissed at him for staring, they'd give him the finger, do guppy lips. Their parents would threaten him and pull out their cell phones, miming how they were calling the police. The Japanese would take a hundred photos of him, blinding him with the flashes until he packed up. He figured the guys in front of the Louvre probably didn't have to suffer through this kind of crap, but who knew, maybe they did.

The kid points at Lash, then moves his hand slightly aside, indicating he should take a look.

Somebody's on the ledge.

Well now.

He thinks for a second that it might be himself. You always had to be ready. You could never be too sure. He does that sometimes, sneaks up on himself. You took what comforts you could afford. It's kind of fun actually, watching himself jump. Unless it's happening to him, with the bastard sort of prancing and laughing behind him.

Iwuvyou begins yipping, tangling into circles, stopping to sniff at the floorboards, then recovering and leaping around the apartment.

It's the kid's mother. Lash knows it as soon as he sees her.

You don't have a story unless you get mixed up in the middle of things. Somehow, he's tripped over an energy curve, a quantum field, a cosmic force that connects the parent to the child. She's running from gangsters, gonna pop in and plead for him to help save her son. Offer herself to him as payment, but he's a hero here, gotta refuse. For a bit. Goes to scope the scene, outwits the mob–the amateur who's more pro than the professional hitmen themselves.

He comes back and the woman has double-crossed him, she spikes his drink. But he's switched glasses. She keels over, gagging, hands about her throat, the blood spiking from her ears. He heads across to the church, discovers it's a money laundering biz, the kid is really a midget with a .45. Lash busts him a good one in the chops, steals the briefcase lying at the pint-sized feet, it's full of cash. But the bills are marked, it's all a waste, he returns to his apartment, opens a can of beef stew for Iwuvyou, thinks about tomorrow.

The lady out there on the ledge is shuddering so badly she might knock herself off. Dressed in a black dinner dress, wearing pearls, she's about a dozen feet away, twenty-six floors up. Her arms are stretched over her head and she's holding onto a gargoyle, gripping it around the throat like a careless weekend lover. The beast is giving Lash that macho barroom grin, telling him, Yo buddy, fuck off, she's mine for the night. Go find another lay.

Rainwater surges into her face and obscures her features. The wet black hair drapes in savage coils and batters her shoulders. Lash opens his window and the storm howls in answer, a thundering thrum roaring above him. On occasion, you can almost believe in God.

"Hi," he calls to her. "You wanna come in?"

She takes a hesitant step into mid-air, leaving her foot out over the precipice, as if considering what it might feel like not to have anything under you. Lash has screwed around like that a little too, on really awful nights. A bottle of tequila in one hand, a bible in the other, some woman loud in his mind and the loneliness turning the back of his skull to steel.

The kid's mother wriggles her toes out there and kicks off her high-heeled shoe. Looks Italian, the pair goes for at least a grand. It fires down like a missile and clunks a street sign. A shadow darts from behind a garbage can and scoops it up, vanishes again.

The sigh at the back of her throat is violent yet reassuring. He knows what an overpowering sensation it can be, to have to force yourself to find reasons not to let go.

She puts her foot back on the ledge and does the same thing with the other one, taking the endless step, shirking out of her shoe. Lash thinks, Okay, this here lady, she has a few issues to deal with.

Who're you to get in the way of that? Nobody gets in the middle of yours.

He closes the window, looks over at the words on the wall and tries to decipher them. This is an equation with theme and substance but no context. His father used to do this all the time. The man, a part-time poet, would wake up in the middle of the night and scrawl on a notepad beside his bed. In the morning asking Lash, Can you make this out? Is this an L or a K? This say recitation or resuscitation?

He opens the window once more, tries again. "Hey, if you want me to help you, just tell me, all right?"

She turns towards him but all that hair still flies wildly around her head, a miasma of her own delirium. The kid continues making faces, maybe at Lash, maybe at his mama. The church clamors with blaring pipe organ hymns, prayers reaching over the drenched spires and steeples. You finally have your soundtrack. Iwuvyou is digging the music, hopping along on his back legs.

Lash is tempted to go out there, show her how it's really done. Think about it. The savior, giving her his hand, reaching while she flinches and shrinks away. This could be one of those really whacked-out lovers' moments here, like a suicide pact between strangers. So you go, Okay, how about this? We'll try it pretty much together. Me first. Taking that step over the big edge, giving her a nice smile, demonstrating to her how there's nothing to it. Now that would be a change. That would be something. She follows maybe a second behind you, the both of you twisting in mid-air, fighting and clawing towards each other as you fall, until you embrace a fraction before you hit.

He shuts the window.

Perhaps this is a chance to get back to the work. WOMAN ON LEDGE: SERIES FOUR; *In Varying Shades of Blue*. She can wait there posing for him while he paints, going, Don't move now. Try not to shiver so much. The light is fading. Come inside, we'll hump each other into the dust bunnies under the bed, and then we'll resume tomorrow.

There are priests down on the street now. Folks in robes. Lash always thought they dressed in black, but there they are in vestments of red, blue, brown, gold, and white. Several are hooded, with their arms folded across their stomachs, hands hidden within their oversized sleeves. The restless souls of Benedictine monks float from the chapel, passing harsh judgment on all of humanity. Other children are dressed like the kid in the window, unwavering and stoic. A doorway filled with pre-teen ghosts.

Nuns gape and wave. Not even frantic waving, but the Hey, how're you doin' type. Lash nods back, gives a Come on up gesture. They all frown and move away.

Lightning seizes the sky and ignites the world. You're tapped into the elemental design of the universe, with your hand on the lever that works the turbine of the abominable engine, and you've got about nine bucks in your pocket. Your jeans don't fit right around your hips. Your elbows are covered in dead skin. The heavens shake their fists in your face, promising further pain. You are tied to the fountain of souls by your endless common dread. There have always been heinous wraiths under your bed, at the back of your closet. Incantations and maledictions are scrawled in your high school yearbook. Your friends were set in place by the infernal arch-dukes to trick and deceive you. You recall your father's poetry and realize he was trying to warn you about this.

The woman is at the window.

She's crouched there, pressed against the glass, staring

at him through all her hair. She snorts water. Fingers clawing, she's perched and gawking. He leans closer. The nuns
and monks and kids are all screaming up at him now, shouting words that might've held meaning once but no longer
contain enough humanity for him to understand. There are
tongues not meant for a mortal mouth.

"You want me to let you in?" Lash asks her.

She shakes her head, body as solid as the gurgling
stone spitting up beside her. He still can't see her eyes. She
has weight, this lady, intent and function. If she's got a message for him she's certainly taking her time delivering it.
He maneuvers against the pane, trying to be as fluid as the
downpour on the other side.

So, she doesn't want to go over and doesn't want to
come back inside. Then what?

From one moment to the next we make our moves.
Even if you're only thrashing in your nightmares, you're
still on the go. What's he supposed to do now? Paint her that
way, hunched over and about to be washed off the rim of the
world?

They're chanting below, and there's enough of them
now on the street to be heard over the madhouse thunder.
He really doesn't want to see how many maniacs that might
take, but he looks anyway. Christ. If it's sacrifice they need
from him, they won't get it. He can just imagine. He's
God's right hand, the avenger, the bearer of the flaming
sword. He spins and the woman is actually the embodiment
of hell taking over the city, with a heart of pure eternal darkness made reality. The sword is tied across his back and he
snakes it free, bears up beneath the hideous weight of right-
eousness. The point is perfect blue fire, holy and eternal,
and he rams it through the window into the center of the
abomination. Poison spurts and gushes, scalding his hands
as he hangs on. She opens her enormous, fanged mouth and
lets loose with a screech made up of all mankind's sins. The
sword is torn from his grasp. The tempest sweeps her up

into the merciless ashen sky and suddenly a ray of warm sunlight slices through the oppressive darkness. He drops to one knee and his mother—golden and forgiving—wafts down on iridescent wings and blesses him. She heals his blistered hands.

He stares at the woman and says, "It's time for you to make a decision, lady. Today you must make a change."

But she's set in grim determination and hunkers down on the ledge, watching him without eyes, the coiling hair writhing in the rain. Her kid, multi-colored and outlined in the stained glass across the way, a martyr who doesn't shave yet, glares at Lash and sticks his tongue out again.

"Fine," Lash says. "See if I give a damn. What, like this is my fault? You think I'm to blame? Is that it? You've got it wrong. We're just alike."

The pane rattles viciously in its frame. Cracks appear but the window holds. Maybe it's merely another test of wills. The things out there being forced in, and him trying to hold up under the barrage. No different than yesterday. He waits for her to crash into his arms. Two minutes go by, seven, nineteen, but it doesn't happen. Iwuvyou curls up beneath the radiator and gnaws a chew toy. The cracks divide, scuttle in other directions, and abruptly stop.

A meeting is inevitable but his patience is beginning to lag.

He clenches his teeth, trembling with anxiety, and swings to the canvas. The paints splashed on it are still fresh, and he uses a brush to swirl them together, slowly urging a pattern from bedlam. He lets his subconscious ride the wave of anguish that's been building since his dog tore out his heart. Lash shuts his eyes, turns his head up, loosens his shoulders so his arms flop this way and that, just close enough that he can touch the canvas while he sways.

After an hour, he opens one eye and squints at what's there. It's a self-portrait of a sad man trying desperately to smile.

A hand clasps his shoulder and Lash spins to face himself. He's standing there with his tongue out, facial muscles contorted, giggling like a moron. Lash punches himself in the mouth and knocks himself down. He sits on the floor pouting, starts whimpering and sobbing, looks over and holds his hand up, like Iwuvyou. Look at me, I'm so cute. No wonder the girls in the bars think he's an asshole.

There's a storm inside. The woman is in the same position, but the cracks have grown more jagged, and they're beginning to take the form of his father's handwriting. Is that a D or a V? Is she spelling redemption or revulsion? He listens to himself weeping.

Lash lies on the bed prepared to dream with a new and luminous intensity. He gets up off the floor and struggles to the easel, stares at the bed and wants to kill himself. Perhaps a little later, as soon as he finishes making this face. Next time that Lash wakes up thinking, This is it, you're finally dead, maybe the sorry son of a bitch will be.

Geoff Cooper

*Geoff Cooper ("Coop" to his friends and foes alike) is a new writer who emerged from the short-lived "gangsta" horror movement of the early years of this century—think of the Splatterpunks from the 1980's, only with a less incriminating wardrobe. As you might guess, the "gangsta" movement was built on fiction that was street-savvy, profane, violent, and genuinely angry. Coop's fiction was all that and more, as he has gone on to prove with the release of his superb novella, **Retribution, Inc.***

The following story may surprise those readers who think they know what Coop is capable of. I couldn't help but be reminded of the dense, poetic work of Clark Ashton Smith as I read this spellbinding dark fantasy.

—JNW

FOR WHOM WE MOURN

✠ BY GEOFF COOPER ✠

Gustav and Dimitri were close, once, before Dimitri opened Mother's grave and left behind an empty casket. After that, lumps of shame burned in Gustav's throat; rage smoldered in his chest, brotherly love twisted to rancor.

He held himself responsible for her desecration. If only he'd stopped Dimitri sooner. If he acted those years ago, he could have saved Mother much pain. He should have. He should have when he identified the darkness within his brother. Within them both.

Gustav did not because he was thwarted by an emotion most evil, sent upon his heart as a curse by some god the two had blasphemed. He loved his brother—as only men like himself could love—and hesitated pulling the trigger. In more lucid moments, Gustav understood Dimitri's actions. It was an addiction, one he knew well: the brain screamed, and the body reacted. *Feed me*, it cried, and it was hard not to obey…to find a book or ancient scroll and begin to read. Then the madness' thirst for darker knowledge grew insatiable.

If Gustav were in the grip of their madness, he would seek out the tomes, find the black incantations hidden between paragraphs mundane to unlearned eyes. Once the brain saw the secrets, it would recognize them in places most ordinary: proof of the madness in others. Sometimes he saw them still, but their meanings were never as apparent.

Dimitri understood what he had read, had learned. That's why he took Mother's remains. With them, he would seek the places of power. It was going to be a long journey. Gustav read a little before he gave chase. A little—enough to heighten the thinking, raise the consciousness. To tingle the brain. Tease it. The madness whispered within his mind. He stopped before it started to scream.

Before he left, Gustav checked his Makarov pistol—a good, Russian-made model. He packed extra ammunition, because it was scarce and expensive. He hoped he would not need the weapon, but packed it anyway. Just in case.

He saw the old man wandering the streets in Istanbul, narrating events no one around him could see, asking questions no one but Gustav, Dimitri, and a handful of others could answer. The old man's left hand was a stump. Its bandages were new.

"You've seen him," Gustav said.

The old man turned. Gustav looked into his eyes. He Saw. Yes. He Saw too much, Saw that for which he was unprepared. Madness swam into and out of focus in the old man's stare.

"My hand. He stole my hand. And a bottle of my best brandy."

"When?"

"Two nights ago. I was asleep in my bed. The bed I made. I'm a carpenter. Was. My hand and my brandy—all that I needed. Why would he take an old, callused hand? Why would someone steal that? And to take my drink afterward, that was mean," the former carpenter sobbed. "That was mean to take my brandy after my hand."

"Show me."

The man led Gustav to his home, reeling from the Sight, asking far to many questions. Once there, Gustav demanded to be shown the bed, and inquired about the brandy. The man seemed oblivious to Gustav's tears.

"I hope you catch him," the man said. "I was a carpenter. I used to build houses. Now I see them falling. Falling down. He builds, too, doesn't he? He builds with bones."

Gustav nodded, placed his hand on the bed. Mother had lain here. The carpenter's eyes were heavy on him, patiently waiting an elaboration. Gustav wiped his hand on his coat. "You ask questions you do not understand."

"Teach me, then."

"Kneel down."

The old man's joints creaked as he knelt. He looked up at Gustav and clasped his hands, expectant. "I knew you would come," he said. "I Saw it." Gently, he placed his hand on the bed, where Gustav's own had set a moment before. He closed his cursed eyes and opened them again. "I Saw Her, too," the madman said, "I Saw Her through the eyes of the sphinx."

Gustav nodded—made sense.

"Will you teach me now?"

"Yes." Gustav leveled the gun at the old man's head, aimed through tear-blurred eyes.

"Thank you," the carpenter smiled.

The blast blew out his brainstem.

MASQUES V

Gustav followed the trail of whispers through the desert to the Temple of Isis at Philae. Before he entered, he removed his boots and socks, his belt and weapon, setting them carefully in the sand outside the sacred boundary. From his pack he removed a book and fought the urge to open and read on the temple's stone steps, though his brain screamed. Not this time—too many men had died for this book. Its cover was the skin of a scapegoat slaughtered outside a Jewish settlement long ago. The goat would carry the villagers' sins out into the arid waste, but this one never made it: The Arab waited outside Gomorrah on the eve of the ritual, and took the goat and its burden of sin to bind this book. Its words were enlightenment—and damnation.

Gustav lowered his eyes as he entered, holding the book before him. He made his way past hieroglyphs depicting Nectanebo II with offerings of incense to Osiris, to the inner sanctuary where the Waters of Life originated and Isis herself dwelled.

He dropped to one knee, raised the book over his head, shut his eyes, and waited.

"Is this...?" Not even Isis could bring herself to mention the book's title.

"It is," Gustav said.

"This..." She stared at the book in amazement. "This is the original...complete?"

"Every page as The Arab penned it."

"You bring me this—a true offering. Much power is here. Won't you miss it?"

"Few gods—and no men—should ever read those words."

"But you have."

"Yes. Dimitri as well."

Isis grew angry at the mention of his name. "He was at Ghiza, looking for *The Book of the Dead*."

"I'm sorry," he said. "I had hoped to stop him before he reached your land."

There was nothing to say, so Isis smiled. "I would send you off with my blessing, but…"

"I know," Gustav nodded. He was too corrupt. "You cannot. I thank you for considering it."

She accepted his words with a nod, opened the book. A purple glow came from inside to cast an eerie light on her face. She began reading the ancient text.

Gustav watched her turn the pages in silence. As each moment passed, her expression changed—from awe to contemplation, contemplation to realization to disgust to horror. She shut the book after only a few pages, weeping.

Gustav's heart ripped in two. A woman's grievous tears were powerful in their own right. A Goddess's were far more precious. He accepted them as he could not her blessing, and felt unworthy of the gift. When he left, Isis knelt with her hand to her head. Gustav wondered for whom she mourned. He almost asked, but dared not.

Gustav followed Dimitri's trail of desecration across the desert. Holy cities were stained with his passing, the tombs of prophets and madmen opened, their remains drained of power and knowledge. Sometimes, he missed his brother by only a few hours. At other times, he lost the trail, and had to waste valuable days to recover it.

Dimitri slaughtered a sacred bull near Samrala, India. He and Mother's corpse had lain in the carcass. The villagers still wept when Gustav came upon them, but he left them to their grief, because he had only one way to cure it, and not enough bullets. Makarov ammunition was scarce in these impoverished lands. He refrained from expending any, until he reached Laos.

Eighteen of them were skinned alive and tied to bamboo stakes. Water dripped from buckets atop each onto their tongues; they could not dehydrate. When Gustav reached them, they all stared down at the small heaps of unusable flesh at their feet and watched leafy shadows creep across their skin. Dimitri had taken quite a bit with him: choice cuts.

Gustav needed no magic to see the root of their madness. They all babbled in their language, but Gustav understood nothing of what they said. He did not speak Lao, but could not mistake the pleading tone to their slippery, incomprehensible words. They reeked of deceit.

Flat tongues lingered maliciously over lipless mouths as they spoke, lidless eyes stared at his pale skin with hunger far deeper than sanity. They wanted to wear it. Like the crones sharing an eye betwixt the three, his flesh would be passed between eighteen.

Gustav shot them one by one. He paused only to reload and weep.

Gustav lost his brother's trail in Asia, but knew the general direction: north. There were many places Dimitri could go first, but Gustav knew where this journey would end: Lake Baikal. Gustav remembered how dreamy mother's eyes grew when she talked of Baikal: a dream never realized. Many her age wanted to make the journey at least once. Dimitri defiled her dreams and Gustav's soul bore the weight of shame at the mockery of the goals she never achieved.

Strange lightning came from Olkhon Island, where monks' bones lay unburied—not Dimitri's doing: it was the custom. Gustav thought of Dimitri amongst all those holy bones and his anger flared. He cursed himself for permitting this to happen, but another curse on his soul was redundant.

The Siberian people believed Burkham, god of the lake, was angry, and families went hungry from the hoards of food and vodka sacrificed to appease Him. In the fishing towns on Baikal's shore, orders to sail were refused, and refused so often that they were no longer given. No one ventured past shore, much less to Olkhon to inspect the source of trouble.

When Gustav inquired of passage to Olkhon, he was met with skepticism and distrust. Some refused to acknowledge him because they thought him mad—(how correct they were)—while others looked at him suspiciously, as if he caused the strange lightning in the sky, as if he were responsible. How correct they were, too.

Unable to find passage to Olkhon, Gustav bought a small rowboat with an outboard engine. The man who sold it to him did not ask his destination. When the deal was done, the man took both Gustav's hands in his and said, "May Burkham keep you."

"And he you."

The depth of the man's stare betrayed his understanding. He knew. He knew and was not touched by the madness. He knew, and had a family. He knew, and held his humanity around him like a badge of station.

Gustav knelt before him as he had before Isis. The man let his shaking hands go, and bade Gustav to leave. When Gustav left the room and stepped outside, he wondered what god he had touched—if it were Burkham himself.

Outside, the weird lightning flashed soundlessly across the water. The lightning was green this time. Then purple. Gustav looked across the massive lake to Olkhon Island, could barely make out its rust-colored rock from the cold, dark waves.

He hefted his bag of supplies down the ramp, loaded it into the boat, and draped a plastic tarp over the ancient texts to keep them dry. He was as ready as he could ever be for a confrontation with Dimitri.

It rained harder.

MASQUES V

❖ ❖ ❖

Silent thunder followed a flash of orange lightning. Unease quickened Gustav's pulse. Cold Siberian rain dripped off his beard to his neck, bleached his skin a frigid shade of white.

The waves grew, and as they slapped the boat's hull with muttering voices: *"Back. Don't. Back. Don't."* Each wave's voice was unique: like snowflakes, no two alike. As Baikal's water's roughened, the waves' voices grew proportionately louder: with meter-and-a-half seas, they were deafening.

Lightning flashed blue, red, and yellow, and the Siberian skies spit cold rain. The screaming waves tossed the tiny craft to and fro. Puddles sloshed about the boat's deck, soaked through Gustav's boots. His toes went numb. Gustav was no seaman, but he stayed his path as best he could: rolling with the waves, trying not to let the silent lightning or the loud voice of the waters distract his course or cause. *Nerpa*, the indigenous Baikal seal, regarded him with brown liquid eyes as he passed a group. Their expressions questioned his sanity: *Where are you going, man? This is not your element.* Gustav could almost make out warnings in their dog-like barks.

Cold wet wind collected in the wrinkles of Gustav's coat and boots, ran in rivulets off his brimmed hat, soaked through his gloves and froze his fingers. The boat bobbed and swayed across the ever-roughening waters, its small engine barely audible over the screaming waves. On top of the growing clamor, the *nerpa* joined in, calling him a fool and a failure, telling him to go back to shore, where he belonged. Gustav ignored the *nerpa* and kept his course, adjusting when could see the island over the rising and falling bow.

The boat shuddered violently as the water thickened to the consistency of molasses. The tiny engine strained, trying to propel the craft forward through water suddenly too thick. He gave it more gas, tried to raise the prop to ease the load, but nothing helped. The engine started getting hot. Gustav shut it down before it blew and left him stranded.

All was silent. *Nerpa* opened and closed their mouths mutely. The rain splashed on the water without sound. The waves flattened out. Dead calm.

The boat floated steadily toward Olkhon Island across a smooth and silent span of water. Gustav took the Makarov out of its holster, jacked a round into the chamber, and let the boat drift. His spine shot out warnings to his system and his eyes darted from peripheral to peripheral. Something was happening, but he did not know what. Until he saw the billowing clouds on the water.

At first, Gustav thought it was merely a reflection of the sky above but these were not clouds of rain or snow; these were clouds of silt—

(As above, so below)

—from Baikal's bottom.

The water's surface bubbled and rolled without sound. Gustav smelled millennia of decayed fish in the Baikal mud. His nose attempted to curl back into his face to hide from the reek.

The boat began to sway. Bubbles from Baikal's bottom burped noxious gas. Mist loitered around him, shut down visibility. The unearthly lightning cast glows about the scene and threw distance and depth into confusion.

The boat lurched to port. Gustav fell to his knees, held on to the Makarov with his right hand, the boat's railing with his left. The stern spun around, kicked to starboard.

A hand-shaped wave smacked the bow. Wet fingers disintegrated, sprayed Gustav in the face, clung to his cheeks and beard. It tasted awful, smelled worse. His nose filled with methane reek and rotted aquatic life. He gagged from the smell. His stomach pitched its contents to the back of his throat. His eyes dripped stinging tears as he reswallowed vomit.

The boat lurched again, spun violently. Waves shoved against the starboard side of the bow—dirty, reeking waves, shaped like hands. They pushed. The small boat spun. Gustav held on, screamed demands for order, and in anger called out his brother's name.

The hands reached over the deck, fingers stretched out, splayed palms. Gustav felt the cold wetness seize him, pull him toward the edge of the boat. He screamed as they lifted him over the rail. He splashed into the freezing water turned black by silt and mud. Watery half-formed arms reached for his ankles from the dark waves. Their grip was not tight, but he could not kick them away. They dragged him feet-first.

Rancid waves flooded his face. Water shot up his nose. They stripped his weapon away, and the Makarov sank to the bottom like a stone. Gustav fought the progress, tried to sit up, breathe, suck air, kick them away, but the wave-hands did not relent.

They pulled him toward the shallows. Olkhon's shore: jagged rock the color of dried blood, erupted out of the water before him. The hands gripping him dragged him ever faster toward the blood-red rock. Gustav screamed before they threw him against it—afterward, he could not: the force of impact expelled his breath from his lungs and ignited pain in his spine. Warm blood flowed over his cold forehead, stung as it dripped into his eyes, salty in his mouth. The waters of Baikal drank from the gash and the hands that assaulted him matched the color of the rock.

He was thrown onto the rocky beach. It hurt to moan. Even breathing caused pain. His fingers clawed at small pebbles cast atop the larger rocks as he tried to pull himself away before the water could grab him again, drag him back in.

Slowly his breathing stabilized. The flaring pain throughout his chest dimmed to throbbing. It hurt only when his heart beat.

He crawled up the beach for safety, groaned with every

aching movement and realized the silence had been broken. Besides his own voice, the first sound that registered was the handwaves reaching for him. They smacked and slapped at the rock and behind him, the *nerpa* called him a fool, told him to come back to the water where it was safe, that there was nothing on the island good anymore, his element be damned.

Gustav turned toward the water. At first, he thought the hands had left, but after a moment he saw their outlines skimming across the cove like the dorsal fins of mutant sharks. The seals congregated *en masse* out further, and continued to speak amongst themselves.

As he watched the seals and hands in the water, and thought about the lost pistol, the *nerpa* became restless. A visible wave of panic passed through them as the group scattered. The hands ceased to hide in the waves: arms shot out of the water, looking like lunatic reeds. Their every movement was menace. Green lightning crackled across the sky.

He smelled the smoke. It wafted toward him from over the rise. He turned his nose into it, forcing himself to rise and trace it back to its origin.

The makeshift hut was dilapidated. No wall was plumb or square. Its roof leaned to the left, collecting rain in its deep bows. The thick smoke rose slowly through a chimney-hole to hang low in the damp air. Gustav recognized the smell: he could never forget the scent of burning bones.

He stepped over protective circles drawn in the mud around the perimeter and rapped on the door. It swung open.

The first thing Gustav saw was the glow emanating from the pyramid of skulls burning in the fireplace. Tongues of flame wagged and moaned. The monks' remains lamented their predicament and they cried out to deaf gods for mercy. The room they showed was impossible: its proportions too large to be contained inside the hovel. A harpsichord—Mother's favorite instrument—rested in the corner, amongst rich tapestries and original art in gilded frames.

He saw a late sixteenth-century Dutch clock on the other wall, the type with only the hour hand. Dimitri must have worked hard to so alter the ramshackle lodging: such lengths were unlike him.

Gustav stepped over the threshold, calling his brother's name. He was answered only by the monks' remains in the fireplace, pleading with him to end their torment.

In the flickering shadows, Gustav saw an easy chair and endtable, a lamp, and behind that, a shelf of books, many of which were unique; handwritten copies of the unaccredited author's manuscript; most were in languages never meant to be spoken, and few were in any modern tongue. Gustav knew them all by sight. Many he had memorized in their entirety. His brain tingled as he saw them and his madness screamed. He approached the shelf, and from behind, heard the door to the hut slam closed.

Gustav spun, instinctively reached for his pistol, but his hand came up empty as he remembered the weapon was at the bottom of Baikal.

"What would you do with it if you had it?" Dimitri asked as he approached.

The question hung in the air between them, and Gustav let it hang. "Where is she?"

"So nice to see you too, dear brother."

"Where is she?"

"Where is who?"

"You know damned well."

"Mother," Dimitri called, "Gustav wishes to see you."

Gustav started a word of protest, but it fell from his lips when he saw her enter the room. She shuffled slowly and felt her way with one hand on the wall. In the other, she held a knitting-basket and several skanes of yarn. Dimitri had resurrected her, repaired her flesh with that taken in Laos. Except for her eyes. They were absent from their sockets, but Gustav did not know whether that was Dimitri's omission or the logistics of rot.

Dimitri walked over to Mother, took her hand, led her to the chair. He did not bother turning on the lamp. Her hands drew up her needles. Their clicking was not the sound Gustav remembered from his childhood, but there was no reason it should be. The familiar aluminum needles she used to use were replaced with fine, rune-carved needles of bone.

"What have you done?" Gustav asked his brother, though his eyes never left the shambling incarnation of his mother's reanimated corpse.

"I brought her back."

"Why, Dimitri? We know you *could* do it; that was never in question. What purpose could this serve? What benefit could come from it?"

"Mother can knit," he said. "I thought you would have remembered."

"Yes, of course she could, but..." Gustav stopped as the significance overwhelmed him. One of the most ancient forms of magic, back to the Fates. How foolish of him to never have considered it before. Mother would be easy for Dimitri to control; the bond between mother and son does not stop with the cessation of life. With her resurrection, she could keep on knitting until Dimitri told her to stop, and that order would never be given. She could knit his fate, his victories and his accomplishments, his life everlasting. As long as he kept her secret — and well protected.

Dimitri whispered in Mother's ear. The harpsichord in the corner began to play. At first, the notes were random, then, as she started another loop of yarn, a melody took shape. Dimitri stroked her hair, smiling at Gustav.

"You've enslaved her," Gustav said, distaste on his tongue. "After all she did for us, you've enslaved her."

"All she did is nothing compared to that which she shall do."

Gustav looked at his mother's ever-moving hands. The flesh on her knuckles as thin, racked by fissures from which protruded blackened, drying flesh and bloodless veins. Everything those hands had worked for was gone, her life's work betrayed by her youngest son. Gustav glared at his brother as a surge of hatred renewed itself, a grudge held a lifetime. "I should have shot you when you were eight."

Click-click click, the needles tapped out the seconds. *Click-click, click.* Dimitri returned the glare with a parody of a smile, a showing of teeth.

Click-click click.

"Then who would have taught her so much? Mother lived, died, and never realized anything outside of the mundane. She was unlearned, ignorant. She never got out of St. Petersburg, much less to the places I have taken her."

"You took her there for your purposes, not hers."

"Partially true. Why would I have come here? To Baikal? To come here and see it was *her* dream, not mine. I could have gone anywhere."

"If you wished her to see it, you would have given her eyes," Gustav advanced a step. Dimitri was within arm's reach.

"Go ahead," Dimitri said. "Do it. I see the thought in your mind. Anyone could. You wish to see me bleed. You wish to choke the life from me, the dangers to yourself be damned. Oh, noble, noble Gustav, you always were—"

Gustav could control himself on longer. Rage flashed out his arms, wrapped his hands around his brother's throat. Hate clenched his fingers.

Dimitri's hands went up to block the attack, too late: Gustav drove him to the ground by his neck. He rammed his knee into Dimitri's sternum and pinned him, then lifted his head and rammed it into the floor. Dimitri's vision unfocused with the shock of impact. Again and again, Gustav slammed the back of Dimitri's head on the floor in perfect time with mother's needles—

Click-click click
SLAM

Geoff Cooper

Click-click click
SLAM
Click-click click
SLAM

—until Dimitri's body went limp. Gustav paused, wondered for an instant if he had killed him, but after a moment, he felt Dimitri's chest rise and fall. His tenacious will to live drove Gustav deeper into his rage and he squeezed Dimitri's neck, grabbed his larynx and twisted, until he felt the cartilage crack and splinter. He pummeled his brother's face with his fists and yet, Dimitri still breathed.

Click-click click

Wheezing, blood-wet, breath continued to draw past Dimitri's lips, and in his mouth, his tongue rolled back, as if it tied to fan what little air it could into the ruined throat.

Click-click click

The raggedness of Dimitri's breathing grew fainter, the rhythm stronger. The blood stopped pooling in his mouth and the lips, ruined by Gustav's pummeling, wove themselves back together, drawing the smallest pieces of skin back from where they were knocked out of place.

Gustav's shock overtook his senses and he stared mutely at the magnificent transformation.

Click-click click

As he looked up to Mother, whose expression never altered, Dimitri began to laugh under him. Slowly, Dimitri pushed himself up off the floor. Gustav tried to hold him down with sheer force, but Dimitri was gaining strength. He crashed his fist into the side of Gustav's head and knocked him senseless, and, while Gustav was dazed, he landed another fist to the underside of Gustav's chin, knocking his sense of balance askew.

Then Dimitri pressed his advantage, and heaved his body upward while pushing Gustav away. The next thing Gustav knew, he was being kicked in the ribs and screamed

293

at for every perceived wrong he had committed toward Dimitri in all of his life, from the time they were eleven and seven, when Gustav first got hold of the black tome from grandfather's study and would not let young Dimitri read it, too; to the fist grave they violated together, when Gustav asked the first and last questions of the corpse and claimed his right to do so was based on his being the older brother; to the girl Dimitri had a lust for when he was fifteen and whom Gustav had lain; and the meddling and foiling of countless schemes and plans and dreams, and with each accusation, another blow landed.

Gustav shrank back from the ferocity of his brother's assault, struggled to regain his feet, but Dimitri's kicks pre-empted such action. He curled on his side, tried to protect his soft throat and belly. Dimitri's kicks kept coming no matter what he did, so the only thing he could think of doing was scuttling away as best he could, rolling on the floor or crawling, whatever permitted an inch or two of safety from the ever-continuing barrage.

Click-click click

Gustav's retreat was halted by the wall: backed into a corner. He looked up through one eye, for the other had swollen shut. The skulls' flickering light from his left cast a dim glow on mother's back. Her hair was disheveled, fallen from her glamorous funeral style. She did not seem to notice. Instead, she mindlessly knit as they tried to kill each other, oblivious to all that occurred around her.

Dimitri's right leg kept coming in to his field of vision, a dark blur against the glowing backdrop that careened into his chest, his gut: a pendulum of pain. Dimitri saw his brother's predicament: against the wall, he could go no further. Lying on the floor, he could not rise. His tactics changed, then, and he rose his foot to stomp down with his heel.

The first landed in Gustav's midsection, its power explosive. He tasted the pain on his tongue, felt it roll with the waves of nausea through his torso. He doubled over, dimly aware that his arms that protected his face were useless against Dimitri's full weight should it come crashing through his skull. In his vulnerability, he became acutely aware of the cold, hard, unyielding floor beneath him, and how it would absorb none of the shock—the proverbial hard spot and the rock-hard bootheel, his braincase an egg between them.

Dimitri lifted his foot again, and Gustav reached up. His right hand missed, but his left caught the inside of Dimitri's pantleg, slowing the ascent long enough for the right to grab hold of Dimitri's ankle.

Dimitri shook his leg in an attempt to dislodge Gustav's grip, tried to shuffle back. Gustav held on, drew both of his arms around Dimitri's leg, pulled them to his chest. He felt himself pull away from the wall as Dimitri dragged him across the floor, felt the muscles in his brother's leg strain with the effort. Then he let go.

With Gustav's weight no longer restraining him, Dimitri's full-force backstep betrayed him. He lurched in reverse, off balance, and his arms went out to try and stabilize himself as he went down. His right grasped nothing. His left grabbed the bookshelf. Instead of halting his fall, it tilted forward.

As the top books slid off onto the floor to crack their spines and tear the endpapers away, the light scrolls in cases crushed beneath the heavier, older volumes, Dimitri regained enough of his balance to leap out of the way.

Mother did not. The shelf smashed the lamp and table. Shards of glass and splinters of ancient wood cascaded to the floor, and the shelf came to rest on top of her frail corpse.

The harpsichord ceased its performance. The *click-click click* of her needles did not punctuate the seconds' passing. The sixteenth-century wall clock with the single hand melted into the wall on which it hung; the walls began

to slide forward and lose their fine finish, fading to dilapidated wood that was neither plumb or square; the ceiling
overhead faded to reveal the low-hung, bowed roof which
let through columns of water through to collect in puddles
on the earthen floor. The ornate hearth above the fireplace
disintegrated, as did the *bric-a-brac* collected on its top,
revealing a stone fire-pit. Smoke collected in the single-
room hut and obscured vision: the skulls of holy men still
burned and their tongues of flame softly lamented.

Gustav listened for Dimitri but heard nothing from his
brother. The only sounds in the hut were the spattering of
rain on the roof, the moaning monks and a tapping sound
from the pile of broken books and crushed scrolls. Gustav
labored to rise. His head spun, and he reached to the wall to
keep himself upright. The nausea he experienced with
Dimitri's crushing kick to his kidney returned. Every movement aggravated it further. His eye was swollen, blood was
in his mouth every time he spit but he could not tell if it was
from his lips, cheek, or nose—or any combination thereof.
Every breath was accompanied by a stabbing speculation of
a broken rib. He moaned in chorus with the dead monks.

He leaned on the fallen bookshelf with both of his
arms, hanging his head to dispel the nausea and drain the
blood from his mouth. A sticky strand dripped off his lip to
stain a page a hundreds of years old and partially obscured
a passage regarding the elementary principles of creation,
destruction, and the manipulation of the two. Gustav
remembered it from his studies, though he had not seen the
book since he was a teenager and lost it to Dimitri in a
wager on Olympic hockey. The corner of the book's spine
rest in a growing puddle of muddy water stained the red
shade of Olkhon.

After a few moments of recuperation, Gustav made his
way around the bookshelf, leaning his weight upon it for he
could not trust his own legs. As he approached the top corner of the shelf, it teetered: Mother's chair its fulcrum. The

sudden weight shift surprised him, and he let go for a moment. Standing by himself, he could see Dimitri on the far side of the shelf as he lay crumpled on the floor. The wounds healed by mother's knitting had reopened, the magic fueling his chateau and life gone. All that remained were his creations: the shelf for the books, the chair, and mother's unnatural life. The rest he left to her to execute at his command. Dimitri had always looked for the easier way.

Gustav sighed. Part of him mourned.

Mother was closer, so he reached her first. She was pinned to the chair, her hands trapped on opposite sides of one of the shelves. Her eyeless face did not look at him, but still her hands worked the bone needles. They tapped against the wooden shelf as they tried to complete the loop she started when the shelf fell. She still wore her wedding band on her left hand. Gustav was happy to see it. It reminded him of her life, when she would turn it over on her finger as she thought of a suitable punishment for the boys for them when they were naughty.

(Boys will be boys.)

Somewhere, a dark god laughed at the irony.

"Mother," Gustav said. "Can you hear me? At all? Mother?"

Slowly, her head turned toward him, and her eyelids opened to reveal black rot and Dimitri's shadow magic. There was no love in her eyes, no acceptance. Only the grave's empty wisdom, and that, he already knew.

Gustav wondered about the carpenter's mother in Istanbul, whom he never knew. About Horus's—sweet, sweet Isis, and the tears she cried. About the mother of the Arab, about the mothers of the scholars and prophets…how these men all needed their mother's wisdom, how they all must have remembered mother's words in times of need. A single word from her would help.

"I'm sorry, mother," Gustav said.

The stare he received in answer was blank.

Gustav reached down and removed the bone needles from her hands. Despite their absence, she continued to try and complete the final loop. Gustav almost broke them over his knee, but the runes upon them caught his attention. To destroy these would be a sacrilege: he owed both Isis and the god at the lakeshore more than that.

The skulls in the fireplace muttered their approval.

Gustav reached forward, laid his hands on her face. He said something more, some small word of apology, barely muttered as he twisted her skull from her neck.

The *nerpa* outside wailed.

The magic powering her died, the flesh of the Lao fused to her own fell away. Gently, he carried her head to the fire. The dead monks within accepted her quickly, flickered their tongues over her face in passionate kisses. Within moments, her bare skull rest on top of the pile, and her voice joined the chorus. She did not speak, but she did sob.

Gustav almost asked her why, but dared not.

From the fire, he turned, and went to where Dimitri's corpse lay cooling in puddles of water from the leaking roof. Gustav kicked the books out of his way and crouched down before him. In death, his brother looked kind: how looks can deceive.

He sat there for a long time. The roof leaking on his face concealed that which ran from his eyes. His loss, guilt, and grief crushed all thought, overwhelmed most of his senses. He was aware of the wetness only because it reminded him of Isis, the tears she cried. He looked up, through the holes in the roof, and let the rain shower his face. As he cried into the grey sky, he wondered why, and for whom he mourned.

George Ibarra

*I have come to the conclusion over the years—based on those Texas writers who have appeared in the five **Masques** collections—that there must be something in the water down there that gives them deep insight into all things (in the dictionary sense) odd. The following story has done nothing to dispel this notion.*

George Ibarra is a new writer whose appearance here marks his first professional sale. Don't be surprised if the following story reminds you of another Texas writer, Joe Lansdale, who first raised in me the suspicion that there must be something in the water down there in Texas. At least now I know what it is...

—JNW

ATOMIC POSSUMS

✠ BY GEORGE IBARRA ✠

Bubba smiled when I bent down to pet him between the ears. Weren't no pretty smile neither, him having one eye, a half-bit ear, and his lower left jaw exposed to the flesh. Still he was my dog, my Bubba, brothers to the end and all.

Weren't always so ugly. Was a time all the bitches were hot to trot for some loving from the mutt. Old Lady Celia's retriever had three litters from Bubba's juice stock 'til she finally had her dog fixed. I'm telling you he wasn't always so unsightly.

For that reason it took some time to get used to his ugly mug, but good hunt dogs are hard to find, and harder to train. So I kept him on after the possums used him for Sunday brunch. No need to terminate a mutt who can still run a scent. Around here, that's worth more than a worm farm. Least of all that's what I tell those folks who ask why I don't put him out of his misery.

See, even when the fishing's good down at the creek, can't eat but one cat from the water. Thanks so very much to the nuclear energy plant they built nearby. Times those fish look like they've been sprayed with Da-glo. You know that ain't safe.

Fact is, we'd been fishing the day of Bubba's run-in with the possums. Lazy summer day if I recall. My clothes of choice were my blue dungarees and a John Deere cap to keep out the sun. Clothes play an important role in fishing. You got to be comfortable.

We hiked through the woods for a good hour, using the creek on our left as our guide. Bubba arrived at the clearing while I made way through the rough. The strong scent of animal urine made my nose hairs stand on end. I decided Bubba must've smelled it too from his jumpiness.

Bubba's ears perked when his attention fell on something in the high grass. From my position, I saw him skirt and slowly trot circles around an indentation in the meadow. He barked a few times to let me know he'd found something curious. I ran to him and discovered the object of his interest.

The bones of six squirrels were arranged in the shape of a pyramid. The meat from the skeletons picked clean, but not cleanly enough to leave the indentation of teeth. Sharp teeth.

I kicked the bones and muttered some objections to myself about kids these days. Bubba barked for agreement. The carcasses scattered over several yards of unkempt nature. I scratched the dog's ears and offered him soft 'dillo jerky. He inhaled and swallowed the treat.

Bubba calmed with my presence, but I shook with the thought of people disgracing the tranquility of nature. This far from town, I did not expect such dishonor. In years past, fear kept us from disturbing the peacefulness of the creek.

George Ibarra

The place stood like a sacred monument to God. However, times change and so do our gods.

There's darkness in the modern world that makes me glad to live in a town of two thousand. Even so, sometimes that darkness stretches some feelers into the sticks. Makes people sick in the head. Or maybe they were already sick, and the darkness only reveals a path for them to pursue. Can't remember that sickness ever stretching out to the creek. Not until that day.

Who'd do a thing like that with a handful of squirrel carcasses? Not someone from town I hoped. Most people here live simple, God-fearing existences. Once in a while, we sent someone away to college. Mostly they were good people after the experience, but sometimes there'd be a bad apple in the bunch. Lorna Hughes returned after her first year at university with a craving for alcohol and colored boys. Her daddy took care of both those things with a heavy, calloused hand.

Forgive my rambling, sometimes I think on a subject and I got to say my due. Besides I can't say I didn't have eyes for that rump on Lorna. Had to play her righteous though, being that Pop served a stint with her daddy in Vietnam.

Anyhow I'm getting far away from the story, and the doctors tell me it might do me good to recollect. They think I might remember more about that afternoon. We'll see.

We left the skeletons and headed for the creek. Bubba ran himself tired and took to napping under the shade of a dead oak. I parked my behind on a stump and commenced my fishing with a .22 and a case of Bud.

After the first hour I'd blown two cats out of the water, and was in the middle of aiming my sights at a hot-pink colored bottom feeder, when I heard Bubba howl like a little girl. This ain't like my dog, understand. His growl can put the fear of God in a mountain cat. So I ran to my friend, and what did I see but two possums holding him down while a pack of baby possums gnawed at his face, and another was hunched down by Bubba's legs.

Imagine my dismay when I witnessed the possum sticking his prick in my dog's asshole. Poor Bubba shrieked, but I wasn't sure which pain he felt the most—that on his face or his pride. If that weren't bad enough, the sexually inclined possum popped the top on one my Buds and chugged it like a rebounding alcoholic.

Bad enough to rape a man's best friend, but to drink his beer? Might as well piss on my boots and shit on my heart. Action was necessary.

I steadied the sight of my rifle at the offending possum. They engaged in their little party while I looked intently, stunned by the unfolding events. Bubba shot me a stare, tears in his eyes, but it was his helpless cry that awakened my senses. I didn't want to hit my dog with a stray bullet, so I put a shot into the oak.

The possums looked up at me. Now if you ain't seen a possum bearing teeth, you should know they look so ugly they make Anna Nicole look like a fine piece of grade-A beef. Even so, these fuckers got more ugly than usual. Possum eyes don't usually glow bright street cone orange, and their teeth are never covered in neon lime brightness.

The ploy worked, though. Their attention distracted, they left Bubba, and hissed and bared fangs in my direction. Bubba used the opportunity to curl into a ball. The possums measured my worth as an opponent, or so I thought by the way they looked me over.

I broke the standoff by firing a slug into the possum with the hard-on. The shell exploded in it's eye. He fell screaming out something that sounded like language. It died with his penis gripped in it's paw.

The other howled, while the smaller of the adults ran for me, its front paws flinging to and fro with mechanical grace. With no time to reload, I bore the butt of the rifle into the charging possum. Teeth and blood sprayed from its mouth. It stood but reeled uneasily from the blow. Before it gathered its senses, I delivered my boot into it's most private area and sent it flying into a tree.

Tree and possum exploded in dust and splinters. I reloaded. They scattered, but formed a semi-circle around me and Bubba. I calmly walked to my dog and lifted him into my arms. The last adult and the baby possums squealed while I steadied my rifle in the crook of my shoulder to take a shot. Bubba barked a warning in the direction of the meadow.

In the meadow, the undisturbed grass broke and spread as several possums came to their friends' rescue. Their heads bobbed up and down, revealing pairs of pink possum ears. A sigh of relief came from the oldest beast. Ahead of me a dozen possums closed the gap on me and Bubba, while to my right the remaining possums emitted a high pitched cry. It sounded like an appeal.

Places to hide are scarce near the banks of the creek, and this part is murky enough you don't want to step in the water unless you got on high boots. It's infested with water moccasins and whatnot. So I had no choice but to run alongside the creek, Bubba and the rifle safely in my arms.

Despite my long stride the possums managed to stay a few feet behind. I heard their little legs slap against the hard earth, while dried twigs and leaves popped and snapped beneath their paws. From my side, I saw them closing me in, trapping me against the creek.

I ran faster, but with the sun above my face, the weight of Bubba in my arms, and having already hiked a distance, I felt my knees buckling. The tree branches whipped at my face, and warm blood flowed down my cheeks, pooling on the shoulder straps of my dungarees. Pulling Bubba over my left shoulder, I swung the rifle forward like a machete. The brittle summer-dried twigs easily gave way.

Two possums swung down from their tails a few feet in front of us, their teeth exposed. I steadied the rifle and fired at the one in our path. It swung back from the blast spinning around the branch like an olympic gymnast, his tail still gripping the branch, his face well on its way to the next tree. A well placed blow from the barrel of the gun gave the second one a need for some plastic surgery, and cleared the path for me and Bubba. So I thought.

Up ahead I could see the twelve-foot fence surrounding the nuclear plant. Barbed-wire hung over the top waiting with its jagged teeth. Rumor had it the fence went underground a few feet. The creek also met the river here, leaving us cornered between the fence and the radiated water. River wasn't much wider than the creek, but much deeper.

This was no good place to die. I thought of the squirrel skeletons arranged, pointing towards the sky. The thought dispersed, replaced by an image of my bones joined with those of Bubba in some mad possum architecture.

We'd have to make a stand.

I'm no expert on possums, but most animals don't take kindly to water, so I made for the river. Water moccasins be damned. The run-off here was hot from the nuclear plant, but not unbearable. Weren't supposed to be any fishing here, but no one listens, and the fish are much fatter even if a bit odd-colored.

Nothing splashed behind me so I turned to look back and found the possums chattering and dancing on the shoreline. They looked pissed. I fired a round at the one nearest the water and put the bullet in its paw. It screamed then ran for the bramble.

The remaining bastards gathered at the water's edge. I'd never seen so much anger in the face of a wild animal. The silver of their eyes (don't ask me why they weren't white) burned a deep red from the pulsing blood vessels and their lips broadened into a wide grin, revealing sharp, vampire-like teeth.

One of them stuck its foot in the water. I swear it was testing the temperature.

I let go of Bubba, and he knew enough to swim for the other side of the river. My own feet argued in a struggle to fight or fly. Even so, soon as the first possum stepped waist deep in creek water, I turned and ran.

Two feet into my stride and I found a channel. It took forever to fall in. Underneath I saw man-sized catfish of all colors. You might think I'm crazy, but there were fish in all sorts of rainbow hues.

I struggled to keep my head above water, but I'm no swimmer. Just before I went under I looked to the shore and saw the possums pointing and laughing. I thought then I should be laughing, I was the one getting away.

If you can call it that.

I don't remember anything after going under. I woke with Bubba pulling me out from the neon green jaws of pink, polka-dotted catfish. Sometimes it's best not to recollect some things.

I think God made it merciful that way. We aren't meant to understand or remember all the events this universe provides for our education and experience. There's a story I got that from, but I don't remember the name, and I'm sure I misquoted something fierce like the uneducated red neck, country boy I am. Still, my doctors think it would help for me to remember. It don't matter much to me what they say. I know what memories are important.

On the other hand, some experiences are meant for savoring. Moments shared with friends, family and lovers especially. Me and Bubba, we'd been tight a long time, but never tighter than after that day. See, Bubba saved my life. It's what friends do. The only appreciation necessary is more friendship.

S'been months since the incident, and people still ask me why I keep Bubba around. I just shrug an "I don't know." They don't understand a man and his dog. The relationship between man and dog is a sacred bond built from years of trust. A conviction exists that can't be found in any other bond, be it man and man, man and woman, or man and beast.

Dogs like that aren't just found. Takes years of companionship to develop that sort of trust and understanding. It's not too much unlike a marriage, 'cept without the benefits of the sexual aspects of a relationship born from matrimony.

Besides, after being mauled and raped, you'd think the dog would have all sorts of problems. You'd think he'd need a friend, but he just goes on. He ain't got time to feel sorry for himself. Dogs are like that. They don't think beyond their next meal. We could take a lesson or two from dogs, you'd have folks less depressed. Still, if ever he needs a friend, I'll be there.

So I let them question the loyalty I display and feel for poor Bubba and his hideous face. I pay them no mind. Besides, those possums may have left him ugly and mentally scarred, but I still think he's the fortunate one. Unlike me, lucky dog got away with his limbs.

❧❧❧

Mark Powers

Here we have yet another "first" story for this edition of **Masques**, *this one from a young Illinois writer who sent us one of the most enigmatic and disturbing depictions of genuine madness we've seen in quite some time, made all the more disturbing by its matter-of-fact brevity. Ladies and gentlemen, please allow us to introduce...*

—JNW

MR. HANDLEBARS

~~~~~~~~~~~~~~~~~~~~~~~~

✠ BY MARK POWERS ✠

T he ward door buzzed.

"Oh! It's Handlebars. Hi, John," said the oriental nurse, Joanne, standing by the nurses' office, smiling.

Her eyes met obese nurse Dorothy's, seated by the ward window, while, with raised eyebrows, she withheld a grin.

He looked in at Dorothy.

"Is there anyone special I'm supposed to talk to?"

"No, John," she said, sighing. "Just begin your inspection of the rooms."

"Okay."

He looked at Joanne, as she was about to go down the hall, noting lips. He looked at Dorothy.

"What's the problem, Mrs. Conners?" he asked.

"Come on in, John. And close the door."

John complied.

"Have a seat please…"

He sat by the door.

"John…" she said, picking up papers on top neatly stacked folders on the desk. "Several patients from here have written letters…" She slid on glasses hanging on her chest. "…they report that you, *you* only—no other staff—mistreated them here." She watched him over her glasses.

"…here a man says that while lying on the floor in the day room, next to the sofa, asleep—you *kicked him*! She frowned. "John, I don't know *what* to make of this!" She sighed. Read on.

John entered a place, blanking her out: "La-la-la-la-la-la-la…you fat farty cow…you enormous *pig*! La-la-la-la…"

"…that fat ass saying that stuff!" John said, dipping mop into dirty water; sliding it into the flat wringer hooked to the bucket's side. He squeezed—*forcefully*. Here's your head, *bitch*! I'll show *her*. *Goddammit*!

Mop plopped on a dry part…have to be more careful…pick on those who won't squeal, he thought…Ones that are passive, vulnerable.

After all, I'm *Mister Macho*…stroked his handlebar mustache. Smiled. He plopped the mop.

He began whistling.

He was playing a ferocious game of Ping-Pong in the day room—losing—to a schizophrenic, when he saw:

"Is that the guy that arrived this weekend?" John asked Phil, a big muscular black man.

"Yeah. Sur is," Phil said, slurred, as if with mouth stuffed.

Maybe it *is* stuffed, John thought. Never know about these fuckin' wackos…

Mark Powers

"Damn!" John said, as Phil slipped one out of range in his opposite corner.

Phil grinned missing front teeth. "Maybe dis just isn't your game, D'zohn."

John looked over. He was young—about 20. Lead by a nurse, he walked slowly to the sofa in front of the TV.

Wait until *he* screws up, John thought. Practice remedial reality on a loony...

He stroked his mustache, delivered a quick one to Phil's left corner. "Got you, Phil," he said, grinning.

"Damn! You playin' like you mad."

The ball sprung, rolled to the sofa.

"I'll get it," John said. He watched the man.

Nearer his front, he said: "Hello. I'm John...Did you just arrive?"

"Yes." He slowly faced John, avoiding eye contact.

John looked steadily. I can't watch him intensely; appear friendly. He smiled.

"What's in your lap, a *Bible*?"

"Yes."

Eyes twinkling. Mind working. He said:

"It's okay to just watch TV...By the way, what's your name?"

"Ron," he said, hollow.

"Well, Ron, go ahead and watch. I'll see you later...Ron?"

Ron looked. "Yes."

He leaned, close to ear; said in hushed voice: "I know Him too, Ron. I've known Him for two years." He backed away. Ron looked surprised; John knew.

Hesitating, said: "Three for me."

John smiled; stroked his mustache.

John saw him two weeks later at dinner. John had been on vacation. Entering the day room to catch football scores on the news, he was sitting to his left, on one side of the far end of a long recreation table. It paralleled the Ping-Pong table's length. John almost laughed. Ron sat opposite a young, blond, girl who eyed him with disgust.

A problem—with *medicine*!

Tapioca pudding drooled down his chin into his plate. "Oh, God!" the girl said, rising, taking her tray.

John returned to the TV, as she passed him and sat in front. He watched the scores—grinning, stroking his mustache. He saw him try chicken.

What the hell, he thought, lips lining faint grin. He frowned, removing the smile, and walked behind him.

"It's okay, Ron," he said, kneeling. Mouth to ear, he whispered: "God understands. He won't judge you, even though that *bitch* did..."

Eyes wet, pudding on chin.

What the hell. He selected napkins; wiped the pudding. Standing, he delicately removed knife and fork and began slicing the chicken smaller. Oh, *well*. Pursed lips; slight wince.

"All the time you want, Ron..." he repeated. Dr. Kaswell and his *amazing* pharmaceutical house-of-horrors, he thought. How does it feel being a vegetable? He nodded approval as Ron, with difficulty, swallowed. "That's *good*, Ron. Every time means we have less left, less to go back to..."

The remaining table members ate quietly, not looking. Lenny, a ten year old, finished and played Ping-Pong with Kelly, one of the teenage girls, as John and Ron watched.

Everyone else long finished as Ron ate.

They were playing checkers later that week.

"Do you mind that I always win, Ron?" asked John, removing Ron's remaining pieces.

"No, I don't mind. I think..."

"What did your doctor say about being in touch with reality?" Eyed Ron. "Are you ready for another game?"

"No. Go ahead."

John set his. Ron did likewise; slower.

"You want to be black?" John asked.

"Okay."

"So, what did he say?"

"He…said…he'd give me medicine…to get me in touch with reality," Ron said.

You need a good swift kick.

"So you think it's working…getting you in touch?"

"I think so…I mean, it is, but…" Drew breath. Sighed. "It's rough…but, like…I used to get an *erection* when I played Ping-Pong with Kelly…I…wasn't used to — *girls*…But now, with *reality*, doesn't happen…I'm even afraid…"

"Of what?"

"…I might not like…girls…" Ron asked; grimaced. He rose. "It's personal. I should only be telling my *psychiatrist*."

John touched his arm; held a hand there. "I think you like girls, Ron," he said.

"You do?"

"Yeah, sure." Cocky grin. "Yeah, man. I've seen you look at girls." He smiled.

Ron avoided his eyes.

"Have a seat, Ron."

"You know, liking girls is okay, Ron…according to the *Bible. Song of Songs*, man." He patted Ron's arm; held his hand there. Sensing discomfort, removed it. They played, watched TV; Ping-Pong.

"You think…God would try to…take back sexual feelings?" Ron asked. John stared; mind running.

"No, Ron…I don't believe so…" I've got to finish these and I'll have won every game, but I'd better not right now. "...You see...the fact is, Ron, it's okay to like girls...but (head shaking) I don't know about *lusting*, Ron." I said *that*?

Surprise!

Ron insisted his desires were normal!

John nearly smiled; held it. "Ron, *come on.* You said yourself that when you played Kelly you got *an erection!*...Isn't that extreme? What would the *Bible* say?"

Extreme pain; mouth opened, closed, opened: "I'm going to watch TV" He rose.

"Okay, Ron," John said. "But think about it, will you?"

A few days later, John was glad to hear that Ron was having a rough time, but was angry—bewildered—Ron wouldn't talk with him. He'd seen him quietly, obvious agitation, walking hallways, playing checkers with patients and staff: On an evening his parents had visited, he wanted sedation to quickly sleep to escape anxiety.

"What's bothering him?" he asked nurse Sarah. They were in a small snack area.

"Well..." She surveyed the activities room. "I shouldn't tell you," she said, hushed, "but nurse Genaro said he simply *had* to speak with her last night. He didn't trust other regular staff. Seems he has some obsession about becoming a...homosexual. Uh..." A nervous smile creased her lips. "...for some *religious* reason God is trying to take away his feelings for women...Crazy, huh?" She laughed.

"Completely," John said, smiling. "What does she think started this?"

"Who knows?" she said. "He couldn't wait for his doctor this morning. He rushed into his office. But he came out a little calmer. His face wasn't so tense..."

While John was mopping the floor, Ron passed. He let him circulate more.

Catching eyes rounding the corner, he said: "Hey, Ron, I heard you've had a rough time. I feel pretty bad about it..." Ron passed—tremors evident; walked the other hallway. "Want to talk, Ron?"

"Shit!" he muttered. I *can't* let him reveal our discussion!...*He's got to understand*!

He passed again.

"Ron..." Silence. "You can't keep avoiding me..." he called. "We've got to come to an understanding...."

Halfway down the hall, he slowed, returned; stood a few feet away, facing him.

"...it's rough now, Ron," he said, pleading. *Shit, I really* am *pleading*. Ron looked, bleary-eyed. "You've got to understand that everything I shared about God and...*lust* (shit!) was...to *help* you. You know, one brother to another..."

"What does God want?" Ron asked. "He's too unknowable...I don't *know*."

"I don't know, Ron. I'm no minister, or psychiatrist..."

"You're a *source*," Ron said; eyes black, shiny mushrooms. "You spoke God's *thoughts*—a Christian! I *know*. Who am I?"

"That's right, Christian brother. But this place is secular." He thought quickly. "...they don't tolerate Christians in the secular world, you know." Moist beads lining eyelid ends, smoothing over eyes, he nevertheless peered in a strange, detached way.

Approval: please! I'd like to ring his fucking neck!

"I don't know," Ron said dreamily. "Something's pushing me—can't say. Damn!" Face convulsed. "Things...blurred from this medicine. Bright *lights* in this place! Got to go. Keep walking..."

John grabbed a shoulder.

"Please, Ron. Secret's ours. Okay? Brother to brother." Ron jerked; walked.

Down the hall, before entering the activities room, he smiled strangely back; said: "My psychiatrist represents

God…I think—*hope*. I can't deny him…my…best…efforts.
I can't deny God. I can't deny him…anything…"

John touched his forehead and knew he'd been
sweating.

On entering the ward some days later nurse Dorothy
instructed him to wait for Ron Thatcher's psychiatrist to
speak with him later that morning.

John stroked his mustache.

❧❧❧

Ron Horsley

*Ron Horsley is a writer/artist/editor who currently resides in Las Vegas. His fiction has appeared at **Dark Planet**, as well as the excellent Canadian magazine **On Spec**. He is the editor of the acclaimed anthology The Midnighter's Club and co-creator of the extremely funny on-line comic strip Tastes Like Irony (**www.tastes-like-irony.com**).*

"You never get a second chance to make a first impression" was a phrase that kept creeping into my mind as I read the following story about individuality versus familial identity, and the extent that some of us are willing to go to in order to be loved and accepted.

—JNW

IN THE EMPTY COUNTRY

✠ By Ron Horsley ✠

S he never knew it was to be the day that everything she thought of as identity, and comprehension, about family and loneliness, would be flung into her face. Ripped to paper and ribbon shreds before she could repair herself.

A glorious day; she'd looked forward to it with all the joy and dread and ultimate terror a person will feel when mentally marking down a calendar towards something so desirable as to be horrifying in its realization.

"I can't handle this," Sharon insisted, looking out the car window as the house snuck itself closer and closer to their approaching car. The car's interior, originally blessed with air conditioning, now seemed instead the cold she exaggerated in her mind to share in common with concentration camp-bound trains in Nazi Germany.

"Sweetheart, they're going to *love* you." John chided,

beginning the slow turn to park the car against the curb in front of the house that held throne at the furthest arc of the cul-de-sac. The car slowed; suddenly everything held a tangible clarity, screaming for her attention: the brightness of the half-overcast day, sun struggling to come out from behind the clouds, gravel crunching under the wheels, the whir-hum of air vents from the climate-control console hanging above her blowing on her goose-pimpled skin. *Too much*; it all seemed to speak in a dozen different languages, all translated to *Go home, go back home with your handsome fiancée and don't tempt the Fates by meeting the people responsible for his being in the world for you and you alone. Go home and don't tempt them by finding out the truth.*

That was silly. Her mother's voice, talking in her head. Telling her not to go out, not to risk anything, stay at home where it's safe.

She'd spent every day since high school graduation—from the very first decision to go to college out of state instead of attending the community college in her mother's hometown—fighting that voice. It was the same voice that had made her accept dates, accept sex, accept John when he finally stumbled into her life her first day working as a paralegal, his as a courier. The voice was behind her fear, and with that realization she found the sensory deluge dulled to whispers; she could settle that nausea in her stomach with a clenching of teeth, a forced smile.

"I'll be okay. You're right." She turned to the man driving. God, it was amazing. A lot of women (and many men too) would have called John Veritas Smythe a plain-looking man. Not unattractive, she imagined them clucking, obviously no Mutant or Ernest Borgnine, honey. But no Brad Pitt, either.

Well, who'm I, then, she secretly smiled, *Tyra Banks*?

He had a head of dark-brown hair, between the brown hues of chestnut and the pitch of a rich mahogany. It was kept short with a little cowlick he was always trying to keep down with styling gel and never quite making it. As his hands slid across the black-leather steering wheel, she noticed again how good and strong his hands were— smooth-knuckled with fast, deft fingers (oh, she knew how deft those fingers were, all right, to ever pore and sinew's reach).

He caught her looking and gave her a sunny grin; the kid's grin she'd liked when, standing in her boss's office, amidst shag carpet and wood paneling in bicycle shorts and short-sleeved T-shirt with the logo "HERMES COURIERS" stenciled on its right breast, he'd asked her out on a date after she'd signed for a package.

She put a hand out to his arm, holding them both in a pause of time just after he put the car in park, about to get out.

"Are they going to care, you know — ?" her eyes wanted to finish the question instead of having to make it real by finishing it out loud, and risking a real answer.

"About you being black?" he said, his sunnyness faltering.

"No, I know they wouldn't care about *that*, you've already made that clear." She smiled softly; it didn't reach her almond eyes. "I mean about...the doctor visit."

His hands reached out, clasping her, enveloping her hands in those agile fingers. He was warm, but there was always a cool edge to his touch that oddly attracted her on top of everything else. "Sharon, endometriosis isn't something you chose to get. It isn't anything you asked for. Do you really think if they don't care about your skin color, that somehow they're going to take exception to you having a disease?"

"I realize what you're saying, but..." her eyes were wistful. She had a heartbreaking inability to lie that had always, she suspected, been the quality he liked best in her. "This isn't like AIDS or diabetes or something. I can't have kids now, John. The doctor said too much distortion of my tubes took place before the pain drove me to get treatment. I was stupid and now we can't have any kids of our own. People whose sons can't give them grandkids...especially when it isn't the son but the daughter-in-law's fault—"

"Be quiet about that right now." John gripped her hands tighter. "You told me yourself you thought the first pains were just related to your periods, you've always had heavy times around the end of the month. So you didn't realize that you had it until it caused the damage—so what? That'd be like me blaming a man who got hit by a bus for not seeing it sooner. There's no point in seeking blame, and there's no blame in my opinion to find a home for. So don't go looking to let it get adopted in my parent's house, okay?"

His eloquence never surprised her. He'd composed a poem for her on their first date; the one and only first date of its kind: she'd bedded him without worrying about commitments or disease or anything of that kind. It'd been the last time she'd felt completely good about herself, because three weeks after that, it'd been the cramps, and the nausea...then the doctor: kind-faced, grim. Sitting there with charts in his hand and Johnny's hand in hers...

She bowed her head, closing her eyes, feeling his warm-cool-to-the-touch hands.

"You're right." She choked a little. "You're right."

"And even if somehow they *did* take exception, which they *won't*," he corrected hastily, "then to Hell with them anyway."

"John—"

"Don't worry. They won't mind."

"If you say so, then I know it's true."

"Okay then. Ready for soda and bratwurst?"

She smiled wide, affected her Butterfly McQueen parody that was their private gag. "Law, sir, ain't there-be no greens n' chitlins for alla Gawd's chillun?"

He laughed—it always caught him off-guard.

"Yessuh, Mammie, soon's I get some'a *yaw's* sweet greens," and he gave her a quick, riotous tickle against the side before evading her retaliation, hopping the car and hurrying around the Blazer to help her out on hers.

She took a breath she hoped he didn't see, took his hand, and was led up to the house that now seemed less ominous—just a nice, brownstone ranch after all, with yellowing white trim, and a ceramic cupid bird fountain in the mulched flowerbed that ran alongside the front veranda porch.

He pulled open the screen, leading her in with his other hand. There were the sounds of pool water, splashing. Kids, laughing; parents murmuring, telling dirty jokes. Somebody spilling a beer on their shirt, somebody else yelling for *Marilyn, bring those damned* hot-dogs *over before the grill gets cold.*

Then he was opening the front door (she marveled at that—she came from a neighborhood where it was unfathomable to ever leave a door unlocked, much less the front door to your house) and pulling her in, calling out their arrival.

"Mom?" he shouted. There was a mild cheer as his voice was recognized.

He smiled, turned his head back to Sharon.

"Welcome to the Smythe family," he laughed, blowing away the last vestige of her Mother's voice in that joyous chuckle.

Mother Smythe was *Marilyn* to her, Sharon was told. *Just call me Marilyn.* Yes, Sharon smiled warmly, She of the Damned Hot-Dogs. She was given a surprising hug by the woman, who was at least a head-and-a-half shorter, red-haired and bright-faced, wearing a flower-print dress and sagging-fat arms like some old-world Mama in an Italian farce. But her face and dimples were all Welsh-Irish-German mutt-American, according to John's talks about his family beforehand.

She held Sharon's hands in her hand, pulling her arms apart slightly to regard her.

"Well," she said to John, "it looks like you *finally* picked someone that *you* need to work be worthy of, instead of the other way *around*, Johnny."

"*Mom.*" An old language; the language of Embarrassed Son, Happy Mother. Often spoken, never well-translated except to those the Son is embarrassed in front of.

"Never mind, dear. Welcome to our family." She hugged Sharon again, then heard the holler of the hot-dog barker. "I have to go, dear, Johnny's father is a great grill-cook, but he's the definition of short-order, as in short on *patience.*" A lithe giggle; with a whisk of dress hem, John's mother was off to the kitchen.

So it continued. John had a smattering of cousins, direct *and* once-removed (*Get the whole variety pack*, Sharon mused as a herd of various-headed children ran past, wearing damp bathing suits and swim-trunks, running from the back hallway with water pistols in hand to wage war in the crystalline-blue pool she saw glints of through the kitchen and dining room windows).

He introduced her to Reba Clandike, one of John's ex-girlfriends.

"Oh, don't worry about it," Reba answered the momentary stiffness in Sharon's smile that had unconsciously risen once the introductions were made in full. "It's not like I'm going to go stealing this *troll* away from you. I found myself a *much* better way to spend my free time."

She referred to the gentleman who, smelling of spilled

beer on his golf shirt, walked up behind her and gave her a goose that she yelped at and slapped his chest for. He was dark-haired, similar to John, but with a gaunter face and more seams around his eyes. His hazel eyes glimmered with a mixture of humor and Old Milwaukee.

"Pleasedtomeetchou," he blurred, holding out a hand to be shaken. Sharon took it, looking to John.

"This is Eddie," John said, patting Eddie on the shoulder.

"Your brother?" Sharon smiled more genuinely at the clarification. Eddie was the halfhearted troublemaker— John's older brother by two years.

"The very same black sheep you've heard and admired," Eddie said, attempting charm.

"How many of your ex-girlfriends am I going to meet at this shindig, John?" Sharon asked.

"Just Reba," Eddie proffered, "unless you're hiding a whole closet *full* of 'em, Johnny." Eddie made a salacious wink that looked ugly and twisted to Sharon. "Didn't realize Johnny liked a slice of the ole' rye loaf."

"Let's get you in the living room, Eddie." Reba took Eddie's arm.

"But I wanted to tell this joke I heard—"

"Let's *go*, Eddie. You've told your best joke already."

Eddie was led away as Sharon turned to John.

"I already know that look," he said, hands upraised, palms out to her.

"I can take a redneck brother." Sharon gave John a kiss on the cheek. "Just don't start drinking Old Milwaukee and go laughing all over the place, okay?"

"Deal."

"In hindsight, I should've expected your family couldn't all be perfect."

John smiled, trying to lighten her up. "Hindsight is what Eddie Smythe's all about. C'mon and I'll introduce you to Dad."

Bill Smythe was a titian-haired man with a smile that cracked his face, but by the laugh-lines at the sides of his nose, smiling wasn't an alien concept to him. Sharon had plenty of uncles that helped her to identify Bill Smythe as the Loving Curmudgeon. She could see the stamp of Bill's features in Eddie's as Eddie brought his dad another beer. Bill nodded to her during the introduction, one hand holding the beer against his paunch while the other hand turned burgers and bratwurst on a grill roughly the side of a Buick.

"Nice to meet you." He smiled a thin grin that was more to John than her. "Want a brat?" He proffered one with a nudge of his grilling tongs.

"I'll get one soon, thanks." Sharon looked at the pool that dominated most of the small backyard and patio.

The cousins were shouting, spraying each other with the water pistols. There was a tow-headed child, two brunettes who could have been twins, a red-headed waif-in-training with a rash of freckles across the entire length of her pinched face. She cried as water got down the back of her bathing suit.

"Kind of reminds me of Eddie's camp," John remarked, seeing her glance and trying to change the subject.

"Really?" Sharon asked. "You never mentioned being a summer-camp kid."

"He wasn't." Bill took a draught from his beer. "Johnny-here got measles the summer we were going to send him to Camp Sakoset. Eddie went while Johnny stayed home, sick and throwing up half the summer. He got an ear infection right after, so by the time Eddie got back in July, Johnny was run-through just about every prescription the pharmacy had in stock."

"I'm going to go talk to some folks," John said, hugging her. "You going to be okay for a little while, alone in this madhouse?"

"I'll be fine," she returned his hug. "I'll just chat up your ex-girlfriend and the donkey that amazingly resembles your brother."

Even Bill laughed at that, though he kept his eyes on his smorgasbord of grill offerings.

"Marilyn, I was wondering if I could see some of John's childhood photos."

Marilyn was mixing egg salad at the kitchen counter. A cousin screamed outside as they cannonballed into the pool, Bill hollering at them not to splash water too close to the grill.

Marilyn smiled sadly. "I only wish we had any, dear. We lost Johnny's baby pictures in a fire when the boys were young."

"High school photos?" Sharon asked.

Marilyn shook her head. "No. He didn't pose for any. The poor boy was incredibly shy about his acne, you know how that can be." She continued mixing egg salad.

Sharon had wondered about it, only because she'd seen so many framed photos of Eddie around the house, especially in the short hallway between the front living room and the kitchen.

Eddie with Bill, fishing. Eddie with Bill, holding a string of caught smallmouth bass. Eddie, in a graduation robe and mortarboard, tassel bright gold against navy blue, the school colors for Dennison High, where he and then John had graduated. Eddie, in football jersey and padded pants.

"Not quite as handsome as your catch, but close."

Reba stood behind her as she looked at the pictures in the hallway, hanging on neat little brass-plated nails that no doubt their father had griped and fumed his way through mounting to the wall.

"Hi," Sharon turned.

"I'm sorry about Eddie," Reba breathed heavily. "Get more than half a beer in him, he's an utter fuckwit."

Sharon giggled at the obscenity, unable to help it. Reba smiled at her sound.

"So how are you two doing?"

"We're alright," Sharon nodded. "It's been rough since—" she stopped.

"Okay, *give*," Reba said, frowning politely. "Is there a problem? Seriously, woman to woman here, you don't know me from Adam and I understand, but I'd like to try and be your friend now that you're family. What's wrong?"

"I can't..." Sharon swallowed. "I mean...a couple of weeks ago, John and I found out I'm unable to have children."

Reba's face opened wide, eyebrows going up in a pained expression. She took Sharon's hands in her own, a weird mirror of John earlier in the car.

"I'm so sorry, sweetheart," Reba cooed. "It's terrible. Is there...is there a way around it?"

Sharon shook her head. "The problem isn't John, it's me. Endometriosis."

"Oh." Reba tilted her head to a side; for a moment Sharon felt anger. Anger at Reba for being so sincere (or even insincere, it didn't matter to her anger), anger at John for being so loving about it, anger mostly at herself...and that Mother's voice in her head.

"I suppose it's good then that you've got a guy like John with you."

"It is. It really is. Even when he's trying to make me laugh with that silly voice of his."

"What?"

"That Tennessee Williams impersonation he does, like Big Daddy from 'Cat on a Hot Tin Roof,'" Sharon saw Reba's confused expression. "You know, he always does it when he's being silly, because the voice is so exaggerated like Deep South?"

Reba shook her head. "Must be a thing between you two, hon'."

It wasn't. John had done it to a waitress at a restaurant once, when the girl was new and felt bad about messing up their order. He'd done it again during a party at work, celebrating his getting the new job, when he'd been kidding with the other architects.

"I guess so," Sharon said.

"What's going on in here, ladies?" Eddie came into the hall, a waft of beer-stink. Reba intercepted him in a half-hug before he got in front of Sharon.

"Just girl-talk, sweetie." Reba squeezed him around the stomach.

"You going to be ready to go soon?" Eddie asked. Reba nodded. Eddie noticed a photograph over Sharon's shoulder, and pointed it to it with a hand holding a near-empty beer can. She could hear liquid slosh inside. "*That* was a hell of a summer. Johnny tell you about that?" Sharon turned to see he was pointing at the picture of Eddie and their father, holding up the string of fish.

"Yes," Sharon replied, not thinking of the conversation. "It looks like you guys had a good time."

"Yeah. Dad felt bad about me being too sick with measles to go to Camp that summer, so while Johnny was gone, when I finally started feeling better, Dad took me out to Huron Reservoir to catch some smallmouth. Caught hell from Mom about taking me out after just getting well, but Dad didn't seem to mind her yelling that much."

"Wait. I thought *you* went to Camp Sakoset when you were twelve, and *John* had to stay at home with measles."

Eddie frowned, then smiled good-humoredly at her. "No, no, that's mixed up. I stayed home with measles. *Johnny* got to go to Camp Sakoset, with the counselor who kept throwing up during the canoeing lessons."

Sharon found Marilyn in the dining room, serving Dixie cups of fruit punch to the cousins who clamored with their dented cups for refills before running off to find other distractions.

"Marilyn, it's funny, but I don't know John's birthday, exactly. I mean, the details of it. What was his birthdate exactly?"

Marilyn laughed as she poured the last cup for the red-headed cousin. "That's so crazy of him. Johnny was always such a *bear* about making sure everybody knew his birthday. There was some movie or other he saw as a kid, where everybody forgot this girl's birthday no matter how many times she tried to get them to remember. And he got this idea in his head that nobody would remember unless he made sure he told them all. Anyway," she grinned, continuing to serve punch to the cousins, "It's June 17th, 1974."

"What day of the week was that?"

"Uh...I believe it was a Tuesday." She went to the kitchen to put away the remainder of the punch in the refrigerator. Sharon followed her.

"What time of day? Morning or evening?"

"Well, I'm sure I can't recall." Marilyn spoke distractedly, then turned directly around to face the kitchen window and called out, "Bill! Do you need more hamburger patties?"

While Bill yelled back of course, he needed more goddamned hamburgers, Sharon left the kitchen; a worried frown tried to chew its way from her brain to display on her lips. It got tangled up in an artificial smile that she held long enough to get past the cousins and some other snack-foraging neighbors at the food table in the dining room.

She went to the living room, which was mercifully empty of Eddie or anyone watching sports. She went to where her purse was left on the front table and got out her electronic day-planner.

The day planner had a calendar function on it, able to backdate any calendar date entered. She dialed in June 17th, 1974.

The machine gave her the date information for that year.

She looked at it, her face going still, and then silently put the organizer back into her purse.

I'm sure I can't recall.

She looked carefully in the bathroom mirror. Mother's voice reminded her that when you saw cracks in your face in the mirror, you were going crazy. Not because you had the cracks, she said—because you were looking for them.

No cracks. Except maybe in her head.

She splashed cold water on herself, then tried breathing deep. It did nothing except leave her damp and hyperventilating.

John went to camp but didn't. He dated Reba but she didn't remember anything about him like that over-used Foghorn Leghorn voice he liked to make when he was joking. His mother knew his birthday but couldn't be sure of the time or day.

A mother didn't forget birthday information. She just *didn't.* You didn't go through the "Ring of Fire," as the head breached the cervix, and forget what day of the week *that* little gem of a moment occurred on.

These people remembered things that hadn't happened to them at all, and then could tell things about John that he knew in only the vaguest terms, more like...

...more like what he'd heard other people describe, rather than lived through himself.

"John?" He was in the kitchen talking to a neighbor who was a childhood friend...or so she'd been told at the introduction. "Could I ask you to help me with something outside? In the car?"

"Sure." He followed her outside to the front sidewalk. She stopped when they were almost to the car, safely (she hoped) out of earshot of the house, and turned to face him. Surprised, he managed to catch his foot to stop from bumping into her, and took a step back.

"What's up?" His smile showed a frown in his eyebrows, a total-sum look of perplexity there.

"John, who are you?"

"What?" It was the classic question of fake curiosity. The question had been heard, and heard clearly.

"I asked you who you are."

"What's that supposed to mean?"

"What day is your birthday, John?"

"June 17th—"

"No, the *day*. The day of the week. Was it a Monday? A Wednesday?"

His head turned, looking at her sidelong, a half-grin trying to poke out of his lips. "What kind of gag is this, honey? A Tuesday, you know that. Ask my mother—"

"No, I *don't* know that. And neither does your mother. Is she your mother, John?"

"Of course she is!" John huffed a laugh, shaking his head. "Is this a gag of yours, something Eddie—"

"What *about* Eddie, then?" Sharon stepped forward. "There are photos of him all over the house with his father, but none of you, not a single one. And none of your mom, either. She doesn't even look like Eddie or you at all, no family resemblance whatsoever."

She looked back at the house, seeing it now as something horrendous again. A looming, lurking thing making its den at the end of this otherwise-cozy cul-de-sac neighborhood.

"And it was Eddie that had measles, John. But you said *you* had them, and that *he* went to camp. And Eddie made another comment, about a counselor who was always throwing up, but how would he have known about a counselor at a camp he never went to, John?"

John waved his hands in the air, making a show of exaggerated surrender. "I give up, Sharon! You got me—I'm a secret agent with the K.G.B, and I'm actually here to infiltrate secret government bicycle courier services and architectural firms, and to mate with the superior race of women!" He gave her his usual gamin grin. "Now c'mon—"

She recoiled from him. "What about Reba? She doesn't seem to remember anything about you, but you two dated for a while, didn't you?"

John's smile fell as quickly as it had built. "Sharon—"

"Don't 'Sharon' me anything, John. I've heard a lot of things from a lot of your family and friends today, and they just don't add up. I'd think that you were all having a joke on me, or just a lie or something, a way of introducing me to your quirky family, but it's more than that. Simple questions like your birthday--"

"I told you that!" John shouted. "It was a Tuesday! You can ask Mom—"

"John," she closed her eyes, "June 17th of that year was a *Monday*. I looked it up."

John stopped protesting.

His body went rigid; Sharon saw something she'd never expected: a blue-white glow flickered out from around him, like someone behind him had momentarily turned on-then-off a powerful spotlight, illuminating a viscous gas around him.

The flicker went away, and John was subtly different. He seemed smaller, he looked less handsome; less *bright* was the only way she could have described it. His hair looked more disheveled, his skin splotched like someone with pellagra, or early-stage melanoma.

"You're not..."

Her eyes slitted, trying to see clear again; the afterglow of that momentary halo still had her vision blurred around him. "You're not even...what *are* you, John?"

A cry, like an egg breaking to reveal a baby bird, a bird

with broken wings right from its release. The cry whistled out of John's direction, though she didn't see his mouth open. He looked at her with eyes like shards of summer sky—the only part of him unchanged.

"I don't know what I am," he replied quietly. "I started out...somehow...I can't rightly remember just how. I don't even know just how old I am...June 17th was as good a day as any...it's the same day as Eddie's birthday, actually—"

"What have you done to those people in there?" She felt her Mother's voice edge in her thoughts—*told you so.* "To me?"

"Nothing, really. I was just...oh god, I was born...I mean...whatever it was you could call it for me...I came into being with nothing: no form, no memories, no family, just...just some floating bundles of thought I called 'me,' and a few wisps of energy tied together around a mess of protons and willpower."

"I don't understand."

"I'm not sure you ever could," he answered. "It's been so long since I was in that state...I don't really know how to convey it to you. But...I felt so empty. So lonely. I had no voice, no hands, no way to touch...I wandered and tried things...tried to find scraps of acceptance, of place. I somehow found myself here...with a man who had lost his wife to breast cancer, and a son who resented his father, thought he'd ignored his mother until the illness was too late. I...found myself able to ingratiate myself into their lives."

"Bill? And Eddie?"

John nodded, a slow bob of his chin.

"I have something...it's what fantasy books and fairy tales would call a glamour. A way to hide things. Not quite like the old fairy tales, of course. I don't make pots of gold shine at the end of the rainbow or anything. But I can make people remember differently. I can look different, depending on memories. I can shape and change people, the way they interact and think, and then use that to ingratiate myself."

"Why would you manipulate people you love like that?" Sharon demanded.

"Because it's the only way I can really exist with a definite form, a definitive life." John shrugged, holding out his hands to her. "As I take their pre-existing memories and shape them around myself, it gives me the solidity to start making them remember me, so that I can be more and more real. It's a cumulative effect. The more people I interact with, weave their minds around each other, make the realities bend a little more, the more leverage I have to keep myself grounded, and real. After Bill and Eddie, I was able to bring Marilyn in as my...our mother and Bill's wife. It made Eddie love his father again, and gave Bill something of his life back. When that pain was threatening to ruin things, I made them forget their first woman completely. It works better with Marilyn their since the beginning."

"What are you, really?"

"I can't..."

His lips quivered, his eyes were wet, gleaming. And past that...something else.

A shine, not quite the color of old pearl necklaces, not quite the glint-flicker of sputtering neon, in his eyes. It held for a flicker's beat, then was gone again.

"I don't know. Maybe a wish? An angel, fallen from heaven? An alien, something from another dimension? All I know is not where I was from, but I know what I was. I was lonely. So lonely and so empty I couldn't begin to draw you a picture in your mind of it."

The *real* him, inside, was something she tasted on the air between them; an aroma of sweat and honey, of dust and moth's wings stirring up early evening pollen from flowers...faint, so faint that the next breeze almost completely erased it from the air. She realized the full meaning of what he was: there was *nothing* to him, no body or eyes to look at her with, no hands to hold hers in, without those same things.

And the reverse of that: she remembered how suddenly *cold* she'd felt, how hard and hollow she'd felt in the pit of herself when the doctor had made his announcement to her in a clean, smug clinic office...she could sense on some level that the loneliness, the empty that John described, was something so massive it made her own pain like a divot in a golf course, next to the massive chasm inside him.

"Then why all the problems?" Sharon asked. "Why the little mistakes, like your mother not remembering just when your birthday was, or the fact that Eddie was the one who was sick with measles and not you? Or the fact that there aren't any photographs of you in the family? At that rate, there must be a hundred little things that someone could've discovered—"

"*I can't keep it up, don't you understand?*" John's face collapsed. "It *hurts*. It sucks a little more of me out when I have to reshape my life to each new person. I can't *help* the mistakes I made—think of them as flaws in a stage rehearsal. I've tried to use them to sort out the flaws, clean up the mistakes—the more people I can weave together into a family to shape me, the more they can correspond with each other, strengthen the effect. But—" he waved his hands in the air to emphasize a frantic, paralyzing frustration.

"But it also means more people to add things up and find the gaps where you fit in, doesn't it?" Sharon finished. John lowered his hands and nodded.

"The more people, the more glamour, the more *energy*. I get some of it back, sort of like the way a farmer's effort yields him food and crops in return. But soon...the effort was outweighing the energy I was getting back. My parents...Eddie...cousins...neighbor kids and *their* parents...so many different people I was weaving together, making fit around me...can you imagine if you only had so many bolts of cloth to make a suit, but you kept getting bigger and bigger, the suit gets tighter and tighter? And pretty soon…you run out of cloth. But you *keep* growing…something was close to bursting, even though I had shape and form. So I thought…well, I didn't think, I *knew*…I was lonely, still…I had no one with me in the nights, or when I was home from work…I had to still find something to define me in a way nobody else did…"

"My god, John, is that what *Reba* was? What I—" her hand went to her mouth, an 'O' of shocked realization. *"Is that all I am to you? Some mirror for you to work from?"*

"Sharon, don't ask me that—"

"Am I? Damn it, *am* I? And tell me the truth, I don't want your *glamour* or whatever-you-call-it."

Sharon looked more carefully. Had he had thicker hair when they'd first met? And hadn't she just remarked the other day, while seeing him shaving in the mirror and getting ready for his job interview, that he was looking better, a little meatier around his previously-thin arms and thighs? Had he been constantly changing, even with her, to make himself an identity more in line with her own inner desires for a certain man, the *right* man?

"When I met you…I needed identity. Yes. So yes. That's your answer. My family was able to keep me alive, keep me semi-solid long enough to try and find a life. I could try things like meeting other kids in the street, going through puberty, growing up. But it wasn't enough. I still didn't have any full existence. I'd given my family each other, but I needed someone to define *me*, and me alone."

"Reba?"

He nodded. "But you've met Reba. Reba barely knows herself, what could she really do for me? She wanted somebody shallow and thin like her, somebody who no more defines themselves than they shape the events they read about in the newspaper each day. I had to use her for a little while, long enough to give me more *self*, long enough for there to be the John Smythe you met and liked."

"So he's a fiction, then? Part of your power? A complete fucking *lie*?"

"*Nothing* I am is a lie!" He wheeled on her. Then, seeing her own pain and anguish illustrated, a mirror of his own mercurial furies, he shrank back. "I mean...I *don't* lie. I...seam together things that didn't normally meet. People who didn't normally know each other. I make a metaphysical overlap into the world, and situate myself in its pocket. That's all. What's *truth*, anyway? If it's what you can remember, then that's mutable. Better to write down your thoughts, but someone can easily erase and edit to their own liking what you've written, can't they? I'm not a lie, Sharon—I was never a lie, not you, not to *anyone*. But especially not you. I was simply...more truth than you would have ever found on your own. I became the man you love, and I *am* the man you love. Don't you realize that when I say I would give my life for you, when I say that I will stand and swear before God that, richer or poorer, sickness and in health, I will be with you, that it *has* to be the truth? I can't lie when I don't exist without your reality to define me! They..." he swept a hand at the house. "They're like a collection of old toys to me, now. Some pile of things I played with, then grew out of."

"So you made me love you."

"No, Sharon. You made *me* love *you*. More to the point, you made me *to* love you. And I *do*." He dared to step close to her, coming to within shared-breath range. "I always will." Silently, he reached for her hands. She didn't resist. He raised them to his lips, kissing them.

"I'll tell them all."

He froze in mid-kiss on her ring finger, where the half-carat diamond winked.

"What?" Barely a breath.

"I'll go right back in there and tell them everything. The lies, the mix-ups, the jangled memories they think are of you but are really each other's. I'll take your pretty patchwork life and I'll rip it to separate little cloths again. You've got your power, but it's still a lie, no matter how pretty you cover it up. And I'll tear it to pieces just to set those people free of you. You'll stop completely without them."

She felt the temperature in his hands drop perceptibly. He felt like he'd been holding ice cubes before gripping her fingers.

"Why…" he sucked in the words, trying to gasp hem out like valuable air, "why would you d-do that, Sharon?"

"*Unless*," Sharon continued, biting each word so that it would seem as sharp as her resolve was soft, "you can do something for me."

He smiled.

She read his look immediately. "No. No lies. No *wishes*. You have a power, a power to change things, right? A power to, what did you call it? 'Overlap,' and make yourself fit in that space. You can change things to make a better identity for yourself, is that true?"

He nodded.

"Good."

It was the *real* smile this time.

Sharon brought the cake in with a sigh. It was a hot day, *damned* hot. A breeze blew through the kitchen's screen door, and that helped, but she was going to finally press John for air conditioning to be installed for individual rooms next week, when his bonus check came in from the architect firm's new commission.

She looked over the dinner table, resplendent with its frosted cake, ice cream dollops in a ruby-red punch and cut-crystal serving bowl, hamburgers, buns, cheese slices, a deli-tray of vegetables and ranch dip…a whole summertime assortment, as befitted any good party.

She was about to check the banner to make sure the heat wasn't making it come unstuck from over the double-doors of the dining room when she heard the clang-chime of the doorbell. She gave a quick glance—it looked all right—and went to answer the door.

"Hey, there, Baby Jane!" Marilyn beamed. 'Baby Jane' was somehow the affectation that the woman had come to indelibly write over her mental image of her daughter-in-law. Sharon didn't mind--she was used to the family humor now. "Here you go!" she dumped into Sharon's grasp a massive Pineapple spice cake that was redolent of cream cheese and cinnamon. "Are we first?"

"Of course we're first, you damned fussbudget," Bill Smythe chortled, brushing into the room. He gave a quick bow-and-half-shoulder-hug to Sharon, and then swung his free arm around to reveal a six-pack of sweating Budweisers. "You mind I put these in the fridge? They've been in the car for the last twenty miles from the Easy-Go, and I'd like to keep them cool."

"You know where the kitchen is," Sharon grinned. To Marilyn: "Let me put this on the table with the rest of the food and we'll see about getting hold of John on the phone."

"He's late?" Marilyn asked, following Sharon into the dining room.

"Not really. It's just that he said he'd be home earlier for today, you know, so I asked him to make sure to pick up a few last-minute things. He should've been home by now, though."

"Smythe men are always coming in last," Marilyn laughed brightly.

Not always, Sharon thought. *Not always, if at* all.

Just as the Pineapple cake was relegated to its place on the dinner table, another front-door sound—that of it opening. There was a clunk of briefcase against the floor molding by the foyer table, and then the shout.

"Honey? Mom and Dad already here?"

"Yes!" she called out. "Your Dad's stocking us with booze as usual."

"The hell I will," the resultant hoarse cry came from

the living room, where already the sounds of a football game on the television were coming from. "I'm not buying my son booze when he can afford his own damned condo."

John was smiling as he came into the kitchen. Marilyn had already joined her husband, so Sharon and he were alone in the kitchen.

He came up behind her as she was putting out cocktail napkins, and put his arms around her in a hard embrace. "Love you," he whispered against the back of her neck.

She reached up behind her to pat his cheek. "You, too."

A cry came from the upstairs. A baby-bird sound.

"You check," John said, kissing her. "I've got a few gifts to put together, if I can get Dad's attention away from the Steelers."

"Okay."

Upstairs. Bedroom to the left, across from the master bath.

A room, decorated in soft blues, with little red, yellow, and navy bears cavorting in repeating patterns against a background of white and blue stripes. Thick carpeting that now sported an assortment of plastic toys and a stroller.

She leaned over to touch his cheek. Immediately, Peter's cries stopped. He gurgled happily up at his mother.

"Who's the lucky birthday boy?" she asked with a baby's coyness.

Peter looked up with adoration at the moon his mother was in his pleasant toddler life. A thin line of thrilled drool cascaded milkily down his chin. She took hold of his bib and wiped it off.

He had light olive skin, and black, shining hair curled in a bob around his sweet, round head. When he smiled, however, he was all his father: sun and rays in that smile.

MASQUES V

And a shine, not quite the color of pearls and not quite the glint-flicker of sputtering neon, in his eyes when he looked sidelong at her, grinning with baby-mischief.

"Miracle baby," she whispered, smiling at him. "Little miracle baby, you're your father's boy, you know that?"

Peter *did* know that. He smiled, *ooh*ed, and slapped his pudgy hands together merrily.

❖ ❖ ❖

During those first nights, after the hospital delivery, she'd worried. She'd feared that when he wasn't crying for food or to be changed in the middle of the night, it was because he wasn't there at all. Just an empty bassinet and a mobile that spun lazily over empty air. That her own sleeping, her own not-thinking of him, would somehow make him fade away like an old movie special effect.

But that fear had passed when she'd realized that, like his father, Peter too, needed someone to help him find the world. Maybe not as dramatically as John did, but in the way all children need their parents to help them feel and smell and begin to understand the abstract shapes that will become their lives.

And as she looked down at Peter, and began hearing the sounds of Bill and John argue over putting together a toddler bicycle (Peter's prize gift), she considered that, maybe together, all three of them could seek out what it meant to be alive, to be loved, and to be with someone who defined you, who made the world yours.

As family.

"The family is the country of the heart."
Giuseppe Mazzini
(1805–1872)

John Maclay

*As well as being a life-long friend, John Maclay has enjoyed a long career as both a publisher a writer—witness his skill at the short story in such collections as **Dreadful Delineations**, **A Little R Book of Vampire Stories**, **Night Tales**, and **Mind Warps**. John graces the pages of **Masques** yet again with this unnerving gem about the thin line between fantasy and accountability.*

—JNW

ACTION FIGURES

✠ BY JOHN MACLAY ✠

He was thirty-five and single, but he didn't have a bad life. There were his job at the computer store, a couple of male friends for drinks after work, and his parents' house in the suburbs to visit on the weekends. His apartment in an old loft building wasn't bad, either.

And there was Judy. Small and dark-haired to his blondness, she was an adequate sex partner from time to time, though neither of them wanted to commit to anything further. Still, he was finding more and more that something was missing, especially in that department.

Quite frankly, the sameness was boring him. And when a man was bored, he had a little trouble being a man. Even if he did succeed, it wasn't as good as it should be.

So he began looking around. And what he found wasn't another real woman, or a surrogate from the street or a strip club.

No, what he found wasn't real, or the same, at all.

❖　❖　❖

One day after work, he was walking along a downtown street, taking his time getting home. He was glancing idly at the shop windows when he suddenly stopped in front of a toy store.

Being single and childless, he hadn't thought of entering such a place in more than twenty years. What had caught his attention, though, wasn't a bike, a chemistry set, or even a computer game.

It was a tiny figure—an action figure, he knew it was called—in a clear plastic bubble on a brightly printed card.

But it didn't represent a hero from the latest science fiction epic, as such figures always used to.

Instead, it was of a heroine. And she was scantily, or provocatively, clad as someone in a men's magazine.

What's going on? he asked himself. *Is this supposed to be a toy? Who's its audience? Surely not a child.*

Intrigued now, he went into the store, finding himself again in an innocent world of model trucks, dolls, and mechanical animals. But the action figure section was something else, indeed.

Here, along with the usual macho males, were even more plastic, six-inch women. They were dressed, or undressed, as lady wrestlers, or military types, or warrior amazons. Shrugging, he reflected that they had to be, to be true to type.

But he couldn't help knowing that another thing was operating. And a sudden, visceral feeling told him what it was.

Intentionally or not, dirty mind or not, this was sado-masochism in a toy store! Nor, while he tried to laugh it off, did the three other customers he noticed beside him deny the truth.

They were men, grown men. One was a fat, pimply, myopic guy of about twenty, whom he visualized spending his time reading SF magazines and making the excuse that the female action figures were in line with his interests. The second was a fortyish, business-suited man, who might have replied, if asked, that these "toys" were for his kids.

But the third, who silently told their real story, was a balding, mustachioed, leather-jacketed, sweating fellow, whose eyes devoured the little plastic women as dominatrices...or as prey.

Feigning casualness, he studied the three men, and the display. But then, obeying what was below his belt, he reached out, took a figure from the rack, walked to the cashier, paid for it, and left the store.

He would take the thing home and study it, he decided. Far be it from him not to be open to new experiences.

But this new experience would take him somewhere he never wanted to go.

Sex, for him, had always been a beautiful thing. It never had any edges; instead, it had been relaxing and almost holy. His times with Judy and the others before her, their soft bodies moving sweetly under him, had taken him as close to heaven as he ever hoped to get.

Now, though, there was this need to break the peace, the sameness. And he surely found it in this unlikely little woman—*devil?*—he had bought.

Sitting on the edge of the bed that night, he tore the clear bubble from the card. And what fell into his hand, making him involuntarily start with excitement, was a barbarian princess, wearing a tiny brown leather bra and thong.

However, there was more. She also had on arm gauntlets, knee-high boots, and a studded collar. And as if to banish any thought of innocence, her package also held a plastic knife and sword.

This is silly, he thought, as he again felt the stirring, total now, below. *Or pathetic*—am I to be aroused not only by sadomasochism, but this *form* of it?

But he was beyond thought now, and besides, what really was the harm? Alone, in the privacy of his home and of his mind, he could do anything he wanted.

So, fitting the sword and the knife into the tiny hands, he set the defiantly smiling princess on the bedside table.

Then he lay back and undid himself, as he had many times, in between real sex.

But he didn't reach into the drawer for a magazine, as before.

And the intensity of the experience that followed—the three-dimensionality, however tiny, of the object, but above all, the violence of her—left him, scarcely a minute later, with his head throbbing, and gasping for breath.

He was totally gone, and amazed. It had never been like that, nor had he imagined, in his wildest dreams, such sharpness of sensation. It was as though a door—to where?—had opened in his mind.

And yet, on the bedside table, there was the little figure...still smiling, brandishing her weapons, leading him on...to more.

During the weeks that followed, he paid more visits to the "toy" store, amassing quite a collection of miniature women. He tried to convince himself he was doing only that, and he even bought a glass case for them.

But, on the nights he lay on his bed indulging his fantasies, he knew better. They were still only fantasies, true, but they were taking increasingly bizarre turns.

There was the time when he bought flesh-colored paint at a hobby store, and made one of the figures totally nude.

And the time when he, well, made on of them touch him as he found his release.

The ultimate time, though, was when he discovered the power of two or more of the figures together.

He had read somewhere that men welcomed the spectacle of women fighting with or dominating other women, since it was a less guilt-inspiring form of what they wanted to do to the women themselves. Be that as it might, it was wildly exciting to him.

Now, on the bedside table, there were not only objects, but drama. The swords were directed from one figure to another, and the knives were at each other's throat.

Then—the female figures seemed to have a life, or death, of their own—two or more of them would simply gang up on another, and kill her, all pretense at a fair fight gone.

And he would help by painting blood on the naked, prone, weaponless victim, or by cutting off her tiny head.

In what world would this be taking place? he asked himself. In some violent, futuristic society, or in ancient Rome?

But he inwardly knew it was a perverted world of his own making, one in which he was increasingly becoming lost.

He tried to concentrate more on his job, his friends, and his parents. While less frequently now, he still made dates with Judy and had sex with her. And after a particularly warm, loving session, he was moved, the next morning, to throw some of the action figures away.

But he only bought new ones. And now, even *his* reality took a violent mental turn.

One night, while engaged with his lover, he chanced to look at the bedside table. Suddenly he realized that something, or someone, was missing. Much as he tried to concentrate on his real partner, he could scarcely perform without one of the tiny, violent women there.

So his mind simply made the transference, but also the next, inexorable step toward his ruin. He thought of Judy, first nakedly waving a sword...but then, which was far more perversely exciting, as a beheaded, bloody corpse.

From that time on, he could never have normal thoughts about sex again. And he made far fewer dates with his lover, since he didn't want to abuse a real woman, even mentally, and what little was left of his own conscience, in this way.

Still, he wasn't quite over the edge. He had his job, his friends, and his visits with his parents to partly counteract what was growing inside of him. While he knew—was yet sane enough to know—that his soul was deteriorating, not a single criminal thing, in actuality, had happened.

One evening, on his way home from work, he scanned the faces of the men he passed. Who among them guessed, he asked himself, what was going on in his sexual mind? And how many of them harbored evil fantasies like his own?

He shrugged then, and even smiled. Maybe his fears were unfounded, after all. Thoughts were not deeds. So long as one didn't really do anything, any fantasy was all right. It might even be the mind's way of answering a need, for novelty or the like.

So long as one didn't really do anything...do anything...

But then came the time when even the fantasy wasn't enough.

He wasn't conscious of it happening, but it did; that must be the way with obsessions. He withdrew from his friends, and made excuses to his parents when they called. He didn't see Judy at all, and didn't miss her. He only went through the motions at work, only because he needed the money.

To subsist...and to buy more figures. The rest of his hours, he spent in his apartment...where there were now hundreds of them, standing defiantly on every surface.

Late one night, when he was selecting one with which to gratify himself, he was able, for a rare moment, to draw back. What in the world *are* these things? he asked himself, as he had that first time in the store, what seemed like ages ago. Why are these little women—with their muscles, their leather, their weapons—*like* this?

And yet one of them—still his trusty favorite, a young, blond barbarian who was always smiling joyfully at her deadly craft—seemed to answer.

Because we're meant to fight and die, she seemed to say. *You and those like you have made us so. There simply isn't any other kind of woman for you.*

Nor was there, he knew. Not only could he no longer have normal sex, there was no such thing. And, he realized chillingly, there wasn't anymore even a shred of guilt.

But even worse was to follow.

To put it bluntly, that night he found himself unable to perform. Far from reaching the revelatory sharpness of the sadomasochistic sensation, he couldn't even summon the prerequisite for it.

Nor could it be guilt, nor any realization of his now definitely pathetic state, that prevented him: those were indeed now long gone, banished by the patent sharpness of the thrill.

No, it was the fact that he was jaded: not only by the sameness as before, but now also even by the sado-masochism. And if the figures couldn't do it for him, then what was beyond them that could?

He lay back on his bed, feeling a desolation the depths of which he could scarcely believe. Was he to have no more sex, ever—and not because his conscience couldn't bear the evil fantasy that was required, but because even that was uninspiring? If that was the case, he knew that he valued sex enough that his life might as well end.

Just then, however, he glanced at his favorite action figure of all. And she seemed to speak to him once more.

The answer is simple, she seemed to say, with a logic that finally damned him to Hell. *I'm a fake, and fake doesn't work for you anymore.*

But you are real, so you need to make it real.

You can do everything with her that you did with us—get ready for lots of blood, the little devil woman seemed to conclude, with her usual smile. *And whether you do turn it on yourself afterwards, or they kill you for it...I promise that your last time will be incredible.*

And so, initiating an act that would be even worse than the end of his own life...he reached for the phone and called Judy.

Then he got up, walked in a trance to the kitchen...and found a long knife in the drawer.

Thomas F. Monteleone

Thomas F. Monteleone's novels and short fiction have been gracing the field of speculative fiction for nearly four decades. A multiple Bram Stoker Award winner, Tom is co-founder (along with his wife Elizabeth) of Borderlands Press, and co-editor of the acclaimed and hugely successful series of **Borderlands** *anthologies. Tom's first* **Masque** *appearance is as quintessential a* **Masques** *story as we've ever seen, and one that will have you remembering old TV shows with something less than sweet nostalgia.*

—JNW

HOW SWEET IT WAS

✠ BY THOMAS F. MONTELEONE ✠

Most people can't remember a time without it in their life.

Not me.

Even if just barely. I was a little kid, maybe four or five, who spent most of his time playing with stuff like Lincoln Logs and Tonka Toys on the living room carpet. Until the day my mother opened the front door to let two workmen lug this big, polished mahogany box into the room.

"Where'd ya want this, ma'am?" one of them asked.

And the question kind of perplexed Mom, because she obviously hadn't thought of the answer ahead of time. So she paused, scanning the living room with great pensiveness, then said: "There. You can put it right there."

The workmen nodded and lifted the heavy piece of

furniture to the wall beneath the staircase. Its height came level with the sixth step, and it was then I noticed a single, thick-paned window in the front of the box. It was like a glass eye, looking back at me.

My mother thanked the men and they disappeared forever from my world. I asked Mom what the one-eyed box might be, and she said it was a *television*.

"What's it do?" I said.

"We can see pictures on it," said Mom.

"What kind of pictures?"

"Let's turn it on."

So I watched her insert a plug into those two slots in the wall—the same place I'd jammed a dinner fork a couple of months ago. I got what my dad called a "shock," and he got to go down into the pitch-black basement, where I heard him cursing a lot while he tried to find the "bad fuse." It sounded scary, and I didn't want to know any more about it.)

Anyway, watching my mother, I studied her movements as she turned a knob on the left beneath the glass window. It made an audible *click!* and there was a flash in the dark window, then it began to glow brighter and brighter. I stared through the glass and saw a matrix of intersecting lines, circles and a picture of an Indian. A humming sound came from the box.

And that was it.

"It doesn't look like anything's on." she said. "Let's try some of the other channels."

My mother reached for a larger knob under the right corner of the screen, and it made a harsh, yet muffled, *clunk!* as she turned it. The screen flashed, the speakers sputtered and hissed with static.

"I don't get it," I said, which is what my father would always say when he didn't understand something.

"Hold on, here's something…"

And there was…

Like nothing I'd ever seen before. The images remain

burned in my memory as if I saw them yesterday: black and white cartoon of a cat being chased by really dumb-looking dog, choreographed to some tinny, Thirties dance-band music. I sat transfixed by it all, including the primitive commercials for a kitchen cleanser called Ajax and some local appliance dealer called Luskins. The cartoon show was called *Film Funnies*, and it became, for little while, my favorite pastime as I sat cross-legged on the floor looking at the tiny screen over the television whose name I learned was Emerson.

But I soon learned to "change channels" with the big heavy knob on the right, and I discovered old Republic serials, quiz shows, and other stuff for little kids. As much as I loathe television today, that's how much I *loved* it back then. Wow, looking back, I can still feel the afterglow of the pure magic it was for me. It was my private window into a larger universe about which I knew practically nothing.

And so the shows curled over me like waves hitting a beach. Hour after hour, day after day, I watched and I learned. So much, so fast. Polio, Wonder Bread, The Big Picture, Chevrolets, Hula Hoops, rock-and-roll, Punch and Judy, the New York Yankees, the atom bomb, and Ovaltine were just a handful of the icons which imprinted me, shaped me.

I watched everything and anything the Emerson would find for me, but my favorite was *Mr. Curiosity*.

Despite being enhanced by the nostalgic lens of memory, the show's production values were cheesy—even for its own era. Mr. Curiosity was this guy dressed in a set of mechanic's overalls and an old football helmet, which were supposed to look like a spacesuit. The show would always open with him sitting at the controls of his rocket ship (which looked, even to the younger me, like a red wagon with some plywood panels in the shape of stabilizer fins drilled into the sides.). And his ship always had a few extra vessels in tow, which made it look more like a train, which he rolled across the sound stage accompanied by some bouncy piano riffs. He would sing this song which told me you "Gotta Get a Sense-a-Wonder 'bout the World!" and then he would spend the rest of the show telling us kids about the strange and wonderful world we lived on.

To this day, I can't remember *anything* specific Mr. Curiosity showed me or taught me. And that is very weird because I do remember absolutely *loving* the show, and counting down the hours until it would be on the air. All I can recall is that I believed Mr. Curiosity told me things I could never learn anywhere else, and that there was something special, something magical about the show which appealed like nothing else on television.

As I grew older and my parents sent me off to first grade, I guess I stopped watching *Mr. Curiosity*. I don't remember doing it with any sense of importance or ceremony, and if the show cancelled or pulled from the airways, I don't recall hearing about it. As time passed, the show just kind of passed out of my life, and I accepted it with the calm sense of the inevitable that allows all children to buy into the massive machinery of being and nothingness without going insane.

That was it. One day, *Mr. Curiosity* was no longer part of my life, and I didn't give it much thought. But every once in a while something would occur that brought an awareness of the show back into my thoughts. And it was always the same event.

As I grew older and learned the arts of conversation and beer-garden philosophy, the talk among friends would occasionally tip towards old television programming and favorite shows. Whenever this happened to me and my cohorts, something odd always followed: I would mention *Mr. Curiosity* and everybody would look at me with blank stares.

Nobody had ever heard of it—much less remembered it.

At first, I didn't think much of it. Some of my friends

were younger, some didn't get TVs into their homes until much later, some lived in different cities. And besides, I had no idea if *Mr. Curiosity* had been a local, national, or syndicated broadcast. But as more time passed, and I grew older, presumably wiser, and a lot more paranoid, I began to wonder why I was the only one who ever remembered watching Mr. Curiosity ride his rocket-train—knees high and wobbly—across the dull linoleum of a sound stage.

Once, while browsing in a B. Dalton's, I found a coffee-table book called *How Sweet It Was*, which purported to be the most comprehensive compendium of every television show that aired up until the time of its publication. It was thick and cyclopedic in appearance, and as I picked it up, I was reminded of the show that none of my friends remembered watching. I went to the table of contents, confident I could solve the mystery of my forgotten show. The book was divided into chapters which listed shows by type—variety, westerns, sit-coms, quiz shows, and of course, children's programming. In the back pages, I noted an exhaustive index.

This should take care of business, I thought, as I flipped through the book, seeking vindication.

But I was wrong—there was not a single mention of *Mr. Curiosity* within the book's 600-plus pages. Nothing. I spent more than a hour, standing at the bargain table, carefully perusing the pages, studying each photograph and caption. Was it possible, I had the title confused? Had some network "Suit" changed the name of the show when it went into syndication?

No. And no.

That prompted me to deepen my search, and in those pre-Internet days, it wasn't easy. Not every neighborhood library had the reference volumes that would contain the definitive information I craved. I tried alternate resources such as universities and their repositories of popular culture, museums of technology, and even letters to various television "pioneers." This took time, and progress proved grindingly slow. Years passed, filled with the obligations and obstacles of life—job, bills, wife, kids (you know the drill)—and my quest took a backseat to lots of other things. But I didn't quit, and by the time "to google" had become a verb form found in any contemporary dictionary, I was all but convinced there was no record anywhere of *Mr. Curiosity*.

So what was really going on? If there had never been such a show, the only sensible explanation didn't seem terribly appealing to me—I had hallucinated the entire program. Could I have been so creatively loony at such a young age?

No way. Impossible.

Gradually, despite any supporting evidence, I dismissed the notion I'd imagined *Mr. Curiosity*. I knew I'd seen the show; it had been *real*.

I began treating its existence the same way I did *gravity*—I knew it existed, but couldn't really prove it, so I just stopped thinking about it.

Things went along like that for years. I stopped counting. But it all changed when I was reading an anthology of short stories.

In one of them, a character waxed fondly of lost innocence and made a passing, quasi-literary reference to old television programs being the techno-equivalent of biblical parables or other cultural mythologies. His exact words: "Is it possible our *Winky Dink* or *Mr. Curiosity* will become the Aesopian lessons of a stainless steel future?"

While not exactly the poetic prose of Bradbury, the line struck me with the force of a Martian heat-ray. And its single, searing message covered me in its smoking ash: *This guy knows!*

My hands trembled as I tried to keep my place on the page. Other, less pleasant sensations included my tongue turning dry and thick, my eyes stinging. I felt a swell of abyss-staring fear rise and fall within me. I was panicking, and I wasn't even sure *why*.

I calmed myself by planning my next step.

The writer's name was Vincent Manzara, and while not one of my favorites, I knew his work well enough to know he'd been at his business for a while now. Certainly long enough to have remembered a show called *Mr. Curiosity*. The guy had a website for email, but I wanted to *talk* to him.

The publisher was a small press in Maryland. They had a website and a phone number on the dust jacket. There was only one thing I could do. After bugging the publishers, I tracked down the editor of the book in Ohio, and who, after some badgering, gave me the contact info on Manzara who also lived in Maryland, a couple of hours from me in Central Pennsylvania.

Piece of cake.

"You know," said Manzara. "In one sense, I'm not at all surprised to hear from you. And in another..."

"Yeah, I know what you mean," I said. "I hope you don't mind talking about this."

"No, not at all. I mean, you're not the first, actually."

"What? How many others?"

He tried to laugh, but he sounded nervous. "Well, I don't know. But a woman from Michigan sent me an email about two weeks ago—all freaked out because...well *you* know why..."

"So there's three of us?"

"So far. I guess I put that line in the story as a kind of bait. I wasn't sure it would have any effect, so I was really shocked when I got her note. That got me thinking *if there's two of us, maybe there's more*."

"And here I am."

"Yeah," said Manzara. "But you know what—now

that I know there's more of us, I actually feel *worse* than when I was feeling like I was the only one."

"I know," I said. "I'm kind of scared myself."

"Do you know *why* you're scared?"

I thought about that for a minute. "No, but I can't help the feeling."

Manzara paused, and I could detect a vacuum in the phone line, as if there was some other entity hanging silent in the space between our words, sucking up all the energy.

"Well," he said finally. "I've been thinking about this a lot—obviously—and I think there might be more to it."

"Like what?"

"I'm not sure how to start this, but I'll try." Manzara cleared his throat, then started up again. "Have you ever heard or seen something that…that gave you a weird feeling? A feeling that there was something *special* about, but you had no idea what it could be?"

I considered his question, but wasn't sure where he was going with it. So: "Can you give me an example?"

"Sure. A couple of years ago, I was watching the *History Channel* or *National Geographic* or one like that, you know? I hate most of the crap on regular TV."

"Yeah, me too," I added. "Go on."

"Hold on…I've got some notes on this stuff," he said. "Can you hang on while I pull them up?"

I said sure and waited through a few minutes of dead air, wondering what was with Manzara. He certainly sounded like a regular guy…but isn't that what all the neighbors always say about the donut who walks into the local hardware store and starts shooting everybody because they sold him the wrong size finishing nails?

"Still there?" he said. "Sorry, I had to remember how I'd filed them."

"I know the feeling. So go on—what's up?"

"Yeah, anyway, I was saying—I was watching one of those shows on cable, and I saw this show about ancient archeology."

He paused for dramatic effect, and I wondered where the hell this was going—although there was a part of me that had a damned good notion.

"One of the sites they started talking about is this island off Okinawa," he said. "And back in 1988, some scuba divers found this huge fucking structure under the water near this island called...let me see here...'Yonaguni'...yeah, that's it. Anyway, some professors finally got down to take a look at it a few years later, and they figured out what it was—a gigantic step-pyramid, a ziggurat, around the size of the Great Pyramid at Giza."

"That's pretty big," I said, realizing I sounded like an idiot.

"Yeah, but there's more. Various geologists have placed the age of the site at anywhere from ten thousand to thirty thousand years ago. That's at least *ten times* older than we'd imagined there was any civilization on earth advanced enough to build anything *close* to that thing."

Pausing to digest what he was telling me—because it was intriguing on its own merit—I also tried to figure what this had to do with me and why I'd contacted him about an old TV show that very few people remembered. So I asked him.

"It's connected, man. Believe me. I'm getting to it. C'mon, what's with you—you have a short attention span, or what?"

That kind of pissed me off, but I said "Okay, I'm listening."

"Right, so anyway, I'm watching the show, and all of a sudden I get this *weird* feeling all over me. Like a chill, but deeper, colder. Like some vibration was struck somewhere and it went right *through* me, like every atom in my body had been touched. I...can't describe it any better than that, but that's what it was. And I knew it was because of this strange set of ruins they'd found in the Pacific. That's what I meant when I asked you if you were ever affected by something you *knew* was…weird, and somehow special to you…"

I listened to his words and realized they were creating an odd somatic response in me. Like the way you feel when you recall a near-miss auto accident or some other moment of hideous danger that somehow passed you by, left you unscathed but terrified.

He must have sensed me hanging like I was, so he pushed on: "The primitives on the islands around there, they have this legend about an old god named…let's see, 'Nirai-kanai,' who supposedly rose up from the sea and 'allowed' the natives to 'live.' You ever heard anything like that?"

"Lots of cultures have similar myths," I said. "You know, like Noah and the flood."

"Yeah, but this is different," said Manzara. "And you *know* it."

He didn't say anything, as if he *knew* I had something similar to share, and was willing to wait."

He was right. And I told him so. "Okay, how 'bout this. I read this book a couple years back about ancient civilizations, and one of the places they talked about was this huge structure in Lebanon—at a place called Baalbek."

I paused to see if he recognized it, and he jumped in. "Yeah, I know about it. Nobody knows how old the place is…but the quarry where the stones were cut is like twenty thousand years old, and is almost fifty miles from where the platform was built."

"Yeah, that's it," I said. "When I started reading about that place, I remember thinking that it all sounded somehow *familiar* to me. There were photos of these gigantic stones with weird writing on them, and I'm telling you, I kept thinking I'd seen it before."

"You *have*!" said Manzara.

"Huh?"

"You saw it on *Mr. Curiosity*…"

I didn't say anything for a moment because I guess I'd

already figured that one out, but again, it was one of those things I didn't really want to deal with. I mean, none of it made much sense. I told Manzara.

"Of course it doesn't make sense! It's...not part of us. Part of us humans."

"Okay, now you're starting to sound nutty," I said.

"Don't you think I don't *know* that. I scare myself when I think about this shit."

"Obviously it's on your mind a lot."

"Well, how 'bout this, man...How long have you been interested in ancient civilizations?"

I shrugged unconsciously. "I don't know. I always have, I guess. Just one of those things that catches your interest, you know?"

"*Sure* I know!" said Manzara. "Same with me. Same with the Michigan lady. So what's that all about?"

"I'm guessing coincidence isn't high on your list."

"What're you—kidding me? C'mon, man..." He spoke in a softer conspiratorial tone. "There's a lot more to this than any of us can probably imagine."

"Well, how do we find out what's going on? What do we do next?"

Manzara paused for a minute. "I might have been just fooling around when I put that reference to *Mr. Curiosity* in my story. But now you and Miss Michigan have got me going on this. I think I'm going to take out some classified ads in the papers, and maybe in USA Today. I'll bet there's a lot more of us out there."

"Sounds like a plan," I said.

"Give me your phone number and your email. I'll be in touch."

I did, and he was.

About six months later, in early May, I got a cyber-note asking me to attend a special meeting at an address in the small Maryland town of Jarrettsville. The invitation was from

Vincent Manzara, and I knew what it was about. Since I ran my own business and did a little real estate on the side, I had no trouble scheduling the time and the trip, and after checking MapQuest for their usual half-assed, semi-inscrutable driving instructions, I headed south.

Jarretsville hid itself in the middle of Maryland's thoroughbred horse farm country, and my destination must have been one of the nicest in the last century: uncountable acreage of rolling meadows, punctuated by the occasional copse of shade trees, and surrounded by miles of rail-fencing all painted neatly white. In the center of this pastoral stateliness, lay a larger friendly-looking house and about six outbuildings such as stables, barns, and servants' quarters. There was a mile long driveway up to the house and there were cars parked along both sides. Behind the barn, an expansive field held a lot more vehicles, enough to make it look like a very successful auto dealership.

I went inside and met Vincent and the owner of the property, a woman about our age named Virginia Bourner. Mrs. Bourner had recently become a widow when her horse-breeder husband rode his Lexus underneath a flatbed truck that had suddenly jackknifed across I-95 right in front of him during a thunderstorm. His vehicle's roof, along with his head, had been sliced off in an instant. After she told me this, I expressed my condolences, then allowed her and Vincent to escort me outside where a huge tent had been erected, enclosing enough chairs to run a small college commencement.

"I told you there had to be more of us," said Manzara.

"Looks like you were right."

He smiled wryly. "Gee, why does that not make me feel all that good?"

"So what's going on? What's this all about?"

"You'll see," he said.

Eventually, after some attaching of nametags and a little

punchbowl conversation, we all convened under the tent in an attempt to understand what had happened to us...and perhaps the more important corollary question: *why us?*

I won't try to catalogue the events or reconstruct the many dialogues that emerged from the day-long convocation. There was way too much of it, and until the moderators learned to keep things focused, there tended to be a lot of ranging off into the fringes of rational thinking...which we all know is bounded by lots of quicksand. Suffice to say many of the attendees had shared very similar experiences regarding the interest, affinity, or arcane understanding of ancient archeological mysteries.

Remember what started all this. I saw a show on TV as a kid that only a miniscule, fractional percentage of the population remembers. So what does it mean or portend?

Several notions arose from the mass meeting that transcended the status of "feelings" or "opinion." Here they are:

1. The program, *Mr. Curiosity*, did exist. The odds of all of us experiencing a mass hallucination in different parts of the country, in different time zones, and wildly different cultures and households was not even remotely possible.

2. We all learned "stuff" from *Mr. Curiosity*. We were fed information by this guy and it was bolted down in our subconscious where it remained unused until this day. It was like stumbling into a sub-basement in your house, and finding all this weird machinery there, all covered in tarps and oilcloths and not having clue what any of it might be used for.

3. We're not sure yet exactly *what* we were learning from the show, but we intend to find out.

4. There seems to be little question *Mr. Curiosity* had some

connection to, or association with, evidence of ancient civilizations on the planet.

5. All this stuff is getting pretty scary.

After suffering through a logistically challenging "outdoor cook-out," we all re-convened to witness our attempt to get some answers. Since our numbers included doctors and other scientific professionals, we had a chance to examine a variety of research techniques. Some would require months of highly focused research and/or experimentation (in the spirit of the hallowed *scientific method*) and we assembled volunteer teams to begin the torturous process to make them happen. Other ideas were attempted that evening, and they ranged far afield of mainstream investigative techniques. I sat in the front row brimming over with skepticism at what I was going to see...or *not* see.

The first subject was a man from New York who worked for the Long Island Railroad. I watched as he sat at a small dais, rigged with a wireless microphone, calmly waiting for another guy in a black turtleneck and matching pants to inject him with syringe of clear liquid. A tall, red-headed woman, accompanied by short balding guy, stood behind them.

"I'm a salesman for a pharmaceutical company," said the man. "I get lots of free samples."

He paused as very nervous chuckles susurrated through the crowd.

"What I have here is a big favorite with the 'alphabet agencies.' It makes the old thiopental sodium cocktail look like Kool Aid." He paused, looked at the Long Island Railroader. "You ready?"

"Shoot," said the seated subject.

And Black Turtleneck Salesman did just that.

Ping. Mainline express via the biggest vein in the subject's arm. I was amazed at how fast it reached his brain — maybe five or six seconds — and he started to nod around, neck muscles loose and swiveling.

That was the cue for the redhead and the bald guy to come around to the front, where the latter checked vital signs. He looked like a doctor, and probably was. Going under the supposition we'd tapped our population for specialists in every instance, I figured the redhead to be some kind of psychological pro (or an intelligence ops type.)

She sat directly in front of Long Island Railroad, spoke softly to him. "You are five years old. You are watching a show called *Mr. Curiosity*, can you see it?"

Pause. Then: "Yeah, I can..."

"Can you hear him?"

"Yep."

"What is he saying?"

Another pause. Then he spoke slowly, as if parroting what he was hearing: "Today we're going to hear...about a shipwreck...in a very cold place. A story about a boat. The boat's name is...the *Wilbur Whately*..."

We all listened to a short simple tale about a sailing schooner, which lost a mast and drifted into the frozen south polar regions, where it became locked into the eternal ice. The crew became infected by a strange spore, which either killed them or...transformed them. The survivors were picked up by another ship called the *Emma*, but the ship vanished before making safe port.

In one sense, it was a tale almost nonsensical and silly, but I knew it was hardly typical material for a kid's TV show—especially when you factored in how utterly unsophisticated programming was back then.

No, this was weirdly compelling. Unsettling. And dripping with déjà vu.

We didn't know what it meant, but on a purely instinctive, atavistic level most of us felt it was something *bad*.

The redhead continued to probe, and Long Island Railroad offered up one more oddity: "I tell you this...every day...because it is important. Most of you will never remember this story…or any other. We only need those of you who *will*."

And then Long Island Railroad's head dipped and he dropped off into a near anesthesia-like state. The doctor checked him, then gestured for some help to get him off to a more comfortable place. As for the rest of us, we all sat there looking at each other with expressions ranging from puzzled to terrified.

Just exactly what did *that* all mean?

Inexorably, we extracted more information from a series of injected volunteers and questions. The interrogations unfolded like a strange, absurdist stage play. Someone spoke of a race called the Yithians. Another mentioned an ancient city, Pnakotos. At first I felt like I was watching a parody of a cheesy bible-thumping TV extravaganza— where they bring people up to the platform to bear witness to God, then carry them off when they become suffused with the power of the Holy Spirit.

But it was a lot more than that.

We had become miners in the ebon tunnels of our deepest memories, our darkest fears. As I sat in the audience, I swear I could sense this kind of Jungian, collective consciousness that webbed us all together in some unarticulated way. Despite the obvious physical and intellectual differences that defined and separated us all, there was some as yet unknown commonality here. We had become this large hive-like entity, this gestalten *thing* whose spiritual excrescence would surely absorb us all. Something was happening to us and an unspoken awareness flooded throughout the group: none of us would ever be the same.

Perhaps the most frightening revelation came from the evening's final volunteer—me. I felt the seductive sting of the needle in my arm and the white-heat rush of CIA soup taking the carotid express to the gray room. I felt the tumblers to lifelong locks tripping into place and terrible truths fall from the vault of my now-empty soul.

The redhead whispered to me and I spoke to her in the ancient tongue I learned at the altar of my Emerson television. The words leapt from me as if finally escaping the prison of my flesh to become flesh of their own.

That's when it started...

At first just a low frequency humming, then it gradually built itself into a true sound, a cadenced emission of unintelligible words, a chant. It grew like the insect-song of an unseen chitinous horde.

But it was coming from *us*.

As if I'd been some kind of trigger, some kind of primer to the alien cacophony, now everyone, the enclave of "special ones" (as one of our more optimistic attendees had called us), began to unwind like spools, and the strangeness unraveled from us unending. We were helpless to stop the unknown language as it streamed from us. As I sat there, drugged to my eyelids, enthralled by the rhythmic chant of arcane syllables, I was suddenly struck by this almost-funny image: someone hitting the *play* button on some monolithic recording device.

And then, with a hot, whirling drill-bit immediacy, a searing truth bore into my thoughts. I had somehow stumbled upon part of the truth. And suddenly a memory from Mr. Curiosity rushed in to fill a bit more of the vacuum of ignorance still with me—with the great passages of time, absorbing the catastrophic changes of our world, they were losing their repositories of knowledge. Their libraries, along with the rest of their great cities had been pressed against the grinding wheel of time, reduced to dust. New vessels were required...

...and were found.

And so, it seems we've only lifted the corner of the sheet. We've only just barely glimpsed what lay beneath it, what reality hints at its shape and substance.

And there's one more thing.

Something I haven't been able to make myself share with the others. Maybe because it will make it more real if I give it voice…I don't know. You see, when I was in that trance, I caught glimpses of things that I wish I never had. A simple thing like the configuration of a doorway can tell you a lot about the shape and size of what it allows to pass through it. And the insane geometry I saw was only a warm-up for those who'd devised it.

You see, they were not like us. They *are* not like us. Us and our thin, transparent flesh, our stick-like limbs, our knobby little heads. No match for the achievement of their biologic tyranny.

My group does not yet know the old maps were true: *here be monsters*…

What they do now know is not pleasant, not at all. It appears that something is probably coming to reclaim its place on this world, and it has selected some of us to ease its passage, while discarding the rest.

Call me crazy, but I keep thinking *we* weren't the lucky ones…

Tim Waggoner

Tim Waggoner has been making a name for himself since the release of his first short story collection, **All Too Surreal***—an unjustifiably overlooked gem that showcased Waggoner's talent for combining audacious imagery with deeply thoughtful subject matter...not to mention solidly-crafted writing. His most recent horror novels include* **Pandora Drive, Like Death,** *and* **A Nightmare on Elm Street: Protégé.** *He's published over seventy short stories in the fantasy and horror genres, and his articles on writing have appeared in* **Writer's Digest, Writers' Journal** *and other magazines. He teaches creative writing at Sinclair Community College in Dayton, Ohio. After reading this, you'll be wanting more Waggoner, so visit him on the Web at* **www.timwaggoner.com.**

—JNW

WATERS DARK
AND DEEP

✠ BY TIM WAGGONER ✠

W ater roaring in her ears, pushing heavy against her ear drums. Hands clawing for purchase, feet kicking, trying to find something, anything solid to stand on, but there's nothing—nothing but water. She opens her mouth to scream, takes a deep breath first, but instead of filling her lungs with air, liquid rushes down her throat and a shower of bubbles bursts from her mouth. Her lungs feel full and heavy, as if they're filled with concrete and it's weighing her down, down, down...

My camera! she thinks. I can't lose my camera! Mom and Dad will kill me!

She looks up, sees a scattered diffusion of light some-where above her—five feet? Five hundred?There's no real difference at this point. There's a whole world of air up there, if only she could reach it. If only she was wearing a life jacket, if only she had learned how to swim...

A small shape slides toward her through the gray murk: sleek, scaled and streamlined. It's a fish of some sort. Daddy would know what kind, but she doesn't. It turns as it nears her face, displaying its flank, a cold black eye looking at her with supreme indifference as it passes, and then it's gone, returned once more to the darkness it came from, and she's still going down, down, down...

"It's all right! You're all right!"

Tina struggled to catch her breath. She was sitting up in bed, covered in sweat, chest heaving. Carl sat next to her, hands firm on her bare shoulders as if he were trying to hold her down. The bedroom was dark; it was still night. The darkness made her think of her dream—of the water—and she shivered.

"Light," she managed to gasp out. "Please...turn on the light."

Carl removed a hand from her shoulder and leaned over to switch on the night stand lamp. Soft yellow light illuminated her small apartment bedroom, but the corners remained dim and shadowy. *Murky,* she thought. *Like water.*

Carl began gently kneading her shoulders. "You had a bad dream."

Tina's pulse was racing, and she felt as if she couldn't catch her breath, but she still managed a soft chuckle. "No kidding."

They were both naked; normally she slept in a nightgown, but not when Carl stayed over. The sheet was thrown back, the blankets twisted into knots. She must've thrashed around quite a bit before Carl woke her. Without thinking about it, she leaned forward and began straightening the covers.

"Same one?" Carl asked.

She nodded. "That's the third time I've had it this week. I don't know why. I mean, I used to have it a lot when I was kid, but I haven't had it for *ages*." She paused, checked the sheets and covers, gave them one last smoothing with her palm. There.

"Until now," Carl added.

"Yes." She turned toward him and forced a smile. It wasn't hard to do. He was a boyishly handsome man who kept himself trim by working out and doing a little body building. Maybe he was no Mr. Universe, but he sure looked good with his clothes off. Besides, she loved him like crazy, which was a good thing considering that they were engaged to be married.

"Maybe it's just stress. You've got a lot going on in your life: your job, getting ready to start on your MBA..."

She smiled. "And don't forget our impending nuptials."

A flicker of something passed across his face, a hint of an expression that was gone before it could be fully born. It was his turn to smile then, but it was a thin smile, one that hardly counted as a smile at all, really.

A second passed, then another, before he answered. "Right." The word seemed toneless and devoid of meaning, like it had been emitted from a computer speaker rather than the mouth of a man she intended to marry.

She wondered if something were wrong, if she should ask him if everything was okay, but then she glanced at the digital clock on the night stand and saw that it was sixteen minutes after four in the morning. He was probably just tired and out of sorts from being woken by her thrashing about. That's all.

She snuggled into his arms and they lay back on the bed, holding each other.

"You know what I say about stress."

He sighed, but smiled. "'Pressure makes diamonds.' I think you've attended one too many corporate training seminars."

She ignored the dig. "It's all a matter of whether you let things get to you or not. Anything can be controlled—including stress—if you work at it hard enough."

"It's a good life if you don't weaken, eh?" He kept one arm around her as he rolled halfway over and reached for the lamp.

"Carl? Could you...leave it on? Just for a little bit, until I fall asleep?"

He hesitated, but then said, "Sure," and rolled back over to kiss her. It wasn't a quick kiss, but it wasn't exactly a lingering one, either. "Night." He disengaged from her and turned over on his side, his back to her. She felt hurt, even though he slept like that a lot of the time. But after the nightmare she'd had, she could've used a little extra TLC.

Her lips were still moist with his saliva, and it felt...funny, thicker than it should, cooler. She touched fingers to her lips, brought them to her nose, sniffed—

—and smelled the faint, brackish odor of lake water.

Tina hoped she wasn't sweating too badly. It was late June, and in southwestern Ohio, that meant high humidity. She could feel moisture being sucked out of her pores with every clack of her high-heel shoes, and she wished she hadn't worn her blue blazer and skirt today. The fabric was *way* too heavy for summer, but it was the nicest outfit she had, and she wanted to make a good impression on the doctors at this practice. Maybe free samples were what really sold pharmaceuticals—and her case was bulging full of those today—but looking good in the bargain sure didn't hurt. *Especially* when the practice was staffed by all male doctors, like this one.

As a pharmaceutical sales rep, she was always careful not to park too close to the entrance of a physician's office. Docs hated it when you took up spaces they thought should be reserved for their patients. Ordinarily, it wasn't much of a hassle, but the office park was crowded today, and she'd been forced to park her Geo Metro in front of an orthodontist's the equivalent of city block away. The way she was sweating, by the time she got inside, she'd be lucky if she didn't look like a drowned rat.

She remembered the dream she'd had last night, and despite the heat of the day, she felt a chill ripple along her spine. Maybe *drowned* rat wasn't the best choice of image for a simile.

Tina heard a soft *squeeek-squeeek-squeeek* of turning wheels. She turned toward the sound and saw a small woman—*really* small, so tiny she looked more like an ambulatory doll than a creature of flesh and blood—pushing herself across the parking lot on a stainless steel scooter. Tina wondered if there were something wrong with the woman's legs, if they were too weak to support even her minimal weight and she needed the scooter to get around.

The woman had blonde hair down to the center of her tiny back, and she wore a white dress and shoes that were so small they looked like they belonged on a doll rather than a person. The woman's head was out of proportion with her body, so much so that it seemed she might topple over any moment, her head dragging the rest of her body down to the blacktop of the parking lot. She was so small, so thin that Tina imagined she wouldn't make much of a sound when she hit, no more than a child's stuffed animal dropped onto carpet. The little woman held onto the handlebars with stubby sausage-link fingers as she half-walked, half-scooted toward Tina, wheels *squeeeeeking* softly.

Tina felt the flesh on the back of her neck crawl as the woman approached, and she almost turned around and hurried back to her car. But she stood her ground, afraid of hurting the woman's feelings and, more to the point, blowing her sales call. Besides, if Tina avoided contact with the woman just because of her appearance, that would make her a...what? Not a racist. A height-ist? Something like that.

As the woman drew near, Tina relied on her years of sales experience to conceal her true feelings. *Just act like you're talking to a customer.* She took a breath, released it, forced her body to relax and put on a "you don't know me yet, but we're destined to be good friends" smile.

The little woman reached the sidewalk, stood and half-lifted, half-walked her bike onto it, sat back down, and then rolled right up to Tina, the front wheel of her scooter bumping into Tina's left shoe. Tina didn't wait for the woman to speak; in sales, it was vital to get the first word in yourself.

"Hi." Opening lines flashed nervously through her mind and were discarded just as quickly as they came. *Nice day for a bike ride...Doing a "little" shopping?...How's the weather down there?...*

But whatever Tina might've said died unspoken when she took a good look at the woman's face. Her skin was pale, almost grayish-white, her lips round, the flesh puckered and tight as if they didn't belong to a mouth at all but an entirely different orifice. Worst of all, though, were the little woman's eyes. They were large, moist and black, like ebon marbles with petroleum jelly smeared on the surfaces. Tina had the impression that she'd seen these eyes before, but she couldn't...

And then she remembered. They resembled the eyes of the fish that had swam past her face when she'd almost drowned as a kid. These eyes had the same cold alien quality: detached, distant, and utterly devoid of any shred of human emotion.

The orifice that served at the woman's mouth irised open and she spoke, her voice liquid and phlegmy. "In the end, control is a fragile illusion. The more you struggle to hold onto it, the more easily it shatters in your grasp." Her mouth opened and closed once, twice more without making any sound, as if she were gawping for air. She scooted backwards a foot, turned the front wheel of her tiny bike, and then advanced, making her way around Tina, wheels *squeak-squeak-squeaking.*

Tina turned to watch the little woman continue down the sidewalk away from her. The woman's cryptic words swirled around in her mind, but they weren't what bothered Tina the most. What truly disturbed her was the glimpse she'd gotten of the little woman's hands as she'd pulled her bike back and then moved forward. She'd seen that those stubby fingers were connected by gossamer-thin webs of skin — skin covered with glistening scales.

She felt dizzy, nauseated, and then Carl's words from last night returned to her.

Maybe it's just stress. You've got a lot going on in your life: your job, getting ready to start your MBA...Not to mention the wedding, which Carl hadn't. But maybe he was right. She *was* under a great deal of stress, more than she ever had been before. So she had encountered a strange little woman on her way to a sales call — what of it?

What about those eyes...those fingers?

Stress could do funny things to a person's perceptions. The little woman on the bike had been real enough, and she'd said those words, whatever the hell they were supposed to mean, but the eyes and the webbed fingers? Uh-uh. Not a chance they were real. A trick of the light, the mind, or both. Best to just forget about them and move on.

She continued down the sidewalk, passing office fronts — real estate, financial planning, an optometrist's — on her way to the doctors'. The encounter with the little woman might have shaken her a bit, but at least it hadn't put her behind schedule.

She was mentally rehearsing her opening spiel for whichever doc might be available to see her (and trying to decide if it would be too obvious if she undid another button on her blouse), when she felt a tightness in her chest. It wasn't much at first, just a sensation as if she were wearing constricting clothes, but then it worsened, and her lungs began to feel heavy, as if they were filling with fluid. Breathing became more difficult, until it felt as if she were trying to suck air through a mouthful of wet cotton. Her pulse rate soared, and she could feel her heart pounding in her ears, the sound not unlike the rushing-gurgle of water.

Panic surged through her. She dropped her sample case and ran toward the doctors' office, high-heels clack-clack-clacking on the sidewalk as she wheezed and gasped for air. Her vision began to go gray around the edges (a gray that resembled the murkiness of silty lake water) and she prayed that she'd reach the office doors before she lost consciousness.

Almost there, almost—

Tina drove away from the doctor's, embarrassed and angry at herself. She was a professional woman, goddamnit, not some simpering little thing that let her "nerves" get to her.

I suggest you make an appointment with your regular doctor to see if he or she would like to run some more tests, but based on my examination, I'd say you experienced a mild panic attack, brought on most likely by stress. Not a lot of fun, of course, but nothing serious.

The doctor had smiled then—a patronizing smile, Tina thought, one that said "There's nothing wrong with you, so leave now and let me get on with seeing patients who *really* need me."

He'd also offered to write her a short-term prescription for anti-anxiety medication until she could get in to see her regular doctor, but she'd declined. She hated the idea of taking pills to alter her emotions. They were *her* emotions, and if they needed to be controlled, then she would be the one to do it, not some damn medicine. Not exactly an attitude her supervisor at Pharm-Tech would approve of, maybe, but that's how she felt.

The words the little woman (the little *fish* woman, she couldn't help thinking) had said came back to her then.

Tim Waggoner

In the end, control is a fragile illusion. The more you struggle to hold onto it, the more easily it shatters in your grasp.

"Bullshit," she whispered, but without much conviction. She continued driving toward her next sales call and tried not to think about the little woman's cold, black eyes. Tried very hard.

When Tina was twelve, she almost drowned.

Her family had been vacationing at a state park that summer: her father, mother, little brother and herself, all crammed into a tiny tin can of a trailer for a week. She'd never been the outdoorsy type and was well and truly bored after the first couple days. Besides, there really wasn't that much to do, not with her parents. Her dad like to go fishing, but her mom was too afraid to get into the boat—she was worried about tipping over, about getting sunburned, about getting eaten alive by mosquitoes—so she remained at the trailer, staying inside and reading or watching the portable TV they'd brought, even though they could only pick up two local channels out of Cincinnati. Her brother liked to fish, too, so he accompanied their father, which left Tina (who *loathed* fishing) with only two choices: stay at the trailer with Mom or roam around the park and see what trouble she could get into.

And on the last day of their vacation, Tina found trouble all right. Found plenty.

She wandered down to the boat dock, hoping to see the cute guy who worked at the nearby food stand. He was a teenager—sixteen, maybe seventeen—and, at least in Tina's eyes, he was movie-star handsome. She had no illusions that the boy would fall in love with her. At twelve she was coltish and awkward, and besides, her family was leaving for home later. But she just wanted to see him one last time, and maybe, if she was lucky, snap a picture of him with the camera Aunt Karen had given her for her last birthday.

But—rotten luck—the boy hadn't been working that day, so bored *and* depressed now, she walked to the end of the dock, thinking maybe she might see a crane or something flying over the water and get a picture of it.

Her mother would've had a fit if she'd seen, because Tina had never learned how to swim and, despite Mom's advice, she wasn't wearing a lifejacket. There was no way Tina was going to wear one of those bulky orange things. Not only would she look like a big geek since all she was doing was walking on the dock, they were itchy and uncomfortably hot. She wasn't stupid; she'd be careful not to get too close to the water. And even if she did fall in, she'd be so close to the dock that she could pull herself out easily.

So she stood at the end of the dock, sandals hanging over the edge by a half inch, and she looked down and saw a school of small darting fish in the water. They weren't exactly a crane, but she figured they'd do. She brought the camera (which was hanging by a black strap around her neck) up to her eye and gazed through the lens, struggling to focus it. She wasn't sure if she'd be able to get the picture—would the camera be able to shoot something that was under the water? Maybe if she leaned down a little…a bit more…just a—

And then the world swayed, tilted, and she was in the water.

She went down once, twice, and was about to go down for the third time when she felt a strong, sure hand close around her wrist and pull her up. *Let it be him*, she thought, hoping that the cute food-stand boy would turn out to be her savior. But it wasn't. She was saved by a fat little man with bad skin and a sunburned bald head. Still, she wasn't too disappointed. She was alive, after all, though her camera was completely ruined.

Her T-shirt and shorts were still sopping wet by the

time she got back to the trailer, and her mother nearly had a heart attack when Tina explained what had happened.

She hugged Tina so tight she could barely breathe and said, "I'll never take you to such a dangerous place again!"

And she was true to her word. Tina's family never went on vacation after that, not even a simple day trip. Before long her mother didn't want to go anywhere, for any reason. By the time she died of congestive heart failure when Tina was twenty-five, her mom hadn't left the house for over a decade.

Tina had been terrified by the experience of nearly drowning. The complete and total loss of control—not being able to breathe, unable to stop herself from sinking—had shaken her to the core. But when she saw how her mother reacted to the incident, Tina decided that she wouldn't let it get to her, wouldn't let her fear make her retreat from the world. She took a paper route, saved her money, and signed up for swimming lessons at the Y. By the time she entered high school, she was good enough to be on the swim team, and by the time she graduated, she was able to go to college on a partial swimming scholarship.

Tina first heard the phrase "pressure makes diamonds" from her swimming coach in high school, and she liked it so much she decided to make it her personal motto. Whatever happened to her, no matter how bad it was, she would handle it. She'd taken control of her life, and she was never going to let it get out of her control again.

"C'mon, c'mon…" Tina urged the driver ahead of her to go faster. The idiot was barely doing twenty, even though the speed limit here was forty-five. Yes, it was raining, but not *that* hard. It was—she glanced at the dashboard clock—six thirty-seven. She was supposed to meet Carl at the restaurant at six thirty.

She slapped her palm on the steering wheel and swore. The windshield wipers arced back and forth, back and forth, moving at their highest setting, but even so water rippled across the glass as if the wipers weren't even there. The car ahead of her (the slowpoke!) was little more than a blurry outline with a pair of reddish smears for brake lights.

She looked at the clock again. Six thirty-eight.

Carl would wait, of *course* he would, and he wouldn't be upset. Being exactly on time was one of her things, not his. But that didn't make being late any easier to deal with, especially not after everything that had happened today. After her encounter with the little woman on the bicycle and the resulting panic attack, Tina had tried to make the rest of her scheduled sales calls, but while she managed to fit them all in, her timing was off. She was hesitant, unsure, unfocused, and the doctors she saw (when she got to see any; a number of receptionists didn't send her back) were short with her, cutting her off in mid-spiel and asking her leave her samples and go, they hated to be rude, but they were especially busy today, just swamped. Summer allergies, summer flu, check-ups before summer vacations. A shrug, an apologetic smile. *You know how it is.*

She knew, all right—knew she'd had her worst day on the job since she'd started with Pharm-Tech. She was furious with herself for letting that weird little woman get to her. She'd been no diamond today. Hell, she hadn't even been a cubic zirconium.

And to top if off, now she was late for dinner with Carl. Tonight was supposed to be special, the night they made final decisions on the wedding, everything from the invitations, to the reception and the honeymoon. She had a notebook filled with ideas, samples, and brochures that was she eager to finally show him. Like a typical man, he'd been ducking the detail-work of the wedding, but she'd finally pinned him down on making some choices over dinner tonight. She could've just gone ahead and picked whatever she wanted—she knew exactly what her preferences were – but she was determined to get Carl's input. After all, it was *his* wedding too, right?

But she wasn't going to get his input if she didn't make it to the goddamned restaurant!

She took a hand off the steering wheel, intending to lay on the horn so that the driver ahead of her would either speed up or pull over to let her by, when she noticed the way the water undulated across her windshield. It didn't look like it was coming down in drops anymore. In fact, it almost looked as if she were driving *under*water.

She gripped the steering wheel more tightly, eased off the gas, and concentrated on taking slow, deep, even breaths as she continued driving toward the restaurant at a crawl.

And if out of the corner of her eyes she saw dark, streamlined shapes moving gracefully through the dimness beyond her car, she told herself it was just an illusion conjured by the rain, that's all.

Breathe in, two-three-four. Out, two, three, four...

Cocooned in water, arms and legs thrashing as she sinks, unable to stop her descent. She's a damn good swimmer, but her training is no use to her now. Her body's deadweight, falling down to darkness.

The water is murky-dim, but she can still make out objects floating around her: foil-encased sheets of pills, all different colors, shapes and sizes; decongestants, antihistamines, anti-inflammatories, antibiotics...loose wedding invitations on creme-colored paper, tumbling slowly end over end. Come celebrate the wedding of Ms. Tina Gensen to Mr. Carl Lockhart on Date Yet to be Determined.

A fish emerges from the outer darkness and comes swimming toward her. Its head is larger than it should be, long, fine tendrils trailing behind as it swims. No, not tendrils, she realizes. Hair. Blonde hair.

The fish swims up to her face and matches her descent so they can remain eye to piscine eye. It opens its tiny pucker of a mouth, and even though they are underwater, its voice comes easily and clearly to Tina's ears.

"Control is a—"

Tina doesn't want to hear. She covers her ears with her hands and tries to scream, but there's no air left in her aching lungs.

"—fragile illusion."

Tina woke up, fists jammed tight against her ears. It took a moment before she realized where she was—her bedroom—and what had woken her—the ringing of the phone on the night stand.

She sat up and reached for the phone, but before she could pick it up, the answering machine clicked on. She listened to her own voice greet the caller and ask whoever it was to leave a message at the sound of the tone.

A pause, then, "Tina? If you're there, pick up." Another pause. "All right, you're probably mad at me for standing you up tonight, and I don't blame you. I just...well, I was going to say I got tied up at work, but that's an excuse. The truth is I'm...not entirely comfortable with getting married. I know it's a cliché, the man getting cold feet, but that's not it. At least, not all of it."

A third pause, this one so long that Tina thought Carl was going to hang up, but he didn't.

"It's just that you can be so...I mean, you always want things to go a certain way, and I don't...Ah, hell. Forget it. Blame it all on me if you want. The bottom line is I don't want to get married. Not right now." A fourth pause, not very long this time. "Not ever." *Click.*

Tina sat there, struggling not to cry. Finally, a single tear rolled from the corner of her left eye, slid down her check and onto her lips. She told herself it didn't taste like lake water.

It had continued to rain on and off all night, and the parking lot was covered with puddles. Tina sat behind the wheel of her car, waiting. She'd been here since five a.m., telling herself over and over again: *We can make this work, we can make this work, I KNOW we can...*

At eight forty-eight, Carl's certified pre-owned Lexus pulled into the lot. Tina got out of her car as he parked and hurried toward him, running shoes splashing through puddles. She reached him just as he was closing his door, and she called out "Carl!" She tried not to sound pathetic, upset and needy, but she couldn't help it.

He turned toward her, car remote in one hand, briefcase in the other, and whatever emotions she'd expected to see on his face—joy, anger, confusion, irritation, disgust—there was nothing. His expression was completely neutral, and that was far worse than anything he could have said or done to her.

She was suddenly aware of how she must look to him. Carl was a mortgage broker, and he was dressed for work in a gray suit and maroon tie, while she wore a faded green T-shirt and jeans that were frayed at the cuffs. She hadn't washed her hair since yesterday morning, and it was a matted tangle. She hadn't put on any make-up either, and her face looked pale and washed-out, her eyes bloodshot and puffy from lack of sleep. There were other people pulling into the lot, parking, getting out of their cars, walking toward the office building, looking at the two of them and no doubt wondering who she was and what she was doing here, confronting one of their professionally attired brethren looking like trash. But she didn't care what anyone else thought; all she cared about was making things right between them.

"Don't do this to me, Carl. Don't do this to *us*."

"Jesus, Tina. There is no *us*, okay? Not any more. I'm sorry, I really am, but that's the way it is." He started to step around her, but she grabbed his arm and stopped him.

"Don't walk away." She spoke through clenched teeth. "We're still talking."

Now anger did twist Carl's features and he pulled free of her grip. "No, we're finished. In every sense of the word." Then more gently, "Just let me go to work, okay?"

Tina became aware of a faint sound coming from somewhere behind her, a soft *squeeek-squeeek-squeeek* of wheels turning. She ignored it. "Not until you agree to try to fix things between us—and we *can* fix them, Carl, I *know* we can. It'll take some work, and some time, but in the end it'll be as good as before. Better, even!"

"This *is* the end, Tina. Accept it and move on." Carl gave her a last look that was a mixture of love and regret, resentment and pity, before walking toward the entrance of his office building.

Squeeek-squeeek-squeeek. Louder now. Closer.

"It's not over, Carl!" she shouted. She took a step forward until she was standing at the edge of a large puddle. "Do you hear me? It's NOT!"

Other people heading into work turned to look at her, but Carl wasn't one of them. He just kept going.

The *squeeeking* drew up behind her and then stopped.

"I'm not going to turn around," she said, almost smugly.

She heard a rustle of cloth, a soft grunt of effort, then shuffling footsteps. The little woman had gotten off her bike. She hobbled to Tina's side and they stood there, silent, watching as the last few men and women made their way into the building to begin their workday. Moments later the parking lot was empty except for the two of them.

"It's not an illusion," Tina said, still stubbornly refusing to look down at the little woman. "Control *is* possible; all you have to do is—"

"Work hard enough," the little woman finished for her in a mocking voice.

Infuriated, Tina turned to the woman, intending to...to...she wasn't sure what, but intending to do *something*. But when she saw the woman's face, she froze. She was more fishlike than before—eyes wide, black and empty; cheeks covered with a scattering of scales; tiny gill slits on each side of her neck, opening and closing as they struggled to extract oxygen from the unforgiving air. But there was something else, something familiar about the shape of her nose, eyebrows, forehead, cheekbones, chin...Then Tina realized where she had seen those features before: on her mother's face—and in the mirror every morning.

The little woman's pucker of a mouth stretched open in a hideous parody of smile, revealing twin rows of tiny sharp teeth. Then with a swift, sleek motion she dove head-first into the puddle, sending up a splash of water that smelled like rotting algae and dead fish.

Tina watched until the ripples subsided and the surface of the puddle grew still once more.

Walk away, she told herself. *Just turn around, go get in your car, and go home.*

But she didn't. The puddle was just a puddle, not even an inch of rainwater over blacktop, and she was going to prove it.

She took a step forward.

Water around her, below her, above her...dark, so dark...but she's not scared this time. She's not a kid anymore, and she can swim, swim like a goddamned fish. She's in control.

She kicks toward the surface. Her wet clothes make swimming awkward, but she concentrates on remaining calm and strokes harder. Soon she's rising through the black water. Up, up, up...and still there is no light, only darkness surrounding her on all sides. Her lungs begin to burn for air, but she ignores their need and keeps swimming.

A thought occurs to her then: what if there is no surface—just an endless ocean of Nothingness above her?

She dismisses the thought immediately. There is a surface because she says there is, and she'll reach it. All she has to do is work hard enough.

*She senses unseen shapes moving in the water around her, circling, keeping pace with her, but she pays them no attention, continues moving her arms and legs, continues rising toward where the surface is—where it **has** to be.*

Rising...rising...rising...

Richard Christian Matheson

Novelist, screenwriter, producer, prolific short-story writer...R.C. Matheson is so busy most days you're lucky to catch a glimpse of him as he speeds past, but we were lucky enough to have him stop long enough to give us the following tale that—like those found in his benchmark collections **Scars and Other Distinguishing Marks** *and* **Dystopia**—*proves what a master craftsman can do with a minimum of words.*

—JNW

MAKING CABINETS

✠ BY RICHARD CHRISTIAN MATHESON ✠

Ice water; a diamond stalk on white linen.

The clearness tastes warm, red. The thin woman chokes, covers mouth with napkin.

One table over, a boy eats pie, eyes unblinking. Watches her hold menu in pale hands.

She scans gourmet adjectives. Imagines soups, meats. Their dark succulence, piquant sauces.

All of it horror.

She searches more dishes, stomach a sick pit.

Maybe a salad, no dressing.

But the tomatoes; the cook would slice them open, their seeded flesh unprotected, seeping helplessly.

The waitress approaches. Perhaps the special of the day? Lamb. Unspiced; a meticulous blank.

The thin woman's stomach twists. She imagines the dead flesh using her mouth like a coffin; fights nausea.

Why hadn't she heard them?

The waitress tilts head. The thin woman needs another minute. The waitress nods; the same conversation everyday.

A couple, at the next table, excavate lobster, amused by lifeless claws. The busboy sweeps; a metronome.

The thin woman sees the boy eating pie, his lips berry-blue like a corpse.

Electric saws, pounding hammers.

Maybe the vermicelli. Plain.

But the long strands, like fine, blonde hair.

She tries to sip water, again. But the cubes have melted; water like dread-warm saliva.

His gentle smile, serving his recipes. The perfect husband.

The waitress reminds her she must eat. She loses more weight everyday. She's so pretty. It was almost a year ago. She must move on. The thin woman listens, nods. Tries not to look at the boy.

Making cabinets, he'd said; basement door always locked.

The thin woman looks up at the waitress. The young woman's lipstick resembles a tortured mouth.

She imagines running between the red lips, down lightless corridor, to the banned door. Inside, music deafens. She presses ear to door. Hears blades severing. Pounds on door until it gives.

Finds two little boys, hanging upside down from ropes, screaming through gagged mouths, half peeled. He turns, goggles freckled red, black rubber apron stained. The stove behind him gurgles with spiced stews.

The thin woman tells the waitress she's lost her appetite.

Maybe tomorrow.

Richard Christian Matheson

The boy's smile falls as he watches her leave, bones and veins visible through her starved skin.

❧❧❧

William F. Nolan

*William F. Nolan—another **Masques** regular—is an award-winning author, biographer, screenwriter, editor, and racing enthusiast. Author of the novel **Helltracks** and countless short horror stories, Nolan returns with a short, tongue-in-cheek tale about the consequences of ignoring your conscience.*

—JNW

KILLING CHARLIE

✠ By William F. Nolan ✠

The first time Dot killed Charlie was in Oakland, across the Bay Bridge, at an amusement park. They had an argument and she pushed him out of their seat on the Ferris wheel. Charlie went crashing through the roof of the ticket booth below, and there was a lot of screaming, with people running around like headless chickens.

A week later, when Dot (back from a trip to our local Sure-Save store) opened our apartment door, there was Charlie, sitting on our big overstuffed sofa. He smiled at her.

"Hi," he said. "Hope you brought home some of those yummy frosted cinnamon rolls for me. I'm really in the mood for a frosted cinnamon roll."

"I thought you were dead," my wife said. Her legal name is Dorothy, but I've always called her Dot.

"Nope. Still alive and kicking," said Charlie.

"But I saw you smash through the ticket booth." She was staring at Charlie, standing there kind of frozen, still holding the sack of groceries.

"Yeah, that was quite a shock," said Charlie. "Kind of hurt when I hit the roof."

"I thought you were dead," my wife repeated.

"I *was* shook up," Charlie admitted. "Had me some busted bones. Broke my nose." He touched his face gingerly. "But everything healed fast and here I am, fit as a fiddle, back in my happy home."

"I don't want you here," Dot said. "This isn't your home anymore."

"Hey, now...let's us try to get along," said Charlie. He shrugged his shoulders in a way that had always irritated her. "I forgive you for pushing me off that Ferris wheel. What the heck...I'm willing to let bygones be bygones."

"Well, *I'm* not," said Dot.

She put the groceries down, walked over to the desk, took out a loaded .38, and shot Charlie in the head. He fell off our sofa onto the rug. There was a lot of blood.

"Have to buy another rug," Dot sighed. "This one will never clean properly."

She dragged Charlie out through the kitchen and pitched his body off the fire escape. He landed with a *plop* in the alley.

Another week passed—and when Dot opened the driver's door on our Buick Roadmaster, Charlie was in the back seat, curled up and snoring.

"Wake up, you bastard!" shouted Dot. "And get the hell out of my car!"

Charlie sat up, blinking. He scrubbed at his eyes and yawned big, the way a cat does. "I didn't have the apartment key," he said. "Must of lost it when I hit the alley."

"I shot you in the head," Dot declared. "And it's a three-story drop from our fire escape."

"Yep," nodded Charlie, rubbing the back of his skull. "Bullet messed up my head for sure, and I broke both legs in the fall. Took a while for things to mend, but I feel all chipper again."

We lived in San Francisco, a few miles from the Golden Gate, and Dot drove out to the middle of the bridge and made Charlie jump. From that height, hitting the bay water is like going head-on into a concrete wall. Charlie sank fast.

Dot watched until she was certain that he didn't bob back up again.

Then she drove home.

Everything was fine for another week — and then Charlie sat down in the aisle seat next to Dot in the AMC Multi-Plex where she was watching a new war movie starring Tom Hanks.

"Hi," he whispered, patting her knee. "How ya doin'?"

"This is crazy," Dot whispered back. "I *saw* you hit the water. You never came up."

"I know," nodded Charlie. "And boy, was it ever *cold*! Brrrr! I get the shivers just thinking of how cold that water was. Freeze the balls off a brass monkey." He chuckled at the old saying.

"How did you get here?"

"The tide washed me ashore," he said, keeping his voice low. On the screen, Tom Hanks was killing Nazis with a machine gun. "Had to buy a new suit. My other one was ruined, being in the salt water so long. My shoes, too. Had to pay for a new pair."

"I don't understand any of this," said Dot. "I keep killing you, and you keep showing up again."

"Guess I'm just mule stubborn," Charlie said. "Or maybe I should say I'm like a rubber ball. I keep bouncing back." And he chuckled again. "But I harbor no hard feelings against you."

"I don't give a damn about your feelings," Dot told him, causing the woman seated next to her to protest. The woman couldn't hear the dialogue with all their jabber.

Dot stood up. "C'mon," she said to Charlie. "We're leaving."

They walked out of the Multi-Plex and Dot pushed Charlie in front of a bus on Market Street.

"Dear God!" cried the distraught bus driver. "I *tried* to miss him, but he just popped up, right in front of me. I just couldn't brake in time."

Charlie was crumpled under a rear wheel.

"He's dead, that's for sure," said a sleepy-eyed cop who was on the scene.

The bus driver shook his head. "My first accident. Wow! I really clobbered the guy. This is not going to look good on my record."

"A lousy break," agreed the cop. His eyes were almost closed.

Dot was watching them from the doorway of Mel's We-Never-Close Drug Store. No one had seen her push Charlie in front of the bus, but her stomach was rumbling.

She bought a packet of Tums for her tummy from Mel, walked to the garage where she'd parked the Buick, and drove home.

Charlie was sitting on the apartment steps when she got there. He looked pretty beat up. His new suit was ripped in several places and the left coat sleeve had been torn off.

"How did you get here so fast?" Dot asked him, plainly vexed.

"Took a taxi," said Charlie. "Woke up in the meat wagon, and when it stopped for a red light, I hopped out and found me a cab. Lucky I had enough money to cover the tip."

"I don't want you here," said Dot.

"But I *live* here," he said.

"Not anymore," she declared.

Charlie looked sad. "Getting whacked in the street by a bus in no fun," he told her. "I need to lay down for awhile."

"It's *lie* down," she corrected him. Then she sighed. "All right, come on up and I'll fix you some hot chocolate."

"Great!" said Charlie, following her inside.

Dot put a saucepan of milk on the stove to heat, then got a box of rat poison from the top shelf in the pantry. She poured it all into the saucepan, then followed up with a couple of heaping tablespoons of cocoa mix.

"Whew! This stuff is *bitter!*" exclaimed Charlie, making a face. He held out his half-empty mug. "What'd you put *in* here?"

"Rat poison," said Dot.

Charlie convulsed, then collapsed on our new rug. No blood this time. She checked his wrist.

He was dead, all right.

She dragged the body out to the stair landing, and was about to pitch Charlie over the rail when he sat up.

"Look," he said to her, "I've ignored a heck of a lot from you lately, but this is the last straw. That stuff tasted *awful.*"

"I put in enough poison to kill a whole *house* full of rats," she said peevishly. "How come you're still alive?"

"Simple," said Charlie. "I'm immortal. Seems to me you'd of figured that out by now."

"What makes you immortal?"

"About a month ago I was down in the Marina district, kind of kicking back," he said. "Then I spotted this funky shop, just off the main drag. Dark little place. Musty. Full of cobwebs. With all kinds of weird stuff inside. Run by a freaky-looking humpbacked guy with one eye and a club foot. Asked me if I wanted to live forever, and I said sure, that would be swell. Cost you ten dollars, he said. Okay, that seems fair enough, I told him. Once I'd handed over the cash, he went to the back of his store and came back with a beetle."

"A *beetle*?"

"Scarab, actually. He told me that scarabs guarantee immortality. An ancient fact, discovered by some Egyptian guys. Took a dirty pestle, ground the scarab into powder, dumped the powder into a cup of root beer, and—Pow!— I'm immortal. All for ten bucks."

"That's ridiculous," said Dot. "I don't believe anything like that could ever happen in San Francisco."

"Well, it did," nodded Charlie. "But lemme get back to what I was saying—about that rat poison being the last straw and all."

"Go ahead," said Dot.

"My patience is exhausted," said Charlie. "I don't think you love me anymore."

"I *hate* you," snapped Dot. "Absolutely loathe and despise you."

"That's pretty darn obvious," said Charlie. "But the point is, I can't let you go on killing me the way you've been doing. It's ruining my clothes. And bottom line, it's really annoying me. So…"

"So? So *what*?"

"So I'm going to have to put a stop to it."

That's when I drove my pocket knife into Dot's heart. She gurgled and slumped forward, sprawling out along the landing like a big rag doll.

She was dead. And my wife is not like me. She'll *stay* dead.

I pulled the knife out of her chest, wiped it off against the leg of my pants (they were ruined anyway), and put the knife back in my pocket. It has nostalgic value—Dot gave it to me on my thirtieth birthday.

By now, I'm sure you know who I am. Well, gosh, isn't it plain as pie? I'm Charlie. Been playing a little word game with you. Just to prove I haven't lost my sense of humor, despite all that's happened to me. And since I'm going to live forever, I *need* a sense of humor.

I thought about me and Dot. Strange how quick a good marriage can go sour. I'd been convinced that, deep down, she still loved me. But I was wrong. *Dead* wrong. Ha! Ah, well…

I left our apartment building and took a cab back to the AMC Multi-Plex on Market. Bought a ticket to the war movie with Tom Hanks. I'd liked the part I'd seen with Dot.

Worth another look.

Ed Gorman

Ed Gorman is, in our humble opinion, one of the 10 finest writers working today. Primarily known for his superlative mysteries, Ed has the uncanny ability to seamlessly fuse together several genres at once while not being obvious or showy about it. The following novella ranks up there with his best short work—and that is no small feat. It is an honor to present this story for the first time.

—JNW

INTENT TO DECEIVE

✠ BY ED GORMAN ✠

She sat, so prim and perfect she might have been a statue, in a wooden chair in the reception area of the Mayor's Community Affairs office, pretty without fuss, silken dark hair, dark melancholy eyes, slender figure flattered by the inexpensive cotton dress, which was some sort of riff on the color emerald.

She wore no nylons, of course. Everywhere you went there were signs begging women to turn in their nylons, the material vital to making parachutes. There was, after all, a war on.

She had slim white legs. A lot of women colored their legs with this goop that was supposed to look like nylon. But this girl knew better.

When she heard Delancy come out of his office door, she set aside the *American* magazine she'd been reading. It was, like most magazines, filled with inspirational tales of how well the war was going to for Yanks.

But, as she could see for herself, Nick Delancy's limp was proof that the contrary was true.

She said, "I'm sorry to bother you."

"You're not bothering me at all."

"But your door was closed so you were probably hard at work and—"

He took the final steps toward him, still self-conscious about his infirmity. The docs all told him he'd get used to it. He should've asked them for a guaranteed date as to when that would happen.

"Are you all right, Mr. Delancy?"

The wince. Sometimes when the edge of the prosthetic cut into the bone and flesh of his knee, he winced. He was rarely aware of his wince though obviously other people were.

He smiled, not a handsome man but one with an open, freckled prairie-boy face that people trusted. "I'm fine. Still getting used to my new leg, I guess."

The twenty-three-year-old had enlisted three days after Pearl Harbor, leaving his job as a police detective. In August, he was involved in one of the first raids on Japanese-held islands near the Solomons. For his trouble a machine gunner he'd charged took off his leg below his left knee.

He'd spent almost three months in a Michigan military hospital learning to walk on his prosthetic. He still hadn't mastered it and was embarrassed now as he approached the woman.

"The war," she said. "The damned war." Then shook her had with solemn disgust.

Only when he was closer to her and saw her face in the golden glow of Indian summer sunlight through the wide window behind her did he see that she wasn't the dead girl he remembered from her autopsy photo. She was either older sister or mother.

She offered a slight hand and after they shook, she said, "I should've called for an appointment. I'm sorry. But I just decided I needed to talk to somebody responsible. Somebody said you were a good man to talk to. So I just thought I'd try and slip in."

Nona, his secretary, had told him there was a woman to see him before she fled for lunch. Radio station WYHA was broadcasting live over the noon hour in celebration of the warm, exuberant seventy-degree weather the city of Prescott, Illinois was experiencing. If you gave a quarter to the bond drive you were eligible to win $25 of free clothes at Maurer's Department store. Nona won stuff. All the time. There was almost something supernatural about it.

"Well, if you're in a hurry, we can talk right here." The Mayor's Office of Community Relations was a recent development. Prescott was a quiet, conservative town ninety miles due west of Chicago. Until six months ago. That was when the U.S. Government decided to construct a boot camp on the northern outskirts of the town. The population now included 8,000 mostly young recruits who had to know, given the headlines, how many Americans were dying in this year of 1942. So they pursued girls, liquor and other assorted pleasures with a desperation that sometimes became violent.

The local citizens had so many complaints about the Army base that the Mayor, who hoped to win re-election in two weeks, created this office and manned it with a man he knew he could trust as both investigator and negotiator. He was the liason between the community and the camp. He couldn't offer Delancy his old job back—department rules didn't allow for a crippled cop—but this was the next best thing. He had also seen to it that a request for Delancy's private investigator's license had passed through quickly. As a private investigator, Delancy had certain legal privileges that helped him do his job.

"My name is Beth Hewitt, by the way. And I'm afraid you may not like hearing what I have to say."

"Well, why don't you say it and we'll see how it goes."

"Your police department is either corrupt or stupid. Either way, they've let my daughter's killer go scot free." Some of her quiet appeal disappeared in the taught and angry look of her face. "And if you won't help me, then I'm going directly to my uncle."

"Is that somebody I'd know?"

"Oh, I think so, unless you're stupid as everybody else in town. He happens to be the governor of this state."

2

"They're out there again," Donna Wainwright said.

"I know. I saw them when I walked down the hall," Laura Tierney said. "I'm just glad I don't have windows in this office so I don't have to look at them all day."

Donna, a heavy woman given to black business suits, touched long fingers to her attractive face. "My cheeks are still burning."

"From what?"

Laura Tierney ran Safe House, a former two-story hospital that had been converted into a shelter for the runaway kids who had crowded the town as soon as the army base went into operation. Safe House was always overcrowded with teenagers who'd left homes and school because they'd bought into all the myths about army towns. They would find wealth, excitement and sex. Not a thought to what might happen if it didn't work out that way. Not a thought to what the future might bring.

What virtually all of them found was danger, venereal disease, poverty and despair. Many of them turned to prostitution to survive. And about ten percent of them killed themselves. The police had recently arrested a twelve-year-old for selling her wares in the area of the city known as the Zone.

When they'd run out of hope, they came to Safe

House. Laura immediately contacted their parents. Sending the kids back home—even the eighteen-year-olds who were technically old enough to make their own decisions—was always the first choice. But for those whose home situations had been intolerable—Laura had been shocked by the number of incest stories the girls had told her—Laura tried to place them in home situations here in Prescott. A good share of parents were lonely for children—theirs being overseas fighting a war.

"So why is your face still burning?" Laura said.

"One of the picketers said I was a disgrace for working here. You know, with you."

"You mean 'Satan's Mistress?'" Laura laughed.

"You think it's funny?"

Donna was perfect as a counselor for a certain kind of teenager, one who thrived on daily melodrama. Donna's office was rarely without a soap opera playing on the radio in the background. She loved emotional problems the way Mr. Bela Lugosi loved blood in his role as Dracula.

"If they give you any more guff, Donna, just remind them about the statistics the county health board put out this morning."

"Good?"

"Venereal diseases reported in the 15-21year old category down twelve per cent last month. So you can tell them for me—or I'll tell them myself—that I'm very glad I did what my cousin did in Akron, Ohio."

Her cousin Tina, who ran a similar shelter in Akron, was so appalled at the rate of VD among teenagers that she asked for and got permission to purchase prophylactics are bulk rates and to make them available everywhere teenagers hung out.

The problem was nationwide. And it wasn't just runaways and street girls who were driving the rate up. A lot of "good girls" felt it was their patriotic duty to give themselves completely (as all those Frankie Sinatra songs always sand about) and not worry if their parents approved or not.

Well, maybe the girls only gave themselves to two or three boys but the young soldiers might have slept with more than a dozen bar girls who weren't careful at all. Venereal disease was now such a problem that even the Red Cross made prophylactics available to soldiers and town kids who wanted them.

"They're going back to the city council tomorrow," Donna said. "And try again to get it overturned."

"I'm assuming that the council will split the way it did last time, with one vote in our favor."

"I hope so. It's scary to think what'll happen other-wise."

Laura was glad her phone rang. She was tired of the subject. She was a controversial figure in this community— "A pretty, spoiled rich girl who thinks she can push every-body around" a city councilman was quoted in the paper recently—but she was willing to put up with the scorn and mockery—even the occasional death threat—if it would help not only her own charges but the young people of the whole community.

Donna waved goodbye as Laura picked up the phone, her clear blue eyes resting on the framed photograph of her husband David. It was a head-and-shoulders shot of a sleek, blond young man in a captain's uniform. He was presently island-hopping as the American started making fragile headway against Japanese strongholds.

Before she had time to think about it, the voice on the other end of the phone gave her a momentary jolt of pure pleasure—somebody she was happy to hear from. Then came the realization of what the voice symbolized—her doing something of which she was ashamed—and she was not happy to hear the voice at all.

Nick Delancy said. "This is a business call."

She hesitated.

Which gave him time to say—"I'm sorry about the

other night. It was all my fault and it won't happen again. We have a good working relationship and that's all it'll be from now on."

"It was my fault as much as yours, Nick. But let's talk about something else." She felt flushed, anxious.

"Good enough. I wondered if I could swing by and look at your file on Sarah Hewitt and maybe talk to a few of her friends at the shelter."

"Sarah? You mean the police are actually going to investigate it? That would be something."

He could understand her anger, even though he knew it was misplaced. The Prescott crime rate had quadrupled since Pearl Harbor. Between home grown teenage thugs, runaway teenage thugs and young soldiers who seemed determined to get into serious trouble—maybe court martial and prison were preferable to facing the war—crimes such as assault, car theft, mugging, breaking and entering, robbery, arson and murder had overwhelmed the local cops. At the moment, one of his former detective pals had told Delancy, they were dealing with twelve open homicide cases.

"They do their best."

"Not in Sarah's case, they didn't."

"Well, I'm going to start my own investigation. But I'll need your help. Would you round up a few of her friends? An hour be all right?"

She reached for the small green roll of Tums that was always on her desk. The best friend a harried runaway shelter manager ever had.

"An hour. Fine. See you then."

3

"Hi, Nick," Donna Wainwright said.

"Hi, Donna. I'm supposed to see Laura."

"Afraid she had to go to this meeting downtown all of a sudden. But we found two girls for you to talk to."

Delancy tried to read her face pleasant face for the real truth but Donna she was too practiced at looking sweet and innocent.

I'm getting out of here before he gets here, Donna. I'd appreciate it if you'd cover for me.

He was pretty sure that something like that had been said. He was also pretty sure that Donna would have pushed a little to find the reason for the tension between Laura and Nick who had, after all, been working together effectively for more than a month. But Laura would give nothing away. In the propaganda movies where Japanese soldiers tortured Americans, many of the Yanks (excepting the hero, of course) gave up their secrets. But it would take weeks of round the clock brutalization to get anything out of Laura. She was that private.

"Well, fine, let's get to it then," Delancy said, hoping his tone didn't sound contrived. He wanted to keep his disappointment secret.

The ground floor of the shelter was set up for relaxing, studying and taking meals. There were three table model radios, a junior-size pool table, a ping pong table and small tables for playing checkers and chess. The offices were also on this floor.

Bunkbeds took up two large rooms on the next floor, one room for girls, the other for boys. These were at opposite ends of the upper level. Each room had its owner toilet and shower facilities. A youth counselor from Mt. Prescott college sat in the area separating the rooms from ten o'clock till five o'clock. He did homework.

This time of day, most of the residents were out working at various jobs or getting themselves ready to return home. The place had echoes of its hospital days, ghosts; the smell was of tobacco and soap with disinfectant.

Donna led Delancy to the counselor's desk and said, "I'll be right back."

She returned moments later with two girls. One was

dressed in bobby-soxer fashion—white anklets, black penny-loafers, blue skirt, white blouse with Peter Pan collar, blue barrette in her blonde hair. She looked crisp, friendly, bright. She looked like the daughter of the middle class.

The other girl was more of the street-girl stereotype. Shorn hair, a small face set permanently on belligerent, a sweatshirt that revealed ample breasts for somebody who was probably fourteen or so, and a pair of dungarees that were the tightest fit Delancy had ever seen.

Once the girls were seated at the table, Delancy took out the type of nickel notebook he used back when he was a detective.

"By the way, Nick," Donna said, pointing to the blonde girl. "This is Angie Coleman and her friend is Mike Foster. Mike for Michelle."

"Mike," snapped the girl.

"Mike, it is," Donna said. "So I'll leave you alone. I need to get back downstairs and answer the phone, anyway."

When Donna was gone, Mike said, "I shouldn't be here anyway. I don't like cops."

"I'm not a cop."

"The same thing. Some kind of invest-igator. And I couldn't stand Sarah. She was a lying bitch."

"I kind of don't blame her for saying that," Angie said. "She took Mike's boyfriend."

"He wasn't my boyfriend. I never liked him all that much."

"Is that why you told me you were in love with him?"

"How about you, Angie, did you like her?"

She thought a moment and then pointed to Delancy's package of Old Golds on the table. A book of matches sat on top of the smokes. He shoved them both to her.

After she got her own cigarette going, he pushed pack and matches to Mike.

Angie said, "She pretty much thought she was better

than everybody else. But I think she was like her mother. Kind of insane. Her mother had been in and out of mental asylums a lot ever since she was a teenager. And she wasn't real nice to anybody."

Mike said, "Except for boys. She was always nice to them. If they had a girl friend."

"It was kind of a game with her. She did that with a couple of the boys I liked here at the shelter."

These two were supposed to be friends of the dead girl's. Her enemies must really be bitter.

"Did she talk much about why she ran away?"

Mike shrugged. "Because her dad killed himself and she blamed her mother. She hated her mother. She said she'd do anything to get even with her."

"Any idea why she blamed her mother?"

Angie started to say something and then stopped herself. "You're really not supposed to speak ill of the dead."

"I'm glad she's dead."

"No, you're not, Mike," Angie said. "Not deep down you're not."

"You were going to say something, Angie," Delancy said.

She glanced at Mike then looked at Delancy. "Her mother was having this affair with a family friend and she wouldn't stop. Sarah said her father couldn't take it anymore."

A curly male head edged into the frame of the doorway then jerked back before Delancy could see much of it. Somebody listening.

He decided to go on with the girls as if he wasn't aware of the kid at the door.

"How about boys Sarah saw around here? Anybody special she talked about?"

"She must've been seeing somebody who had some money," Mike said. "She bought a lot of clothes."

"She looked older than seventeen." Angie inhaled

deeply, let out a stream of smoke blue in the stream of sunlight through the window. "When she got dressed up, she didn't even get carded at bars."

"Any idea which bars she went to?"

"Out in the Zone." Mike said.

"She had this ribbon once," Sarah said. "Some kind of military insignia. Probably from an Army jacket or something. As soon as I saw it on her bunkbed, she grabbed it and hid it. She was in one of her moods so I didn't ask her any more about it."

"Could you describe the insignia?"

"It was just a gold bar in the middle of this patch."

An Army second looie.

He had already filled a page and a half of his notebook.

"Anybody else you can think of?"

"That guy in that Packard, remember?"

"Oh, right, Mike. This big new Packard pulled up about half a block down from the house here. We were just coming back from the picture show when we saw it. You don't see a lot of cars like that in this neighborhood."

"How do you know Sarah was in it?"

"She got out of it then leaned back in and talked to the driver for a few minutes. They were having an argument. Sarah got pretty loud and nasty when she was mad."

"Could you hear anything of what they said?"

"No," Mike said. "Then she slammed the door and the Packard flipped a U turn and took off real fast."

"Then she walked up to us and said not to say anything about the Packard to Laura because Laura would start asking questions."

"Did either of you mention this to Laura or to the police after they found Sarah's body."

"Not until now," Mike said and for the very first time—national holiday—smiled. "You smoke my brand of cigarettes so I told you." She was even a bit flirty.

"I've got a carton in the car," he said. "So you can keep these."

"Gosh, I don't believe this." Angie held the pack up to check out how many cigarettes remained. It was nearly full. With the war on, smokes were as precious a commodity as gasoline and meat.

"I might have to call you with some more questions but this is a good start."

Angie laughed. "I feel like a stoolie in a Jimmy Cagney movie."

Mike scowled at her friend. "Nothin' funny about bein' a stoolie. Nothin' at all."

The impulse was to jump up from his chair and move on the kid at the doorway. Surprise him. But the impulse died as soon as he stood up and the edge of his prosthetic leg but into his flesh.

He put a finger to his lips so the girls wouldn't give him away and he hobbled to the door as quickly as he could. The kid was running down the hall by the time Delancy reached the doorway. The kid's feet slapped hard against the wooden floor.

"You know a curly black-haired boy, slim, maybe five-six, five-seven?" he asked the girls when he came back to the table.

"He was probably listening in," Angie said. "His name is Dwight Abernathy."

"He was real scared when the cops came," Mike said. "A lot of the kids told the cops that he got into an argument with Sarah the night before she died. More stoolies. He's a good kid, though."

"He was really in love with her," Angie said. "He used to write poetry to her. He found her diary once and wrote about twenty poems to her. She got really mad. She always hid her diary."

"The police didn't find it?"

Mike said, "But they couldn't pin it on him because he

had an alibi. Him and a couple of other kids went to a picture show and all the kids stuck up for him. And they couldn't find the diary, either."

Delancy got everything down in his notebook, thanked the girls and left.

4

Single working girls shared apartments—sometimes as many as a dozen girls in three rooms—because while one group was working, another group could be home sleeping. Or getting an early buzz on in one of the nightclubs.

Delancy parked his car near a plant that had once manufactured farm equipment but was now making tank parts. He had to pass in front of the main gate to reach the coffee shop he wanted. Two armed guards in Army uniforms looked him over carefully as he limped past. Saboteurs could be anywhere.

The coffee shop greeted him with the inevitable sound of the Andrews Sisters on the juke box. Their relentless cheeriness depressed him as did most of the propaganda lies. He knew that keeping spirits up was a critical part of the war effort. But after coming close to dying in combat and then seeing the wasted remains of hundreds of soldiers in the military hospital—

Thankfully, the song ended just as he was seating himself in a booth near the back of the small, clean place with a six-stool counter and the smell of fresh pies that brought back sentimental memories of visiting his Grandparents near Rock Island. Benny Goodman came on next, which was fine by him.

He felt a spasm of anger when a cute girl in her factory uniform walked in with a handsome guy in a white shirt and blue trousers on her arm. The guy looked plenty healthy. And that was the source of Delancy's anger. He knew he was probably being unfair and he didn't give a damn. All the corpses he'd seen in the Pacific; all the near-corpses he'd seen in the military hospital and here lover boy courting a chick. He was probably her supervisor at the defense plant. For all the positive publicity the plants got when the women took over, there was, as in any human enterprise, a lot of secrets that few cared to know about.

A number of Rosie the Riveters had sex right at work, in storage closets that contained a cot and could be locked from inside. Their partners were men who'd been declared unfit to serve—sometimes legitimately, sometimes because It wasn't the single women Delancy cared about. It was the engaged and married women. He'd seen too many Dear John letters he'd in the trembling hands of combat soldiers learning that their fiancés and wives were calling off their relationships because they'd met somebody knew. If he was drunk, Delancy might have gotten up and gimped over to loverboy here and smashed him in the mouth. Of course, with his luck, when he sobered up he'd learn that loverboy here had a heart condition and probably wouldn't live another six months. Much as he wanted to, he restrained himself from punching people. The least they could do was carry their medical recorrs are so Delancy could se if it was all right to slug them.

While he waited for his black coffee and slice of peach piece, he lighted a cigarette and scanned two war posters he hadn't seen before.

He still read pulp magazines so his favorite posters were those that looked like pulp covers. The war bond ones were usually the best for drama. His favorite today was of a soldier parachuting from the sky with a machine gun in his hands. This could have been a Doc Savage cover.

His art appreciation was interrupted by a softly seductive voice saying, "You're a patient man. I like that."

As Beth Hewitt slipped into the booth seat across from him, she smiled and said. "I loved my husband very much. But he wasn't what anybody would call clever."

He thought of what the two shelter girls had told him, Sara believing that her mother's infidelity had driven him to suicide.

The waitress came. All Beth wanted was coffee.

When they were alone, she said, "You've changed."

"I've changed?" He smiled. "We've known each other maybe half an hour. How could I change in half an hour?"

"You started looking into things and you heard something about me and now you don't see me the same way as you did back in your office."

He wanted to keep smiling it off but her observation was true. He'd seen her as an innocent while they were talking before; now, after talking to the girls, he saw her as—what? That was the power of gossip. Even if a story wasn't true, simply hearing it altered your perception of the person being discussed. *Even if it wasn't true.*

"I went to the shelter."

She slumped back in her seat. She really did have the kind of good looks that snuck up on you. The longer you looked, the better *she* looked. That melancholy little face, the eyes that so easily reflected pain.

"I imagine you talked to some of her friends."

"I'm not sure I'd call them friends. But they told me what they knew about her."

"I'm sure they told you that I caused Sarah's father to kill himself. That's what Sarah would have told them. She told me that twenty times a day before she ran away." She reached into her purse next to her on the booth seat and withdrew a package of Chesterfields. She had her own lighter. She took a deep drag which she French-inhaled, the smoke in elegant tendrils escaping her perfect nostrils.

"That's why you don't look the same. I'm some kind of whore to you now."

"Whatever happened or didn't happen isn't my business unless it helps explain her murder."

"Well, you may as well know the truth," she said bitterly. "It's true. I was having an affair with my husband's best friend and I planned to leave him because of it. I told him that and very soon after he killed himself. Sarah blamed me, of course;' I would've done the same thing in her position. The only thing I had was the family respectability. She wanted to destroy that so she started to do everything she could to humiliate me. She started sleeping with everybody she could. She started drinking. She got into two car wrecks within a month of getting her driver's license. She was lucky to live through them. She quit going to school and she started hanging out in hotel lobbies. The police were nice enough not to officially charge her with prostitution. She'd apparently slept with as many as a dozen older men That's what the officer told me, anyway. Then she started shoplifting. This time it wasn't kept out of the papers. I hate to say it but I do care about the family name—more than I should, I know—so I really had it out with her over that. The next morning, she was gone. Two weeks later Laura, from the shelter, put her on the phone and we talked. We were very cold to each other." Her tears were glycerin-pure standing in the corners of those soft dark eyes. "But I'm not making any apologies.e. I didn't go looking for an affair but I was obviously ready for one."

"What I need to figure out," Delancy said, easing the conversation to Sarah's more recent behavior, "is if Sarah carried on the same way here she did back home."

"I wouldn't be surprised. And when I said I don't have any apologies to make, I meant about my husband. Not about Sarah. I was a terrible mother and I can see that now. I just assumed she was old enough to accept what was going on." She shook her head. "I've been in and out of mental hospitals all my life for depression. I don't deal well with things—and neither does Sarah."

Delancy let her finish her gentle crying. She had thick supply of Kleenex in her purse.

He was thinking about a wine-colored Packard and an older man. Maybe the same type of older man she'd solicited in the hotel back home.

"I don't suppose this has been much help," she said. "I just wanted you to get my side of things, too. As soon as you said you were going to that shelter, I knew what you'd hear. That's why I called your office and asked you to meet me here." Nona had given him the message when he'd checked in earlier.

"Does a red Packard mean anything to you?"

She gave one of those small but telling starts, as if somebody had prodded her with a sharp stick.

"Oh, God, a red Packard?"

"You know somebody who owns one?"

"Of course. Ted Carlson. My lover. What about it?"

"Well, Sarah was seen getting out of a red Packard a few nights before she died."

"But why would Ted come here? How did he find her? We tried for weeks and didn't have any luck."

"I was hoping you could tell me. Now that I've got his name, I'm going to start looking for him."

She still looked shaken. Could the news have been that startling? "Are you telling me everything? I need as good a sense of your daughter as I can get."

The small face was composed again. "I just want you to find the man who killed her. I didn't do much for her the last year of her life. That's the only thing I can do for her now. So that means I'll tell you everything I think that's pertinent."

5

He was popular at the police station. A few cops beat the draft by having the city proclaim them vital to local safety. While this was legitimate, it was understandable that a large number of officers who had to serve were resentful of the cops who got to stay home. The cops who went to war far outnumbered those who stayed behind, which was another thing the press got wrong in its reporting. There were a lot of young cops who'd been rushed through police training and who still didn't know what the hell they were doing. But in a town that had turned into one big rising crime statistic,

Delancy was proof that not all soldiers resented cops. Here was a man who'd not only seen combat but had been wounded. And he walked among his old friends without a hint of bitterness.

He came in the front door so he could pass by all the office workers. They were his friends, too. Everybody waved, smiled. He grabbed a Pepsi from an ice-packed chest and went on back to the detective bureau.

Until Pearl Harbor, the most popular topics of discussion in the bureau had been which guy had seen the biggest breasts that day, which guy was foolish enough to bet on either the Cubs or the Bears, which guy was likely to become chief of detectives when fifty-four-year-old Bob Casey retired, and which guy was having the most problems at home because of all extra hours he had to put in. After Pearl, all those topics got shifted downward by one. The war was now the first thing the detectives talked about.

There was only one cop present when Delancy walked in that afternoon. Fortunately, it was the cop he wanted to see, Tom Gibson, the slender, red-haired dapper man who wore Sears suits. But somehow, on him, they looked as if they'd come from an expensive Chicago men's store. The trouble was, Gibson was the resident expert on the Zone and the thugs, grifters, hookers, drug addicts and killers of the Zone probably didn't have an eye for male fashion. Gibson was the expert because he'd had the bad luck to have grown up in the Zone where his old man had been a bartender in one of the most profane of all the Zone dives.

Gibson was a wry man. "So you're going to show me

up and find out who killed that girl from the shelter, huh?"

"I'm sure going to give it a try."

Gibson nodded to Delancy's leg. "You used to be quite a dancer. Think you can still handle it?"

Delancy knocked his knuckles against the hollow leg. "I'm already entered in a jitterbug contest." He smirked. "Sure I am." He got out his smokes and put one between his lips. "You pissed?"

Gibson grinned. "Yeah, I'm real pissed. I got six open murders right here on my desk, the stooge they gave me as an assistant had a nine-day course in police procedures, and this morning that rag of a newspaper criticized the police chief for letting the Army push him around. Why would I want a trained detective with a lot of experience behind him to help me out?" He shoved his hand over to Delancy. "You're savin' my ass on this one, Nick. And I appreciate it."

The newspaper reference revealed how bitter the tension had become between townspeople and the Army camp. Two members of the city council wanted to ban the military entirely from entering the city limits. The only place soldiers could pass the time was in the Zone. Any soldier caught in the city would be fined and jailed for forty-eight hours. They buttressed their arguments by citing the stats on auto theft, vandalism, assault and rape. The newspaper was all for the ban. The chief of police, a wise and calm man, had pointed out that a) such a ban wouldn't stand up in court b) he didn't have enough men to enforce such a ban and c) was this any way to treat young men who were being sent into war?

"You interviewed a kid at the shelter named—"

"—Dwight Abernathy. He sure looked good for it. But—"

"—he was at the movie with friends."

Gibson sighed. "I even checked out the ticket lady and the usher at the movie house. They remember him coming with four or five others kids and leaving with them to."

"No chance he could've snuck out? That theater isn't that far from the shelter."

"The usher said it was a slow night and he would've remembered the Abernathy kid leaving."

"No fire exit?"

"How about this crap? The fire department has given them three or four citations over the past year to get it fixed. I tried to get the door open and I couldn't. The frame is wood and it's warped from rain and snow over the years. I couldn't budge the damned thing. And it's in plain sight, right to the left of the screen. You'd notice anybody who tried to wrestle it open."

"How about a red Packard?"

"Hey, that's not fair," Gibson said.

"What isn't fair?"

"I worked on this for a week and didn't hear anything about a red Packard."

Delancy smiled. Gibson and he had always felt casually competitive with each other. Even after all this time, it felt good to spring a surprise on him.

"I'll let you know what I find out."

"Gee, thanks. Maybe being a private eye is making you smarter."

"I was wondering if you'd found out anything more Sarah Hewitt."

Gibson sat up straight, eager to get involved again. "I was in court testifying four days in a row so didn't have time to follow this up yet. But I heard whispers about her working for that Justice of the Peace—Cyrus Banning."

"How the hell did he get to her? With her background and everything, she was way out of his class."

"Kiddo," Gibson said. "She may have come from money but she managed to turn herself into just another street kid who'd put out for cash and might even have picked up on drugs. Very angry; almost like she was trying to kill herself."

"This thing with Banning--you're saying she was an 'Annie?' That's the word I picked up from a few people in the Zone. But as I said, because I was in court so much—I had six cases I had to testify in—I never really got a chance to find out, for sure."

An Annie, Delancy thought. Life forms didn't get much lower than that.

6

"Because I was worried about her. Why the hell else would I drive all the way over here?"

"And stay for two weeks? You're a successful trial lawyer, Mr. Carlson. How can you spare this much time?"

Ted Carlson was a well-dressed gray-haired man whose looks were just starting to fade into fat. There were only two excellent hotels in Prescott. He hadn't been hard to find. Delancy called his room and asked him to meet in the coffee shop downstairs.

The waitress had just served them coffee. Carlson had a plum Danish even though it was afternoon.

"I'd say it as my business. And tell me again just what your professional interest in this is."

Delancy had assumed that the man would go lawyer on him so he produced his ID from the mayor's office and then the his private investigator's office. "Take your pick."

Carlson gave the IDs a quick legal look then shoved them back to Delancy's side of the booth.

"I'm sure Beth told you all about our history together. We each broke up our families. I'm not proud of it and neither is Beth. But in the course of it, Sarah became like a daughter to me. I cared about her very much."

"That sounds nice, Carlson. But Beth didn't know you were in town here until I described your car."

He smiled, a toothy effect that he probably used with great success on juries. "I probably should drive something a little less inconspicuous, shouldn't I?" He took a bite of his Danish. "I didn't really need that now, did I?" He patted his stout stomach. "I'm not the golden boy I used to be." He wiped a napkin across his lips and said, "She didn't know I was in town because I didn't tell her. And the reason I didn't tell her is because we haven't spoken in more than a month. All the misery we caused our families—and we've both been having problems ourselves. She almost broke it off. And then so did I."

"She told me you're still lovers."

"She's more optimistic than I am."

"Why say it that way?"

"Is that really any of your business? I mean, no offense, but you're not a real cop."

"If you want to talk to a 'real cop,' I have the authority to hold you here and then walk over to that payphone and ask a 'real cop' to come out here.'"

That Broadway smile again. "I doubt you'll believe this but she found out I was interested in somebody else. She found that out on her own. And shw won't let go of it."

"I thought you were so deeply in love and all that."

He frowned. "I'm something of a libertine, I admit. But I do have a conscience. I got to the point where every time I look at her, all I can think of is all the people we hurt. We were pretty damned selfish, when you come right down to her. Her husband committed suicide; my wife's been seeing a psychiatrist for months. My two kids were straight A students. Now they're grades are bad and they get in trouble a lot at school." The frown, this time accompanied by a solemn shake of the head. I then realized that he was playing to a jury—of one—me. "I can't look at her and feel good about myself. I know she hates me but I can't help it."

"I still don't understand why you're here?"

"You don't? Isn't it obvious. To get Sarah to go back home. As miserable as my kids are, they still have their home environment to fall back on. She is—was—over here. In a frigging army town for God's sake."

"So you saw her?"

"Three or four times. I was planning to see her tomorrow night. She didn't tell me all the things that had happened to her while she'd been here. But I assume they were pretty bad."

"How did she feel about you being here?"

"Better than I'd hoped. She was resentful at first. She was pretending to be this adult. I was a pretty good reminder that she wasn't. But we had a few good talks. I could see that deep down she wanted to go back. This has got to be a scary place for a girl her age. She was very sheltered back home."

Delancy slid out of the booth, left a dime for coffee, a nickel for a tip. "Because I'm not a 'real cop,' I can't officially make you stay in town for at least another day. But I can get a real cop out here fast if I need to."

"I'd planned on leaving tomorrow, actually."

"Make it the day after."

His blue gaze assessed me with no pleasure at all. "I suppose you get a lot of sympathy from that leg. War heroes are very popular these days."

"So are guys who sleep with the wives of their best friends."

7

Laura took a quick, late lunch. When she got back to her office in the shelter she found a sheet of plain paper folded over and sitting in the center of her desk.

After glancing at it, recognizing the scrawled penmanship and taking note of the message, she walked over to the stairs and climbed to the second floor.

The kids would be back from school or work soon. She wouldn't have long for her search.

The residents had no private space except their bunkbeds. Therefore, the item in question had to be somewhere on or under the bed. If the note was accurate, anyway.

She found it quickly. A long slit had been opened up on the underside of the mattress and then clumsily sewn back together. Before she tore the item free, she felt the shape of what she was looking for.

It took less than a minute to free the object the note had told her was somewhere in the shelter.

It took her less than two minutes to get back downstairs and to put in a call to Nick Delancy's office.

8

It was said that old Cyrus Banning, Justice of the Peace in the area known as the Zone, had broken more laws than existed in the county code.

At sixty-eight, he weighed some three hundred pounds, was said to smell so bad that most folks could pick up the stench from a hundred feet away, wore the same pair of bib overalls and stained white shirt he'd been seen in for at least twenty years. He was partially blind.

Because of his blindness he had his nephew, who resembled a malevolent beaver, do all the chores that required sight. His nephew was forty-three and had never married. He got the girls free gratis at the bawdy house old Cyrus was said to own down the street. The madame there had a Demerit blackboard, upon which was noted even the slightest bit of irritation she'd received from any of the girls. On Wednesday morning, the madame tallied up the demerits. Whichever girl had the most had to sleep with old Cyrus' nephew who was said to smell almost as bad as his uncle and have a gas problem as well.

Nephew, in his own bib overalls and own white shirt, answered the door. The green fuzz on his bucked teeth looked a little darker than usual. Knowing that he would have to go inside, Delancy gulped and steeled his stomach for the worst.

The word was that at one time—while his wife, who

died under mysterious circumstances (i.e., the police believed Cyrus killed her but couldn't prove it) was alive—Cyrus had let her run an antiques store out of their house. But after she died, Cyrus just begun to accumulate piles, stashes, mountains of God-alone-knew-what. A Shirley Temple lamp sat atop a stack of musty Harper's magazines from the 1880s; an upside-down German helmet from WW 1 was stuffed with a coin collection; fine china, busted Tom Mix drinking glasses, bustles, books on treating ringworm, a signed copy of an H. Rider Haggard novel—somewhere in the piles that filled all rooms but three (the tiny living room where an enormous RCA radio console stood; the dining room where he married people; the toilet where none but the foolhardy would venture)—somewhere in this ungodly tornado-ravaged heap lay treasures unimaginable.

Nephew said, "You got a warrant?"

"No, but I've got this." Delancy kicked Nephew hard in the shin bone. Nephew shouted and fell back.

Delancy walked straight to the dining room where old Cyrus was applying dirty and sausage-like fingers to an adding machine.

"Just think how much money the government would have if you ever paid taxes on what you made, Cyrus."

Delancy and Cyrus were ancient enemies. Like every other Prescott cop not on Cyrus' payroll, Delancy had spent his street days trying to bust Cyrus on anything he could.

Cyrus looked up, his eyes ringed with some kind of rash. "My least favorite cop. You know how sorry I am about your leg."

"Uh-huh. I want to know about a girl who died a few dats ago. Sarah Hewitt. I'm hearing that she worked as an Annie. And that means she worked with you."

"Allotment Annies" were girls and women who married soldiers about to be shipped overseas. The Annies would then get the soldiers' $50 a month check that the government sent wives and widows. It was a system begging for corruption and corrupt it was. The record holder thus far was a New York City Annie who'd married thirty-six soldiers and was getting a substantial monthly income.

Locally, Cyrus ran the Annies much the way pimps ran prostitutes. Girls who tried to be Annies on their own were soon visited by Nephew. For every drunken scared soldier (he knew he might be dead in a month; the idea of having a little woman waiting for him back here gave him great comfort, the poor sad dumb slob), Cyrus gave the girl $25 that night and then had her fill out all the necessary papers so that the monthly checks came to various addresses he used as drop boxes.

"The name doesn't sound familiar," Cyrus wheezed.

"What if I told you I had two eyewitnesses who saw her come here the night she was murdered?"

Cyrus laughed. "You hear that, nephew? Two eyewitnesses? He lost his leg but he sure didn't lose his bullshit."

"He's gonna get his someday. You see how he kicked me in the shin?"

"I'll tell you what," Cyrus said, "beings how you give up your leg for this country of ours. I'm gonna lay it out for you because I don't want to be involved in no murder investigation. Them Army bastards are tryin' to get my JP license lifted because a couple of Annies worked here for a few nights."

"You going to tell me Sarah Hewitt was an Annie?"

"Don't tell him nothing, Uncle Cyrus."

"You got yourself an enemy, Delancy."

"I'll manage to live with the shame. Now what about the girl?"

"She needed money. I offered her a berth in the crib but she didn't want it. Then I told her about how I arranged for Annie. We worked out deal where she got $100 for all three and then signed everything over to me and one of my drop boxes. "

"She was a fast worker."

438

"You ever see her, Delancy? She was one of them little dreamy ones. Scared young boys gonna be shipped overseas—you bet they wanted to marry her. I even had a photographer out here, took a couple wedding shots so the boys could have them in their wallets. But it had to be a fast playoff. They get back to base and started showing them pictures around—comparin' notes and everything before they shipped out—well, pretty obvious ain't it?"

"What is?"

"Whoever killed her. Had to be one of them soldier boys who found out she was an Annie." e of them caught on to her and killed her."

"I want their names."

"Two of them already shipped out."

"What about the third one?"

"He wasn't no soldier," Nephew said.

"You be quiet." Shook his outsize head, wheezed. "Nephew thinks she met some civilian who wanted to marry her."

"I asked him about them guns they use in the Army," Nephew said. "He didn't know diddly squat."

"I keep tellin' you he was an officer."

"He'd still know about guns, Uncle Cyrus."

An invading force landed on the front porch, a force of drunken laughter, a bottle of some kind that dropped and smashed, and somebody who was trying hard to play the Wedding March on harmonica: "You don' think I can play it do ya, Shirley?"

Pounding on the door. A girl's voice: "Open up in there. We wanna get married!"

"Yeah, an' I'm gonna play the wedding march on this here harmonica."

They fell against the door.

Nephew said, "Sounds like Shirley's got a live on. She's one Annie who's gonna make a lot of money."

"Not around here, she ain't," Cyrus said. "Four husbands in three weeks. She's pressin' her luck. You get her that bus ticket like I told ya to?"

"I sure did, Uncle Cyrus."

"Good. 'Cause this is her last one. The others got shipped to four different bases for overseas. She lucked out. But her luck can't last much longer."

More laughter. A few strains of the Wedding March. Falling against the door again.

Nephew opened the door and the happy couple damned near fell through.

For the next few minutes all Delancy did was watch. Shirley turned out to be a bottle redhead with long nice legs in a short black dress and a goofy hat with a birdcage on it. The soldier's uniform was soaked with what was probably booze and he was so drunk he had to keep refocusing his eyes. She wasn't much good at pretending to be drunk but the soldier was so drunk he couldn't figure it out. She looked at Cyrus and winked a couple of times. Nephew helped drag the shorn recruit with the soft downstate drawl into the living room where he —after dropping his harmonica—he bellowed: "Ain't she the most beautiful thing you ever seen?"

No sense sticking around for this farce of a wedding. Nor any sense reporting it. Cyrus knew way too much about too many powerful officials. He would laugh at any charges that Delancy helped to bring against him.

He said to Cyrus, "I'll call you later tonight. I want the name of the one who didn't get shipped off."

"I appreciate that, Delancy. But right now we need to get on with the sacred ceremony of marriage."

At which point, the poor soldier started to fall over backwards. Shirley and Nephew propped him up. He returned the favor by vomiting all over himself.

Delancy decided that this would probably be a good time to leave. He needed fresh air. Lots of it. And fast.

9

It was nearly nine o'clock by the time Delancy and Laura

caught up with each other in a downtown coffee shop named Kilroy's. The place was crowded with shift workers on dinner break. They ordered hamburgers and coffee and took them outside to sit and eat on a bus bench.

Delancy was nervous. Being with her he had to face his terrible truth all over again—that he was half-assed in love with her. Just the way he doted on her face in profile—it had happened without him even being aware of it. He'd seen her three times and there it was. His fate. He loved her and hated himself for loving her. She was a married woman with a husband fighting overseas. He was the kind of man all combat soldiers hated even more than the krauts and nips—the bird dog. Thank God she wouldn't reciprocate. She was saving him from himself.

"It's such a beautiful night," she said. She raised her elegant head to take in the scents of the Indian summer evening, the thick heady smell of leaves burning, the tang of the clean breeze, the oddly pleasant smell of bus fumes. A lazy round prairie moon only added to the allure of the moment.

Then she turned to him and said: "I need to get back, Nick. We've got two new residents and I really need to work with one of them. I haven't even had time to look through the diary." She reached into her coat pocket and lifted out a small red diary with a broken lock. It was a cheap little Woolworth's item and for some reason that gave it an endearing quality.

He slid the diary into his own coat pocket and said, "I want to apologize again for the other night."

She stared at him. Her expression was unfathomable. His heart pounded against his chest. Even with the noise of passing traffic, he was sure she could hear it.

"I'm going to be honest with you, Nick."

"All right."

"My marriage wasn't all that good for either of us. We'd talked about divorcing. I think Don enlisted as a way of getting away from me. We both come from prominent families and both of them wouldt have been angry if we embarrassed them by divorcing. my husband." She hesitated. "You know I'm attracted to you. Or you should, anyway. But I'm still married and I'm going to remain faithful. If something should happen to him over there—I owe him being true to our marriage vows."

She stood up. "So no more after-work drinks, all right? Strictly business and I'm serious. Very serious. All right?"

She turned to walk back to her DeSoto coupe. Then she glanced back at him: "I hope that diary helps you."

10

Delancy walked down the street to a telephone box. He looked up Cyrus' number in the phone book. He dropped a nickel in the slot and dialed Cyrus' number.

Nephew answered. "He's marryin' somebody. Number three for the night. And she ain't no Annie, either."

"You can help me, then."

"What if I don't *want* to help you?"

"Then I'll drive out there and beat your face in."

"You think you're pretty hot stuff just 'cause the krauts shot your leg off."

Delancy laughed. "I was in the Pacific. That would make them Japs."

"Oh."

"You said you didn't think the third man Sara Hewitt married was military. Why not?"

Nephew hesitated. "Well, he wasn't wearin' no uniform, for one thing."

"Do they all wear uniforms?"

"Well, no, I guess not. A lot of them wear civvies."

"Anything else about him that didn't strike you as military?"

"Well, he wasn't in great shape. And he was older."

"How old would you guess?"

"Forties, prob'ly."

And then good old Nephew said it, delivered the one essential fact that set Delancy on the right path.

"Never seen no military man drivin' a red Packard."

11

Delancy had to knock three times before he got an answer. When Ted Carlson opened his hotel room door, he was dressed in a blue silk robe that was a tad fancy.

Delancy didn't wait for an invitation. He pushed past the taller man and stepped into a room that was warm from the glow of small table lamp. Dance music played faintly on a table model radio. Glen Miller.

Delancy went over and dropped into a chair. Carlson seated himself on the edge of the small sofa. The furnishings were tasteful if a bit dull.

"I'm sure you're going to tell me why you're here."

"First of all, because you're a dumb sonofabitch. You couldn't even see that she was using you. And if anybody wanted to push it, you probably could've gone to prison for sleeping with a seventeen-year-old."

"That's what you're here about? That I married Sarah? I'm not ashamed of it. And what we did is perfectly legal."

"I've got her diary, Carlson. She was paying her mother back. She didn't love you. She thought you were kind've stupid, the way teenagers always think older people are stupid."

Carlson inhaled raggedly, as if he'd just been hit hard in the stomach. He opened the teak cigarette box on the coffee table in front of him and then closed it again without taking a cigarette. He was trembling.

For the first time, he glanced at the bathroom door. It was closed. He looked back at Delancy. "I know that, too. Now. She told me on our wedding night. When she wouldn't sleep with me. She knew I was in love with her, as foolish as that sounds. She tried to sound happy about it. S he got drunk and kept saying that she'd paid both of us back. I wasn't in love with her mother any longer. And now I was in love with somebody I couldn't have—just the way her father was with her mother." This time he took out a cigarette and lighted it with a stick match. "I actually felt sorry for her—hated her for how she'd lead me on—but now that she'd pulled it off she was miserable. That's the terrible thing about vengeance—it's rarely as satisfying as we hope it'll be. She broke down and just wept for a good twenty minutes. I set her on the bed and covered her up. I pulled a chair up and held her hand until she finally fell asleep."

The second time Carlson looked at the bathroom door, Delancy took his gun from his shoulder holster and pointed it at a spot right above the doorknob.

"Come out of there right now."

"Go easy on her, Delancy. She's been through hell."

Delancy knew who it would be. Beth Hewitt emerged from the dark rectangle of doorway. She wore white silk pajamas. Her mussed blonde hair Harlow-erotic.

She said nothing. Crossed the room to the sofa. Sat down. Picked up a cigarette from the box. Got it lighted and then sank back in the couch.

"Just get it over with, Mr. Delancy. Then you can call the police and they can charge me. I killed my daughter."

Carlson snapped, "Be quiet, Beth. You know damned well I killed her."

She had started to cry and he slid his arm around her and brought her to him. "Beth came to town. She'd figured out that I was seeing Sarah. She found Sarah, who was only too glad to tell her all about it."

He leaned forward to stub out his cigarette. "Sarah called and said she wanted to meet me by the river. She was insane that night and I mean that medically. She attacked me, slapping me and kicking me and spitting in my face.

She kept screaming that if I hadn't seduced her mother, she'd still have both of her parents. I tried to leave but she jumped at me from behind. She missed me and smashed her head against a stone pillar. She was dead in less than a minute."

Even from across the room, Delancy could see the tears in Carlson's eyes. "She's dead, my best friend committed suicide, and I betrayed the woman I was supposed to love."

When he stood up this time, Carlson looked more formidable than he ever had. He walked over to the phone, lifted the receiver and said, "Yes, connect me with the police department. Thank you." He voice was steady, somber. He nodded to Delancy's gun. "You won't be needing that, Mr. Delancy. I'm turning myself in."

Which is just what he did over the course of the next few minutes. Talked to Detective Gibson, told him who he was, what he'd done, and where he could now be found.

When he put the phone down, Delancy said, "Mrs. Hewitt, I'd like you to put on a robe and go downstairs and get us some coffee. And I'd like you to do it right away."

She leaned over and kissed Carlson on the cheek. There was a white silk robe on the bed. She went to it, slid it on. "You need cigarettes, too, Ted."

"Thank you," he said.

When the door was close, and the flap of her slippers could be heard going down the hall, Delancy said, "I'm pretty sure that Sarah died just the way you said. With once exception. She wasn't fighting with you, she was fighting with Mrs. Hewitt."

"That's your opinion. You can't prove it."

"You won't let me prove it."

"That's right. So don't waste your time. Beth has been in and out of mental hospitals for most of her life. Prison would kill her. I'll probably draw five-to-eight and only serve four. I'll have my health and still be in my forties. It's not much of a price to pay for what I've done. Sarah was right; I seduced her mother, she didn't seduce me. And then I went for Sarah."

He walked over to where Delancy was sitting. "I've been a selfish bastard all my life. Let me do something good for once. All right?"

He put forth his hand. Delancy put out his own hand and they shook.

Then there was a knock on the door. Carlson went over and opened it. A pudgy young uniformed cop came in, one of the ill-trained tribe that had been forced upon the police department.

"I got a call from Detective Gibson of homicide," he said. "He told me to come up to this room and stay with a Mr. Carlson till he got here. Are you Carlson?"

By now, Delancy stood with the other two at the doorway. Carlson said, "Yes, I am."

"Well, Detective Gibson, he said, I should cuff you." He reached around to the back of his belt and began wrestling his cuffs free. "I haven't had a lot of experience with cuffs, so bear with me, all right?"

Delancy couldn't help it. He laughed out loud and then said, "Let me cuff him, kid. Then we'll all sit down and have a drink and wait for Gibson to get here.

The young cop was obviously embarrassed but he after hesitating a long moment, he handed them over and then watched, impressed, as Delancy cuffed Carlson in seconds.

"Hey, you musta been a cop sometime," the pudgy man said.

"Yeah, that's what I used to be, all right."

Then he limped over and poured himself one hell of a drink of bourbon.

⚜⚜⚜

J.N. Williamson

J.N. Williamson is an award-winning editor and writer whose contributions to horror were awarded the field's highest honor in 2002 when he was presented with the Horror Writers' Association's Bram Stoker Award for Lifetime Achievement. The author of over 40 novels and hundreds of short stories, Williamson's work has always been notable for his seemingly effortless ability to illustrate the clash between ancient myths and modern sensibilities. The following story—quintessential Williamson—is no exception.

OUTCRY

✠ BY J.N. WILLIAMSON ✠

T he baby did not make Helene and Phil Doric wait long at the hospital before orchestrating his grand entrance into the world. They had been told that first babies often took quite a while before arriving, and frequently caused the mother a lot of difficulty, pain, delay, and frustration, but not little Alex; his birth—while typically un-pretty in the physical sense (Phil could not bring himself to look at the last little squirt of placenta from Helene's vagina, despite having seen it in countless informational films she made him watch as they prepared for this day)— went quickly and smoothly, not unlike many of the plays Phil had called during his glory days as a professional quarterback.

What pleased Phil the most, however, was that Alex's crying sounded exactly like the high-pitched squalling he'd winced away from with all the other infants he'd heard in the birthing films, or on TV, or the few he'd encountered in real life. It was merely incomprehensible caterwauling, not *that sound*, the one he'd heard last night, right before Helene's water broke.

That sound, that terrifying sound, was still very much in the forefront of Phil's memory, and as he looked down at his newborn son, so pink and still wet, he couldn't help but think: *You made that noise, didn't you?*

Then the nurse handed newborn Alex to his father, and Phil's heart, rather than soar, skipped a beat.

He caught Dr. Alatius in the hall outside of Helene's room. "Do you have a few minutes, Doctor?"

Alatius smiled and gripped Phil's hand. "Congratulations, Philip," said the tall, dark-haired man. Milo Alatius had a head of black hair that kept him looking in his mid-forties, even though Helene had told Phil that Alatius had delivered her into the world. How the man kept himself so vital, so young-looking, was a mystery, and one that Phil had no interest in exploring right at this moment.

For a moment, neither man said anything, simply stood there in the hall with hands clasped together. After a few more seconds of awkward silence, Alatius released Phil's hand and spoke, his voice softly concerned. "You have a healthy son. Why don't you appear as excited and overjoyed as your beautiful wife?"

"That's what I need to talk to you about."

Alatius checked his watch. "I can give you five minutes. Sorry, but I've got a busy day."

"Five minutes is fine."

Alatius led Phil to his private office on this floor and closed the door behind them, gesturing for Phil to have a seat in a plush leather chair facing a mahogany desk that, had it been any bigger, could have served as a landing strip for small airplanes. Alatius sat behind the desk, assuming the position of a man ready to spring up and flash into action. "So, how about answering my question? *Why* aren't you as excited as Helene about Alex's birth?"

Phil fumbled for an answer. "I don't know, exactly. Maybe it's because I haven't been around babies much and I thought...when the nurse handed him to me...I thought I would feel some kind of *bond*, you know? I looked at him with Helene and I could it see there between *them*, that *instant* bonding, but when I was holding him I felt like we were a couple of strangers." He started to say something else, and then stopped himself. He needed to get to the heart of the matter, to plan a play to break through his own defenses, and if that meant sounding weak to Alatius, then, so be it.

Still, Philip Doric was a man of pride, a man whose ego from the glory days had not been lessened any by the passage of time. He never showed weakness on the football field, and had never shown it in life.

Alatius leaned forward, sneaking a glimpse at his watch as he did so. "It's not uncommon for a new father to fell a certain distance between himself as his new child. Helene has been carrying him for nine months, Philip; there's an *organic* bond in place already. You can't expect to feel the same thing right away."

Phil nodded his head. "I know, I know, but it's more than that. Something happened last night, right before Helene's water broke, and it's been..." Once again he fumbled for the explanation.

"Start at the beginning," said Alatius.

"I've already lost almost two of my five minutes."

The doctor grinned. "Make it interesting, and I'll give you five more."

Phil returned the grin. Okay, so the ball was in play; don't fumble it a third time.

"I was laying with my head against Helene's belly,

right, listening to things, waiting for him to kick again, when...and I know how this is going to *sound*...when I heard this sound. At first Helene and I laughed about it because we both thought she'd farted—the sound began with that same kind of low, growling noise like you make right before you really let fly with a big one—and I kept my ear pressed against her belly, but then...it changed."

"Changed how?"

"It turned into a sort of whimper, then rose until it sounded like some distant animal howling in fear and pain. This was coming from *inside* Helene, understand? And for a crazy second I thought, 'The baby is making this sound.' I know how crazy that sounds but, I swear to you, it was the scariest damn thing I've ever heard! And that feeling, that scared feeling I got, it hasn't gone away yet, Doctor. It even got worse when I held Alex in my arms. Have you ever encountered something like this before? Do you have any idea what it could have been?"

For several agonizing moments, it appeared that Alatius wasn't going to respond to the question; he had turned his chair away and was staring out the window, his face expressionless, but when he turned back to Phil, the morning sunlight streaming through the window made the lines on his face seem all the deeper, suddenly revealing his age. "I would say 'no' if Helene and you weren't Greek, as well, but as you know, our people have a long history of mythology."

"You mean Mount Olympus and all that?" asked Phil, wondering what in hell any of this had to do with his concerns.

"In part," replied Alatius. "Our home country's natural features led our people to a certain natural susceptibility to, well...mysteries of many kinds. Caves and groves and volcanic springs seemed appropriate homes for suitably powerful deities. By the way—you bought yourself at least another five minutes, and now it is I who must ask that you not think me crazy."

"Of course," replied Phil, still wondering where this was going.

"Adonis dwelled at the beautiful vale of Aphaca; the sun-god Apollo, at Parnassus; impenetrable waters in gloomy caves housed the Oracle of Trophonius—and many of them had the power to transform themselves or other things around them."

Despite himself, Phil wondered about the ability of unseen infants in the womb to transform themselves, during birth, into a visible human being. The unnatural noise he'd heard last night came to the forefront of his mind once more, having lost none of its power to unnerve him.

"What you heard," said Doctor Alatius, "was the *vagitus uterinus*—or 'uterine cry'. I learned about it not from any medical textbooks but from my great-grandmother, who worked with expectant mothers back in Greece, in the more isolated regions. She told me that my great-grandfather had once heard the sound—what she referred to as 'the outcry'—and was never the same man again."

"*Why?*" asked Phil, feeling even more anxious now.

"Because he was frightened so badly that the terror of it remained with him for the remainder of his days."

"But it's just *a sound*!"

"No," said Alatius. "It is *the* sound, the last, fervent scream of the child in the womb to not be brought into the world of men—at least, that's how the belief goes."

"Your great-grandmother's belief?"

Alatius shook his head."Not just her, but all the women of her generation. They passed this belief on to the following generation, but with each successive generation, the belief became distilled until it was thought to be nothing more than an old wives' tale. But my grandfather and my father both saw what it did to my great-grandfather, how it all but destroyed him, and because I believed them, because I still hold strong to enough of the 'ancient' beliefs of our culture to never dismiss anything out of hand, I am going to suggest that you see a psychologist I know before you allow what you heard last night to damage all of your affairs from this moment on." He grabbed a pad of notepaper bearing his personal monogram and began scribbling on it.

Phil nearly blurted his next words: "But if you're telling me I heard a genuine outcry, and it wasn't caused by my mind playing tricks on me, how can a psychologist help? And *why* is the outcry supposedly so terrible?"

"I'd say it's in your mind *now*, Phil, but logic alone should tell you that just as cheers or boos from a football crowd ten years ago can't conceivably harm you today— unless you allow yourself to *believe* they can harm you, that they've come out of the past and tracked you down—the outcry you heard from Alex before he was forced into this world needs to be put in proper perspective."

"And what the hell *would* that be, exactly?" snapped Phil. "When I held him in my arms, I felt as if he were...I dunno...*angry*. As if he'd come into this world to harm us."

"Listen," said Alatius. "The few cases of this that I've encountered in my life all have certain elements in common. The outcry is heard from a few minutes to several hours before the baby arrives—your sound falls into that time frame, suggestive of a little-known but discernable pattern. For weeks before a child's birth, some studies indicate that it is very much aware of the horrifying event awaiting it."

"You mean its *birth*? *Horrifying*?"

"God, yes!" said Alatius. "The infant begins to receive less and less oxygen, and before it begins its solitary and dangerous trip into the world, he or she has less amniotic fluid. Everything that has been present to give it warmth, sustenance, and comfort is taken away, bit by bit, until it comes into its first moments of genuine awareness. It doesn't want to surrender its comfortable, safe, well-nourished existence for that of the unknown. It is it any wonder, then, that infants so quickly bond with their mothers, or that, alone and terrified, even a full-grown adult will revert to the fetal position?"

"I'd hoped," said Phil, "that I'd have a really close relationship with my son."

"There is no reason why you can't be close—your focusing on the outcry aside."

"I don't follow."

"The old belief about the outcry was simple, Philip: that it contained all of the infant's anger, fear, and resentment at being forced into life, and that, if those who heard the outcry never forget what it sounded like, that memory would serve as a homing beacon for the outcry, guiding it toward them with all the precision of a modern-day missile...and when it found them, it would strike them down. A life taken in exchange for one that was not asked for."

"Jesus..."

Alatius handed Phil the slip of paper on which he'd written the contact information for the psychologist. "You will not be the first man I've sent to him who has heard the outcry, Philip. He knows how to help. I strongly suggest you go to him. He can teach you how to forget. And you *must* forget. If you don't, if you continue to obsess over this, the outcry will find you like a lost ship finds a lighthouse during a storm. And it can be very clever, Philip, make no mistake about that. It can be *very* clever."

Phil wordlessly accepted the paper, thanked Alatius for his time, and wandered back to Helene's room where he stood looking down at the sleeping forms of his wife and son, feeling isolated, unwelcome...and afraid, with the distant echo of a certain sound swirling in the back of his memory.

Over the next few months Phil tried to be a decent husband and father. He tore up the slip of paper with the psychologist's information written on it. A *shrink*! To hell with that.

He learned how to change Alex's diaper, even though the baby seemed to resent him for performing the service — in fact, the baby seemed to resent everything Phil did for it, though there was never anything overt in Alex's demonstrations; it was more a sense of underlying antipathy that emanated from the baby whenever Phil was nearby. He never discussed it with Helene.

He bought stuffed toys for Alex that the baby never played with. He tried to ignore it when Alex threw up on the autographed NFL football Phil left in his crib. He never got angry when Alex would fight against taking his bottle whenever Phil tried to feed him, but couldn't get his lips wrapped around the nipple fast enough when it was Helene doing the feeding. And he tried to not feel jealousy when he saw how close baby and mother became; so close, in fact, that Phil's presence in their lives seemed superfluous...unless, of course, there was something he could do to make things easier for them.

Helene lost all interest in sex; lost interest in everything, it seemed, except for her son. Phil made overtures toward his wife, but she was always so preoccupied with little Alex that Phil might as well have making a pass at the sofa.

So, one night several months later, he located his old little black book, made a date with Minnie Darius, an old football groupie, and began cheating on his wife. Rather than being wracked with guilt afterward, it was the first peaceful night's sleep he'd known since Alex's birth, the first night he'd been able to drift off to sleep without the echo of the outcry's rising howl sticking needles into his brain.

This went on for several weeks until one night Phil was struck by a game-saving idea and shook Minnie awake, his passing arm tingling with the old confidence that his idea was a winner.

"You know that Helene and I just had a baby, but it's not working out, baby. I got a proposition for you."

In the old days, he'd actually considered marrying Minnie, and was suddenly grateful that he now had time to correct the mistake before it was too late.

Minnie sat up in bed and lit a cigarette. "This is the first time I've been propositioned *after* the lay."

"Listen to me. We've always been good together, in the sack and out of it. You *love* football, just like me. You once told me you wanted to have a little baby quarterback with me. I should have taken you up on it right there and then, but I didn't, and I'm sorry. It's important that you understand that, Minnie. I screwed up, not marrying you, and I'm sorry.

"Okay, here's what I can offer you. Financial security for the rest of your life in exchange for you giving me a healthy, athletic son who doesn't look at me like he wishes I were dead. We can have our little quarterback, baby. I'll guide him, I'll train him, we'll get him into a good college and then—*bam!*—right into the NFL. I've still got plenty of connections—hell, they paid me so much on retirement just to make sure I wouldn't sign with another club, they'd take a one-armed retard if I asked them to.

"I'll see a lot of you until you're pregnant, and you won't ball anyone but me, because no way will I pay for a kid with some other guy's genes. But once it's definite that you're expecting my son, then I'll divorce Helene and you and me, we'll get married, and I can have the type of life I've always wanted." He pulled her close to him and squeezed her so hard he actually heard something pop.

"Sorry, babe. What do you say?"

Minnie looked at him for several moments, her face expressionless, then said, very quietly: "Do you love me?"

Phil wasn't prepared for that one. "Sure, I guess—c'mon, baby, what's it matter? We'll be together, and we'll have a healthy, athletic son who'll surpass his old man's achievements on the field!"

Minnie crushed out her cigarette and exhaled a long

stream of smoke. "I'll have to quit smoking, and you remember what I was like the last time I tried to do that, right?"

"God, yes."

She turned toward him, kissed him, then said, "I need some time to think about it. I won't lie, Phil, life hasn't exactly been a joy ride for me these last ten years. I could use the money."

"But you'll get more than the money, baby—you'll get me!"

Minnie smiled. "Nice to see that your ego hasn't suffered any crippling blows."

Phil grinned, cupping the back of her head with his hand. "Speaking of blows...."

The next seven days were agony for him. Playing housekeeper for Helene and Alex while trying to make sure he was within reaching distance of the phone should Minnie call him with her decision.

And he wasn't sleeping well. The echo of the outcry knew just when to strike out at him each night, waiting for that moment that he was wobbling on the edge of sleep, and then screaming into his brain, howling its fury and fear, directing all of its wrath at him.

Then came the night when the sound of the outcry was so powerful he rose from the sofa (he'd taken to sleeping there since Helene insisted little Alex sleep beside her) and strode into the bedroom, staring down at his wife and her child.

Alex was awake, staring up at Phil with a look of such unbridled contempt that Phil knew, finally, that he hated the baby.

If you didn't want to be taken away, he thought, *then why didn't you just die on the way out? Answer me that one, little Alex. If it was so cozy and safe in there, then why didn't you fight it more? Why take it out on me?*

Alex smiled at Phil, but there was no warmth, no innocence, no humor in it.

Phil went back out into the living room and called Minnie. He couldn't stand it any longer.

"Yes or no?" he said as soon as she answered.

"Yes—on one condition."

"Name it."

"We tell Helene together. I don't want to be your dirty little secret, Phil. I want everything to be out in the open."

"Absolutely not," he said, a bit more loudly than he'd intended. "We do it my way, Minnie. That's the deal."

"Your 'deal' makes me feel like a whore, Phil. Maybe I'm not exactly the most pristine woman ever to share your bed, but I'd like to hang on to what dignity I have left. Is that too much to ask?"

Before he could answer, Alex began fussing and crying. Helene was awake immediately, cooing at him, soothing him, cuddling him. Phil's grip tightened around the receiver. A good quarterback knew when to hand the ball over.

"You're right," he said to Minnie. "We tell her together."

On the other end of the line, Minnie began crying. "Oh, Phil, I didn't…didn't think you'd say yes. I didn't think you…you thought that much of me."

"I'll try to be better at showing you respect, baby, I promise."

"I believe you. When do you want to do this?"

Phil thought it over for a moment. He could be packed and out of here within an hour, if necessary. A call to his lawyer, even in the middle of the night, would make sure that Helene only got what Phil *said* she could have, and no more. This could all be done quickly. Tonight, even. It was only a little after midnight.

"Tonight," he said to Minnie. "Now. Give me twenty minutes, then call me before you leave. An hour from now, it'll be just you and me and our new life."

"I love you, Phil. I always did. I know you're not sure whether or not you love me, but you will. You will love me. I'll call you back in twenty minutes, on my way out the door."

"See you then, baby." He hung up, sighed with relief, and turned around to see Helene standing not three feet away from him, little Alex cradled in her arms.

"Who was that?" she said, all of her attention focused on him for the first time in months.

"You'll know soon enough. Shouldn't you be feeding your baby?"

"*Our* baby, you adulterous ass!"

"How nice of you to finally notice me. But it's too little too late, Helene. You don't want me around anymore, and Alex sure as hell doesn't love me, so I don't see what you're so—"

The phone rang. Alex turned his attention toward Phil, his eyes wide, his mouth curling up into a smile.

"Shouldn't you answer that?" said Helene. "Don't want to keep your whore waiting."

Phil stared at Alex for a moment, sending equal waves of silent contempt in the baby's direction, then grabbed the receiver and lifted it to his ear, wondering why Minnie was calling back so soon.

And it wasn't until the receiver was firmly against his ear and little Alex released a loud, long, wet laugh that Phil remembered Dr. Alatius's words: *...the outcry will find you like a lost ship finds a lighthouse during a storm. And it can be very clever, Philip, make no mistake about that. It can be **very** clever.*

But by then the sound was screaming out of the phone and drilling into the center of his brain, freezing him, crippling him, overwhelming all of his senses, reaching down through his body to squeeze the center of his chest, the sudden pain in his heart too great, and he dropped to his knees, gasping for air but unable to let go of the receiver, the outcry was all he could hear, all he was, all he would be, and he could nothing but wait for it to fade away with the pain, to pass away, which it did, eventually.

As did Phil Doric.

❦❦❦

Ray Bradbury

There are some writers who arguably need no introduction, and then there's Ray Bradbury, for whom any introduction is rendered superfluous. Flip through the pages of any **Masques** *volume (or the pages of any anthology published since the mid-1950s, for that matter) and the work of every writer you'll encounter in those pages was influenced in one way or another by Bradbury. His work has influenced all fields of imaginative fiction more so than any other living writer, and we are honored to present this wonderful tale—our second barber shop story.*

—JNW

THE
BEAUTIFUL SHAVE

✠ By Ray Bradbury ✠

He came into town riding fast and firing his guns at the blue sky. He shot a chicken in the dust and kicked it around, using his horse as a mauler, and then, reloading and yelling, his three-week beard red and irritable in the sunlight, he rode on to the Saloon where he tethered his horse and carried his guns, still hot, into the bar where he glared at his own sunburnt image in the mirror and yelled for a glass and a bottle.

The bartender slid them over the edge of the bar and went away.

The men along the bar moved down to the free lunch at the far end, and conversation withered.

"What in hell's wrong with everyone!" cried Mr. James Malone. "Talk, laugh, everyone. Go on, now, or I'll shoot your damn eyebrows off!"

Everyone began to talk and laugh.

465

"That's better," said James Malone, drinking his drinks one upon another.

He rammed the wing doors of the Saloon wide and in the resulting wind stomped out like an elephant into the afternoon street where other men were riding up from the mines or the mountains and tying their horses to the worn hitching poles.

The barber shop was directly across the street.

Before crossing to it, he rechecked his bright blue pistols and snuffed at them with his red nose, saying Ah! at the scent of gunpowder. Then he saw a tin can in the talcumy dust and shot it three times ahead of him as he strode laughing, and the horses all along the street jumped nervously and flickered their ears. Reloading again, he kicked the barber shop door wide and confronted a full house. The four barber chairs were full of lathered customers, waiting with magazines in their hands, and the mirrors behind them repeated the comfort and the creamy lather and the pantomime of efficient barbers.

Along the wall on a bench sat six other men waiting to be cleansed of the mountain and the desert.

"Have a seat," said one of the barbers, glancing up.

"I sure will," said Mr. James Malone, and pointed his pistol at the first chair. "Get out of there, mister, or I'll sew you right back into the upholstery."

The man's eyes were startled, then angry, then apprehensive in turn above his creamy mask, but after a long hesitation, he levered himself up with difficulty, swiped the white stuff off his chin with the apron, flung the apron to the floor, and walked over to shove in and sit with the other waiting men.

James Malone snorted at this, laughed, jounced into the black leather chair, and cocked his two pistols.

"I never have to wait," he said to no one and everyone at once. His gaze wandered over their heads and touched on the ceiling. "If you live right, you don't have to wait for anything. You ought to know that by now!"

The men looked at the floor. The barber cleared his throat and put an apron over James Malone. The pistols stuck up, making white tents underneath. There was a sharp click as he knocked the pistols together, just to let everyone know they were there, and pointed.

"Give me the works," he said to the barber, not looking at him. A shave first, I feel itchy and mean, then a haircut. You men there, starting on the right, tell jokes. Make 'em good jokes. I want entertainment while I'm being shorn. Ain't been entertained in months. You, there, mister, you start."

The man who had been evicted from his comfortable chair unfroze himself slowly and rolled his eyes at the other men and talked as if someone had hit him in the mouth.

"I knew a gent once who..." he said, and word by word, white-faced, he launched himself into a tale. "That gent, he..."

To the barber, James Malone now said, "Listen, you. I want a shave. I want a beautiful shave. But I got a fine-skinned face and it's a pretty face with the beard off, and I been in the mountains for a long time and I had no luck with gold-panning, so I'm feeling mean. I just want to warn you of one little thing. If you so much as nick my face once with your straight razor, I'll kill you. You hear that? I mean I'll kill you. If you so much as bring one little speck of blood to the surface, I'll plug you clean through the heart. You hear?"

The barber nodded quietly. The barber shop was silent. Nobody was telling jokes or laughing.

"Not one drop of blood, not one little cut, mind you," repeated Mr. James Malone, "or you'll be dead on the floor a second later."

"I'm a married man," said the barber.

"I don't give a damn if you're a Mormon with six wives and fifty-seven children. You're dead if you scratch me once."

"I happen to have two children," said the barber. "A fine little girl and boy."

"Don't hand me any of that," said Malone, settling back, closing his eyes. "Start."

The barber began to get the hot towels ready. He put them on James Malone's face, and under them the man cursed and yelled and waved his pistols under the white apron. When the hot towels came off and the hot lather was put on his beard, James Malone still chewed on his profanity and threats, and the men waiting sat white-faced and stiff with the pistols pointing at them. The other barbers had almost stopped moving and stood like statues by their customers in the chairs, and the barber shop was cold for a summer day.

"What's wrong with the stories?" snapped James Malone. "All right, then sing. You four there, sing something like 'My Darling Clementine.' Start it up. You heard me."

The barber was stropping his razor slowly with a trembling hand. "Mr. Malone," he said.

"Shut up and get to work." Malone tilted his head back, grimacing.

The barber stropped his razor some more and looked at the men seated all around the shop. He cleared his throat and said, "Did all of you gentlemen hear what Mr. Malone said to me?"

Everyone nodded mutely.

"You heard him threaten to kill me," said the barber, "if I so much as drew a drop of blood to his skin?"

The men nodded again.

"And you'd swear to it in a court of law, if necessary?" asked the barber.

The men nodded for the last time.

"Cut the malarkey," said Mr. James Malone. "Get to work."

"That's all I wanted to be sure of," said the barber, letting the leather strop fall and clatter against the chair. He raised the razor in the light and it gleamed and glittered with cold metal there.

He tilted Mr. James Malone's head back and put the razor against the hairy throat.

"We'll start here," he said. "We'll start *here*."